ANCHORS TO ASHES

Also by David Caraccio

Tiburcio!

The Back of the Net

ANCHORS TO ASHES

A Novel

David Caraccio & Tom Seeley

ASH ROAD PRESS
Sacramento, California
2025

ISBN: 979-8-218-87526-8
ISBN 13: 979-8-218-87529-9

ANCHORS TO ASHES

PART I:

JOSEPH AND GEORGE

CHAPTER 1

No one can possibly fathom all of the causes and conditions in life that resulted in timber baron George Madison Stevens standing at this precise time and location, but a sprawling, bustling, noisy Seattle shipyard in the year 1916 is as good a place as any to start telling the story of how an American heiress descended into madness.

George Stevens waited for his brother at the spot where the railcar extension connected to the loading docks. He gazed up from under his felt bowler at the towering thicket of masts and white cotton sails of a dozen cargo ships being laden with timber. Heavy autumn clouds flooded the sprawling docks in gray light. White seagulls soared overhead mewing "ha-ha-ha." Workers in dirty overalls, suspenders and tweed jackets scurried across the decks of ships, clambered up and down tangles of scaffolding and checked and repaired the yardarms. Near the vessels, dozens of stacks of thirty-foot planks, twelve feet high, were piled near the schooners. Derricks swung the boards up from the dock and down into the holds. The stacks dwindled by the minute.

George was a principal of Port Seattle Timber Co., an enterprise that reaped cheap, boundless, readily available timber from the vast Pacific Northwest forests and ran the wood through the mills at three hundred thousand board feet per day. Workmen crammed a seemingly endless supply of lumber onto scores of freighters that carried the product to ports all over North America, down to South America and across the sea to the United Kingdom and Western Europe. Inbound and outbound freighters choked the harbor.

As George watched all that wood moving onto cargo ships, his thoughts turned to his reforestation work and studies of crossbreeding plants. He wondered when he might get back to the scholarly work that was his passion. Images of clear-cut virgin forests haunted his mind. He did not want to be responsible for sparse meadows with only stumps visible for miles. He had witnessed the heavy destruction of woodlands from Michigan to Bainbridge Island in Washington, and he knew there was a better way to manage the resource.

Along with his older brother Joseph, George co-owned Port Seattle Timber Co., Stevens & Gibbs Shipping Co., and Stevens Family Investments. He was waiting under a forest of masts and bowsprits and jibbooms that reached halfway over the docks because Joseph had asked to meet him there to discuss some important business. To George, the timing for the confabulation was awful, but he agreed anyway.

Looking down from the foremasts, George thought about the end of an era that was upon them. Shipwrights, like he and his brother, who founded Stevens & Gibbs in 1915 with their partner Teddy Gibbs, were switching full-bore to building vessels from iron and steel instead of wood. Refined steam engines, now more powerful than ever, hastened the transition.

His more outgoing brother drove George crazy sometimes, but he acknowledged Joseph had inherited the business-genius gene from their father and was more like the family patriarch than he was or ever would be. Joseph, who graduated with a business degree from Harvard a few years ahead of George, anticipated macroeconomic trends far before most other businessmen. With the family's timber company already long established, Joseph brought the gentler George into the shipbuilding business as a partner with just under fifty percent of the shares. That's how they operated. Every enterprise was a family affair. After their father, Conrad Stevens, died in 1899, the family investment group passed to the two sons, and they managed the vast holdings together.

When George first came aboard as investor, shareholder and director of the newly formed Stevens & Gibbs Shipping Co., five other shipbuilders plied their trade at the Seattle ports. Competition was intense. The brothers' first move was to acquire one of the shipyard operators and thereby double their waterfront property and capacity. The waterfront rivalry made George appreciate Joseph's high-spirited nature.

Wood or steel, wind or steam, the shipyard buzzed around the clock with the energy of thousands of bees. George looked up and down the crowded and hectic dock to see if his brother was coming. He scanned dozens of hatted heads and faces but did not see Joseph. He found himself spellbound by the constant drone around him. The song of riveters chimed up and down the waterfront. Steam whistles sounded. The horn of a tugboat resonated. Steel ships creaked in the docks. Stevedores and captains and supervisors shouted commands. The clamor enthralled him. The euphony reached into his bones, an ancient symphony playing at a cellular level in his body. Hearing the noise and seeing the action made him stand with pride among the loaders, seamen and shipwrights. In the five hundred-foot-long dry docks, in the drafting rooms, in the fabrication buildings and mold lofts, in the power generating stations and tool sheds, Stevens & Gibbs employees worked their age-old occupation in seeming defiance of time.

Erect masts. Sea mist. Plump clouds.

Then, George's thoughts turned again, this time to his wife Agnes, who was in labor at home. This was why his brother's summons to the docks was so ill timed. No pregnancy had ever been easy for his wife. This one was difficult, too; lots of sickness and weeks-long spells in bed. She had given birth to three girls — but no boys — in nine years. She also suffered through three miscarriages and three stillbirths. George was worried and wanted to be near his wife. But Joseph had asked to meet him, so here he was, waiting.

He hoped the meeting would be quick so he could hop back on the ferry, cross Lake Washington and get home in time to celebrate the birth of a healthy fourth child.

George smelled the freshly cut wood from the sawmill and then caught a whiff of sticky, metallic soot coming from down the dock where ships were being repaired. A dull pain throbbed at the back of his head, and he trembled slightly. Was it the constant Northwest chill sending him shivers? Or did he just have too much on his mind?

He worried a lot lately, fretting over World War I rattling the world's foundation, even from afar. He fretted over the pressures of handling the family consortium of businesses. He fretted over his wife's trauma amidst it all. He pondered endlessly over his voluminous reading and interpretation of tree improvements and hybridization. He either brooded over intrusions of the outside world into his personal life, or agonized about his personal and business life spilling over and affecting the outside world. The double-barreled cacophony of thoughts needled his temples and confused his mind.

Really, the only influence he held over anything in the outside world was the outflow of timber. If he could completely master the harvesting of trees, might he also hold greater sway over the future — his companies', his wife's, his children's, his own?

He heard a shot of steam burst from somewhere down the wharf, and another whistle. The workers — moving around the ships and slipways with tempo, skill and purpose — made his head spin. He wished he could put an end to the gyrations around and inside him.

And where was his brother, anyway?

George drew several deep breaths. What if Agnes lost another baby? What if she left him with no sons, no natural male heirs, nobody suited to take over the business and family investments? Why was he always thinking in terms of losses? Trees gone, children lost, money dwindling. If the war expands and America jumps into the worldwide fire, how many Stevens & Gibbs ships will be lost? How many vessels will be bombed, torpedoed, wrecked? We will just build more, his brother told him when he voiced this concern.

"Stevens and Gibbs grows ships like the forest grows trees," Joseph said. "All the while, no matter what, the Stevens family will keep putting more money in the bank. I don't know why you worry so much."

But what about children? They don't grow like trees in the forest. Agnes might not be able to create any more humans if parturition ends tragically again. Would they even try? Should she even try?

Perhaps his daughters would demonstrate nontraditional acumen in matters of business. More and more, Agnes liked to remind him, women were beginning to take control over family assets and property. Deep inside, however, he knew a son was better suited. He knew Joseph was right.

His brother and four other men had approached and now stood next to him, but George had heard nothing, not even his name.

"George. George! Caught you daydreaming again, didn't I?" Joseph quipped with a sly wink. "You're too cerebral, my brother."

"In my entire life, this might be the first time I didn't hear you coming," George joked, relieved Joseph had finally shown up.

Joseph exuded all of the energy of the dockworkers around him, and his vivacity swallowed up his brother, as usual. Joseph was now talking loudly to his companions: two Navy officers in blue service coats over white shirts and standing stiff collars; a man from the Shipping Board in a tailored wool suit; and the confident and very adept general manager of Stevens & Gibbs and Port Seattle Timber, Mr. Samuel Bass, who wore a black bowler and tweed coat.

Joseph pulled George closer into the circle with an arm around his shoulder and kept talking.

"Samuel and I were telling these gentlemen that we're competing to be one of the fastest shipwrights on the East and West coasts — and we've only just begun. Isn't that right, George? Just think about what we've accomplished in less than a year. Imagine, gentlemen, the feat of engineering it took to implement Mr. Bass's innovative method of ship construction. This modular system is nothing short of a miracle."

Joseph started walking, gesturing for the group to come along with him farther down the waterfront. He was eager to leave what was basically his brother's domain — the cargo quays where ships were being loaded with enough lumber to rebuild several major cities — and go to what he saw as a more exciting area, the shipyards where the vessels were built.

"Look around at these workmen," Joseph exclaimed with a sweep of his arm. "These are the people who really make it all happen. And none of it is by accident, either. Recruitment, recruitment, recruitment. Up and down the West Coast, we invite skilled workers to relocate here. We pay them well above the standard wage so we can attract the best and most qualified workers in the country and leave labor strife outside our gates. Having said that, I must tell you that we could not do it without this man right here. Do you think the Stevens family had any experience building with steel?" Joseph let out a huge self-deprecating howl and continued talking.

"Hell no. We owe it all to Mr. Bass. He has loads of experience with steel. Years and years of experience. He began working at his father's shipyard in Leith, Scotland, before he was ten years old. My father met him as a young man working steel up at the Great Lakes when our family was building wood ships back there. Fifteen years later, we stumble across him working in Bremerton — right under our noses. He knows every inch of these docks, from one end to the other. He implemented the superb technique we are using. I'm not too proud to say I was smart enough to take note of it."

"You're too kind, Mr. Stevens," Samuel Bass said quickly trying to get a word in. "I know my craft, but your family are masters at making maritime money. I simply keep the workers disciplined and the docks running smoothly."

"You're the best, Sam," Joseph said sincerely. "You truly are. Gentlemen, you can see we're proud of the fact that we at Stevens and Gibbs have distinguished ourselves in production speed in less than a year. We just hope we can pass our know-how onto the next generation of Stevens men, just like my grandfather and my papa did in Maine and Michigan long before George and I moved out here and started our seafaring endeavors. Am I right, brother?"

George nodded in agreement, but he was thinking that his older brother could talk without a breath as long as an oboe can carry a note. He also felt a sting from Joseph's insinuation that the family's "know-how" was only passed down through male heirs.

"You see, we've switched to producing steel ships with steam engines," Joseph told his audience. "Over there — those twenty-five acres adjacent to our port — we are buying them as we speak because we know it's inevitable that President Wilson will ask Congress for a declaration of war and it won't be long before the great armed forces of the United States are sent into battle to save the world. The president himself promised to deliver the greatest navy in the world when he passed the National Defense Act. He's increasing the size of the Army, isn't he? And Congress is right behind him, allocating all the necessary funds for building battleships three years out. Stevens and Gibbs just wants to be prepared when the time arrives and our president comes calling. We want to do our part for the country. Hell, I'm not saying I want to go to war any more than the next guy, but if we do, by damn, I might as well make money out of it as well as do my part to help the country. If we begin building commissioned vessels for the Navy, we will expand this shipyard out to eighty acres — or more, once we purchase Tacoma Dry Dock. Gentlemen, Stevens Family Investments has expanded its holdings from being merely a timber company to what is now a major shipbuilding company. We can deliver a freighter in ninety days. That's keel to launch in less than three months."

George saw his brother look at the officers' faces to gauge how approvingly they had accepted his words. They, surprisingly, were as emotionless as a bullet.

"That's ninety days. Hell, George's wife, who is about to give birth any moment, can't deliver a baby in fewer than nine months," Joseph guffawed, searching for some reaction.

The all-business Shipping Board representative asked seriously, "Can S and G handle tankers of up to seven thousand tons?"

"We can build and service freighters and tankers up to fifteen thousand tons, sir," Joseph answered resolutely. "We may be the young shipwrights in the port, but we've grown our capabilities immensely in a very short time. Our slips have fifty-ton floating cranes, one hundred-foot uprights and trolleys that haul the heaviest prefabricated sections you can imagine."

"There are a lot of shipbuilders on the West Coast that the Navy can rely on," one Navy officer said, seemingly unimpressed by S&G. "Many of them are right here in Seattle and Tacoma. And, as you know, the Navy has its own yard right over there in Bremerton. We must wait and see what the demand for ships ends up being — and whether the country actually enters this conflagration across the Atlantic or stays neutral. Our key aim, of course, is to ensure peace for the United States."

"Navy men for peace, huh? Interesting slogan. That has a nice ring to it, but certainly, preparedness can't hurt," Joseph challenged.

"We appreciated the tour, Mr. Stevens," the officer said. "Will you walk us back to the motor vehicle?"

The Navy men took a few steps up the dock but Joseph did not budge. They looked back at him. His welcoming demeanor and mirth were gone.

"Go ahead without us," he responded. "Tell my driver where to take you. I'm going to talk with my brother on our way back to the ferry. But let me leave you with this thought, gentlemen: When the president decides to enter the war and the Navy needs to meet our country's national defense needs, whether that's transporting supplies all over the world or ensuring that the flow of commerce continues on the open seas, you won't have the luxury nor wherewithal to transform, build and expand your little fleet on your own. That's when you'll come running to us, because you know that what I have shown you was more than you expected. You know we are the most modern, advanced shipbuilders in Seattle. It's unprecedented what we're doing here. Fast performance, skilled work, the ability to expand at a moment's notice and the desire to cooperate with the U.S. Navy. If you can't see that is exactly what you and the country need, and what we provide, may God save you!"

The visitors gave an official nod and strode off toward the shipyard's gateway.

"What didn't they like?" Joseph asked his brother and Samuel when the Navy contingency departed.

"Maybe your pregnancy joke," George said straightforwardly.

"I know what it was!" Joseph declared, ignoring his brother. "It was the timeframe. I didn't sell the tempo of the work enough. I worried about it the minute I said it. Ninety days. It didn't sound fast enough. We can do better than three months to build a ship. That sounds way too long.

"Samuel, we are going to get that pace down to seventy-five days. Immediately! That's your primary job, starting right now — to push production limits like the world has never seen. We will get the amount of time it takes to build a ship down to less than seventy-five days. No, seventy days! That's my goal! Seventy days. Can you do it?"

"Absolutely, sir," Samuel consented. "We will need to hire a lot more craftsmen and laborers, though."

"Whatever you need. We're going to get those lucrative Navy contracts."

"Maybe you should catch up to the officers and tell them," Samuel said.

"And maybe modulate your words," George suggested.

Joseph lashed out at his taciturn brother.

"That's stupid advice, George. Stop giving advice on my end of the docks. The tone wasn't the thing. They'll come running back. Nobody can compete with Stevens and Gibbs. At any rate, don't you have a new baby to meet? Hopefully, it's a boy this time."

"Listen Joseph, as long as the baby is healthy, that's all I can ask. Society is changing, whether you like it or not. States are giving women more independent control of businesses and property. So stop with the whole male heir thing. You sound old. Like dad."

"And you sound like your wife," Joseph shouted back. "I don't mind being compared to Big Papa. You should try carrying yourself like him more often. Generation to generation, sons are natural and legal heirs when it comes to this family's assets. That's how it is, from our timber concerns to shipbuilding to our investment group. That's how father wanted it. Why? Because it makes sense. Because it works. Because experience shows that sons are naturally better suited to lead companies. They always have been. Daughters marry and then bugger off to be a part of another family. They become somebody else's problem, while sons keep building family wealth and carry on the legacy. You don't want our wealth given away by diluting the lines of direct control. My boy, Conrad, is already immersed in our company's culture, and he's nine years old. Why must you challenge this? Hope for a boy, or try for another one soon, but don't talk to me about how society and business is changing. Damn it! You've gotten me all riled up. Now's not the time for that discussion. Let's go catch that ferry."

"I just want a healthy child."

Joseph abruptly stopped walking, and George thought he was going to escalate their disagreement. *Perhaps I should have let it go at "let's go catch the ferry,"* George thought.

"Wait," Joseph said, instantly burying the squabble in his mind. "You get back to Seattle and your wife. Give my love to Agnes. Say hi to the girls. Mr. Bass! You and I have something to do right now. Run ahead and grab those uniforms and bring them back to Plant No. 2."

"Why? There's nothing to see there but a dry dock," Samuel said, "not even a skeleton of a hull."

"Listen to me. The speed of production — that's the problem. That's why they were not impressed. We didn't sell them enough on how fast we are going to build their ships. We didn't distinguish ourselves enough from the others around Puget Sound."

"But we're the best."

"We must do better. We need to cut twenty days off our time."

"I must repeat: Our workforce is at capacity, sir."

"No, we *were* at capacity. Not anymore."

"Twenty days?"

"Let's push that modular construction technique of yours to the limits. What do you say, Bass? Hurry! Get the uniforms back down here before they get to the car, and meet me at Plant No. 2."

George had turned into a statue, frozen between being a husband and being a superlative business partner.

"Well? Are you going home to see your baby, or staying with me?"

"I'll come with you."

"I'm going to the employment office outside the gate where the sailors and ship fitters are waiting and looking for work. You go to Plant No. 2 and wait for Bass and the officers." Joseph briefly smirked, but George ignored it.

Around the employment office stood dozens of sad-looking young and old men, most wearing caps, many holding their own rivet hammers. A few school-aged boys were among them, thirteen or fourteen years old, and Joseph noticed at least two women dressed like the men. Standing under the eave of the roof over the entry gates, where the name Stevens & Gibbs Corporation was emblazoned in enormous, white capital letters, he got everyone's attention with a loud, high-pitched whistle.

"I need workers who will help Stevens and Gibbs shatter ship-building records. I'm going to hire fifty of you right now, on the spot. If you prove you have skill and a strong work ethic, you can stay on at remuneration that you would not think possible. Your earnings will be commensurate to the work rendered. That work will be dangerous, arduous, taxing, grimy. There will be long days. You'll be handling shears, punches, saws. You will work inches away from hellish furnaces. But if you show me skill and determination, you'll stay on, earning much more than your daily expenses. So remain where you are standing, and I'll come and choose who I want. Then follow me to the dry dock, where my manager will tell you what to do next and when to report for work tomorrow. The rest of you can come back tomorrow and the next day. We will hire more workers.

"And one more thing. You will learn a non-traditional way of assembling ships. So I need smart, flexible tradesmen, technicians, journeymen" — Joseph tapped one of the women on the shoulder to indicate she had been chosen for the work — "and even some women will be enlisted."

At Plant No. 2, Joseph found his brother, Bass and the officers, looking impatient and inconvenienced, waiting for him. The newly hired workers sat silent and dazed on the stepped sides of the dry dock.

"I'm sorry to delay your departure," Joseph said to the military men. "Thank you for coming back. I want you to look at this empty slip, and these workers. In this very spot in less than two-and-a-half months a new freighter will be built, assembled, joined and ready to hand over to the United States Navy. I invite you back here on December tenth to see the finished ship. We will christen the boat, and then another and another. You will see what we can accomplish here at Stevens and Gibbs. I hope that we won't be at war yet, but even if we are, please tell the Shipping Board that by spring we will have ten freighters built for the U.S. or the U.K — twice as many as any other yard. We launch the first one right where you are standing, in seventy days."

CHAPTER 2

George tried to stay happy, optimistic and unworried as he drove his automobile at full speed up the motor court of his Colonial Revival home on Lake Washington.

The estate sat on five acres. Formal flower, herb and vegetable gardens grew in the front, and in the back, an apple orchard and a small forest of evergreens stretched down to the lake. Even at home, the lumber baron surrounded himself with trees.

He had devoted hundreds of hours to designing the estate, working with a renowned architect to build the ten-bedroom house with its grand entrance separating two symmetrical wings that angled back toward the lake. Its vast interior, well lit and airy, was set off by fine woodwork and high, wood-beamed ceilings. Decorative molding and quarter-sawn oak floors helped complete the grand home.

But the gorgeous surroundings and trappings meant little to him as he raced up the drive, and he gave no thought to all those details he had so carefully crafted. George was arriving home much later than he had promised his wife. Most of the property was enveloped in darkness, and few lights inside the house were glowing.

He emerged quickly from his car, threw open the front door to the house and hurried toward the birthing room, single-mindedly set on seeing his wife as quickly as possible — until a chambermaid abruptly stopped him midway on his ascent up the double staircase.

"Get out of my way," he barked.

Agnes Stevens was giving birth in a canopy bed behind the closed doors of her second-floor bedroom, and her birth attendants did not believe it was time for the husband to be introduced into that raw cauldron of pain and contractions and dilation and opiate stress management.

"No! I'm sorry, sir. But it's important that Mrs. Stevens remains comfortable and calm," the servant said. "The midwife reports that she is doing fine. We have not even felt the need to alert the doctor. Her brother and father are in the game room, if you care to join them."

"And my wife? Shall we ask her?"

"We did, as soon as we heard the motor car arrive. I think you know her answer."

"Where's the doctor?"

"I told you, there is no need for a doctor at this time. Now please, we have more work to do."

George discerned birthing noises and movement coming from behind the closed door of the barred room beyond the top landing. Casting his eyes down the stairway and to his right, he heard the men's voices and saw light leaking out of the doorway of the billiards room. He again glanced past the chambermaid to the top of the stairs, then back down to the game room.

"Perhaps just a whiskey and some eight-ball first," he said, his composure regained.

They met in the summer of 1903. The Stevens family was spending a month at their Long Island vacation home, away from their main residence in Saginaw, Michigan. The beachfront house slept twenty people, and it was a good thing, because the extended family was growing as fast as their wealth. This weekend, though, the Long Island Victorian was not full, an in-between time when many cousins had departed and others had yet to arrive.

George had just graduated from Harvard with a bachelor's of science degree. He was the second Stevens family member to attend college, after his brother Joseph, who received his Harvard business degree eight years earlier. In celebration, George invited six of his closest classmates to the house for a long weekend of celebration.

One of his good friends, Abel Day, said he could only come if he brought his younger sister along, having been put in charge of her while their parents traveled abroad.

"Can't it be arranged for her to stay with the governess?" George asked him as they prepared to leave the campus for the last time.

"They prefer my supervision for some reason," Abel answered.

"Fine, bring her. There will be plenty of activities for her."

So Agnes tagged along. She was 17 years old.

Abel and George's relationship went back to when they were roommates at a prestigious college prep school in New Jersey, and they again shared a room at Harvard. They did not talk much about their siblings, except for Joseph, because he was the oldest, had achieved distinguished status in scholarly circles and final clubs at Harvard, and had taken over the family business at a young age.

Before her trip to Long Island, the only mention of Agnes came when Abel identified her and other family to George in a photograph in a gilded frame that hung in their room.

Abel directed Agnes to make herself scarce during the Long Island weekend because the young men did not need an adolescent girl hanging around, bothering them, getting in the way, hindering their conversations and activities and generally ruining the fraternal mood.

"I'm not a kid," she rejoined.

She might have remained forever unknown to George if he had not glanced at her while she rested on a blanket on the front lawn, reading a book in the sun, as if she were a subject in a Georges Seurat painting. The romantic scene immediately, internally and hopelessly flooded him with intense fondness.

Agnes knew much more about George Stevens than he knew about her. Both families' roots were well established in the Saginaw Bay region, but of the two households, only the Stevens name adorned an opera house and a downtown business district. The Stevens family owned a fleet of boats navigating the Great Lakes and dominated maritime commerce in the region. Their syndicate had pockets deep enough to corner the Midwest salt market at a time when lumber mills were closing by the dozens and fuel to evaporate brine was vanishing.

But that weekend, Agnes got to know her brother's well-to-do, older friend — without getting in the way of the group of friends. The first things she noticed about George were his kind eyes, his soft voice and upright posture. He impressed Agnes as a scholarly, well-mannered rich boy who was a bit on the quiet side and inclined toward the scientific world.

In short, but friendly, conversations and early passing flirtations with her in hallways or on the deck or in the kitchen, George learned just enough to get dangerously close to developing a very deep affection for Agnes, really just a child. A wild aspiration to know everything about her struck him. Being limited to observing, mostly from afar, her comeliness and her intoxicating idiosyncrasies, he was left to fill in the unknowns of her personality with unrestrained and highly pleasurable conjecture. He enthroned her in the brightest light.

He noticed that Agnes filled rooms to the rafters with her soaring spirit and organic beauty when she entered, like a butterfly flitting into view against a backdrop of cloudless, blue sky. To George, everybody else in the room was a mere caterpillar that never could achieve such a glorious metamorphosis as she. Agnes was as ephemeral as a butterfly, too, because of her brother's decree that she leave the boys alone. For two days, she fluttered away as soon as George set his eyes on her. As soon as he put his legs in motion to walk up to her, she was gone. His desire to talk directly to her for more than a few seconds needed to be satisfied. She was chary of allowing this, but George told himself to hell with Abel's restrictions on her, it was his party.

But he did not see her at all on the third day, which was the Fourth of July, a wild Saturday night. The boom! boom! boom! of fireworks cracked like artillery blasts, and rockets streaked across the sky, piercing a thick pillow of smoke above the water before exploding into a blossom of purple allium-like balls and then a mayapple-shaped umbrella of white. A hot, white trace pierced through the abscission of sparks hanging in the air, flashed and disappeared. Smoke hung in patches over the ocean, and fireworks clapped nonstop as if bands of musketeers were running amok all over Long Island.

The boys went to the town center where drunken men gadded from street to street, harassed well-dressed women and tossed fireworks under horse-drawn buggies. In the folly and uproar of the night, fires ignited, buildings burned, fingers were blown off and eyes put out.

For a while, Agnes watched the distant skies from the balcony of the vacation house, and it all looked beautiful to her.

The young men decamped back to the Stevens house, unscathed by the revelry, and once home they slept like rocks as the night wore on and the war-like sights and sounds became more sporadic.

The next night, George finally got a chance to talk to Agnes unfettered. His opportunity came because his and Joseph's mother, Charlene — the family matriarch and widow of Conrad "Big Papa" Stevens — decided to host a reception at her beach house. Charlene's invitations called the party "a refined celebration on the day after the Fourth of July."

Dozens of prominent people came. Many Long Island households had stayed put during the traditionally raucous and boorish Independence Day celebration, which was not for the faint-hearted, and now they wanted to venture out. Many of them availed themselves of merrymaking provided by the Stevens instead of circulating to other Long Island mid-summer gatherings.

The "Sagaponack Smiths" and the "Richardsons of Manhattan" and the "Neighbors of Theodore Roosevelt" and others of the like monopolized chairs in the front and second parlors in the Stevens home. They nattered with pastors and bankers, whaling magnates and textile titans.

Inside was noisy with music, talking and laughing. Outside, Agnes stood alone near the railing on the quieter balcony, facing the ocean. The moon backlit the S-bend of her figure, so soft and feminine in her evening dress. George noticed her like an astronomer finding a new bright constellation in the night sky, and he could not look away. He excused himself from the small group he was with and went out to her.

She heard the French doors open behind her, releasing a rush of voices and music, and then quickly close. She looked back and saw George slowly approaching.

"I hope I'm not disturbing you. I seem to have caught you enjoying a moment of solitude. I'm interrupting. I'm sorry."

"Of course not, although I may not be great company."

"We haven't said much to each other this weekend, but just having you here has brightened the place."

She smiled, and George's heart opened and expanded like the sky.

"I wish we had had more time to talk," he said. "The weekend is nearly gone, and I feel like I've had little chance to get to know you. I wish we could share more time."

"I will be going back to Saginaw with Abel," Agnes responded. "I will be there for the rest of summer, maybe longer. You should call if you're in town."

"That's just the thing. My mother received a telegram from my brother Joseph yesterday."

"Is everything all right? You seem saddened by the news."

"It's complicated. Joseph is the adventurous one in the family. He's been out West for a couple years, in California and Washington, considering possible investments out there. When Joseph was settling my father's estate four years ago, he was being pulled in many directions by our cousins and other investment partners about how to proceed with the estate."

Joseph resisted closing existing businesses or buying any new ones, George explained. He paid out the personal accounts and kept the money in Stevens Investment Company, and he allowed investment funds to work while making no outlays.

"Guaranteed income is what he called it. The goal was to build up the fund before we invested in any businesses, especially mills. It proved to be a brilliant plan. Joseph put the family in great position, and now he just made big front-page headlines out West for buying the largest lumberyard in the world for two million dollars. He wants to move forward with other enterprises, and he needs me to come to Washington and join him. He wants me to come out to Seattle as soon as I can, as soon as the holiday weekend ends."

"That's wonderful. You must be very happy. What a future you will make with your brother."

"He's got the brains for business. I'm just a science guy."

George had been talking more than usual, and he looked into Agnes' eyes, searching for any hint that he should stop. A long, pensive silent ensued.

"You don't seem entirely happy about this new venture, George!" she exclaimed. "What are you worried about?"

"I'm thinking about parts of Michigan and Maine that look like ghost towns now. Mills take raw wood, and they cut it and manufacture boards into lumber for houses and other buildings. So we keep felling trees by the thousands of acres, and we've wiped out many entire forests. Sawmills all around Lake Superior are abandoned and lumber docks are decaying. In the cities, I see houses in disrepair, businesses closing — all in the name of progress. Agnes, I don't want to do the same thing in California and Oregon and Washington and Alaska?"

"Then don't."

"How do I tell my brother all of that in a telegraph?"

"You tell him when you get out there, and then you change the way they're plying the timber trade out there. You take a greater role in the Stevens family businesses."

"But that's not all that saddens me," George said, even though he feared he might seem like a gloomy soul when she was a carefree butterfly. He had to get everything off his chest now, out here on the balcony even as the spirited celebration of the nation's founding continued. "I don't want to leave you."

"Why?"

"In part, because I don't know you very well yet, and in part because I *have* gotten to know you. Either way..."

"Oh, George. You can't stay because of me. As much as I would like that. Your brother and your family — and this country and our natural resources — need you. I would rather you stay out East, too, but if you go I promise I will write to you every week. And I know because you are a sensitive man that you will write back to me. Our relationship is not over. It has just begun."

The time they next saw each other, she was 19 years old, and in the preceding two years, she wrote 52 letters to George. He wrote back 20 times. Not by accident, Agnes' letters conveyed a lot about her social life — and did so for several reasons. First, she hoped to give the man courting her from afar the impression that there were many capable and eligible suitors closer to her, and numerous chances for interaction with them. She also did not want her life to sound dull, as if she were just a sitting in her room reading, sighing and patiently waiting for her lover to return and sweep her away. After all, he had gone West to do great, influential things in commerce and to get rich by the sweat of his own brow.

Most importantly, she sought to give the appearance — not just to him but the entire community — that her family was maintaining their social standing even though their once-significant financial resources had severely dwindled, which was a closely held secret. Her father privately adjusted his spending without showing any outward signs of financial strain, and Agnes continued to engage with the gentry at soirees, visited museums and attended concerts — all the while dressing glamorously and display-ing the most refined manners.

She was not blind to how marrying into the wealthy Stevens clan would be a strategic way to secure financial and social status, but she knew her innermost feelings for George were love and respect.

A typical letter from Agnes:

Dear George,
I do hope that when you visit you will accompany me to the numerous
social events that have kept me busy in your absence. Even though I am

sometimes the youngest woman in the room, I've grown quite comfortable in intellectual circles and am quite the regular guest at the orchestral concerts at Mrs. Schubert's Center Avenue mansion...

If you think about our relationship, is it not like the bellows? There's this emptiness between us, but it's only air and distance, and through just words, we are capable of emitting a serious romance, a spark of love, even across an expansive physical space...

I hesitate to mention this, it's so trite, but my father and mother are pestering me daily to ask you about it. So here it goes. Could you or Joseph write to Abel to see if he's interested in coming West? They think that if there's a job for him with Port Seattle Timber Co. — whether it's in the business office or at the mills, out on the loading docks or felling trees, or transporting the lumber — that it might do my brother some good and give him a fresh start. He's been quite in the dumps since graduation and is at the moment selling shoes downtown. He's so ashamed of his position that he won't show his face in public very much...

There, that's done.

I took a car ride the other day on a road through the old forest land and started crying when I looked around at the devastation there. I am so happy you are trying to find a way to replenish the trees that lumbermen so carelessly chop down until the land looks like a hair brush whose bristles have been burned and plucked nearly clean of the paddle. When will mankind stop taking trees for fuel and stop building without consideration of how long it takes for them to regrow?...

George, I am so happy when you write to me, although I realize your pace cannot keep up with mine. I know you are busy in the mills and shipyards, but do expound on life out on the West Coast the next time you pick up the pen...

George's letters were indeed succinct. He talked mostly about developments in his work ("Joseph just purchased ten thousand more acres of forest land because he says whoever owns the trees will control the mills. But we are just a small part of the industry right now."); he wrote about the beauty of the landscape and the abundant natural resources all around the Olympic peninsula ("I get lost gazing from the perpetual dark green of the forest up to the soft blues and brilliant whites of the snowy Olympic Mountains in winter."); and he noted the weather ("We're now quite accustomed to the bitter winds that whip down from Canada in the winter, and familiar with the less nippy but still gray springtime, where the sunshine streaks through nimbus clouds").

His intellectual, scientific side also often showed as he wrote of his obsession with the study of breeding, what the future would be like if he could make hybrid trees to grow bigger faster.

His words at the end of one letter sent a frightened chill through her, though she did not know precisely why. She felt an underlying unease for days afterward. He had told her that he had become intrigued with the theory that humans themselves could improve through well-managed breeding.

"I have come across the writings of a man who was born not too far from our Michigan home, John Harvey Kellogg. Mr. Kellogg has some interesting notions on eugenics that I want to pursue," George wrote.

Parallel thoughts from the horror novel "The Modern Prometheus" filled her mind.

Agnes mostly dismissed whatever faults she inferred from the words on the sheets. She primarily gleaned from his communication that he adored her and planned to come home to marry her as soon as business allowed — and when he returned, together they would make the journey back to the West Coast. After all, that was George's new home and would be forever more. He may be more reserved in his expression than she would have preferred, but he was a smart, wealthy, kind man, rising in social status and from a good family. He could bolster her status among the elite with the significant means her own family no longer enjoyed.

George wrote:

As I drove home from work today and saw this city's grand mansions sprouting like new pines, I remembered you mentioning the swaths of vast deforestation that haunt you. Among these stately residences, shanties remain like stumps among tall trees in the forest. Here in Washington, there are so many trees you wonder if they could ever all be cut down. I know that is not true, my love (trust me, the smell of sawdust constantly hanging in the Puget Sound air has not affected my brain). My intention is to share one of these mansions with you, as man and wife, in the very near future. I think I might start building our home now.

By the time George and Joseph got on a train leaving Seattle for Saginaw in 1905, both knew that he was going back to propose marriage to Agnes. Joseph traveled with George not just to stand next to him during the reading of the vows, but also to tie up final loose ends to Big Papa's trust.

In 1905, George Stevens married Agnes Day.

With the trust finally settled and the family's investment company running smoothly under middle brother Walter's management, Joseph, George and his new wife turned their backs on Michigan and took off for their prosperous new life in Seattle.

When George first met Agnes, he found her to be the prettiest young woman he'd ever seen from Michigan to Massachusetts. Now, he knew she was the prettiest from East Coast to West. Her round cheeks, the dimples that framed her smile and gave the impression she held a pretty little secret, the big brown eyes, her soft, thick black hair, that graceful walk and — most of all — a strong belief in him and herself all made George's heart and mind jump and scream when he was with her, just like when they met on that wonderful Fourth of July weekend.

George imagined painting the backdrop of Seattle an intense cerulean, something perfect for his monarch to delightfully flit across.

Grunts and groans and frantic screams emanated from the upstairs room and echoed throughout the house. They came in such violent torrents that George's chest constricted in mid-stroke, and he strangled the cue stick.

The pandemonium ended about midnight, and this time no housekeeper or midwife would stop him from entering the room. He dropped the wood stick on the billiards table and went up the stairs two at a time. But once inside the bedroom, he stopped, uncertain what to do next. Standing just inside the door, he gazed at his wife. Her face was splotchy red. He gaped at her knitted brows, glassy eyes, and thick aerie of hair. For the delivery, she had been moved from the big four-poster bed to an adjacent wooden birthing chair where she still gripped the arms with all of her might. George looked at the soiled linens on the butler's folding table as well as a basin of bloody water, forceps and various other medical instruments.

The midwife and attendants helped Agnes to the bed, pulled the covers over her legs and arranged pillows and blankets until she was comfortable and then propped her against the headboard. Finally, George saw the swaddled baby, calm and sleepy, being gently set into her hands. He approached his wife.

"It's a girl!" the midwife announced happily to him.

"Oh, God, I'm so happy," George cried, sitting close to his wife — and it was the truth.

Minutes later, his nine-year-old daughter ran fast into the room on her bare, light, little feet and leaped into the small space on the other side of her mother on the bed. All three dreamily gazed down at the newborn.

"Susan! It's too early in the morning for you to be up!" George mockingly scolded.

"I couldn't sleep. Can Sara come in, too, mother?"

"No, she still has a sore throat, fever and cough. We don't want to get the baby sick. She can see her later."

"Is her name Anne, mother?"

"Yes, her name is Anne Charlotte Stevens."

George kissed his wife on the cheek. She rested her head on his chest and he tenderly stroked her hair. Susan asked a hundred more questions, about names, the noises she had heard coming from this room, immediate plans, and the dreams she had. After a while, the stories and inquiries stopped, and George felt Susan's rhythmic breathing and knew she was asleep. He kissed the top of her head. When Agnes looked up at her husband, she saw his teary eyes.

"Are you happy?"

"Immensely."

"Even though she's a girl?" she teased, gently slapping his chest. "I think your brother will be disappointed."

"It's a miracle. He understands miracles. He performs them every day at work. He was working on one today."

The three of them snoozed close to each other for a few hours. Around 4 a.m., George slipped out of the bed, beaming as he left the room so his wife, oldest daughter and baby could keep sleeping soundly. He planned to go to the shipyard first thing in the morning and boast to Joseph how his new baby girl was just as beautiful as any male heir could ever be. More so.

Down the hallway, he peeked in his other daughter's room. Sara was four years old. When he walked into her room, she was sleeping, but he could tell her rest was fitful. Concerned, he set a hand on her forehead. Her skin felt mildly warm but not hot. Her throat, though, looked reddish and puffy. As his daughter began to stir and wake, George, a scientific man, pondered calling the doctor. First, though, he wanted to gather more evidence of how sick Sara was.

"Honey," he asked her when she finally opened her eyes, "will you open your mouth wide so I can see how that scratchy throat of yours looks inside?"

"Why, daddy?" Sara asked in a frail, hoarse voice, and then coughed.

He grabbed the nickel chrome flashlight from atop her dresser and slid the switch on.

"Just checking something, sweetie," George soothingly said as he shined the light into her mouth. The normally pink soft palette looked greenish gray and coated with mucus.

His chest tightened as if a bear had sat on it. His heart sped up with growing panic, but his voice was steady, his expression a blank slate.

"Try to go back to sleep, my dear."

With his wife asleep and likely dreaming of her beautiful new baby girl at her bedside, George called for the head housekeeper and told her to summon the doctor.

"He should have already been here for the birth," George ranted. "It was a bad decision to keep him away. He could have been here to examine the child. He could have seen her symptoms, comforted her. He could have put the word out that we need an antitoxin. Damn it, I should fire you, the chambermaid and everybody else for your harmful actions, your injurious inaction!"

"What message should I give the doctor now, sir?"

"Tell him Sara has signs of diphtheria and he must get an antitoxin here fast."

As he waited for the doctor, long spells of uncertainty over whether to awaken Agnes ensued. He kept a constant watch on his daughter's restless sleep, looking for any worsening symptoms. By the time Dr. Eugene Phillips arrived, Sara's breathing had become difficult, stifled. It was 7 a.m.

George decided to wake his wife. He told the chambermaid to keep his other daughter away if she woke up, too.

When he reentered Sara's room, she had begun making choking and gagging sounds.

"Her breathing is getting worse," the doctor said solemnly. "The membrane must be obstructing her throat."

"What can you do, doctor? Where's the serum?"

"There's no antitoxin in the entire Pacific Northwest, none that I was able to locate," Dr. Phillips told George. "I've put out the word, however."

"There must be something."

"When your housekeeper told me you suspected there were signs of diphtheria, I threw in my intubation tube, but that's no guarantee. I could perform a tracheotomy, but only as a last result. We're running out of time, but we're not desperate — yet."

Agnes burst into the room looking as untamed and unbridled as when she was in the throes of childbirth. She flew to the bedside. Sara's eyes shot open, and the first thing she saw was her mother's horrified expression. Panic arose in the small girl. Her parents calmed her down after several minutes of her coughing, gagging and trying to talk. Agnes felt horrible and flustered that she had been unable to conceal her despair, and had made things worse.

"Why didn't we have the doctor here already?" George asked heedlessly. "He might have prevented this."

Agnes looked at him with burning eyes but did not say a word. Those poorly considered, unthinkable words of accusation and blame quickly sunk to the bottom of her saddened soul like a rock in a stream. George's words would always be there, a part of her — unchanging, solid and too heavy to bear — even if the river bed of sorrow dried up.

The most harrowing hours followed. Sara's agonizing symptoms advanced. Her heart galloped nonstop. Her body burned to the touch. In her mother's arms, she shuddered and her teeth clacked. She was limp. Agnes looked down at her little bluish face framed by the white pillow as if her head was vanishing into a cloud. Snot bubbled in her wheezing nostrils and her throat gurgled. Her mother only took breaks from holding her sick child every few hours to breastfeed her newborn girl. When the feeding was over, she shoved the baby into her chambermaid's arms and ran back to Sara's room.

It had been twenty-four hours since the doctor arrived, but he could not remain at the Stevens home indefinitely. When he left, the world might as well have ended for George and Agnes, they were so worried. They pleaded and cried and offered to pay him whatever it would take to keep him next to Sara's bed. But it was imperative that he make other house calls, and he assured them that his absence would not be detrimental. He would return as soon as possible. He left them with strict instructions about the importance of bed rest for Sara, drinking plenty of water, consuming broth and vegetables, if she wanted to eat at all, and isolating her from the other children.

However, when he returned, sapped of energy from no sleep, Sara had worsened. Dr. Phillips conceded the likelihood of asphyxiation. Agnes gasped. George's head dropped into his hands.

"It's time. Her airways are blocked and can't get cleared."

There was no response from the Stevenses.

"I must."

George succumbed to the frightful inevitability.

"You know best," he said sullenly, unable to believe his own words.

The doctor opened his medical bag. Agnes could not look, but George glanced at what appeared to him to be obscene torture devices. Gold-plated tubes of various sizes, a scissors-like mouth gag, metal forceps and an introducer, each sinisterly set in their own specifically shaped indentation on a small pillow of red velvet.

The doctor solemnly nodded and took matters into his own hands. He pried Sara's jaws open with the mouth gag and then forced clear a passageway with a long silver introducer before inserting the appalling tube.

The end was horrific: Blood, choking, suffocation. Lastly, only the fatigued, flaccid dead body of a young girl lying there.

Their devastating loss would last long, long past that dreadful morning. Agnes crawled into a dark corner somewhere at the edge of the world where nobody could reach her. She stayed in bed for days, gripping the covers to her chest. She was dreadfully tired and shut everybody out. She did not speak, she hardly ate, and she half slept. She was seemingly half-dead in her chamber, yet she knew she was alive because she felt morbid despair and utter hopelessness pervading her entire mind and body.

George never got the chance to express to Joseph the initial happiness that overcame him the moment he set eyes on Anne. He burned with excessive pride over bringing a fourth girl into the family and the world in light of his elder, patriarchal sibling placing such great importance on having sons. The sum of his mirth shriveled to the size of a grain of sand on a beach after Sara died less than 24 hours after Anne was born. Agnes's life and his were shaken to the core, and George mourned and walked around his home like a living corpse.

What could Joseph do for his brother? Nothing but let time heal matters, he concluded, and he toiled away at the shipyard at the feverish pace of two or more men. He begged George to come down to the shipyard and undertake some task that might offer a little diversion, a touch of solace and a bit of normality.

Joseph knew the dogs of war were coming for America. The country was about to head into battle, and assuring that Stevens & Gibbs Shipping was ready for what was ahead rested heavily on his shoulders. In his brother's absence, Joseph counted on Samuel Bass being at his side.

They spent long days and nights working with engineers to accelerate the pace of construction and solve problems that arose from the building and moving of heavy structures, bulky engines and unwieldy steel panels, all at an unheard-of manufacturing pace.

They kept improving upon the most innovative system of shipbuilding ever seen. Their workers joined and assembled interior sections first, then shaped the hull and constructed the rest of the exterior parts in various fabrication buildings on the wharf before dragging them down to the slipway.

The vessel's superstructure and its inner parts were at last joined, completed and tested, and time came for engineers to open the valves to allow water to fill the dry dock and lift the vessel level to the ocean's surface.

On the day of the ship's christening, a tall stage adorned with red, white and blue, star-spangled bunting was erected on the dock, and below it, a marching band played. Ecstatic cheers from the attendees interrupted speeches. Joseph, several Navy dignitaries and the chief executive of the new Emergency Fleet Corporation spoke before an enormous crowd.

The speakers preened themselves on the greatness of Stevens & Gibbs and how their patriotic shipbuilding would profit America as she entered the war. The mayor of Seattle broke a champagne bottle on the bow of the ship before lines were cast off. The gate opened and the magnificent new ship sailed out.

Just a few months later, on April 6, 1917, the U.S. entered the war and Stevens & Gibbs embarked on its most lucrative years ever.

By May, Stevens & Gibbs was rewarded with its first profitable Navy contracts. By summer, the shipbuilder delivered four six thousand-ton cargo ships and two seven thousand-ton tankers. The company completed thirty-five merchant ships and six oil tankers for the Emergency Fleet Corporation. By the fall of 1918, the company employed a village-size workforce of fifteen thousand.

The shipbuilder's astounding success grabbed front-page headlines. Admirals, presidential cabinet members and movie stars visited Joseph at his home. He took luminaries on all-expense-paid, big-game hunting trips to Alaska and Idaho. He and Gibbs bought a private ocean-going luxury yacht and steamed down to San Francisco for dining and theater before driving to San Simeon to camp with the Hearst family on their new property. While in San Francisco, they set up a sales office there.

George still had not made it across the water to the shipyards since Sara's death. He just walked around his property, enveloped in melancholy, and occasionally shook his head violently, as if he had developed a tic. He did not think about his own behavior or health, but neither did he know what to do about his wife's heart-wrenching, withdrawn behavior, what his role was in the soaring prosperity of the Stevens businesses, or how to react to his brother's flamboyant trips and impulsive and exorbitant purchase of a private luxury excursion ship. Attempts to verbalize his thoughts became jumbled in his mind or stuck in his throat. He was despondent at a time when he should have been enjoying all of this great affluence and comfort.

Joseph sensed that George did not approve of his spending, but he did not consider his lifestyle to be at all profligate. It's just that they were piling up so much cash that he needed to spend some of it; indeed, a lot of it.

Still, he felt impelled to justify the purchase of the yacht to his brother. He told George the company was going to start a passenger shipping line after the war, beginning with voyages down to San Francisco and San Diego and Mexico.

"When the guns and bombs go silent, George, people will be yearning for travel and inclined to spend money after so much hardship and heartbreak," Joseph said one day while visiting George and Agnes.

After that, he did not go to his brother and sister-in-law's house for a long time. George did not blame Joseph for avoiding him. After all, he was a heartbroken, sad, regretful man and not very delightful to be around. In great contrast, Joseph was ascending Seattle's elite social ladders. His wife, Eva, took seats on arts boards and spearheaded numerous charitable drives, including campaigns to finance and build a church and a college. Joseph co-founded a local bank with several prominent figures.

Joseph's passion for big-game hunting and deep-sea adventures were becoming legendary. He began memorializing them in lengthy journals that he liked to share with family, friends and clients. He hoped to publish them as a memoir and hunting guide someday.

When Joseph was away on one of his adventures, forlorn George was called upon to oversee the burgeoning company's day-to-day operations. This responsibility pulled him back into the office. He did not outwardly express his feelings about returning to the flow of a work routine, especially to Agnes, but the diversion eventually served to lift his spirits a great deal.

The death of a young child is tragic, and living with a wife devastated by that death is painfully difficult. Figuring out how to talk to her about getting out of the house for a short walk and some fresh air, let alone ever socializing again, proved to be a delicate balance that George still could not get right. Bringing up the possibility of having another child seemed impossible, so he did not try. Agnes emphatically swore never again to go through child bearing. In her darkest moments, when they were alone, she said she wished she had never had any children. George tried to understand her emotional trauma. She iterated to him her fear of repeating the tragedy. Her trepidation did not allow her even to contemplate such a thing.

Most of Seattle daily life was consumed by supporting the dough-boys, young men heading off to military training, calls for citizens to preserve staples, encouragement to buy Liberty Bonds, patriotic songs and the sight of ships filled with those answering the call to fight. Like the rest of the nation, the Pacific Northwest saw an overwhelming number of men from many backgrounds respond to the country's call to arms. From overseas came constant stories of troop movement, massive assaults, injuries, deaths by an array of artillery shells, bombs, bullets and flame-throwers, swelled corpses lying in stagnant water and toxic muck, the spread of influenza and the overwhelming spending of national treasure.

Throughout the entirety of wartime, Agnes stood rooted in grief and despair. Those who did not know her, and those who only recently met her, assumed her temperament was a sign of stress on the domestic front because of the armed conflict overseas.

On Nov. 11, 1918, the war ended, but Agnes still battled her demons.

CHAPTER 3

After the armistice, the American Expeditionary Forces swiftly demobilized. In Seattle, Joseph felt the reverberation from the end of the war even though his own son was far too young to fight and he had no close family members with boys who had served.

The war touched the edges of his life, nonetheless. He saw more and more returning soldiers in stores and restaurants around town, in church pews and applying for jobs at the shipyard. They looked to him like they were on the older side of soldiering, but maybe two years of hard service had just aged them a lot. In his parish, and through the hushed conversations of his workers, he became acutely aware of the unhappy side of the war's end and the return of servicemen to civilian life. So many households faced the reality of sons who had been wounded, were missing or among the fallen.

In late 1918, Joseph decided to bring his own family together for a social dinner as the Stevens clan had done back in Michigan before Big Papa Conrad died and, more recently, at his Seattle home before their lives were ripped apart by little Sara's death. His brother Walter had moved to the Pacific Northwest, and his sister Loretta, her husband, Gordon, and their children were visiting them through the end of the year. The time seemed right to reassemble the family for the holiday season to ring in the new year with renewed hope for a lasting peace.

When your blood relations reach back to colonial New England, like the Stevenses; when your family's timber enterprise dated to the 1870s and once stretched from the North Woods of Maine to upstate New York, from the rich forests of Michigan to the Pacific Northwest; when your copper and iron mining interests originated on the shores of the Great Lakes and extended across the entire Upper Midwest; when, as a major shareholder in several regional banks, you've founded million-dollar charities — then nothing seems impossible, not even re-setting social behavior.

Joseph understood that American culture was upended. In the throes of wartime and death, families could barely summon the energy or spirit to come together even for a simple feast. Now, however, he resolved to sit everybody around the same table in the same way he was determined to make profit out of trade. He had just returned from a two-week fishing and hunting expedition in remote areas of Alaska, so his mind was calm and clear and he was stouthearted in his plans for the future. He put the family reunion at the top of his list of things to do.

He decided to start small, so he and Eva invited the following people: George and Agnes; sister Loretta and brother-in-law Gordon; brother Walter and his wife Lilly; his other sister Victoria and her husband Michael; and Samuel Bass, who was single, and a guest of his choice. A simple party of 12, no children this time.

Because he was full of verve from tracking big game through the vast wilderness, snagging eight-foot halibut in the deep sea, and hooking one hundred and thirty-pound king salmon in the Nushagak River, Joseph did not even consider Agnes's delicate state of mind. He messengered a formal letter of invitation directly to George and Agnes's home. Without consulting her husband, Agnes promptly declined. She mentioned the invitation to George at dinnertime.

"We cannot turn down a dinner invitation from my older brother, not with all that's going on," George bemoaned. "He's trying to make everything right. He's my business partner..."

"I don't see why not. I don't feel up to socializing."

"It doesn't look good. Everybody wants to return to some kind of normal. We have to be civil."

"I declined, but my reply was not discourteous," Agnes retorted. "It's not as if we are breaking an engagement we've already accepted."

"Joseph is reaching out to all of us with cordiality. We haven't mixed at all since the war. It will be good to do so. Everybody has suffered so much."

"I don't think Joseph has suffered all that much — except in the most incidental ways."

"How can you say that?"

"He's richer than ever before, because of the Navy contracts. He lost no close relatives in the war, because of fortunate timing. I've endured more agony than anybody in this family, and I am not ready to interact. I simply can't, George. Can't you understand that?"

"It's just... It might be time for you to..."

"To what?"

"To get out again. To talk to people. It's been so long. These are people who love and care for you."

"What would I possibly say to anybody? What can I talk about? Hunting excursions? Pleasure yachts? Profiting from war? Personal tragedy? What do they know about the weight of a sorrow so great that it makes you not want to leave your bed, let alone your house? The answer to your brother is no! We are not going."

Agnes was not that same quiet girl who tagged along with her brother to Long Island fifteen years ago and ended up stealing a rich boy's heart, though she carried little influence in the Stevens family. Ingrained in her were a feminine confidence and strong opinions beyond her years, and she never hesitated to show them. But that didn't mean her in-laws listened to her, either. Minds in their hierarchical Stevens family were hard to sway.

Joseph showed up unannounced at their house the day before the dinner party to try to persuade her to attend. George met his brother at the door and nudged him out of the vestibule and onto the porch despite an outdoor chill in the air. George shut the large front door behind them. He did not want Joseph to directly confront Agnes. While George explained his wife's stance on the matter, Joseph urged their attendance.

"She does not want to talk about business, or children, or heirs, or what happened with Sara. She really doesn't want to talk at all."

"She needs to," Joseph countered. "She needs this more than anybody. She needs us. Come on, George, it's the gentlest reintroduction into society you could ever imagine. It's just a dozen of us, mostly siblings and spouses. I will sit Eva and you at her sides and the other women across the table from her. Nobody will broach any subject she doesn't want to hear. You have my word that the dinner conversation will not get lost in personal or business matters."

"Oh really? How will you pull off that feat? Did you forget that business is all that matters to us? In toto. Business is the only thing that ties us together, brother. What else will we talk about?"

"You must trust me. It's the first time the family has gathered all together since the start of the war. I will tell everybody at the door that this a light-hearted occasion, given the grave times we have just gotten through. We have many other things over which to converse — current events, art, literature."

"I will believe it when I see it."

They sat around a lavishly arranged dinner table, topped with an ornate double white damask tablecloth, polished silverware and China plates, all under a crystal chandelier. A dozen, long-stemmed red roses were displayed in a hand-blown glass vase in the center of the table. On one wall, a warming fire blazed and crackled in a fireplace with a brick hearth and wooden mantelshelf. On each side of the fireplace, leaded glass French doors opened onto a broad terrace. On the opposite wall, a large painting of Big Papa Conrad and his wife, Charlene, hung in a gilded frame. The artist had captured Big Papa's kind, close-set eyes and youthful looks. He stood behind a chair with perfect military-like posture. Seated, Charlene was painted beautifully, but everyone knew she was more gorgeous in life than a portrait could ever represent. Behind one end of the dining table, a servant tended to the second-course fare at a side buffet. Oysters and champagne began the resplendent repast. A cream of mushroom soup was next.

Over six courses, guests had refrained from conversation about business and health matters, as Joseph promised. Sitting to the left of Agnes, George thought he perceived her cold demeanor thawing ever so slightly, even though she seldom smiled, and it appeared awkward when she tried. Her replies were guarded. Still, the conversation was witty and sophisticated enough to pique her interest. Joseph told the table he was pleased with how the fresh pheasant and duck from his recent hunting trip was seasoned, roasted and served for the main course. That prompted Agnes to ask him a few questions about his trip to Seward.

After three hours of dinner conversation regarding art, travel, politics, food and wine, Joseph could no longer avoid talking shop. He was too much like Big Papa Conrad when there were urgent matters to discuss. He stood, walked around the table, lay a gentle hand on Agnes's shoulder, squeezed and changed the direction of the discussion.

"It's been a delightful meal, and we didn't mention a word about family business — that must be a first," he boomed. "See, we love each other and can talk freely about all matters, even politics. But let's not pretend to separate our lives from our business. It's an important business, this one we conduct every day to the best of our abilities. Our actions affect many lives, and we want to make an impact on thousands more. We are also building something significant for the coming generations. I take these aspirations seriously."

Agnes put her head down and shut her eyes in anticipation of what was coming. Eva shot her husband an admonishing glance, as if to say, "Remember, dear, this is supposed to be a social dinner only."

Joseph continued on.

"We need to confront, first as a family, at least in a prefatory way before we bring in the other stakeholders, that Stevens and Gibbs is entering an important transitional period. The post-war industrial era has begun. Running a company will get harder, squeezing a profit will be more difficult than ever before and keeping the labor force satisfied and placid more problematic than ever. It's happening now and we need to figure out how we are going to proceed."

Eva gently tapped her husband's hand, which was on the back of Agnes's chair, and stood to considerately announce that the ladies were excusing themselves to retire to the parlor.

"As I was saying," Joseph continued when the women were out of the room and he returned to his seat at the table, "Stevens and Gibbs is entering a new period. We have grown to be the largest employer in Puget Sound. We've set world shipbuilding records. Thirty-two vessels for the Navy came off our docks, a substantial contribution on our part to the war effort. 'Hip-hip, another ship' — and all that."

The men laughed quietly.

"We are too big to fail," Walter chimed in, and everybody turned to look at him.

"Is that a certainty, Walter? You know our books better than anyone, but we are going to see a drastic downturn in the post-war market, no doubt about it. And there's talk of unrest on the docks. If we want our wealth to carry on for generations to come, we must address these impending hardships and decide how best to weather the storm. And it might be a typhoon coming. I want to get us all on the same page. What steps do we need to take? And how do we position ourselves with labor, short and long term?"

The men locked onto the topic. They focused, and tossed suggestions out rapidly.

"I assume selling the shipping line is out of the question?" Gordon started.

"Nothing is out of the question," Joseph answered.

"We might talk to Gibbs about buying us out," Walter chimed in. "We are a more diverse investment group, but he may want to strengthen his own position."

"Interesting," Joseph commented.

"We have the steam-powered excursion yacht," Samuel Bass added. "It's a start for pivoting to a travel company. People are going to want post-war diversions. We keep our waterfront bays, buy some space down in Newport and San Francisco, even San Diego."

"I like that."

"We can concentrate on the timber business," George piped in. "Maybe we sell the mills and ships for cash and focus solely on the growing of trees. I've been looking into ways we can sustain the forests and by doing so make good profit on the growing end, the supply side — even as they cut more and more trees."

"Can that endeavor possibly be profitable?" Joseph asked.

"I think it will pay dividends," George answered. "I am certain that through man-made breeding we can grow new trees faster than nature can. I've even written to the scientist Luther Burbank. Now, he only works in cross-breeding of flowers, fruit trees and vineyards but he's invited me to his home in California so I can pick his brain."

"All great ideas," Joseph said after nearly forty-five minutes of discussion. "We don't need to pick one solution right here and now, but this is a very good start. Let's move to the library and continue the conversation."

Bass took the transition to a new room as a good moment to depart with his female companion.

The remaining kin gathered in the library. They sat smoking pipes in leather chairs around the clinker brick fireplace and expounded on their ideas for another hour.

"You've orchestrated the evening very well, Joseph," George said when discussion of the future of the business started to wane. "I think I saw Agnes relax at one point."

"Until we started talking business again in front of the women," Gordon laughed.

"I'm glad to hear the evening wasn't terrible for Agnes," Joseph said. As he stood and walked to the billiards table, the other men following his lead. "Agnes — she's been through so much. I just need us all to be together again. It's what Papa would have wanted. It's what he would have done. So thank you for coming for the sake of tradition and family and generations to come."

Joseph began to inattentively roll billiard balls across the table one at a time, but he kept talking.

"Yes, I tried to hold up my end of the bargain through dinner by keeping everybody in cultured discourse, just like old times. But George, there is another matter we need to discuss. It's peripherally related to business. I must take this interlude to talk about this larger-than-life matter. The subject requires a tender heart and compassionate mind."

George did not trust where the conversation was heading. He sighed and thought about saying goodnight and leaving right then and there. Had he walked away at that moment, he would have run directly into his wife, who was coming down the hallway from the women's parlor. She was no longer accustomed to long social nights, and an overwhelming tiredness had enveloped her. Minutes earlier, she had told the women that she was going to find her husband, thank Joseph for the wonderful evening, and take her leave.

Instead of walking out, however, George looked fixedly at his brother. He had been reminded all evening how much Joseph's nature and mannerisms reminded him of Big Papa. Joseph directed everything down to minute details. He controlled all outcomes and situations. He set all the underpinning he needed, contrived proper alliances with great patience, and forged intimate two-way trusts with gracious ease. Before you knew it — bang! — he made you think you had been part of the big picture all along, before you had any inkling of what particular scheme or solution he had whipped up.

George sensed that whatever Joseph was about to say, his brother devised this entire evening to do it, from the much-awaited invitation, to the easy-to-digest dinner conversation, to the escalating talk about the future of the family enterprise.

Half seated on the billiards table, one foot dangling and one foot touching the ground, Joseph commenced:

"Let me begin by saying this is an idea that started when we — our brother-in-law here, Gordon, and I — were in Alaska. We were talking about the war and how every American family knows somebody who died serving his country overseas. He then told me a tragic story, and I was confronted with the notion that one might actually redress in a tangible manner, the misfortune he'd mentioned. Hope hooked me like a fish, and I thought, maybe this is just the thing that will encourage Agnes and you to consider raising another child."

"It really is low risk with very high reward," Gordon added.

"What?" George said, throwing his arms in the air. "So we finally come to the real reason you invited us here tonight."

"George, this is not just another one of my pleas for Agnes to try to give you a male heir," Joseph explained.

"Then tell me what it is, because it sure sounds like it."

"Give me just a moment to explain."

Agnes was about to turn the corner and enter the room when she heard the men talking earnestly. She stopped in her tracks and quickly caught the nub of the conversation. A strong intuition to step into the room and end the talk overcame her. She was about to pull her husband away, but instead she abruptly stopped and stood with her back up against the hallway wall, just out of the men's sight, and strained to hear how her George was going to respond.

"I swear," he said sternly to all of the men, "if any of your wives whatsoever know about this plot that Joseph has conceived, I hope to God they say nothing to Agnes, because this is the one subject that she cannot bear to hear anymore. She cannot tolerate this intrusion into our private life any longer. But this family can't let it go. Look, she has made up her mind not to suffer through another birth. We must respect that. Her reasons are sound, and I support her. Her reaction stems from a basic need to survive, literally survive, to go on living the only way she can, for herself and for the girls. Her pain is deep and dangerous and it's an all-consuming pain. She feels a gaping emptiness and a profound sorrow that could, quite literally, kill her."

"Has she?" Joseph asked.

"Has she what?" George asked back, exasperated.

"Made up her mind? On the matter of another birth?"

"Yes. Most definitely. During her pregnancy, the doctor told her this child will make or break her. She survived the birth, and the baby was healthier than anybody would have expected. What overwhelming joy we felt. She was made whole again, right? Wrong. The unspeakable happened only twenty-four hours later. Sara's death is what broke her instead."

"May I, at least, explain?" Joseph asked unflinchingly. "Because I understand. I really do. But what I'm about to say could go a long way to fixing everything, making everything whole again, as you put it."

George acquiesced in body language only, folding his arms against his chest. Then, Agnes swooped into the room like a hawk on the attack, talons out.

"I am not going to listen to you, Joseph — not for a second! — expound on your obsolete biases toward the male gender. Just because you're the patriarch of the family, the only one of Big Papa's children with a son, doesn't mean you can tell others how important it is to propagate a male heir. We have three beautiful, biological children who happen to be girls, and they will grow up to be smart, confident women. George and I love them unconditionally. I refuse to suffer through any more heartache. No more emotional pain. I can live with the physical pain of childbirth but not the wretchedness and internal hurt of absolute loss. No more loss. No more complete sadness. No more days and nights spent in my room, shut away from those who love me. No more profuse unconquerable melancholy. I will not ask my family to endure my rage or my despair any more. And besides, this is a private matter! It's nobody else's business. Not yours. Not yours. Not yours. To hell with your old prevailing gender norms, Joseph."

Joseph replied to her nonchalantly as he pushed one last billiard ball into the corner pocket.

"Since this affair is so well-ventilated, you must let me finish my story. Hear me out, and then I'll say no more. Gordon's brother, whom we have all met, had a best friend who was serving with him overseas in the war. His friend fell in love with an Italian woman while his division was stationed in northern Italy. Under great danger, even as the world was falling apart all around them, he would sneak out of camp just to spend with her the precious little time he had to himself. To make a long story short, leap forward in time. She tells him she is pregnant, so the friend asks Gordon's family for help in paying and arranging for her passage to the United States, where she can safely await his return. She knows the family has the connections and resources to get her safely out of the country for the sake of their coming child and his future. And they do, God bless them.

"The Italian girl arrived in New York late last summer, as planned. Almost at the same time, however, the father died on the beach in Vittorio Veneto. Poison gas from an artillery shell. By the time she arrived on our shores, her child was already fatherless. Nobody shows up at port to welcome her. She's alone. The boy is born to this immigrant mother who doesn't speak English and is suddenly friendless and completely alone in a big foreign city. There's nobody there to assist her. She knows she will never be able to give her baby boy the life he deserves, the life she had envisioned for him, the life she prayed for. The late father's family eventually finds out what happened with the girl, but it doesn't matter. I don't know if they are insensitive, or afraid of what the future might entail, or they're out of their minds in grief. But they refuse to help the Italian mother or get involved in any way."

"And my immediate family doesn't want to assume any responsibility, either," Gordon added in anticipation of possible questions. "In fact, they have great disdain for the situation. They feel they've already done enough, anyway."

"Why can't she raise her own boy?" Agnes asked in a softer, more condoling tone than her husband expected. He looked at her in surprise. "It would be undeniably hard, but at the very least doesn't the little boy deserve to be nurtured by his own mother in this cruel world?"

"It's complicated," Gordon said. "She speaks very little English. She's frightened for her own life as well as for her child's. But she knows she has done her best to find the right place for him for the time being. A safe place. "

"Where is the mother staying?"

"Thank God, the New York Infant Asylum opened its doors to her," Joseph said. "That's where she is staying now. The facility is a charity for poor, unwed mothers and their unwanted children. They offer first-time mothers free obstetrical care, and then try to find wholesome homes for their sons or daughters."

"Why are you so concerned about all of this, Joseph?" Agnes asked, believing she already knew the answer. "What do you get out of this?"

"I remember one of Big Papa's favorite philanthropic causes was donating to the Protestant Children's Aid Society in New York. He visited the institution twice a year and would come home just glowing about the organization. His face lit up with hope and delight. He would talk for hours about the orphans he saw who were being given options better than growing up on the streets, jails and orphanages. They say a thousand orphans are arriving in that city every day.

"Anyway, Gordon told me the story when we were huddled in a tent during an Alaskan snowstorm, chilled to the bone, wind whipping a hundred miles an hour, temperatures below freezing. My brain latched onto the plight of this mother and son and wouldn't let go until I saw a solution — you know how I am. Then, plain as day, I saw how I... you...

we... we could help as a family. If you and George adopt this child, it's the most perfect resolution to so many problems I see right before my very eyes. It's Christmas time, and it would be the perfect way to heal and put everything right again. Taking just one child off those unhealthy, muddy streets in the winter would be a merit so strong that I think the gates of heaven would open up for you and all your loved ones forever and ever."

"Good God, Joseph, you have a one-track mind — and it's relentlessly fixated on finding me a male heir," Agnes said more as a bone-tired statement of fact than an angry remark. "I can see right through you. Now, you've concocted a preposterous plan to manipulate us into doing what you want."

"I know how it sounds," Joseph belted out with passion. "I know the words that came out of my mouth are not as clear as what I am envisioning in my head and heart. I didn't know how to broach the subject. This is a chance to save a life where one was lost. It's that simple. This is a fortuitous situation with benefits all around. This young, innocent boy could be part of a traditional family structure, and not end up on the dangerous streets, joining a gang for protection, eventually getting arrested and locked up.

"If you saw some of the pictures I've seen, of children sleeping in the muddy streets in ragged clothing and shoes with holes in the toes and the souls, hiding in the shadowy, cutthroat alleyways of New York.... It makes you hesitate and wonder about how far you should go to help and how much you should engage your soul in their plight. Through one selfless act, you can be the difference in liberating an innocent soul from doom. You could provide everything for him, where right now there is nothing. Zero. You can give a child who does not have a chance in hell a family, a home, a financially secure life. For the lost spirits of all of the fallen soldiers, for Gordon's brother's deceased friend, for the family of this fighter and hero, for the mother and her poor, poor baby, for all the families waiting and hoping for their sons to come home from the Western Front — I am asking you find a gram of compassion and motivation to consider doing this."

Joseph stopped talking. His eyes had turned glassy with emotion.

"Certainly, you can see how incredibly outlandish your solicitation is," George shouted at Joseph. "If you're so moved by this humanitarian need, why don't you do it yourself? Or you, Gordon. Or your brother, for Christ's sake."

"I could, but I'm pretty advanced in years, as is my wife," Joseph said.

"My circumstances are different."

"You already have a son," Agnes said. "We all know."

"It was insolent on our part, and I'm sorry," Gordon said, ashamed. "The entreaty is beyond the capability of my wife and my family's compassion. Anybody's compassion, for that matter. I'm sorry we brought it up."

"It would be one hell of a compassionate and benevolent gesture, no doubt about it," Walter added in a tone a little too blithe, but he felt compelled to say something in the weight of the moment. "But Agnes, it might allow your pain to melt away just a fraction, while at the same time giving a young, innocent child a chance, moreover, a leg up, in this difficult world. I don't know. Hell, I'll just say it. It might get you to move beyond the traumatic death of Sara."

Hearing her deceased daughter's name, Agnes broke down and collapsed into a chair. Between sobs, she tried to apologize, explaining in gasps that she did not blame anybody in the room for triggering her outburst, nor did she want them to feel like they had done anything wrong in telling her about this sad circumstance and consequence of the war.

Upon regaining some of her composure, she said feebly, "Every child deserves the perfect lives that we have given our children, but we can't save them all, can we? This little boy didn't ask to come into this world. We can't save them all. We can't save them all!"

As she was crying out for the fourth and fifth time, "We can't save them all," George slowly steadied his wife on her feet, collected her coat and handbag from the front parlor and led her out the door. They left the house without a goodbye.

"That didn't go very well," Walter said into the sudden quietness of the airy mansion.

"No, not at all," Gordon agreed. "If George didn't ask about the appearance, health or personality traits of the mother and father, then he wasn't giving it another thought."

"That's true," Walter chimed in. "If he was at all curious, he would have asked if the mother was blond or brunette or if her skin was pale or olive complexion. Was she tall or short? Smart or foolish? With his scientific background and obsession over eugenics, I'm sure these questions would have crossed his mind."

"It was pretty to think we could do something to help, and kill two birds with one stone in the process, but it was always a long shot," Gordon said with a sigh. "I'll tell my brother that we tried to help, but there's no way."

Applying his skill as an entrepreneur with his intimate knowledge of his brother's brooding mind, Joseph proffered his assessment.

"Despite his study of the biology behind producing offspring, George also believes a proper environment can change a child forever. In a short time, with love and discipline the child will become a new kid, very much different from what he would have been on the streets or in the orphanage. George knows this. Lately, he's talked to me about his theories on nurturing. It's one of the reasons I decided to tell the story."

"If that's true, we definitely cannot tell him the police took her to the New York Hospital for the Insane before she was admitted to the New York Infant Asylum," Gordon said.

"Yes, he'd think she was crazy, a lunatic, for sure," Walter said.

"True, he'd be much less likely to get involved," Joseph said.

"But the hospital was the safest place for her to go, having no other place in the world," Gordon said. "Johnny, my brother's friend, said in letter after letter that the woman he fell in love with possessed great charm, incredible beauty and exhibited an energy and buoyancy about everything in life. They fell in love despite knowing little of each other's first language. There's something gentle in nature about that. It's not craziness."

"Even if George wanted to be the knight in shining armor here, we can never tell him she ever set foot in a mental asylum," Joseph agreed. "When she was found on the street being hysterical, the police took her to the hospital for whatever reason. I'm sure they didn't understand what she was saying one way or the other. But the fact of the matter is you can't give birth to a child in an insane asylum so, thankfully, they took her to another facility — one that actually helps unwed, indigent women. Whether she knew it or not, this mother had already stumbled upon some luck in this country."

"Who wouldn't be overwrought, given her circumstances?" Gordon offered. "She was at the end of her rope."

"I know why my father gave money to these charities," Joseph said. "They serve a great need. The New York Infant Asylum helps with child care for the entire first year. But the facility doesn't allow you to make the same mistake twice, so there are limits to its philanthropy. Somebody else must meet the challenge."

"George can be as foolish as he is scientific, but he's not beyond persuasion," Walter remarked. "You should have told him the mother had light skin with hazel eyes and light-brown hair."

"And my brother's friend Johnny was as blond and tall as they come, too," Gordon chuckled.

"Right. The little Italian boy would likely have the same characteristics," Joseph said. "If he turns out to be smart and a towhead, everybody would think he and Conrad were related, maybe even true brothers."

CHAPTER 4

Through his office window, Joseph watched the group of twenty men assembled in front of the company's general store. They were dressed in second-hand work garments and dark denim jackets. Some stood, some sat on crates. They talked loud and brash among themselves and at times engaged store patrons or longshoremen as they walked by.

Joseph could see all the way to the wharf, where nothing out of the ordinary was happening, just the usual congestion of scows, tugboats and cargo ships coming and going on the water.

"Is everything all right?" George asked, poking his head into the office and startling Joseph.

"As far as I can tell. I'm just keeping an eye on some union fellas out here. They want higher wages, but they don't understand the government has our hands tied."

"At least we're making good progress on a compromise deal with the Metals Trade Council. Maybe that will give us something take to the Shipping Board."

"Our workers are worried about a lot of things," Joseph said. "The feds are continuing their wage controls. Inflation hasn't come down. There's uncertainty over the post-war demand for new ships."

George looked out the window. "What are they doing out there exactly?"

"Buttonholing whoever will listen. Trying to send a message to us by demonstrating right in front of my office and the company store."

"The union promised at our last meeting there would be no trouble as long as we're sitting down with labor in good faith. And we are."

"This group is in no hurry to exit the premises, that's for certain," Joseph remarked without taking his eyes off the group.

"Should I have Bass call in the port police to evict them? The action would be justified."

"No. Loading operations are undisturbed. Ships are departing like normal. The rails are still delivering lumber. At my end of the dock, we're on schedule to complete the steel hulls of four more ships under Navy contract. As long as that keeps up, I'll let them blow off some steam. They're keeping a fifty-foot distance from the store, and besides, nobody seems to be paying much attention to what they're doing or saying — yet."

"It's too damn cold out there for anybody to stop and listen to them."

"Let me ask you something, George. Does 1919 feel different to you?"

"This year? What do you mean?"

"The calendar page just turned over, but it feels like something is brewing. Change is in the air. It's not even mid-January and I see storm clouds gathering. There's something sinister in the air, brother."

"Nothing can be as sinister as fighting a world war over imperialism. And the war is over. You're worrying too much."

"But these un-American ideologies are on the rise, and Bolshevik sympathizers are crawling out from under the rocks. Conducting business is getting harder and harder. There's more to contend with now than anything Big Papa had to deal with. Workers are unsatisfied. Unions are emboldened. Politicians are scared."

"Things have changed, no doubt about it," George said, in agreement.

Joseph spun away from the window and clapped his hands.

"But it's good to have you back on the docks, brother. That's a positive development. And it was fantastic to see you, Agnes and the girls at Christmas."

"Thank you. Actually, that is part of the reason I came down here. I have some news about the boy, our boy."

"Your boy! Yes, yes! George, forgive me! I'm rattling on about how menacing life is, and how doomsday is approaching and all of that, and you're about to start raising a baby boy in this world. I'm sorry. I should be more optimistic. He will be the joy and light we need."

How did George and Agnes, once so resolute in their opposition, find their hearts opening to the possibility of adoption? Joseph certainly had wondered about it himself. He knew the world as a whole, and private family life specifically, had changed perceptibly since he had arranged the social dinner in early December. The story he recounted that night about the little Italian boy and his immigrant mother living in the infant asylum in New York took root gradually within them and it found purchase. Joseph never saw it coming.

In the days following the dinner party, Agnes was silent for nearly a whole week, except for a few practical words to her daughters and George.

When they left Joseph's mansion that night, George saw no possibility of them adopting the boy. He started another busy work week without giving it any more thought. Agnes was silent for nearly a whole week following the dinner, except for a few practical words to her daughters and George. There was a reason for her reticence; the boy's sad story had engrossed her.

One morning, Agnes awoke, propped herself against the headboard and told her husband she wanted to thrash out the details. She insisted they consider all the advantages and disadvantages.

"This seems sudden," George said.

"I've been thinking about how to move on with our lives," Agnes said.

"How so?" George asked sleepily.

"I've been thinking about what might give me not only some solace but also the power to live again and prosper. I don't want to just exist. I've been like a house plant stuck in a dark corner of the room. Don't you and the girls deserve more?"

They talked about orphans in all the world's countries who needed homes, something, in the comfort of their lives, neither had contemplated much, let alone spoken of. They talked about the tens of thousands of men who died in the war and left behind widows and fatherless sons and daughters. They talked about how terrified that young Italian mother must have been arriving on a foreign shore in a city teeming with eight million people, and nobody on her side.

Agnes scooted her body down from the head of the bed and dropped flat onto the mattress. Her long, thick black hair was strewn across the big white pillow, her dark eyes radiant. As she spoke she took a long strand of her hair and stretched it to arm's length as if it were a measuring tape, let the piece fall from her fingers and then stroked another strand in the same contemplative way.

"I am so scared to get pregnant because of the complications I've endured, George. Emotionally, physically, I can't. There are so many health risks for me and the baby if we tried again."

"I know."

He saw the tears welling in her eyes, and from her lips fell familiar words of resentment and annoyance directed at her husband.

"You and your talk of natural breeding and your ignorant beliefs about how superior children are produced! Why must you be so scientific, George?"

"Now, I know I should have kept my opinions to myself, and I've been too open about expressing the problem I have with raising children who possess somebody else's unknown, perhaps inferior, inherited genes. To my credit, however, I am reading more and more about heredity, and I am beginning to understand what a critical role environment plays in a child's development, a much, much greater role than I ever imagined. A malicious child placed in a loving, nourishing, moral and peaceful environment will more than likely see his temper change for the better. A normal boy raised by savages, as the argument goes, will grow up to be a savage."

"What are you saying, George?"

"Simply, that that is where we find ourselves, Agnes. We are more compatible in our thinking than you know. We are both afraid of what might happen to you or to the baby if you are pregnant again. And I think that rearing a child, in the very simplest terms, is like cultivating a plant — if you give it the right conditions, plenty of sunlight, water, food and nourishment then it will grow strong and beautiful. I think the question we need to consider is whether a child, any child, will lift your spirits and make you whole again."

"I can't imagine the light reappearing by doing nothing," Agnes said.

"We must strike a match to the candle to illuminate the dark," George said.

Agnes felt her heart, body and mind starting to open. "And God knows these have been the darkest times, so we need to bring light to the darkness. Isn't that right, George? We can't hide from what happened to Sara, or pretend it didn't happen. God knows we can't. Can we mend it, though? Can we somehow honor her memory? Will this act of goodness help heal us, even if I can't see and touch the scar? Those are the questions."

"We don't have to excise the bad completely to have some good," George answered.

"How fulfilling it would be to save a child in plight. How much happiness could be gained. But... do you still blame me, George?"

"Blame you? How? What do you mean?"

"Do you still blame me for not calling the doctor to the house?"

George put one arm on the far side of his wife and perched over her and peered into her, peering into her dark brown eyes that were wide open and sparkling.

"Oh, God. My butterfly. I never blamed you. I never meant it. You have to believe me. My words that night were loaded with fear and the unimaginable. They were wrongly uttered. I should never have said that. I've regretted it ever since."

They decided not to tell anyone yet what they were about to do. They needed to give the idea time to settle deep and lastingly into the corners of their minds. That was when another unsettling occurrence happened.

While George and Agnes were giving the matter serious thought, Joseph's only son, Conrad, was stricken with an illness. He developed a cough, complained of aching muscles and joints and came down with a fever. Extreme fatigue gripped him. The doctor determined he had the Spanish flu.

Conrad, however, was a robust and lively young child, and while quarantined, he responded well to bed rest and to the liquids and aspirin given him. Joseph heaped love upon Conrad during the sickness and was relieved and grateful for his recovery, but he saw the malady as a sign from God that everything in life is impermanent and continuously changing. Joseph heeded this divine warning, applying prayer and seeking to understand the inescapable truth of life. Conrad recovered within three short weeks.

With his prayers answered and the boy recuperated, Joseph knew God was looking favorably on him and his family. Then, another blessing manifested itself: George and Agnes decided to adopt young *Edoardo*, the son of the Italian mother and deceased American soldier.

Joseph and George walked away from the window and stood in the middle of his office.

"So what's the news, brother?" Joseph said.

George passed a letter to him.

"We received this from the New York Infant Asylum saying Edoardo's mother walked away from the facility and was nowhere to be found."

"Did she leave with her boy?" Joseph asked, clearly worried.

"No, Edoardo is still there. But it appears she does not want anybody to find her if... if she's still alive."

"Who sent the letter?"

"The Children's Aid Society, along with a copy of the commitment petition, which his mother signed before taking off."

Joseph looked at the paper in his hands and read:

To the Mayor of the City of New York.

The Petition of Margherita Bianco respectfully showeth, that she is unmarried and resides in said City and County, and by occupation is a Domestic. That she has one child. That she is desirous of committing and surrendering her child named Edoardo, aged 1, to the care and management of The Children's Aid Society. That your Petitioner is unable to support said child or to provide for his suitable education.

"This gives the organization custody of the boy," George explained, taking the letter back. "Therefore, we just have to sign the final adoption papers when we're there. We are planning to travel by train to New York in early February to get him."

"That is wonderful news. Hopefully, we'll have a labor deal by then and we'll be able to fulfill all of the remaining Navy contracts. Then, you can depart."

The next day, Joseph was compulsively back at the window watching the idle men. Twenty more had joined the protest. Their very presence outside his office window taunted him. Every day, to and from his office, he was forced to confront the objectors. They did not touch or speak directly to him. They did not block his way.

But they shouted their various slogans louder whenever they saw him coming or going:

"ABOLISH THE MACY AWARD!"

"WORK CONDITIONS MAIM! MANAGEMENT TO BLAME!"

"HONEST DAY'S WORK! HONEST DAY'S PAY"

Some of the new demonstrators he recognized. Some had been dismissed for various reasons. Some were high-wage earners showing support for their lower-wage fellow workers. Whoever they were, Joseph had had enough of their public display. He called on the union steward of the Seattle Metal Trades Council.

"Bert, this is a provocation by left-wing radicals within your union and must stop. They're deliberately congregating right outside my window and harassing workers and customers. They are getting louder and more numerous by the day. I've had enough!"

"We can't do anything about it, Joseph. It's not an official protest. They are acting on their own. Look, it's your property, you remove them."

"And play right into your hands?"

Upon returning to his office, Joseph immediately called Bass. It was time to bring in the police to break up the burgeoning picket.

The laborers did not follow police orders to vacate. Standing toe to toe in tense confrontation, workers clenched their fists and officers clasped their clubs. The shouting grew louder. There was pushing and shoving. Bass was forced to bark the orders. The cops forcibly seized the demonstrators and dragged them off the premises one unwilling detainee after another. The more stubborn and resistant demonstrators held their ground and fought, suffering bruises and scratches when they ultimately were hauled away and tossed into the streets outside the Stevens & Gibbs gate.

Joseph enjoyed one day of peace before Bass stormed into his office carrying a formal strike notice in his hand. He slapped the paper on Joseph's desk.

"The unions have declared that all work at the shipyards will end January twenty-first and their members will walk out."

"Has this been made public?"

"Not yet."

"That's in three days. What's our immediate plan?"

"I'm not sure we need one."

"I don't improvise when it comes to business, Bass. Do we cut a deal with the metals workers now and take it to the Shipping Board?"

"Look, I guarantee our workers aren't interested in walking out," Bass said. "Most of their wages were grandfathered in before the war rules came down. But just to make my point, I'll take a straw vote tomorrow to find out their opinion. I'm right about this, boss. Trust me. I'll let you know the results first thing on the morning of the twentieth."

"You do that, Bass, but I'm not going to be caught on my heels as I wait for the results of your poll. Convene all the shipyard owners and representatives from the Emergency Fleet Corporation to assess the situation and get on the same page."

Two days later, Bass was waiting outside the door to Joseph's office by the time his boss arrived.

"Ha! See? I told you we have nothing to worry about. Ninety-seven percent say they don't want a strike."

"We'll see what happens tomorrow."

Work continued as normal that day and into the next morning. In the company office, Joseph and George Stevens, Samuel Bass and Teddy Gibbs sat confidently in chairs talking about the future of their business and listening to the familiar and agreeable sounds of a vibrant shipyard outside.

"The future is still bright," Gibbs declared glibly.

When the clock struck 10 a.m., however, a pronounced change on the docks occurred.

It took a few minutes for Stevens & Gibbs' inner circle to notice.

"What's that?" George asked.

"What's what?" Bass replied.

"Ssshhh. Listen," Gibbs said.

It was silence. Powerful silence. No hammering, no riveting, no hand sawing, no steam whistles, no shouting, no rasping cranes, no groaning from engines.

"It can't be happening," Bass said doubtfully.

"What's happening, Bass? Tell us, because you assured me there would be no strike, but the stillness outside feels pretty damn ominous," Joseph upbraided his lieutenant. "You and your damn poll."

For a few moments the only sound outside was the rub of ships in the harbor and slipways, and waves lapping against the docks.

Then came a heavy, rhythmic, pulsating pounding, like thousands of drummers striking the same beat. Heavy, consistent, purposeful, alternating raps repeated over and over again like a slow, systematic parade of elephants.

Stomp-Stomp. Stomp-Stomp. Stomp-Stomp.

Joseph leapt from his seat and bounded to the window to put sight to sound. He witnessed fifteen thousand men walking off the job; he heard thirty thousand boots hitting the wooden walkway.

Stomp-Stomp. Stomp-Stomp. Stomp-Stomp.

None of the workers on the move spoke. None of them turned their heads even to glance at Joseph through the window. They all were jammed together shoulder to shoulder staring ahead — and out the gates they strode.

They marched past the Stevens & Gibbs employment office and flowed into a sea of fifteen thousand more dockworkers pouring out of the other shipyards. They converged in the brimming Seattle streets. Thirty miles south in Tacoma, another fourteen thousand men and women left the docks.

"There they go," Joseph said. "The American Bolsheviks."

"So much for your poll, Bass," Gibbs snapped.

"The poll was correct."

"Shut up."

"I know how my men really feel. Radical union leaders are making them do this."

"They're acting awfully calm for radicals," George quipped.

"Well, now we know. The left-wing leadership of these unions is outsized," Bass said. "They're influencing and intimidating our workers. We won't be fooled again. I predict they'll be trickling back to work by the end of the week."

They were not.

Joseph assembled Stevens & Gibbs' board of directors posthaste for an emergency meeting. "I wanted to ensure that we are all moving in unison before tomorrow's talks with labor. By the way, Central Labor Council and AFL leaders will be joining the assembly."

"What? Why?" a board member asked.

"A general strike might be called."

"They wouldn't dare! It's never happened before in the history of this nation!"

"The longshore unions want to see what kind of leverage they have," Joseph explained. "If the hotel unions, restaurant unions, transit and city service workers — you name it — join the walkout it will greatly consolidate the strength of organized labor."

"So what's our plan?" Walter Stevens asked.

"We still have nineteen million dollars in signed contracts we need to deliver to the United States Navy so we need to attract and retrain workers more than ever," Joseph said as he examined everyone at the table. "I propose we offer the trade council higher wages for most of our skilled workers and see what happens, even if it reduces our profit."

"Come on, Joseph. The Emergency Fleet Corporation and Macy Board won't budge on the government-imposed wage scale," Walter rebutted.

"Probably. But what do we have to lose? Our shipbuilding heyday might be coming to an end as we speak," Joseph warned with a heavy sigh.

Less than twenty-four hours later, Joseph Stevens, Teddy Gibbs, seven other owners of large and small shipyard companies, and a West Coast representative from the government's Emergency Fleet Corporation found themselves on one side of the table in the Labour Temple. On the other side was a formidable bloc of union leaders from the Metal Trades Council, the local chapter of the American Federation of Labor and the Seattle Central Labor Council. But the biggest union cat at the table was the national leader of the Industrial Workers of the World.

Everyone's objective, ostensibly, was to avoid a general strike that would grind the region to a halt. From the beginning of the meeting, however, Joseph saw that not everybody was behind that intention.

Inside the brick-veneered, four-story, block building on First Avenue, the titans and union reps held their places at the large rectangular table. Long, vertical, windows allowed natural light to stream into the spartan hall, where it caught the drifting haze of tobacco smoke. Labor and syndicate bosses sat on wooden chairs around a sturdy metal table set up in front of a boot-scuffed stage. A podium stood next to American and union flags in gold stands. A small collection of badges and pins bearing the letters CLC and AFL with images of clenched fists and tools of the trade were scattered on top of the table.

The room around them buzzed like a command post with union activity. Groups of workers pondered and conversed over stretched-out maps on top of other tables that were pushed against the walls. People constantly entered and left the headquarters through the front door of the hardy building just north of the Stevens & Gibbs shipyards.

"It's like they're planning for war in here," Gibbs whispered in Joseph's ear.

"Gentlemen," Bert Swain, secretary general of the Metal Trades Council, dourly addressed the maritime syndicate. "You're sitting across from a group of labor leaders who represent over one hundred local unions. We speak on behalf of our workmen when we say we've tried for two years running to change the work landscape here in Seattle and Tacoma, and all around Puget Sound, but nobody seems to be listening to us. That's a grave mistake.

"We tried to make you great capitalists understand that workers are struggling on their current wages to feed their families and raise their children and buy the most basic necessities. We tried friendly persuasion. We tried gentle nudging. We tried tender words. We tried to not rock the boat — a metaphor I'm sure you all can appreciate — and still convey our deepest feelings and concern to you. Our hands were tied because of the war. We all sacrificed and we all gave up important things out of consideration for the war. We wanted to be patriotic. You needed us to be patriotic. We were all patriotic, because nobody stood isolated from the hellish hostilities taking place overseas.

"Now we sit here unchained of nationalistic sentiment. We've reached a critical stage. We reject the strict wage control that the Macy Board set up in wartime. You ignore our demands for increased pay. So our dispute remains unresolved. Therefore, we are submitting a general strike proposal by all member unions. This will happen unless you meet our demands of uniform wage increases!"

Swain's words produced a moment of silence, until Joseph stood to speak.

"We have been talking to our unions for two months now. So you'd be better off addressing Mr. Marks, the representative of the Emergency Fleet Corporation, who is sitting so quietly right there. The question of increasing wages, or not, has more to do with his government agency than us yard owners and our workers. His silence betrays what the Shipping Board really wants. The federal government's fixed wages are now unsustainable. Mr. Marks knows that labor unrest, like we are facing here, was inevitable the day the armistice was signed and rigid price controls remained. Mr. Marks knows the fixed nationwide wage scale for skilled and unskilled workers in shipyards has, in effect, reduced wages for most workers. But shipyard owners are bound by terms set by the Shipping Board. If we fail to comply, the government can pull our contracts. If they pull our contracts, nobody will have a job. There won't be enough work to go around. Isn't that right, Mr. Marks?"

"From the beginning, our goal has been to keep shipbuilders in business by protecting jobs," Marks declared. "That's our concern in following the nationwide wage scale. I am only silent because we are bound by the agreement. The solution will be complicated. But if you think the issue is between the Emergency Fleet Corporation and all of the fitters, welders, riveters, machine operators, crane men, blacksmiths and boilermakers on your payroll, you're dead wrong."

"And how is that?"

"Because shipbuilding has peaked and idealistic egalitarians have taken over the workforce," Marks said. "As far as we're concerned, this may be the perfect time for the unions to call for a strike, if for no other reason than we will finally get an idea of how deeply the AFL's left-wing faction has infiltrated the union ranks. I believe the majority of workmen do not favor the strike and simply want to break the whole concept of society, and replace it with disorder."

"Yard owners at this table are bound to the Macy agreement, that's true, but not all equally," Edgar Ames, one of the other yard owners, said to Joseph, "Isn't that right, Mr. Stevens? In fact, you were able to afford higher wages — eight dollars for skilled workers — before the war. Those have been grandfathered in. We will see what your workers do."

"The shipyard strike affects us all, Mr. Ames," Teddy Gibbs retorted before Joseph could respond, jumping out of his seat. "A general strike brings down the whole city. We are all in this together. We all share the American ideals of freedom. Freedom to work. Freedom to earn money."

Walker C. Smith of the I.W.W. struck the table to give himself the floor.

"The ideal of the freedom of capitalism is not consistent with the ideal of making a decent wage in a safe environment without being overworked. Until we get to that point, the government and the capitalists better be prepared for a revolution!"

The mention of revolution intensified the pressure in the room like combining water and coal in a boiler.

"Revolution?" Gibbs asked. "Did I hear you correctly? You're calling for a revolution? Nobody wants a repeat of the violence we've seen recently in Spokane and Everett."

"One war is over, and another is about to begin," Smith declared full-throated. "Our war will be fought on U.S. soil against wage slavery, poverty and child labor."

Joseph could not believe what he was hearing. The unions stood united while the shipbuilders and the Emergency Fleet Corporation were fractured. Ames had made that much clear. The Wobblies were talking about a broad uprising. And the EFC representative seemed to only be interested exposing Russian communist influence on union leadership. Joseph saw no way out.

Marks signaled he was leaving the talks by standing and shoving his chair in with a crash. Before turning to go, he betrayed a confidence: The EFC had come to the negotiating table with only one outcome in mind.

"Charles Piez, my boss and the director of the Emergency Fleet Corporation, will send a telegram this evening to all the yard managers, big and small, stating the U.S. government will consider all wartime contracts null and void if any of your companies grant wage increases," he concluded. "Prewar wage controls will remain in place no matter what!"

"You are tying our hands with the rope of our own commitments!" Joseph yelled. "Do you think this is a game, Marks? Are you really willing to allow the first citywide labor stoppage ever in this country?"

"Sure, let's see if it's true. Are you too big to fail now?"

"We'll hire returning soldiers and train them, if we have to," Gibbs shouted as Marks strode away. "We will break the unions."

Gibbs' threat caused the room to erupt in shouting. Union leaders kicked and tossed chairs and threatened to bring work on the entire peninsula to a crushing halt.

Marks slipped out of the back door of the union hall.

Nobody went to work in the city on the shivery, fossil-grey day of February 6. And nobody left the suddenly silent city.

Hearing news of the impending strike, wealthy households had already fled to Portland, Vancouver, Canada, and other havens until calm returned, while the citizens who stayed stockpiled home supplies. Stores closed, streetcars did not run. George and Agnes hunkered down in their mansion in Medina, next to Seattle, because they could not get on a train to travel to New York and adopt their son. They took a cautious, observing stance as they stayed put.

"Is this a bad omen, George?" Agnes asked, looking down at the date printed on her train ticket that she had placed on the console table a day before.

"I don't believe in auguries," he answered. "But I do wonder if there will be uprisings in other cities along the route. However long we have to wait, we know Edward is safe and well-cared for by the Children's Aid Society until we can get there."

Less than half of the sixty-five thousand union workers across the city who stopped working on February 6 were employed by the shipyards. The other thirty-five thousand souls acted in solidarity, abandoning factories, shops, buses, ferries, city garbage trucks, restaurants, streetcars, theaters, mines and trains.

The citywide general strike was on; the fuse was lit. The U.S. Secretary of War sent National Guard troops into the city. Police set up mounted machine gun posts. Two U.S. Army battalions from Fort Lewis bivouacked in the streets. The mayor threatened to declare martial law.

Ignoring the show of force, the union sent unarmed forces out to patrol working neighborhoods and report to union headquarters. Cooks who had walked out of restaurants in unity pitched tents to run improvised soup kitchens and served tens of thousands of meals each day to striking workers. The Teamsters made sure medical supplies and patients reached hospitals, and the milk wagon drivers union announced in newspapers the locations of milk stations for dispensing quarts to families with babies and to the infirm.

Lines were drawn, but calm prevailed through the first and second day of the general strike. Joseph took advantage of the relative quiet and left his house to visit his brother. He stood at the front door holding three newspapers in his hands. When George opened up, he excitedly thrust the papers into his brother's chest.

"Take a look at the Seattle Times. They are sticking to their guns. One front-page editorial calls for an end to the walkout. Another hails the mayor and supports his call for martial law. This strike will break soon."

"But you read EFC's telegram. The government will still not compromise on wages."

"Yes, they will," Joseph reacted without conviction in his voice.

"That will be good, because Agnes and I could then rearrange our schedule and get to New York. We have something to do that's more important to us than what's going on citywide here in Seattle."

"Wait," Joseph said. "You can't leave."

"What do you mean, 'I can't leave'? Yes I can."

"No, George. Whether this strike ends soon or not, we need to be prepared to take immediate action to save the company. We need the full board ready and willing to act. There is nineteen million dollars in government contracts suspended right now. Nineteen million! Do you know what that means? If the Navy nullifies our contracts, we're out of business."

"I'm talking about a human life, a child's future hanging in the balance," George cried. "We need to go get our boy."

"Even if the strike ends and you can get a train out of here, it's far too dangerous. Haven't you heard? There are wildcat strikes flaring up all across the country. The papers say millions of workers are participating in the disruption to the steel industry, railroads, textiles. You could end up stranded in middle of nowhere. If a gang blocks your rail car in a city like Chicago and they find out you're a wealthy industrialist, you'll be in danger. What good will traveling now do anybody? Have you lost your mind?"

"I'll get through."

"No, you won't."

"Is there something else you want to say?"

"Yes. At all costs, we must ensure the family business survives not just over the next several months or years, but for decades to come. That's our mission. That's Big Papa's legacy. It's our duty to fulfill it. You need to be here to vote on some very important issues regarding our future."

"The Navy needs to overhaul and fix all their ships. That means there is going to be another shipbuilding boom." George seemed to be trying to convince himself. "We'll be out here on these docks for the next twenty years."

"No, George! We won't. You're dead wrong. We're about to suffer a devastating loss of millions and millions of dollars. We are going face some very angry shareholders. If we go bankrupt, what does that mean for Edward and Conrad and the rest of our progeny? I need you here. The company needs you here. Our board will be voting on major financial decisions and strategic moves that will change the course of Stevens Family Investments. We need to figure out an action plan right away. But don't worry, George, we'll find a way to get little Edward here, to us, to his home, as soon as we can."

CHAPTER 5

The Stevens Investment Company board met in a new building in the central district adjacent to a surface parking lot with a gas station. The office did not exude the same prestige and wealth found in the great board rooms of U.S. Steel and Standard Oil in New York City, and it was not in a high-rise building. Nevertheless, the building was newly constructed, and the room's tall windows let the sun illuminate the dark wood paneling and plush carpet. A heavy mahogany table polished to a luster occupied most of the room. The only recognition of the company's blue-collar roots were several hanging framed photographs showing the un-scrubbed mills, lumberyards, shipbuilding docks and laborers who toiled there.

Sitting in that boardroom on a sunny day in early April, Joseph knew better than to take a victory lap. The general strike had resolved itself quickly, never having built meaningful momentum despite all the build-up and preparation on both sides. Missteps by the union's bigwigs torpedoed the strike, those leaders completely misjudging the Seattle mayor's sentiment toward labor. He had showed no support for the workforce and railed against left-wing radicals in speeches and newspapers articles. His words made him famous as an organized labor-busting politician.

Another major error played out when the unions failed to gain the support from the city's major newspapers. The unions' third failure was setting no clear signposts on their journey to attaining higher wages and cleaner and safer job sites. A writer described the botched planning as "one road that leads to... no one knows where." The journey took workers in a full circle that ended back at the beginning.

The general strike had fizzled by the second week of February.

The shipyard strike, on the other hand, dragged on for another month as the government refused to budge on its terms. Joseph and Bass watched dissent spread quickly through the ranks of the union and on March 17 dockworkers were told to go back to their jobs on the slim hope that the federal wage scale would expire and their wages would increase.

To Joseph, the end of the strike and workers returning to their jobs was a hollow victory because the post-war shipyard landscape looked dim to anybody paying attention. As president of the Stevens Investment Company board, he stood in front of the company heads, investors, accountants and lawyers and did not have to worry about overstating the bad news. The indicators were unmistakable, and tension hung heavy in the air.

"The Shipping Board has just billed us for twenty million dollars in unfinished work, and we don't have the money nor the workers to finish the ships even if we wanted to," Joseph told the men sitting at the table. "We've already closed two plants in the past two months. Just last week, we laid off a thousand workers because of the post-war slump. It's industrywide. The Navy is pulling back and overhauling their ships themselves. They now have a bigger presence than anybody in the sound these days. Now they are threatening to discontinue all contracts if we don't pay. We're hemmed in and need a way out."

"Bass is talking to old associates and business connections to get us equipped to start producing civilian ships," George offered as good news. "He estimates we'll need to hire eight thousand men, all open shop. Supporting a union will not be a condition of their employment. "

"What would that payroll be?" Gibbs insisted.

"Twelve million."

"How do we get there?"

"Borrow it."

"Forget it!" Gibbs barked.

"Got any better ideas, Gibbs?" Joseph shot back.

Walter Stevens attacked the partner, too. "You're not planning on getting your San Francisco buddies together again and going behind this board's back in another attempt to take over the company on the cheap, are you?"

"Mr. Director, we have bigger problems than rehashing our past squabbles and differences," Gibbs responded.

"Those squabbles are not that far in the past," Joseph retorted. "It's still raw."

"Listen," Gordon broke in without raising his voice. "In the wake of the government's wartime intervention in business, we need a short-term legal strategy as much as a long-term business one. What's it going to be?"

"The short term?" Joseph proceeded. "We countersue the Emergency Fleet Corporation to pay us in full for preordered work. I propose our lawyers, led by Mr. Davies here, draw up a complaint and get that filed as soon as possible. All in favor, say 'aye.' "

The vote was unanimous.

"That's an easy vote," Joseph said. "Let's get on a roll. What else? George? I know you want us to focus on the mills, but lumber prices have plunged. I don't know if we can keep the mills running at this rate, let alone make them profitable."

"We still own a great amount of forestland."

"Oh, wouldn't that be paradise for you?" Gibbs laughed. "An entire business of just growing trees! But there's one thing wrong with that — it's not profitable!"

"Growing better trees," George corrected.

"How?"

"Our early experimentation and efforts on crossbreeding have been very successful."

"Successful by which measurement? We're talking about how to increase our revenues here. We'd be better off trying to grow better humans. Wouldn't that be more profitable? A nation of better humans, all working for the Stevens family. An abundance of cheap labor working twenty-four hour shifts, seven days a week. I vote 'aye.' "

"Restrain yourself, Gibbs!" Joseph shouted.

"Tell us your far-seeing plans then, Joseph," Gibbs countered. "You're the shrewd son of the great Big Papa Conrad. Lead us to the Promised Land."

Joseph was going to respond but he noticed board members on the opposite side of the table being distracted by something they saw out the window.

"Can you people please pay attention?"

They did not hear him and kept whispering to each other.

"Look at me!" Joseph demanded.

"Yessir."

"In case you missed it, a board member wants to know what I have up my sleeve as far as righting the financial ship of this company. So listen up, I am putting the following motion up for a vote. Stevens and Gibbs will sell off the dry docks and lease them back as needed to finish our remaining work. We will keep ownership of one plant in order to build a luxury passenger ship of one thousand feet, with fifty-seven thousand gross tons of internal volume, for transatlantic ocean travel."

Around the table, mouths dropped and eyes popped.

"That's very detailed," Gibbs noted.

"This new state-of-the-art vessel will be built in conjunction with an overhaul of my private yacht, which I will donate to the company to be revamped for professional use in transporting passengers and cargo up and down the West Coast. Let's vote on the authorization of the plan and funding now!"

At that moment, the sunlight filtering through the windows disappeared and the room darkened. Before a vote could be cast, an office clerk and a salesman flung open the meeting room door and burst inside.

"How dare you barge into a board meeting!" Joseph yelled. "Well? What is it?"

"We're sorry, sir. There's a column of thick black smoke to the north. ... It's our largest mill on fire. It's spreading to our other mills. We heard the bulletin on the receiver set."

Every board member moved to the reception area for a better look out the windows. Orange-red flames in the distance climbed and spit up through the black, heaving smoke.

"Did they give any other details?"

"They said Seattle firemen are helping, and a bucket brigade has been set up, but it looks bad, really bad."

"How about the docks and harbor?" Gibbs asked.

"The wind is blowing on shore," answered George, an avid weather watcher. "We're fortunate."

"That fine sawdust will ignite like gun powder," Joseph said. "And there are boards stacked fifty feet high that will fuel the fire like mad. The flames are going to sweep through the mills and down the entire port. We won't be able to do a damn thing. I pray every worker gets out any way they can, by window, door or log chute. We have three hundred and fifty employees down there."

"We need to haul the ships out to water in the harbor," Gibbs proclaimed, and ran out the door.

Board members, clerks and scriveners rushed out of the building to see what they could do to help fight the fire. Joseph and his brother remained standing at the lobby window watching the roiling smoke and tongues of orange flames.

A man stayed seated at an oak gossip bench near the brothers casually reading a catalogue. He glanced up at Joseph as if expecting a directive of some kind. He set the catalogue down and extended an arm across the top of the bench in a carefree manner. His jacket parted slightly to reveal a handgun holstered in a shoulder harness.

Joseph had hired the bodyguard in January when signs of labor strife started to show. He kept him on as a precaution.

George took a fast step toward the exit but Joseph grabbed his arm.

"They don't need you down there, brother. There's plenty of help."

"There's a lot more that can be done."

"Just hear me out. During these past several weeks, you've stuck by me when I should never have asked you to do so. We are like-minded when it comes to what we need to do to move the business forward into the future. I appreciate you putting aside your personal responsibilities and being here for me, and for the company and our employees. But now it's time to go get your son. It's time to put him and Agnes first. When Edward gets established in his new home, we'll get the shipyards sold and turn our attention to timber, logging and forestry. For now, get home, get the house ready for your new boy's arrival, and make sure all of Agnes's needs are met. When is his train due?"

"Tomorrow morning at ten."

"Which station?"

"Northern Pacific in Yakima. End of the line."

"It's going to be wonderful."

George was anxious. He glanced out the window at the smoke and flames.

"Brother, our mills are burning down..."

Joseph tightened his grip on George's arm.

"They don't need us to fight the fire. You go home, and I'll make our presence known. I will offer the workers' families generous compensation through our emergency relief fund and make sure they are fed and sheltered. You've allowed me to be able to focus on this. Now, go! You have your own family planning to tend to."

They both momentarily stared at the glowing spectacle through the window. From where they stood, they could almost feel the throbbing massive human effort to squelch the blaze. The smoke was blacker and thicker now, rising in great rolling clouds.

"Do you believe in omens?" George asked.

"No. But I remember *omne trium perfectum* from my Latin studies at Harvard: Everything that comes in threes is perfect. We've had two fortuitous events, the end of the general strike and then the end of the shipyard strike. Now, it's time to welcome a new son into the family."

George nervously laughed at his brother's optimism.

"Did you forget an inferno is burning our mills to the ground right now, and our prime shipbuilding days are gone?"

"*Omne trium perfectum.* Let's go make more fortune for ourselves. When you return from Yakima, there will be nothing but harmony in both family and business affairs, and we'll be perfectly complete again."

CHAPTER 6

Joseph took it upon himself to arrange little Edward's travel from New York to Seattle. When everything was complete he allowed himself a brief moment of pride for his efforts. He had managed the details brilliantly, with two primary objectives: guaranteeing an infant's safety and comfort on a three thousand-mile journey across the states; and making sure his brother and business partner was as calm as possible and not a cauldron of worry and emotion while awaiting his son's arrival.

Joseph wrote to a minister in New York, an old friend of his father, to tell him about the child they were to bring out West. He explained to the pastor that circumstances kept the adoptive parents from making the trip to bring their child home, and asked what they could do to unite the family as quickly as possible.

"Because of cross-country logistics and the timing of this adoption, I need to quickly find and negotiate travel options," Joseph wrote to the minister.

"Have you considered a mercy train?" the minister asked by telegraph after receiving the letter. "One leaves for Northwest soon with one hundred kids."

Joseph learned from the minister that the social welfare program sent motherless and fatherless children by rail across rural America to be placed in families for the dual purposes of getting the boys and girls out of New York City's squalor and poverty and to provide free labor for farmers mostly in the Midwest and West.

Joseph did not hesitate to set this plan in motion. In his typical elaborate way of orchestrating a venture, he chartered private railcars, which were to be coupled to the mercy train. The private cars afforded first-class accommodations, such as a spacious cabin, galley, dining car and personalized service for Edward and his caregivers. He hired two chaperones to accompany Edward — a male cousin, seventeen, whom he had not met but longtime business colleagues and church leaders affirmed was mature and reliable; and a young nurse of twenty-five years who came highly recommended by friends and family and hoped to settle down in the West. Joseph considered hiring a private chef so the escorts could enjoy fine dining, but scrapped the idea at the last minute for being too ostentatious.

Joseph promised to cover all expenses incurred by the Children's Aid Society, the charitable institution sponsoring the trip, not just his own extravagance. He added generous additional stipends for the minister in charge of the orphans and his two agents.

With each step of preparation, Joseph became more excited and convinced his little nephew would have a comfortable and safe passage across the country. The resulting bill was incredibly expensive at a time when he should have curtailed excessive spending, but he did not care.

To ensure the safe delivery of the child into new arms, Joseph mailed a cloth tag with the letters SFI to the Children's Aid Society with a note directing them to sew the tag onto the boy's garment at once. He told the organizers of the train that upon arrival George and Agnes would first repeat the letters to the minister in charge and then show their identical matching cloth tag. The child would be handed over only after these safeguards were completed.

Joseph was delighted with his plans and ecstatic for his brother and his wife. George repeatedly told him how thankful he was for the effort and care his brother put into arranging the trip. It was the least he could do in light of their benevolent deed, Joseph replied.

Then, Agnes dashed his ambitions.

"My son will not begin his life flaunting his wealth in the presence of others. I will not let him travel in the greatest of comforts while dozens of poor orphans are crowded into compartments for sleepless nights and long days on end," she scolded Joseph. "George and I did not even have first-class tickets."

"But the boy is eight months old, Agnes. He's extremely precious cargo and requires special care. The conditions in the main compartments might not be any better than cattle cars."

"The other children will see him and he will remind them of how unfair the world is. They are already frightened and alone. They'll feel even more horrible and inferior. They don't know where they're going or what kind of life they will lead, while Edward's predetermined future is comfortable, safe, easy. These other children might become slaves, for all we know. No, he will not travel like a prince in his own carriage."

"It's a five-day trip, for crying out loud, Agnes!"

"That's my final word on the matter."

"His welfare is my utmost concern. I'm offering care and protection for him on every step of the journey."

"He may have his personal attendants," Agnes consented. "But, he will be using the same compartments as the other children. And your chaperones' services and overall supervision must be made available to all the children as needed, and they will help the other agents whenever and wherever needed. It must be emphasized that they are there, as extra eyes and hands, to oversee all the orphans on that train, not just Edward, and make every child's trip as content as possible."

Joseph held his tongue until he met George in privacy. In turn, he upbraided his brother's wife for her stubborn resistance to his plan.

"There is still the fear of strikes across the country — so my arrangement gives Edward insulation and protection..."

"It actually might make him a target, don't you think?" George responded.

"George! Think of the conditions aboard the train. I bet they feed those orphans one meal a day on that train. Maybe they get one trip to the bathroom per day. They're probably packed into small coaches. He deserves better."

"Agnes sees eye to eye with you on adult supervision. He's in good hands. He'll survive. But she is not going to change her mind on anything else, brother. You're the one who got her thinking about all of those urban children abandoned in overcrowded orphanages and living in poverty. You must let her have her way. We must."

"Are you willing to put up with snide whispers, laden with blame and conjecture, as to why one of the wealthiest families in the Pacific Northwest allowed their youngest heir to travel across the nation in such lowly fashion? It's cavalier, by God. What would Big Papa say? We must be conscious of what inheritors of our name will think when they look back at our lives. Imagine what we would have thought of our forebears if they had done the same. It's a shame that getting Edward to us had to come down to this, but I'm trying to do my best to make sure he arrives safe and sound."

George did not say a word, just nodded.

"Fine. I'll let the matter drop. Under the circumstances, it was just a well-intentioned effort on my part..."

"You understand he won't recall anything about the trip, not even if he's surrounded in the greatest comfort and style money can buy."

They laughed.

"Even if he has no idea, he might sense it," Joseph stated with finality.

In New York, little Edward's journey started with a prayer from the minister on the platform. The children were lined up tallest to shortest, and the Stevens relative, who noticed he was not much older than some of the orphan boys, and the enlisted nurse nervously smiled at each other. Edward lay at their feet in a rattan basket with a carrying handle.

Edward wore a long, linen gown with finely detailed embroidery and decorative ribbon trim. His garment was in the fashion of that favored by wealthier families of New York, and likely donated by a rich patron of the orphanage. Its delicate pink and yellow lacing and stitching was in the custom of little girls' clothing. Joseph insisted on knowing what his little nephew would be wearing when he arrived, down to the details of the seams, but there was a sudden shortage of clothing for infant boys at New York's orphanages. If the Stevens family wanted Edward dressed in a newer, more splendid type of outfit — that is, one that had barely been worn at all — then there was more choice among donated baby girl items.

"As long as it's not *too* feminine, put him in it," Joseph wrote to the matron. "Just make sure to sew on the cloth tag. That's most important thing."

The railcars filled quickly. The chaperones boarded with Edward in tow and walked down the narrow aisle to find seats. All of the remaining seats were wooden and faced forward, but the nurse found room for all three together. As the male chaperone hoisted their trunks onto the overhead rack, the minister stood in the front of the car and barked out a litany of rules and instructions for everybody on board to follow: Don't damage anything on board; raise your hand when you need a drink of water or to use the bathroom; be respectful of the chaperones during the entire trip; and when the train stops, stay in designated areas until it is your turn to step off.

It would not have taken Joseph long to feel justified in securing a private railcar for Edward and his guardians. Small amounts of food, bread, milk and apples were distributed sparingly over long stretches of time. Older boys constantly tested the authority and patience of the minister and his agents. Sometimes they set off in packs and roamed the narrow aisles looking for mischief before incurring the wrath of the minister. They made fun of other orphans' names or appearance, took and hid smaller boys' hats, books or food, and sat next to and flirted with girls. An occasional loud belch sent the entire train snickering, and tossed wads of paper came daringly close to smacking the minister and chaperones. When the few adults on board intervened, the boys dared to be kicked off at the next stop so they could go on their own merry way.

For the young nurse, the trip was especially hard. There was bottom wiping and diaper changing and crying and restlessness. Edward fussed and cried from hunger, lack of sleep, or both, waking the other riders, and the restless mob of children stirred Edward from slumber every time they raised their voices. By the third night, the nurse was dead tired and could hardly stay awake because of Edward's fitful sleep or her own fretting. If Edward was awake and in a good mood, he wanted to squirm off her lap. Most of the time, her companion chaperone was nowhere to be found, so she could not ask him for help.

Worse, the air on the train thickened by the hour with the smell of sweat, unwashed bodies, messy diapers, overripe fruit and dirty clothes.

The day the train was scheduled to pull into the Yakima station, Agnes was nervous and thought it was best that she stay home and oversee the preparations for the child's arrival, getting the house in order and readying Edward's room. She still had not gotten through her lengthy checklist, let alone double-checked it.

Joseph offered George his hired gunman to drive him to meet the child.

"Take my guy," Joseph insisted. "He'll basically be your driver. You can just sit back and relax as much as possible."

"Relax? Have you ever noticed how guns tend to nudge people to use them, especially if they're loaded? No, thank you."

"It's just for a little piece of mind."

"Why, exactly, does he accompany you all day, every day?"

"He's been on my payroll ever since the strike commenced. There's still a labor war going on in our city and across the country. We are laying off workers by the droves, and it's not sitting well with some. Then, there's the fact that we didn't have enough funds to help everyone who lost work in the mill fire. Guess who they blamed for that? Me! It's getting ugly out there, George, and more and more fuel is being tossed on the flames."

"Are you possessed with a relentless determination to make Agnes hate you? She'd never allow me to have an armed bodyguard."

"Actually, I'm trying hard to make her like me," Joseph answered while putting his hand in the small of his brother's back and pushing him forward. "Now go. And take him. You'll be glad you did."

George was not prepared for what he saw in Yakima.

He heard the muffled chug and guttural whistle of the locomotive before it ever came into view. With a high-pitch screech of air brakes and gust of steam, the train stopped a little ways down the track from the station platform.

Many of the older male orphans, twelve, thirteen or fourteen years old, hopped off the locomotive before being allowed to climb atop the railcars. Younger children, eight to ten years old, disembarked next and stood together next to the powerful engine in front. Some of them mounted the cowcatcher in front, while the rest scattered themselves down the tracks. The very youngest, four to six years old, stuck close to the Children's Aid Society agents.

The Yakima stop was atypical for the group. The boys and girls did not file into a hall to be reviewed, as they had grown accustomed to on the first leg of the journey, but remained outside near the train, as if the whole event might be quickly called off and the orphans sent on their way. Dozens and dozens of orphans waited in various spots for their new families to come off the platform and walk down the tracks to seek them out.

The girls wore plain white or plaid dresses or skirts with long sleeves and checkered pinafores. Boys wore dark suits or dark dress pants with white shirts. The older boys wore hats.

The children looked out at the crowd of prospective parents milling around the depot waiting for the stationmaster to give the official word for the adults to walk over to view, meet and evaluate them. Many of the children had been forced to leave siblings either in New York or at other stops, and now they felt isolated, confused, vulnerable, scared and uncertain. Yet, somehow, they endured their sad predicament, putting on smiles and standing tall in hopes of a decent outcome, an acceptable fate.

George saw a few were no older than four, and one child seemed to have just learned to walk. He knew Edward could not walk at all, and therefore would be in the arms of one of his chaperones. Of the older children, he saw that males were more in demand than females. After all, boys could provide manual labor for many years to come and scrape by with nothing more than a room in a barn or shed, while young women had to live in the main house. The presence of a young woman under roof could create tension in the household. They needed to steer clear of covetous husbands, and placate spiteful wives. Daughters could be huge burdens.

There were far more people than just expectant parents hanging around the train station platform, George observed. The entire town seemed to have come out to see the mercy train spectacle. He saw optimistic eagerness and rapacious ardor in their faces. Many gripped handbills that announced the date of the train's arrival and explained how the needy children would be selected and how the unwanted would go back on board to try their luck at the next stop.

Joseph's unexpressive bodyguard stood motionless next to George. A gust of wind kicked up and blew dust into the faces of the waiting kids. They squinted, put their heads down and shielded their eyes with their forearms until the flurry let up. George figured he would wait for the crowd to thin until most of them found their selected child and left. Then, he would approach the chaperones Joseph had hired for the wonderful, exciting, prearranged first meeting with his adopted child.

He tapped his pockets to ensure he still possessed the stash of extra money his brother had handed him before they left. The bills, stacked and wrapped in sackcloth, were designated for Edward's dutiful chaperones and for the minister in charge.

"I don't think I'll recognize our cousin, but the nurse will probably be the only one holding a baby," he told the bodyguard, who nodded once.

When the crowd surged toward the children waiting by the train, George thought they must have felt as if a pack of dogs from which they could not run had been let loose.

The unfolding scene mesmerized him. He saw adults prodding the muscles of adolescent males and gazing into their mouths to assess the health of their teeth. Some of the girls' skirts were hiked up above the knees to check for bowleggedness or knock knees. George tried to not stare, but the process was oddly fascinating, especially in relation to his research into selective breeding.

He overheard some men telling a child about how great his new life on the farm would be, with ponies to ride, dogs and cats to pet, sheep to groom, chickens to feed and baby pigs to entertain him. Elsewhere, two brothers despairingly tried to hold onto each other's hands while a man desperately tried to explain to them that he could only take one of them. Their grip was soon broken, separating them, possibly forever.

After twenty minutes, the group of children quickly thinned to ten or twelve. George saw that mostly adolescent girls remained. A few adults lingered, a couple here and there talked to the train engineer or the Children's Aid Society agents or among themselves on the platform. He was immediately ashamed to have stayed back and gotten caught up watching the drama unfold around him instead of avidly running to the train and fighting through the crowd to meet his own awaiting child. What was the matter with him? I guess everything is going to be new to me from here on out, he thought.

That was when the bodyguard nudged him and pointed out what appeared to be a nurse and a male companion scanning the landscape. They looked disconsolate, shaken, fearful, tired. There was no baby Edward to be seen. George and the bodyguard hastened straight over to the pair.

The minister saw what was happening, hurriedly broke away from a conversation he was having with two town officials, and met George and the bodyguard in front of the two chaperones.

"Where's my Edward?" George called out. "My son. Where is he? You have my son, right? These two are supposed to be with him, right? I'm here with the adoption papers. I have all the identifying pieces. But where is he? He's a baby of eight or nine months, wearing pink and yellow lacing. He came all the way from New York. You two are his chaperones..."

A look of great consternation on the minister's face startled George and he waited for an explanation.

"We had to... at the last stop, that is, we..." the minister stumbled in speech, which was not his tendency. "We... at the last stop, we..."

"What is it, man? Out with it! What happened at the last stop?"

George peered at the chaperones' spooked faces, and back to the minister. He looked hard into the minister's eyes for some kind of hint, any inkling that Edward was here, or at least alive somewhere. He felt his heart beating hard in his throat; uncontrollable panic gripped his chest and sweat rolled down from his hairline.

"Where's my child, man?" George demanded. "The directions were explicit to bring him to us in Yakima. I have the paperwork and a corresponding tag to match his."

"Somebody took him," the nurse blurted out.

To George, it was as if the entire world fell silent for an entire minute until he could muster up a response.

"What did you say?"

She pointed at her companion.

"He let somebody snatch Edward at the last stop," she said. "He was supposed to watch him for just two seconds while I used the lavatory."

"I can't believe what I'm hearing. Who snatched him? Who? From where?"

"It was just outside the train at the last stop," the nurse cried. "We were getting some fresh air..."

"Who was?"

"Him and the baby and me... while the other orphans were being distributed to their new families."

George looked at the cousin, who kept his eyes lowered as if examining the laces of his boots.

"Look up! Look at me!" George shouted at him. "What happened?"

"We didn't see who took him. I, I didn't see. I was so tired, sir. You wouldn't believe the miserable conditions on that train. Can't you smell me? I haven't had a bath or any sleep in a long time."

"I smell the tang of alcohol," the bodyguard pointed out.

"By the final stretch, I was so tired and stinky and wretched that... maybe I dozed off for a minute. I don't know what happened!"

The boy could no longer speak, and started sobbing soundlessly.

"It's more likely he was talking to one of the older orphan girls he fancied and wasn't paying attention," the nurse said with great disgust, "or distracted by checking for his stash."

"Now that is God's truth!" the minister barked with a suddenly searing fire-and-brimstone resonance. "May the spirit lead you back to wisdom and wholesomeness, son. This boy you hired, sir, sight unseen by the looks of it, to take care of your son seemed to be more interested in tipping the bottle and flirting with young girls than safeguarding a human life."

"What? What kind of operation is this?" George fumed. "It's not a rolling speakeasy. It's a mission train. A train full of young people in search of a better future. A mercy train full of orphans, for Christ's sake."

"I know. I know. It's unprecedented. Tens of thousands of children and we've never had any trouble, certainly not of this magnitude. Our reputation is stellar. And I can assure you we don't allow alcohol on these trains, and we don't know how he brought it on. We don't tolerate custodians associated with our mission getting drunk and acting obnoxious. We allowed him the transgression early in the trip — once! — on the promise it wouldn't happen again.

"We knew you were a family of great admiration and social standing and importance, so we took that into consideration and gave this boy the benefit of the doubt. Then we found him again in the passageways intoxicated, befuddled, mean-spirited and being lecherous, to boot. We checked every opening, pocket and flap of his travel bags with a fine-toothed comb to see if he had any contraband."

"I can't believe my ears. Was she bent, too?"

"No, no, no. Miss Addison's behavior and manners have been impeccable. After the second incident, we separated them and never let him out of our sight again."

"Miss Addison is equally responsible for this offense," George accused. "After all that had transpired, she trusted this imbecile to watch after my son."

"She cannot be blamed," the minister despaired. "After two days, we allowed them to reunite in their duty so they could be together at the last stop give Edward to you. It was supposed to be a very joyous occasion."

"I didn't do anything wrong except take my eye off the child for one second to look for her," the boy lamented, his body shaking. "I swear. Somebody evil took advantage of my situation..."

"Alcohol befuddles the mind and causes heedlessness, even after you have drunk your last drop," the minister proclaimed.

The bodyguard's baritone voice blasted like a foghorn and made everybody stop and listen.

"Stop pointing fingers. At this point, we need to know exactly how you three went about trying to locate Edward. We have to come up with a plan to get him back. And come up with one quickly."

"I'll tell you what we did," the minister answered. "We looked all around. We walked up and down the track looking for anybody lingering about who might know something. We canvassed the entire station for those waiting for the next train or working in the terminal. We searched the parking lot. There was not a buggy or motorcar anywhere. We checked the lavatories in case the kidnappers were hiding in there. But the station was completely abandoned. We left a note for the stationmaster, who wasn't in his office, either, and finally got a porter to track down a sheriff's deputy."

"And?"

"It was as if the child vanished into thin air."

"This is a nightmare," George seethed. "Why didn't you let us know? We've been waiting like imbeciles for you to show up with our son."

"After all that, we determined the best action to take was to continue to the next stop where we might explain the situation to you in person and devise a plan going forward. This was the fastest way to get you the news. There was no telegraph office at the last stop. It's a branch line."

"What do we do now? George asked the bodyguard.

"Tell me exactly where you abandoned his son," the bodyguard demanded of the three. "What was the stop?"

"Heppner, Oregon."

"That's four hours by car," George cried as panic set in. "Jesus! What do I tell Agnes?"

"She can handle a little white lie, can't she?" the bodyguard asked calmly.

"Oh, God," George groaned.

"Good. Then, I will get a telegram to Joseph. He can tell Agnes the train stopped farther away than anticipated, so we skipped Yakima and drove down to Heppner. We will take these two unreliable, wretched little urchins with us to the previous station, look around and ask some more questions. I have some experience in finding missing people. Somebody in that godforsaken town knows something."

"What will you do with us?" the young cousin mumbled. He had seen the bulge of the bodyguard's gun.

"Do you only think about yourself?" the bodyguard asked. "What happens to you is up to your Uncle Joseph, and he owns miles and miles of property along the harbor in Seattle."

"What... what does that mean?"

"That means I wouldn't be surprised if he dumped your good-for-nothing body in it. That'd be the last anybody saw of you."

Nobody was certain whether the bodyguard was exaggerating or speaking the truth, but the scenario seemed plausible. The delinquent began whimpering.

The bodyguard walked inside the terminal to send the message while George walked as if in a daze to his car in the parking lot. The other two followed. George sat in the passenger seat of his fine vehicle, a newly purchased Nash Touring sedan, blue with gold trim and wheels a smooth cream color, while the young adults sat in the back. The automobile was the one luxury he had allowed himself while Stevens & Gibbs was swimming in money from Navy contracts. He struck the dashboard with his fist while waiting for the bodyguard whom he had not wanted to bring along in the first place in a motorcar that meant nothing to him now that he had lost a child. He sat and listened to his heart beating rapidly under his dress coat. There are presages in this life, he was convinced. He recounted recent omens leading to this moment until the bodyguard threw open the car door and startled him nearly to death.

"We start at the train depot in Heppner," the bodyguard said. "Do you still have the bricks Joseph gave you?"

"Yes."

"Good, I don't think we'll be giving any money to these two for having botched their assignment, but we may need to throw some of it around to get answers in Heppner on the whereabouts of Edward."

"Let's go, then."

Earlier that morning in Heppner
Cooper May used all his strength to roll over onto his back in bed, sheets tangled around his skinny legs. He groaned and tasted sour whiskey and stale cigarettes. A thin, bright streak of sunlight pierced a vertical tear in the threadbare curtain over his bedroom window and stung his eyes. A blurry thought took shape in his head and tried to convince him that it was time to get out of bed. He did not know why. His body was not letting him move, anyway. So he lay there.

He went over a possible sequence of events. He did not need to get crops in the ground because the boys tilled and planted the wheat, oats and barley for him. He did not need to check on farm equipment and tool upkeep because he had trained the boys to make sure the moving parts of the tractor were regularly greased, its nuts and bolts tightened, the plow blades were sharpened and all that necessary maintenance was done. He knew that every foot of fence around the property recently had been mended. Of course, he did not have to worry about the pathetic animals on the farm because it was part of the boys' daily chores to feed the last remaining pig, comb and curry the last remaining horse, milk the surviving dairy cow and two goats, and collect the one or two daily eggs from the nearly abandoned chicken coop before or after school. In fact, Cooper did not do much work at all anymore on account of his arthritis — so why did he need to get out of bed?

Hard times hit the May farm a few years back. Swine fever and bovine tuberculosis killed nearly every pig and cow, while most of the healthy ones were bartered or sold to stave off foreclosure and avoid starvation. Cooper guessed his neighbors were in the same fix. The Wilson Creek flood devastated the entire community, and by the time nearly everybody had recovered from that torrent of destruction, World War I shattered their lives. When the war ended, agriculture prices plummeted, and because there was not enough work for the boys to do on his land, Cooper hired them out to neighboring farms that could afford to pay for extra work. That income helped some. But soon the throbbing, aching pain of rheumatism gripped Cooper, and his miserable life went from bad to worse.

He knew people wisecracked under their breath about his inability to lend a hand. He heard derisive jokes about him sitting on his porch and supervising the farm labor from afar through the thick monocle of the bottom of a liquor bottle; or how he kept abreast of the price of barley, hops and rye crop from a seat in the tavern.

The stepson he took in several years ago and raised as if he were his own flesh and blood gave up the farm life for good as soon as he turned seventeen and now worked behind the desk of a fancy hotel and lived in Portland. A fourteen-year-old orphan boy was now the oldest left at home, and he showed no gratitude toward Cooper for providing him with food and shelter. At every chance, the orphan tormented Cooper with threats of how he, too, would leave the farm when he turned seventeen. The effrontery angered Cooper to the point of lashing out at him with fists and belts. Cooper swore he would kill the boy before losing another farm hand.

He had selflessly saved another orphan from the fate of a cruel life on city streets, this one now ten and responsible for handling domestic chores, such as cooking meals, churning butter and milking the goats and cow, in addition to helping the older boy. He mostly kept his mouth shut, but Cooper thought he was slow and lazy.

Lying in bed, Cooper's sodden memory was jolted. He needed to get down to the Heppner train station or face the wrath of his wife. Another train of orphans was rolling in and, as she had reminded him last night, they did not come around these parts very often. Once every four years, the trains brought to northern Oregon farmers like Cooper May free farm labor in the form of juvenile and adolescent boys. If he could get himself out of bed and to the station on time.

Cooper started to remember pieces of last night, particularly his wife, Willa Rice, passing him the bottle of whiskey they were sharing and shoving a notice from the newspaper into his chest.

He took a dull glance at the leaflet. It said "Wanted: Homes for children"

"That train stops here at ten a.m.," she told him.

"So what? We have enough mouths to feed around here and very little work"

"Just make sure you get down to the station on time."

"What for? We have two boys more than capable of handling all the work around here. We don't need any more mouths to feed."

"I want to adopt a nice little girl to help me around the house."

"Our youngest one helps with household chores. And don't pretend you don't know that — you relinquished your domestic duties years ago in full embrace of the market principle. You'd be asking for trouble, anyway. There are too many rakes living at this domicile to bring a poor homeless girl into our family. You know it."

"I'll protect the girl from the likes of you and them boys."

She snatched the bottle back and took a full swig.

"We're not bringing an adolescent girl home to live on this property," Cooper asserted.

"You know I always wanted a baby girl to bring up. Find me one of them."

"They don't put little babies on them trains."

"Then get me an older girl I can talk to. I don't care as long as I don't have to listen to all the grunts and farts from you boys."

"There's a reason adolescent girls are left behind. Nobody is crazy enough to bring that kind of trouble into their home."

He took the bottle back.

"Then I want a baby girl. You can't help me with that, can you, Cooper? Not with your stiff back and lasting symptoms from the hookworm."

The gall of this woman, he thought, always bringing up my illness and shortcomings; she knows how much that angers me, and makes me feel worthless. Two can play that game, Cooper decided.

"Maybe there is something to be said for getting somebody to help clean up this messy house. This place is a pig sty."

"What are you saying?" Willa Rice prodded while rising out of her seat to seize the bottle again. "I ain't keeping this establishment clean enough for ya? Goddamn, if you ain't like my late husband complaining all the time. All of you are the same. But at least he gave me a child of my own. That man was virile and strong in every way except virtue."

Cooper looked askance at the hole in the screen door, where fat flies passed through all day and buzzed around in the kitchen, landing in thick assembly on food remnants left over from breakfast and lunch. Cooper stood and threw open the screen door, gesturing for Willa to take a good look at the clutter and dirt and garbage inside.

"Take a look here. You see them leftovers and dishes piled up on the table and in the sink. If I want to eat there's not a clean plate in the house. There's layers of grease on those counters a quarter-inch thick, and the last of that bread we used to make sandwiches was as stale as last week's loaf because you left it out all night."

"It's stale because that's all we have to eat because you don't have a cent in your pocket to pay the baker," Willa upbraided her husband. "And those thin bacon dregs we got cheap from the meatpacker don't have enough fat to make grease."

Cooper jabbed his finger at the kitchen mess.

"I can see small pieces of yoke from breakfast floating in cold, murky pan water — how hard is it to throw it out to the pig?"

"I can't always clean up everybody's messes!" Willa yelled. "I'm always giving that boy a piece of my mind about keeping up with his chores. You said he's lazy yourself. But this is the arrangement you wanted. Why don't you take some disciplinary action on him for once, you coward?"

Cooper always feared her volatile hair-trigger anger once she got going. Today, he did not care. He tossed the empty liquor bottle into the weeds in the side yard. Willa pulled a shoofly flask from under the patio chair and cracked the lid open.

"The bottom line is we don't need any more kids around here," he told her. "This so-called free labor starts costing a lot when you have to feed growing boys."

"How much can a baby eat? We have a cow and goats for milk."

"Sooner or later boys start eating like two or three men each."

"Then go down there tomorrow morning and get me a baby girl, Cooper."

"Girls are their own kind of trouble."

"Goddamn it, Cooper. Can't you see? I'm feeling the pull of motherly instinct."

"Give me that bottle, Willa. You're talking nonsense."

"Get me a baby, Coop. Get me somebody else's baby, since you're dried up and can't give me one. You need to get up early tomorrow morning and go down to that train and get me a baby girl. And don't say they don't have any."

"Shut up about that. They don't have no little girls to adopt."

"We just never got one. You need to make it up to me. Even my deadbeat last husband could muster enough jism..."

"You're vulgar, Willa. Why are you always bringing that up? You know my condition. Besides, you can't raise a girl properly talking vulgar like that."

"And you can't even make a plot of land fertile to turn some profit. You and the land, both barren. Why did I ever listen to you and let you talk me into coming out to this godforsaken patch of barren earth in the middle of nowhere?

"I didn't exactly drag you out here. You were out of options and not getting any younger. And you know it."

"You infertile son of a bitch!"

"Shut up. Maybe you're the infertile one."

"I've made kids, Cooper. You haven't."

"I'm taking the rest of this bottle to bed with me. I don't want to talk to you anymore. You're insane."

"Give me that bottle, Coop," his wife seethed. "You need to get up and ride down to Heppner by ten. I will have my baby girl, goddamn you, Cooper."

She ran at him and swiped at the liquor bottle in his grip. He pulled it away from her reach. Not giving up, she scratched the side of his face with her fingernails, drawing blood.

"Get away, you crazy..." Cooper snapped, but she clawed at him again.

He shoved her harder than he intended, and she stumbled backward and hit the decrepit porch's balustrade. The rotten top rail snapped and she sailed off the stoop and hit the weedy ground below with a soft thud and a grunt. Cooper left her on her back gasping for the air knocked out of her lungs.

Cooper knew that once Willa recovered and caught her breath she would come at him in an instant with any number of makeshift weapons lying around — knife, glass bottle, dish or piece of firewood. So while she was down there regaining her breath, he beelined for his room and locked the door. The last thing he remembered was his wife yelling and banging at the door:

"Get me a baby girl, Cooper. You owe me a baby. One way or another, you owe me. If you don't, I'll slice your useless maypole right off!"

Member intact, Cooper slumbered safely behind locked doors right through the rooster's crow. He figured it was ten or eleven o'clock by how high the sun was in the sky when he looked at the south-facing window. He let his arm fall over the side of the bed and his hand hit a hard smooth object. He looked down and noticed he was touching an empty whiskey bottle on the floor, but something next to it caught his attention: the crumpled newspaper advertisement for the train of orphans. He bolted from bed like a chicken from the coop at the sight of a hatchet.

His wife was nowhere to be seen or heard, and neither were the boys. He ran to the shed. The horse stall was empty and there was no carriage next to the other farm equipment. She would not have taken the horse and buggy on her own, would she? She must have, though, because if the boys were using the horse in the fields he would be able to see or hear them even if they were in farthest corner plot. He remembered they had planned to hunt and fish for dinners this week, and did not need the horse and buckboard for that.

Now he knew what his wife was up to.

George, his bodyguard and their wards arrived at a train station that looked abandoned. Not a conductor nor a switchman was to be found. No wayfarers lingered at the benches with traveling bags. The last train appeared to be long gone, and another did not appear to be coming any time soon.

They saw a railroad section gang inspecting rails less than quarter mile down the track. They walked down to where the four men were working. It was as good of a place to start as any.

"Excuse me. This young man and woman here got off a train that came through a while back with a bunch of orphans on it and there was a baby with them. The baby wasn't theirs, but they were responsible for his welfare. Somebody snatched that little child when they weren't looking. We need to find the baby boy."

The men looked at one another. One man started to mumble some words but was stopped by another.

"I'm in the employ of Mr. George Stevens here," the bodyguard continued. "You may have heard of the name. The Stevens are big shipbuilders up in the Sound. The missing child whom we are looking for belongs to Mr. Stevens, and the man and woman who were in charge of the infant are paid employees of his brother, Joseph Stevens."

"So the Robber Baron has lost a baby, has he?" one of the men said.

"Sounds a bit like a Charley Ross-Vanderbilt type of story," said the man who appeared to be in charge.

"OK, you've had your fun. Now we need some information, and we'll get it one way or another. George, show them your burlap brick."

George pulled out one of the covered stacks of bills.

"One hundred dollars for anyone with information leading me in the right direction."

The workers exchanged looks again.

"Did something suddenly come to mind?"

"Well, we heard there was a bit of a fuss among the crowd after the last train arrived," the lead worker divulged. "I didn't see anything myself, except there was a girl of about eighteen or nineteen crying near the tracks before the engine pulled out. Wait, that was you, wasn't it?"

He was pointing to the nurse.

"Some agents from that train lost their mind and started looking around and asking questions, too," another worker said.

"Nobody saw anybody with the baby?" the bodyguard asked. "He's less than a year old. He was in a rattan baby basket with a handle."

"There were a lot of adolescents and juveniles getting off that train but no kid that young that I saw."

"Is there a porter who works here who might know something more?"

"He's probably with the stationmaster inside the office."

George held out two bills, and they were snatched. He, the bodyguard, the cousin and the nurse started walking back down the track with no more questions. One of the section gang came running behind them.

"Allow me to accompany you to the station so I can introduce you proper to the station agent."

"For a fee, I presume."

At the office, the worker popped his head inside and told a man behind a desk that two men wanted to talk to him about the earlier disturbance and might be willing to pay for his time.

The stationmaster jumped out of his seat, yanked the worker inside and slammed the frosty glass door bearing his title closed.

"Are you insane, man? We don't want to be associated with a possible kidnapping, or whatever happened out there. Who would ever feel safe here again? They might close this entire stop and put us all out of work!"

The bodyguard shoved the door open wide and stepped inside. He was about a half-foot taller than the gang leader and the station agent.

"The glass on your door is a little thin. I couldn't help hearing something about a disturbance. I'm going to need to know everything you know and everything you might suspect."

"Make them pay for the information!" the track inspector directed. "That man trying to get his child back is a captain of industry and has wads of money in his pocket."

"He hasn't even met his adopted child. Have some respect, you fool! Sorry about that, George," the bodyguard said, and turned to the stationmaster. "You, what do you know? I want to hear it now. Right now. He's right. We'll pay you if it's true and forthcoming. But I'm losing my patience with doing it this way."

"The only thing I know is I saw Willa Rice — and where Willa Rice is there's trouble."

"Willa Rice?"

"You see, she lives with her deadbeat husband Cooper and a bunch of adopted orphans out near Lena. They're an impoverished, no-good farming family out there. Never recovered from the flood. Never recovered from a drop in crop prices. He can't work due to rickety bones and some lingering illness, or so he says. How they're not foreclosed, I'll never know."

"What about this Willa Rice?" the bodyguard asked, trying to keep the storyline going now that they were talking.

"Yeah, Willa Rice. She's quite a woman, I tell you. I came back in here after the fracas and saw her from out the window driving her horse and buggy like a bat out of hell. She never comes into town on her own, the mean old goose, but I recognized her. She nearly ran over one of the switchmen on her way out. That woman's heavy drinking and terrible temper will be the death of Cooper."

"Did you talk to the agents on the train about any of this?"

"They left a note."

"Where were you?"

"I rode after Willa on the account that she looked like she was up to no good. I couldn't catch her so I came back. She left quite a commotion behind, I found out."

"Was she alone?"

"One of her adopted sons was with her, I think, sitting in the seat with a shotgun across his lap."

"You realized she was involved in a kidnapping after you saw the note, right?"

"I can't say I put two and two together, no."

"George, put two bills on this man's desk. He seems to be suffering from amnesia. But if he can tell us where this Wilma Rice lives, then he can have two more of these bills when we come back this way with little Edward safely in hand."

At supper, Cooper May and his boys sat at their rough-hewn farm table. The younger boy had shot and killed a rabbit to give the family a decent meal. Holding the sleeping baby, Willa Rice stood at the open front door looking westward at the rows of plants shaking in the evening breeze. The setting sun spread an amber light across the quiet farmland. Willa did not believe in magic nor the divine, but she wondered if this precious being in her arms might not be the reason the landscape looked so serene to her right now. Suspended low wisps of clouds in front of the sun painted the horizon in light pink, lavender and peach hues. Frogs whirred in song. An earthy aroma from the soil rose in the air. For a short few breaths, Willa Rice forgot life's hardships.

Then, her husband spoke.

"So you didn't notice that it was a baby boy and not the baby girl you said you wanted so bad?"

"Shut up, Cooper. He's still as precious as they come. When I saw him, I knew he was meant to be mine. Now, we're giving him a new home. A special new home, the rural life as opposed to the mean city life. Look at his delicate features and long eyelashes. He's soft like a girl and as dainty as the pink lace and yellow embroidery on his garment."

That was when the blue Nash Touring with gold trim and cream-colored wheels pulled up and shattered Willa's beautiful trance. This intrusion was so jarring she had a sense that something awful was about to happen. A big, tall passenger and a driver who walked with very straight posture, emerged from the car and strode directly toward the front entrance of the house. Willa knew the strangers could only see a foot or two inside the doorway because of the fading illuminating sunlight and darkness in the back of the house where no natural light filtered in. She pivoted away from the charming rustic scene that had mesmerized her and moved into the interior shadows.

She stared down at her husband and the boys loudly crunching, grinding and slurping at the table. She ordered Cooper to get up to greet the intruders while she took the baby to the large loft in the back of the decrepit bungalow where the boys slept.

"What's happening, Willa? What did you do?"

"Do not — no matter what — tell them we have this young child here," she snarled. "He is ours and will not be taken away. Do you understand?"

Cooper had been tipping a liquor jug after every bite of his meal, and he set it down hard on the table and rose to meet George Madison Stevens and the bodyguard just as they arrived at the threshold.

"Are you Cooper May?" the bodyguard inquired.

"I am. What do you want? What's the meaning of your interrupting our peaceful meal?"

"Where's Willa Rice?"

"She upstairs. Not feeling well."

"Nevertheless, we need to speak to her. Our visit carries great import."

"She can't come. And you need to get off our property. You're trespassing."

"Do you treat all of your visitors like this? What are you hiding?"

"We don't appreciate the intrusion. Especially at suppertime. We live a peaceful, quiet life out here on our land. If we didn't invite y'all, then it cain't be anything good."

"Oh, you're right about that. Let me ask you. Do you have an infant boy in here? A little baby, eight or nine months old, who does not belong to you?"

"No, we don't. It's me and my sons is all. And my wife is resting upstairs."

"Why don't you tell her to come down here?"

"She's ill, I told you, and can't come down."

The enduring poor luck of Cooper May persisted when young Edward let out an ear-piercing scream from upstairs.

The bodyguard pulled his nickel-plated Smith & Wesson Hand Ejector pistol from his shoulder holster and pushed aside Cooper May with his other arm as if he were a stack of sticks. The frightened boys did not seem to know what to do, so they stayed seated and said nothing. The bodyguard ordered them to remain still with their hands in plain sight on the table. George was paralyzed himself; his eyes watched, but his body didn't move. He was grounded to a spot near the door.

"Willa? You up there?" the bodyguard inquired pleasantly.

She did not answer, but the baby continued to wail.

"I'm coming up these stairs. I want you to lay the baby down on the floor in the middle of the room up there, and then you need to back up, all the way against the far wall. Keep your hands where I can see them, and away from the baby. I'm coming up at the count of five, unless you come down here first. One. Two..."

"This is *my* baby, and I'm not going to let you take him!" she yelled.

"That's not true. We can prove he belongs to Mr. Stevens. We know there are the letters SFI embroidered on the cloth of that baby's garment. We have official adoption papers from the Children's Aide Society, signed and delivered. And I don't think..."

In the middle of the bodyguard's sentence, Willa appeared at the top of the stairs as looming and electrically charged as a thunderstorm. She held a Winchester Model 12 shotgun at her right side and swiftly descended the steps. Her eyes glowed with savagery. Halfway down the stairs she caught sight of the big, tall man she had seen getting out of the car and raised the scattergun.

Pap-Pap-Pap.

Three shots rang out from the bodyguard's pistol and Willa Rice dropped like a sack of sugar and rolled down the remaining stairs. The baby screamed at the top of its little lungs from the upstairs room.

George could not close his owl-like eyes even though he was scared to look. His carotid artery pounded in his throat as hard as it ever had. He quickly glanced back at the Nash and saw the frightened nurse staring out of the car window.

The bodyguard swung his pistol around and pointed the barrel at Cooper and the boys at the dinner table.

"Nobody moves!" he commanded. "George! George! Get up there and get your son. Cooper! I need you to rip up some sheets or shirts or cloth, anything, and set them over there by your wife and then back the hell away. Don't even think about touching that shotgun."

He ordered the oldest boy up from the table to get a pail of water and bring it inside. The boy ran out of the house to the well.

Willa Rice was alive, but she had blacked out from pain when two bullets shredded her right shoulder and ripped up her bicep muscle. The bodyguard, keeping his weapon close to him, examined her to make sure the bullets had passed cleanly through her limb. Dunking the ripped cloth in water, the bodyguard cleaned where the bullet had penetrated Willa's body and applied pressure to slow the bleeding. He commanded Cooper to take over the first aid and keep pressure on the cloth over the wound, and make sure Willa remained lying on her side on the floor.

"Y'all did an awful thing," he admonished. "Taking a child from an innocent man and woman. But nobody is going to die today because of it, or so it appears. One of you has already paid a heavy price for the transgression. I will send a doctor here immediately. But when I leave this property I never want to see any of you again. And neither does George. Isn't that right, Mr. Stevens?"

"That's right," George said weakly from the top landing as he held Edward.

"One more thing. I don't take pleasure in disrupting lives and upsetting families whether they are millionaires or sharecroppers. I try to protect all people and I try to fix problems. That's my job. If I can, I make things right and fair for everybody. Therefore, George, hand Edward to me and go set the rest of those bills on the table over there for these folks. They need it more than you do."

On the third floor of Joseph Stevens' Queen Anne mansion on Highland Drive in Seattle, there was a boxing ring. Along a wall hung four pairs of boxing gloves, two jump ropes and headgear. Along another wall, a double-end speed bag was mounted, and a heavy gunnysack bag hung from the coffered ceiling. The room was illuminated by a massive Waterford crystal chandelier dropped from a steel pendant. Joseph called the room's style "tasteful savagery," and liked to comment that it was a perfect room to conduct business, as well as settle disputes.

He stood, sweating profusely, outside the ropes on the edge of the raised canvas ring. Under a satin robe draped over his bare shoulders, he wore short black wool shorts and brown leather ankle-high boots. Sitting below him on metal chairs at a folding table were his brothers George and Walter, his son Conrad and brother-in-law Gordon. His sparring partner waited, perched on a three-legged stool at a corner post, until Joseph told him he was done training and could leave.

"We haven't gathered in here since Edward arrived," Joseph said. "That boy is a Stevens now, though, through and through, forged in a gunfight."

He laughed, and out of habit, George checked the door to make sure Agnes was not standing there listening.

"Good lord, Joseph, keep it down," George scolded. "She's right downstairs with Edward."

Joseph sniggered.

"I'm sorry. You're right. She can't ever find out what happened. But I find it endlessly amusing."

"I'm glad you do," George said with a nervous chuckle. Then his voice turned serious. "But, honestly, I want to thank you for everything you've done for us. We haven't been this happy in years."

"In the end it all worked out. But you don't have to thank me. I'll say this in front everybody: I don't care about being a successful man, I just want to be valuable to people, especially my family. That's why I wanted to, as much as possible, help you and Agnes unite with Edward."

"So why did you ask us to come up to this stinky gymnasium, Joseph?" Walter asked with a dubious smile.

"I want to make sure all family members are on the same page regarding the direction in which the company is heading. I thought an informal setting might allow everybody to feel free to bring up any concerns they have regarding Stevens Family Investments."

They all laughed, knowing the boxing ring had settled disputes by fists before.

"You have the advantage, Joseph. You are already warm," Walter joked.

"We're not doing that today," Joseph retorted with a smile that quickly faded. "But as you might recall, at our last board of directors meeting, I announced that Plant No. 2 was permanently closed. Our final act as Seattle shipwrights was fulfilling the contract with Eddison Lines to build them a six thousand-ton tanker. In doing so, we were able to acquire substantial shares in that shipping line. This is a profitable move because Eddison has begun carrying freight from the Pacific coast to Hawaii and back.

"In addition, our luxury yacht is still on the company's books, but we have an agreement with Eddison Lines that allows them to charter the ship for clients as they see fit. In short, we remain embroiled in an expensive legal battle with the Navy, but, as a company, we are moving on. We have physically left the docks, and a new era has started for Stevens enterprises."

"What exactly does that new era entail?" Gordon asked.

"Well, George has a business plan that is going to save us. He wants us no longer to consider ourselves lumbermen. We are now strictly into timber."

"Again, what does that mean exactly?" Walter inquired.

"We only sell logs off the trees," George answered. "No more mills."

"You're underselling it, George," Joseph blared, shaking the ropes around the boxing ring with the palm of his hands. "You see, it's a brilliant plan. It works like this. We only sell the logs if we know there is good profit to be made. But if prices fall too low, we leave the wood and the stump. It's a fantastic strategy. The profit potential is immense."

"That's right," George emphasized, unable to contain his exhilaration for his work. The fact that his devotion to hybridization methods now was backed by a sound business plan thrilled him. "It's going to take another decade after the earthquake to rebuild San Francisco. Lumber prices, which were kept down after the earthquake, are rising again. Furthermore, the hardrock mining operations in Northern California are running twenty-four hours a day. Those mines are burning a cord of wood an hour to keep the steam engines humming to extract the gold."

"Besides all that," Joseph added, "this country of ours is not going to stop building thousands and thousands of houses and laying miles and miles of railroad tracks and erecting long stretches of telephone poles. We all know that, so we will buy as much land with trees growing on it as we can get our hands on, before the government steps in and starts regulating forest consumption, as well."

"There are a couple more things to consider," Walter piped up.

"Such as?" George asked.

"I'm concerned about treating trees like a crop in the same way a Nebraska farmer regards corn in his fields. Once you cut a tree, it probably won't be replanted. If you do replant, you won't see profit from it in your lifetime."

"But our timber company will resemble a Nebraska cornhusker's farm," George answered. "It will be a tree farm, and just like any old farm, the crop will need to be planted, cared for and harvested."

"You have a plan for how to succeed in doing this, have you?" Walter asked.

"The plan is to shorten the growth cycle of trees."

"That won't happen tomorrow."

"No. But we will own enough forest land to keep us solvent until it does."

"How will it happen, George?" Walter asked. "You're a scientist. I'm sure you've come up with a plan."

"I've been talking to the science and economic professors I had at Harvard. They estimate we need to harvest every three decades, barring a forest fire or some other natural calamity."

"What species of tree is harvestable in just thirty years, George?" Joseph asked as he unstuck and unwrapped tape and gauze from his wrist and hands.

"That's just it. We breed faster-growing trees."

George did not expect his words to elicit the hearty laughter that filled the room.

"Don't laugh. It's all about the breeding," Joseph told the men. "George has mapped it out. You know how he's been pumping a hell of a lot of his own money into the breeding of racing horses on that ranch he bought in California? Well, he's doing the same with plants. It's incredible. Just not as exciting as the ponies."

"You're certainly a man with a fondness for eugenics," Walter chimed in with a laugh. "Why stop with trees and horses, George? Let's breed better humans, too."

"Genetic modification and improvement may be what saves the human race," George answered softly, self-consciously and without any great enthusiasm.

His words dried up because he found it hard to justify the adoption of his own son with his overt participation in distinctively selective breeding. Non-intentional breeding was the very opposite of what he was dedicating his career to — and spending much of his own money in the process.

"You are at the forefront of plant breeding, brother," Joseph said. "You are going to be a worldwide leader in forest sustainability, there's no doubt in my mind."

"Thank you," George responded quietly. "I intend to be."

Joseph peeled off the last of the wrapping and tossed it on the canvas.

"But here's the thing," he said. "How will we profit enough from this business of owning sustainable forests enough to secure the fortune of our descendants? As you know, Big Papa wrote into the corporate purpose clause in the company's charter a paragraph specifically stating our intention to protect and pass on wealth."

George got back his enthusiastic voice again.

"That's exactly what a sustainable forest will do — provide profit for future generations, because new trees will grow on the same stretch of land we own, over and over again, paying dividends again and again, rather than leaving us holding tens of thousands of unusable, worthless acres of destroyed forests, soil erosion and washed-away nutrients."

Although his back was turned to the door while he was talking, George saw his partners' smiles and knew his wife and baby son had just come in. Agnes strolled the baby carriage into the room while he was finishing his oration. Edward was asleep.

"My husband the conservationist," Agnes stated as she walked up and kissed George.

"You look absolutely radiant, Agnes," Joseph told her.

She was a different, lustrous and more vibrant person than six months ago. She was her old self again.

"Thank you, but this room smells of too much male exertion," she half joked.

"Well, it is a gymnasium," Joseph said. "And, yes, that husband of yours is a regular John Muir."

"More of a Luther Burbank, you might say," Gordon added.

"Or Frankenstein," Walter remarked under his breath.

CHAPTER 7

Little Edward's first years, leading up to the Great Depression, were spent in a dynastic family whose business endeavors were evolving. He was not a shipbuilder's son, nor a lumber baron's child. Unmilled timber and oceangoing travel paid for his teddy bears, Radio Flyer wagons and Erector Sets, his pet horses, private tutors and elite preparatory academy.

His mother took a page from her Eastern upbringing and engaged an individual instructor for young Edward so he could establish good study habits, set clear academic goals early in his life and develop acute mental skills beyond the discipline of his school curriculum. A piano teacher arrived once a week to give him music lessons for two hours. He met a riding instructor every other week at the equestrian facility where they rented a stable for their two horses.

While Agnes lay the groundwork for a genteel upbringing, his father introduced him to hiking, nature exploration, and the appreciation for plants and methods of growing flora.

His Uncle Joe instilled in him a great appreciation for and love of hunting, fishing and camping. Before he was six years old, Edward was an old hand at road tripping and camping in national parks. He accompanied his uncle and cousin Conrad on outings to boundless properties owned by wealthy acquaintances where they pitched tents next to wild rivers and on remote beaches.

At a young age he became familiar with moon cycles and telling time by the sun's position. He knew intrinsically that wind was magical but also unpredictable in its timing, speed and gusts, and he marveled at air currents, whether they felt dry or carried moisture on any particular day.

He often roamed and hiked in the mountains among the sturdy Douglas fir and red cedar. By the time he was nine, he was as familiar with red foxes and spotted owls as he was with some of his classmates, and he was unafraid — but respectful — of wolverines, wolves, lynx and grizzly bears. Before he was four feet tall, Edward had hooked more than his fair share of salmon, trout and steelhead.

He grew up in the Jazz Age, although little of what defined the period touched the Stevenses. No spirit of rebellion had caught hold of Edward just yet, only a feeling that the world was immense, wild and fun. His was a blessed and innocent life.

Around the house on the lake, he helped his father in the garden and his large personal arboretum. He wheelbarrowed mulch and manure to where it was needed. He did not fully understand everything his father was doing, but he carried potted cuttings for him, as asked, into the nursery and greenhouse where George quietly busied himself grafting plants and organizing and carefully labeling pots. He held tall ladders for his father as he positioned pollination bags for experiments with evergreens. Edward liked gathering pine cones and became adept at knowing which ones were ripe. When Edward was older, George introduced him to fundamental plant breeding techniques and a basic understanding of eugenics.

His father was never far from his journal, he noticed. George filled book after book with his accounts, testimony, theories and conclusions. Edward saw his father pack up the journals before departing on trips that sometimes took him away for as long as three weeks. Edward later learned his father often traveled to Northern California, where he had purchased fertile land north of Sacramento to breed his new tree species.

When his father was absent, Edward spent time with his sister Anne Charlotte. He liked to show her around the garden and arboretum and displayed how much he knew. He was surprised that she seldom was there in their father's company.

When the Depression struck, the timber business fell into a downward spiral. Nobody in the family panicked, but neither were they certain how the difficult times would resolve, or if enough wealth would remain for subsequent generations. The family took measures to brace for the downturn. They sold their remaining mill properties and two Bainbridge Island lake homes. George's race-horse business did not suffer, even creating extra income that came as an unexpected surprise. The family investment plan for the next few years, it was decided, was to maintain a lifestyle that matched current earnings. They would hold their vast forest acreage while George continued researching how to grow insect- and fire-repellant trees, and keep their financial stake in the Eddison-operated passenger and freight shipping line.

Joseph did not let the Crash of 1929 get him down. He carried on as normally as possible. One evening, in 1931, as many extended family members gathered for one of their traditional suppers at his Seattle mansion, he invoked the elegant words of poet-novelist Robert Louis Stevenson to express how he thought they should all view the troubling times that were upon them. He stood at the head of the table with all eyes turned to him.

"Just like a bird singing as the rain comes down, let's remember and be grateful for the good times we've always shared. I, for one, will continue to enjoy what we have, while we have it."

In the decade after the stock market crash, the Stevens family lived mostly insulated from the devastation and ruin of the Great Depression. They benefited from a diverse business portfolio of land management, timber resources and their substantial early investment in Eddison Ocean Lines, which kept transporting people and goods in and out of Puget Sound.

Joseph had more time on his hands than ever. He had arranged his business affairs to allow for days and weeks to slip away on grandiose hunting safaris, fowling adventures and fishing expeditions — to the Snake River in Idaho, up to Jackson Hole in Wyoming, to British Columbia and farther north to Alaska's Kenai Peninsula.

George plugged away at his work on breeding trees and horses. Agnes and Joseph cautioned him not to pump too much of his own money into his pet projects. He listened to them politely but kept writing personal checks to finance both interests.

Joseph's son Conrad was three years older than Edward. By 1932, both boys were teenagers and inseparable. They always could be found together during recess at their private school. They participated in the same sports, and both were especially enthusiastic rowers. In the open water and on Washington lakes, they regularly competed in regattas for the rowing club. They felt strength and endurance grow in their youthful bodies by the day.

Edward's hair darkened to a sunlit brown color and his eyes held a slightly deeper shade than Conrad's, but the likeness in their bearing and easy smiles often led strangers to take them for brothers — even though they were not related by blood.

They were handsome, wealthy and strapping boys, eager for adventure, keen on achievement and able to tell captivating stories sprinkled with an abundance of humor, and they attracted many girls. Despite the difference in their ages, their eyes and ambitions sometimes fell on the same admirer. When neither altered his affections and found himself tripping over the other to gain the attention of a single sweetheart, they both knew it meant one thing: time to settle things in the fairest way possible. They ran to Conrad's home, bounded up the stairs to Joseph's boxing ring, put on the gloves and headgear, and sparred until somebody capitulated. These displays of pugilism typically exposed the truth that one young man's romantic feelings toward the girl in question were not as strong as the other's. In these cases, one of them would come out swinging with relentless fervor while the other danced around the ring. If nobody threw in the sponge, the strictly enforced rules stipulated they must stop after three rounds of three minutes each and neither of them would pursue the crush further, leaving the flower on the stem. Afterward, hurt feelings never resulted between the cousins.

By the time eighteen-year-old Conrad left for college in 1935, three childhood experiences had shifted the ground under Edward. The events did not overwhelm him, but they tripped him up from time to time. The memories colonized in the recesses of his mind and no doubt shaded his perception of himself and the world around him. The evocation of these events provided lifelong lessons.

The first ordeal happened about 1932, while he was on a trip of a lifetime with Joseph and Conrad in Alaska's Aleutian Islands.

The idea for the trip emerged at a Sunday family dinner when Joseph reminded those gathered that the family still owned an ocean-going steel yacht. Since they all seemed to have abundant time on their hands, he suggested, why not take off on a three-week big-game hunting trip deep into the wilds of Alaska? All present at the table were welcome.

"I'm not talking about the Kenai Peninsula," Joseph made clear. "I'm talking about going much farther. I'm talking about going where few men have ever gone before. This is something I started thinking about five years ago, and in the past two years seriously started plotting out."

"I want to go!" Edward cried out immediately, his 13-year-old mind and body caught in wave of excitement and anticipation.

"Then you, sir, are the first man in!" Joseph declared.

That promise hatched an experience that would permanently hitch Edward to the life of the outdoorsman, and arouse in him the long-lasting appetite of an adventure-seeker.

"Hold on! Just one minute," George reacted with fatherly protection. "He is far too young for such an escapade!"

"He is not, I can attest," Joseph countered.

"I'm going, too!" Conrad yelled.

"See? My son is on board and will look after his younger cousin. Won't you, son?"

"Absolutely."

"This sounds like it involves guns and killing and danger," Agnes argued, "and requires time away from his lessons. I'm opposed!"

"It will give him great confidence."

"Agnes is right. It is a long time for a young schoolboy to be gone," George agreed.

"Nonsense. Look, we have guides and substantial shelter. We stay in fortified barabaras. The expedition amounts to hardly more peril than a long auto camping trip. We can even bring a tutor along, if you like."

Conrad and Edward had been on hunting and fishing adventures before with Joseph, but never one of this immensity, one that would last much longer than eight or ten days. As a rule, Joseph did not like to take Edward away from his father for long periods, so he tried to time his excursions for when George was at his California horse property and arboretum stations, or when he was visiting universities on the West Coast and in the Southwest. There he shared with educators his research on cross breeding and gathered information from intellectuals about the increasingly popular field of eugenics.

"When Gordon and I took that safari to east Africa, the boys griped night and day for six months about being left behind," Joseph told George and Agnes. "When we returned from Tanzania, I felt so miserable about leaving them behind I decided I would make it up to them in a big way. Now I am. This will change their lives and shape them into men. We've extensively covered the Pacific Northwest's game fields and all of the

Alaskan Kenai Peninsula, so it's time to stretch out our wings even more and head into distant horizons where few have wandered!"

Conrad and Edward cheered and shouted their support for such an adventure.

Two years in the making, the trip would send them on a long sea voyage to the rarely sailed and remote Bering Sea side of the Aleutian Islands to hunt mammoth-sized brown bears that roam that region's heavily forested, snowy mountains. Joseph repeatedly emphasized that they would be hiking so deep into wilderness that only a handful of non-native people had ever stepped foot there.

"So, I submit again: Who wants to go on the grandest adventure ever conjured up and bring home the biggest bears the world has ever seen?"

The boys shouted for joyfully, jumped from their dinner chairs and hugged each other, profusely thanking Joseph for the opportunity. They promised they would act like grown men and prepare for the trip like adults and help and support each other every minute of the excursion.

The boys knew how much this trip meant to Joseph. He also planned to take his closest friends and travel partners, with whom he shared powerful bonds of trust and loyalty, so his invitation to join those "real men" nearly overwhelmed the teenagers. This was a call for them to prove their manhood. Joseph believed in his son and nephew. He had watched how their confidence grew with each journey, and he was certain they were ready for the most monumental trip yet.

Conrad and Edward were being called upon to act like adults in every way. They were told to prepare themselves physically for thirty- or forty-mile-long hikes with packs of great weight on their backs through snow and mush over rugged terrain. Joseph made them swear they would be their own bosses starting now. They familiarized themselves and executed hundreds of step-by-step preliminaries before the trip. They needed to trust themselves and he needed to trust them. They needed to acquire, on their own, the clothing and outfits required to ensure survival in any weather condition — and to pack and haul their kits themselves. That is the utmost responsibility, he said.

"You will get ready for the expedition as if I am staying behind and you are going alone," Joseph said. "If you want to eat and drink on the trip, you must determine the right amount of food and water rations to last you the entire duration. Hunting for food will only complement what you store. You need to box up enough ammunition and at least three different guns to get through three or four weeks in the wild. You don't want to run out of bullets or have the wrong rifle in your hands."

Jabbing a finger into the tabletop, he emphasized that the boys must learn and become proficient in all four positions for firing a rifle. He demanded military precision.

"I will not allow a second of incompetency, or even one complaint, nor will I tolerate low spirits during this entire trek," Joseph spelled out. "We are going into savage territory where brown bears stand twice as tall as a man — and our lives will depend on our superior marksmanship skills."

The boys took their firearms training seriously, even though they could never have foreseen themselves enlisting in the military and fighting in the next global war that was to come less than a decade later. Brain shot, shoulder shot, kill shot — Conrad and Edward became capable of executing the vital zone shots with great accuracy.

In the years after World War I, Joseph befriended some former soldiers who frequented his rifle club. Now, many years later, he asked them for a favor. Under these veterans' supervision, the boys sharpened their shooting form as if they were snipers. They learned basic ballistics and became proficient in sighting.

By the time they stepped off the boat in the untouched home of the great brown bruins, Conrad and Edward had cultivated a keen sense of patience and quick thinking, and had developed superb reflexes in tandem with a calm detachment. In short, they acquired the expertise needed to pursue and kill big game. Joseph explained to the boys the lessons learned were greater than that — they were the foundation for future success in higher education and business.

Spring arrived, and Joseph was extremely proud of Conrad and Edward. After months of planning and anticipation, the unforgettable trip from Seattle to the Bering Sea commenced.

With their provisions stored safely below, the party waved goodbye from the deck of one of Eddison's old but sturdy one-hundred-foot wooden steamers, a vessel originally built by Stevens & Gibbs. Thrill and anticipation shone in their eyes.

From Puget Sound the sportsmen headed north.

They took the majestic Inside Passage north to the flourishing renegade Alaska salmon village of Ketchikan and pushed off in a cutting gale. After two days of shuddering cold, they rounded the Gulf of Alaska and steamed along the edge of the immense sea. Snowy saw-toothed mountains perforated virga clouds and stabbed at the heavens. As the vessel surged eastward toward the vast open sea, massive islands rose out of nowhere off the bow. The boat pitched and swayed but churned on.

Along the way, bald and golden eagles hunted above, and other crying seabirds — cormorants, gulls and tern — wheeled and dove. Migrating orcas breached on the horizon. Fur seals barked at harpoon-safe distances. Tons of red salmon darkened the surface of the water, chased by peckish sea lions. From the deck, Joseph captured the scenery on his Eastman 4.

They arrived at a remote outpost, and the captain maneuvered through the seiners to find a berth at the wharf. Conrad and Edward took in the scenery with bewilderment and awe.

"Now that the winter gales have passed, these channels are busy," the captain called down from the bridge.

It was time for the hunters, cooks, guides, captain and crew to switch from the Eddison vessel to the tighter quarters of a gasoline-powered boat so they could better navigate the shallows and outcroppings of False Pass. They might have been only the first or second vessel that year to make it over to the isolated Bering Sea side of the islands, and the boys' wonderment and excitement mixed with trepidation. The entire crew paused, spellbound when a loud cracking sound followed by an even louder boom made by a six hundred-foot-tall massive chunk of calving glacier rent the crisp, quiet air. Awestruck, they watched an iceberg shoot off the glacier into the frigid water toward them, as if out of a cannon. The iceberg pitched upward then advanced no further, but the frosty waves continued rolling toward their boat. The swells struck the hull broadside and their boat tilted and swayed for several minutes.

Two hours later, the captain found a bay and anchored off shore. Gear, food and munitions were offloaded onto dories and taken to dry ground. After flat-bottomed rowboats successfully transported all men and supplies ashore, the hunting party watched, with some apprehension, as the captain weighed the anchor and his boat faded into the distance. They were cut off from civilization, alone in big bear country. Edward and Conrad smiled with great happiness.

Does, their fawns and caribou walked the tundra with them as they searched for a place to set up camp for the night. Tired and eager to get a good rest before their first full day on land, the eight men set up camp in an acre-sized grove of alders. They ate canned baked beans, ham, potatoes and rice. Then everybody, except Conrad and Edward, smoked pipes before bed. The crux of their journey was about to begin.

Joseph filled the time between bagging bears by observing and capturing on film all means of wildlife, a pursuit he treasured. The bag limit was three bears per person, and by the end of the first week, he already had the type of pelt he wanted to bring home: the right size, color and length of hair. There was one particular spot in his house where he had always wanted to lay a bear rug. One of his kills, an animal with a long, cream-colored pelt, was perfect for the space, and he was eager to get the hide to a taxidermist.

He skinned the bears immediately where they had fallen and returned in the morning light to retrieve them. Once back at the camp, he salted the hide and hung it to draw out the moisture. Each pelt was packed and ready for transport to his favorite tannery once they returned to Seattle.

The second bear he killed measured so large from its right hind claw crosswise to its left front claw that he was keen to get it officially recognized as a world record. If his steel tape was true, the bear stood nearly twelve feet upright and weighed more than seventeen hundred pounds.

Edward ended the trip with a personal collection of two bears, but for the rest of his life he would remember in a persistent, vivid way, the killing of the second one.

The pursuit started in ordinary fashion. He, Joseph and their guide saw the bear lumbering down the bank across a river. When the bear waded into the water, Edward considered taking a shot, but they remained crouched in long grass, waiting. Midstream, the animal immersed his big body in the water and began swimming toward them. The bear's little dip did not last long; he straightened up on his hind legs and trudged unsuspectingly toward the hunting party.

"He's not seeing or smelling us," the guide whispered.

The bear came out of the river onto the sandbar, and moved closer to them. When it was within one hundred, twenty yards, Edward raised his .405 Winchester and concentrated on aligning the bead with the rear sight notch. He squeezed the trigger smoothly and the gun boomed. Dozens of shorebirds took flight behind him. A herd of caribou fled into the hills. The bear slowly dropped to its hind leg knees and softly came to a rest with its forelegs extended. Its head sank until it rested on the back of its front paws. It was over in three seconds.

"I believe you shot him dead with just the one shot," Joseph said proudly.

Edward excitedly bounded out of the grass without working the bolt to eject the spent round and cycle in a new, live one. Joseph and the guide thought Edward was too excited and over-celebrating as he sprinted to the fallen animal. They realized the boy had forgotten half his training. He had kept his nerves steady before firing but did not remain cautious afterward. In the grip of blind pleasure and tremendous elation, Edward did not hear their commands to slow down! Stop! Wait!

Thirty yards from the bear, he finally halted. The boy was stock-still, apparently watching for any signs of life in the animal. Joseph, breathing heavily, had fallen far behind the guide, who had taken a slight angle in chasing down Edward and now stood twenty yards away from the boy with his own rifle raised.

In an instant — one rapid motion — the bear rose and bolted at Edward. The muscular beast reached full sprint in just a few strides.

Later, whenever Joseph recounted the story, he always finished by saying the incident demonstrates why to this day he only uses and pays top dollar for the best guides in the country — also, why the guides insist on carrying 9.5 Mannlicher take-down rifles.

The bear closed within twenty feet of Edward when the guide fired. With one bullet that penetrated both lungs, the creature went down a second time. The clean double-lung shot was the most expert marksmanship Joseph had ever seen. The target area for the vital organs was minuscule, yet no other shot from that angle could have killed the bear with such needed speed. There was no time to spare.

Edward fell to his knees and broke into sobs of terror. He cried for a long time afterward, scared but thankful. On the way back to the central campsite, he grew fearful that his cousin Conrad, who had been hunting in another location with the other men, would hear about how he had con-ducted himself and relentlessly tease him for the remainder of the trip, and probably the rest of their lives. He did not want to relive what had hap-pened and grew increasingly bitter when he was forced to listen to advice about what precautions he should have taken and how close he had come to being mauled and killed.

Conrad did not make fun of his cousin, but fumed over how stupid Edward was and how he probably had jeopardized their chances of going on any more serious adult hunting trips like this one.

"You need to grow up," Conrad told Edward.

Edward was most upset for disappointing his uncle.

"Uncle Joseph, will you still take me on hunting trips?" he asked tearfully when they were alone outside the tent.

"Yes, Edward. You're a young boy. These are the dangers your mother was worried about, but sometimes we need to learn lessons the hard way. It's not entirely your fault, either."

"It's not?"

"No, I got too excited, too, and should not have proclaimed you shot him dead with one shot. That was incautious on my part."

That was nice of his uncle to say, he thought, but the distressing ordeal stayed with Edward his entire life with concomitant consequences.

When the boys returned from the Aleutian Island trip with Joseph, he made them promise they would concentrate on their studies and help their parents with the chores around the house. Their vows to obey were not easy to keep. How do you finish the tedious chores of everyday life when your mind is racing back and forth in time; when your body still quivers with surplus exhilaration; while elevated levels of stress bubble up internally and muscles still ache from daylong bouts with hunger and extreme cold; as your heartbeat still accelerates on a moment's notice; with the near-constant presence of fear lingering? The thirst for a daily rush of adrenaline, followed by a need to quickly tamp down nerves, remained unquenched. The enormous weight of absolute exhaustion fell upon them unexpectedly. Euphoric, rapturous daydreams stopped any momentum.

They again were home and comfortable once again. They tried to readapt. They were able to tame the ambient light, temperature and noise around them whenever they wanted, but the monthlong vexation of uncontrollable cold and wind and unstoppable direct sun — coupled with nature's constant loud racket in an unforgiving landscape — was not easily suppressed or forgotten. The close, fraternal companionship of guides, captains, cooks, packers and natives, and the close proximity of predators and prey, were not instantly displaced by a habituated array of family members, friends, teachers and household staff.

Eventually the boys adjusted, of course. But the impulse for adventure throbbed forevermore.

Edward was fifteen when he was touched by another profound, unforgettable occurrence. The house was still, quiet both upstairs and downstairs, in the kitchen and outside. He did not know why, but his mother and father had arranged for everyone to be gone. They invited him to come down to the living room. When he got there, everything felt contrived.

Then they told him he had been adopted.

George and Agnes expected Edward to handle the disclosure with emotional maturity and to understand the reasons that they had adopted him, and how their love for him was as solid as a rock.

Instead, he was devastated.

His identity as a person and a member of this large, wealthy, well-rooted family shattered in an instant. They had kept a fundamental part of his life secret for a long time, and now he was confused.

"You betrayed me!" Edward lashed out. "How could you? Do I even belong here? Do I belong in this family? Who is my family? Where are they? Who's my mom?"

His parents expounded on the reasons they chose him to be their dearly loved son, and how they loved and adored him from the day they first saw him. They tried to describe his mother to him in the most positive way. To the best of their ability and sensibility, they explained the life he faced had they not embraced him, and why his biological mother had to give him up. They said they did not know who his father was, only that he was an American serviceman who died before he could marry the Italian woman he loved.

"How do I know you're telling the truth?" Edward asked through teary eyes.

"About what?"

"Any of it. All of it."

"We are! You must know we are!"

"Must I? You seem to be able to keep deep secrets for a long time around here. So tell me how. How can I trust you? You may be hiding something else, lying to me right now, even while you try to appease me."

"We have always told you the truth, Edward. We thought it was best to wait until you were old enough to come to grips with all of it," Agnes said, reaching her hand out to touch his arm as he pulled back from her reach.

"We waited until you better understood who you are, Edward," George said.

Edward studied his father's face as if he wanted to penetrate all of the thoughts shrouded behind those normally kind, tender eyes. Edward tried to formulate words to frame what was a very complex thought, but he was overtaken by emotions. Tears rolled down his face as he ran out of the room to the comfort of his bed.

He did not come out for the entire night despite gentle coaxing from his parents from behind the door. Neither did he emerge from his bedroom in the morning. All night, questions roiled in his mind. Dark scenarios played out in his imagination. How alone was he in this world? Who was his true family? Did his parents love him as much as they did his sisters? What was his mother like? Pretty? Happy? Confused? Lost? Was his father handsome? A hero? The questions did not stop. The answers were all invented; there were no truths.

George and Agnes were reading in the library after dinner when their son appeared in the doorway. They both shut their books and gave him their complete attention. Edward took a seat on the edge of the sofa facing them.

"I am thinking of all the questions I might have asked you, while you were working on plant breeding in your conservatory, had I known all of this," he said, trying to keep his feelings in balance.

"What? What kind of questions?"

"Oh, perhaps about propagating better species with fewer problems, by reproducing the best genes in each strain and leaving nothing to chance. You are always trying to make quick-growing, strong, disease-resistant types of trees. You said the problem lies in the fact that nature is too slow to evolve and too random. You said the same could be applied to humans. Did you not?"

"I suppose, I meant..."

"So, your son is as random an offspring as you'll ever find in a species. What's wrong with me? What problems have you now inherited? What weak genes in me do you wish to eradicate? What disease do I have that you'd like to get rid of?"

"Everything is not about genetics!"

"You've dedicated your life to genetics. I think it is."

"There's more to life than that, Edward. There's love and nourishment and the right environment."

The disquisition tapered off, a slow fade instead of an explosive disintegration. Edward simply walked away without saying another word, and Agnes and George wondered if such a non-cataclysmic ending to the conversation was the worst of all outcomes.

The sore and lasting rawness of the encounter had not eased at all when a third significant — and not entirely unrelated — event happened to Edward.

He came across a letter tucked in the back of a drawer in his father's bureau that he found while rummaging without permission for information about his biological mother, father and infancy. He was starved for more details, anything that might give a morsel of clarity.

Instead of finding clarity, he found confusion and more questions than answers. He wondered if his life had been reduced to a science experiment.

The correspondence contained a letterhead that told him it was from the Better Human Foundation in California. The typewritten communication was clearly addressed to George Stevens.

It read:

Dear George,

It's always an added pleasure meeting with you when we can discuss our mutual passion for conducting research and working in the field of selective breeding; your specific interest being in forests and mine in lemon and orange groves.

I wanted to follow up on setting a time when you can come down to Arizona so I might share more on what our organization has been doing since we last met. We now have extensive data on the personal and social effects of eugenic sterilizations (thanks to a collaboration of ours) and are cultivating a close relationship with the new German regime to understand the reproduction of racially fit humans and, conversely, preventing the reproduction of those we might consider genetically inferior.

During the past three decades in California, institutions have sterilized nearly 12,000 patients regarded as insane or feebleminded. I've included in this envelope the results from case study of these sterilizations. Please let me know your thoughts.

Until we can meet face to face I would like you to consider taking a trip with me to Germany to come together with our counterparts there. I think the trip will provide an inspiration as we come up with a model for our own racial policies. The Nazis are finding our information valuable as they practice applied biology to building a superb race.

Lost in thought, he let the letter drop from his fingers to the floor after reading it.

He looked fixedly down at the letter at his feet, thinking about the words he had just read. He instinctively knew there was more to be discovered here. More of what, exactly? More evidence of his father's commitment to the Nazi's "applied biology?" Reams of literature on the subject hidden somewhere? A trove tucked away in a concealed room, or maybe at one of George's pieds-à-terre in California?

Looking around the room, he vaguely remembered seeing his father use a jib door with a touch latch locking system. It was an amazing system. What had he pushed? Was it a figurine or a bust? Edward scanned the bookshelves in the office. He moved a picture here, a statuette there.

But no, George did not hide what he was researching. It was out in the open. It was on the shelves of his office, right at eye level. Edward's eyes scanned all of the shelves in his father's office, and he saw almost too much Nazi and fascist literature to bear: an early — and no doubt monetarily valuable — edition of *The Myth of the Twentieth Century* by Alfred Rosenberg; a book by Ernst Glaeser; a 1933 publication by Houghton Mifflin of Adolf Hitler's *Mein Kampf*; and a lot more.

He heard a sound coming from down the hallway. Before leaving the room, he placed the letter back where he had found it.

CHAPTER 8

In 1937, Edward Stevens started feeling alone, isolated, abandoned. Life at home was changing for several reasons.

Money was tight. His parents did not curtail his or his sisters' activities and pastimes, but they knew, in the way that children know while going about their lives anyway, that the household budget was being squeezed and many luxuries abandoned. At least two domestic servants were sacked, and the family had not been away on a vacation for two years. Plans to modernize and redecorate part of the house were put on hold, and an entire upstairs renovation was stopped midway through.

Joseph had restricted business expenditures and frozen all new ventures through Stevens Family Investments. Major shareholders were called on to reign in their spending on corporate accounts.

Life got quieter around Edward's house and Uncle Joseph's place, too. Family gatherings were smaller, fewer and farther between. Social calls dropped off, as well. Joseph was now a member of Congress and spent several months of the year twenty-seven hundred miles away in the nation's capital.

Two years earlier, he had cashed in on his connections and relationships in Seattle's influential social circles to make a run at a seat in the Washington state Legislature. By tapping into the enormous fundraising vein of the region's wealthiest donors, he amassed significant campaign funds and gained access to top strategic advisors. With that advantage, he was elected by a landslide.

Next, he set his eyes on the U.S. Congress. In 1936, two years after his first political victory, he ran for a House seat. The main plank of his platform was opposition to Roosevelt administration policies on three fronts: taxation and spending, organized labor rights and overreaching land conservation. The legislative battle was personal and profound because Joseph did not think his own company could survive another term of Franklin D. Roosevelt. He shared his views with everyone every chance he got.

On the campaign trail, Joseph made headlines by calling the president a Marxist and a hypocrite. When Roosevelt came to Washington to expand federally protected forests in the Pacific Northwest, the president saw what clear-cutting had done to the land and attacked Joseph and his profession by calling the deforestation an "ugly legacy of voracious timber barons." Joseph buttonholed a newspaper reporter to point out that Roosevelt himself owned thousands of acres of land back east that was marred by clear-cutting.

"The president shouldn't cast stones," he told the reporter. "Print that!"

His tactics worked, and he easily won. As a congressman, he was burdened by the demands of constant long travel and keeping an arduous schedule.

His son Conrad left the state, too, not for politics but for an education. Conrad departed for Harvard University, his father's alma mater, in the fall of 1935. His going away deprived Edward of a confidant, sparring partner, hunting companion, rowing mate and an accomplice in romantic pursuits. His and Conrad's grooming to be the next leaders of the Stevens dynasty was put on hold, like all other future business matters, or so Edward thought.

If Edward's sense of abandonment had not been absolute after losing his close companion and an adult mentor, then his father's frequent absences finished the job. George's three major interests required him to travel frequently to California for long spells. There were the citrus trees he grew in Southern California. There were the horses he raised and bred in Northern California to set world records. And there was the work in forest genetics, selective cutting and advanced timberland-thinning practices that he presided over at his institute in the foothills north of Sacramento.

Edward suspected his father also spent a great deal of time with colleagues at the Better Human Foundation, which had growing influence. Ever since he found the letter from the organization addressed to his father, Edward came upon what he saw as more warning signs in newspaper articles and on radio broadcasts reporting that racial hygienists in the United States were influencing leaders of the Nazi Party and justifying that regime's pursuit of eugenics policies.

Edward needed to do something to combat his feelings of isolation and the inability to influence much of anything in this world. He did not lock himself despairing in his room. He did quite the opposite.

He immersed himself in rowing, taking to the sport with fervor. He practiced long hours in both a single scull and with his club in eights. He rowed on Lake Washington until his muscles ached all the way down to his wrists and hands, until his legs knotted up and he could not lift his arms or walk straight. Always, the next day he was back at it, oar in hand, refining the catch, the drive and the length. Regattas came, races were won and ribbons accumulated.

He may have appeared to be thoroughly absorbed in sculling, but he relished other activities nearly as much, especially if they helped him connect with others and find new companionship. Drinking beer and smoking cigarettes on out-of-the-way beaches around the lake were among his favorite pastimes. With Joseph and Conrad thousands of miles away, he regularly snuck out to the boat house and slipped the sleek Gar Wood Speedster powerboat onto the lake. Once he was out of sight from the property, he gunned the boat's muscular military-style engine, and he and his friends flew across the water with the freedom of sky-bound falcons. Wind tossed their hair, and their laughter was muffled only by the clamor of the motor and the waves smacking the bow.

Like the boat's motor, an internal engine constantly sped in Edward's head. Everything moved fast in the summer of 1936. He thrived on thrills and ceaseless movement. In his social groups, he found new independence from the tradition-bound Stevens family and he created new rules and pushed boundaries to live daringly, act up and ignore convention. Away from the lake, he snuck off to dance to swing bands and listen to Black jazz music in clubs until late at night. When he was out at night, his chest felt like it might explode with uncontainable energy, and he found it hard to hold back on anything pleasurable, whether dancing, drinking or making love. And, for the first time, he noticed his charisma was seductive to those around him.

After summer, he hurtled through the fall semester at the academy, driven to get good marks and succeed in all of his studies. He was determined to be accepted at the University of Washington. In the spring of 1937, he received his letter of acceptance into the university and at the same time a recruitment letter from the rowing coach acknowledging a spot on junior crew. If he made a good impression, he might even have a chance to make varsity.

After graduating from prep school, his mania peaked as the summer of 1937 came upon him. For all of June, July and August, he wanted to do more and more — more running, more rowing, more drinking, more smoking, more sex, more speed boating, more dancing. To Edward, life could not go fast enough, and a day did not seem long enough to accommodate all his desires.

College reared up like a granite mountainside that Edward would either slam into and shatter upon, or scale with great alacrity and tempo. When classes started in the fall, he climbed to the top of that mountain, hitting a stride that seemed unachievable to most.

The biggest challenge in college life came from athletics. He joined the rowing team the year after the University of Washington varsity crew won the Intercollegiate Rowing Association national championship, and the team hit the apex of the sport. Against all odds, the Huskies beat Italy and Germany in the men's eight event to win a gold medal for the United States at the 1936 Berlin Olympics. The team returned the next year largely intact. Edward would have to wait for his chance at varsity crew.

In 1938, a few varsity spots on the team opened up, so he figured he would throw himself into that. He accomplished his first goal by making the varsity squad and next set out to win a college championship. He spared no effort, but he and his seven teammates in the shell fell short. The dominant University of Washington's streak of titles ended and the crew lost the championship to Navy in Edward's first year racing on the Hudson River.

The disappointment sent him on another trajectory, but he was still in ascent. At the party after the championship race in Poughkeepsie, New York, a young cadet told Edward about life as a Navy midshipman. He suggested Edward transfer.

"Tell me why I should," Edward said with a smile, just to hear the argument.

"For one, you could be a hero. You know the country is heading to war, right? Tensions are growing. We're already making preparations, and there's a huge rise in military recruitment."

"I can see that," Edward joked.

"It's our duty to defend our country if war breaks out," the cadet continued. "America is allied with Britain against Germany. There's a growing threat from German aggression and they're expanding in Europe. Stopping the spread of Nazi ideology and militarism is an honorable and heroic endeavor."

Edward remembered the letter to his father from the Better Human Foundation but said nothing. The cadet continued, full force now.

"This threat must be stopped. If you join us, there's a great camaraderie we all share. We serve together. And it will give you a big jump in your career. There are so many advancement opportunities if you join the academy."

Edward's collegiate rowing days ended before Washington won another championship. He entered the U.S. Naval Academy in Annapolis after his uncle directly nominated him for admission. By 1942, his career as an airman in the U.S. Navy had begun. His new home was Moffett Field in California.

That is where he met James Sizemore. Sizemore told Edward about the Navy expanding its lighter-than-air airship program.

"You should take the training!"

"What do the blimps do?" Edward asked.

"Anti-submarine patrols and convoy escort along the coast."

"It sounds like an easy assignment."

"It's not. It's wartime after all."

Edward dove headlong into acquiring the skills and experience to fly both L-class and the larger K-class blimps. He had not been as excited since he first dropped into the scull at the University of Washington. Everything about airship instruction fascinated him — from becoming familiar with instrument flight rules and radio communication, to managing buoyancy by adjusting gas and ballast and finding favorable winds. Aerial gunnery training enthralled him and James, too, whether it was mastering the anti-aircraft defense system, identifying enemy positions or judging ranges for the fifty-caliber machine gun and three hundred, twenty-five-pound depth charge.

The war was raging in the Pacific, and Edward and James were eager to do their part. Time flew so fast that Edward thought little about what might be happening back home, and he lost touch with family. If he had taken time to write an occasional letter to his mother or father, he might have mentioned how the government's ramped-up production of war blimps reminded him of Joseph's stories about when Stevens & Gibbs accelerated its World War I ship-building efforts under contract with the Navy. He might have told them how Congress had authorized the rapid construction of two hundred airships by June of 1942, when the Navy's fleet had started with only ten. But he never wrote a word.

On the afternoon of their thirtieth mission together, a clear October day in 1943, Edward and James watched their awe-inspiring K-22 non-rigid airship, which was as long as a city block and as tall as a seven-story building, emerge from the towering doors of Hangar No. 1 at the northern end of Moffett Field near the edge of San Francisco Bay.

The friends had been flying the smaller and lighter L-class blimps on coastal submarine patrols, where they were the only two crew members aboard. But the K-class carried a larger crew and a full payload, so eight other enlisted men were joining them this time, a full complement of ten men. Edward and James were accustomed to their intimate two-man operation and the roles both played, but now Edward was assigned as co-pilot and James as gunner. The crew served under command pilot Lt. John Greeley.

As the airship prepared to launch, an unspoken, undefined tension came over the crew. Nobody knew how long the mission would be. Only Greeley knew the exact patrol radius. It felt different, classified and shrouded in secrecy.

The enigmatic assignment came after a cluster of flights where Edward and James never saw a Japanese submarine or ship, but they both believed they would encounter one this time. If so, Edward told James, Greeley and the rest of the airmen better have their shit together.

As ground crews made final preparations, Edward watched the low, late-afternoon sunlight beam off the sheeny skin of the blimp, the words U.S. Navy emblazoned on its side. With the airship still moored to the ground, he and James climbed the wide ladder into the gondola. There was a gentle lurch just before the airship started to rise as the mooring lines were detached. When ballast was released, the blimp rose smoothly and steadily.

They were soaring, floating on the air, and working their individual duties as one cohesive unit. Once they were aloft, the mission's dual purposes were revealed: to check out reports of active Imperial Japanese Navy submarines within their stated patrol radius, and to locate enemy mines planted in Pacific shipping lanes. The heart of the operation began at nightfall.

When the full moon had risen over the black sea, activity inside the airship's gondola picked up. The navigator monitored the on-board radar system to detect enemy subs. Ordnancemen prepared their weapons for the possibility of deployment. Radio operators communicated orders to the command chief, pilots and co-pilots, and sent position reports over the airwaves. The rigger and mechanics kept a close watch on engine performance.

"Altitude: one thousand feet. Tracking one hundred, eighty-nine degrees true; speed forty-seven knots," the navigator called out.

"We have one allied freighter and one allied tanker ahead, sir," the radar operated informed the lieutenant in command.

"Men, high alert," Greeley ordered. "Enemy submarine activity has been reported in these waters."

Their voices were cold and emotionless — until the radar screen lit up at about 10 p.m. and showed an object in the water.

The radio operator called Edward over.

"Enemy I-400 class sub," Edward informed the crew as he watched the radar blip. He tried to keep his voice steady.

"Aft lookout, do you have eyes?" Greeley shouted to James in the tunnel gunnery position.

"Not yet, sir."

"Copy. Do we have a U.S. Navy convoy in sight?"

"No sir. The only detected friendly vessels are allied merchant ships."

"Sir!" James bellowed from his rear seat without dropping his binoculars. "Permission to report on enemy position."

"Affirmative. What do you see?" Greeley called back.

"Visual contact. I've picked up the submarine's wake astern," James informed the commander. "Enemy vessel is above water, in the moon path."

"Our good friend, *la luna*. Look at her perfectly silhouetting their sub. Is she painted purple in the moonlight?" Greeley asked in a singsong voice.

Nobody responded, or even knew how or whether they should.

"What's the enemy position?" Greeley barked, immediately serious again.

Edward's eyes were glued to the radar screen.

"Twenty miles from the allied tanker and freighter," Edward informed the lieutenant. "Ten miles to port of K-22."

"Any sighting of a U.S. Navy convoy in the area?"

"No, sir."

"Maneuver to intercept!"

"Sir?'

"Maneuver to intercept! Do you copy?"

"That's not procedure, sir," Edward informed the commanding officer.

"This isn't L-class, lieutenant,' Greeley shot back. "Maneuver intercept!"

"It's just a bit aggressive, sir. As co-pilot, I advise we stick to recon, track the submarine and request to vector additional surface assets to engage the enemy."

"We're alone out here, Lieutenant Stevens! Are you advising we let the Japs sink our cargo ships? Do you want to just sit here watching as the enemy destroys allied vessels? I'll have you court-martialed for even suggesting that!"

His patience running out, Greeley glared at Edward ferociously.

"I withdraw my counter proposal, sir," Edward capitulated.

"It is our duty to protect nearby merchant ships at all costs," he called out to the entire crew. "There are no other Navy vessels on these waters. The enemy submarine we've encountered is in a vulnerable position, down moonlight. Approach straight on. That's an order!"

"Yes, sir!" the second co-pilot at the controls affirmed.

"What's our ETA on crossing at two hundred yards?"

"Eleven minutes at fifty-five knots, sir," the navigator said.

As the blimp glided toward the sub, the pilots maneuvered skillfully to keep the submarine in the path of the moon. Greeley smiled. They were so far undetected in the cover of night.

"They don't see a goddamn thing," Greeley said under his breath as the blimp drew within a mile of the sub. "Surprise, you sons of bitches!"

"One-half mile to port side, sir," Edward said, but a moment later exclaimed, "Oh, shit!"

The submarine was rapidly pivoting to a ninety-degree angle with the blimp. Greeley was not smiling anymore.

"Steady! Press on!" Greeley roared. "Attack mode!"

"We're coming in hard!" the navigator cried, his voice cracking higher. "Altitude of attack two hundred, target angle two hundred, seventy-nine degrees. Range two hundred, fifty yards."

"First action — crush anti-aircraft counterattack. Gunners ready?"

"Yessir."

"Bombardiers ready?"

"Yessir!"

As the blimp bore down on the submarine, the enemy opened up its twenty-millimeter deck guns. Orange arcs from tracer rounds glowed across the darkness as the relentless flash and explosive cracking of gunfire shattered the night.

"Engage! Engage!" Greeley shouted. "Fire! Fire! Fire!"

The blimp's gunners lashed back at the sub with their own Browning fifty calibers. Dozens of tracer rounds screeched up and down in the moonlight. Edward listened to the loud, uninterrupted popping for a full minute, maybe two. In that span of time, he estimated the Japanese gunners had fired nearly two hundred rounds at their airship. Then, he heard the harsh sound of bullets ripping through the blimp's envelope and puncturing the helium gasbags and his heart sank.

The gunfire stopped just as the combustible electrical system went up in flames, and fire in the gondola grew with a fury.

"Keep the flames at bay, men!" Greeley yelled.

Edward activated the carbon dioxide system to blow inert gas into the space.

"Fire contained, sir... for now," he shouted back.

The pilots aligned the airship directly over the sub and Greeley was smiling again.

"Well done!" he exclaimed.

But the Japanese warship did not hesitate. The sub descended underwater in a flash and disappeared.

Optimism mixed with relief overcame Edward. He knew exactly what orders were coming next. Greeley directed the bombardiers to release their entire arsenal of depth charges on the boat below. Edward and the crew waited for the hydraulic shock waves to reverberate. But the thunderclap never sounded.

"Launch mechanism malfunction!" the ordnanceman reported. "Depth charges are stuck."

"What did you do?" Greeley accused loudly. "God damn it, man!"

Nobody answered the commander, because the blimp was losing its ability to remain aloft. The submarine's anti-aircraft barrage had torn into the starboard engine, and the shell started deflating. Edward felt the significant drop in altitude.

"Major helium leak, sir!" he cried.

"Flight controls aren't working," the second co-pilot shouted.

Unable to control the airship, the crew stopped all activity and gave themselves up to the inevitable. The radio operator put out a distress signal, but it was too late. The K-22 and its aircrew plunged into the dark water.

The partially inflated balloon cushioned the impact, but the gondola, still attached to the rubberized skin, suffered damage and started to sink. Bruised but alive, some of the men scrambled out of the foundering control car into the water and grabbed hold of the airship's large envelope that had partly spread over the surface of the water as it fell. Greeley, Edward, James and the rigger remained inside the cabin as it descended into the shadowy, dark green sea. Greeley ordered the rigger and James to secure and inflate the life rafts.

"We need to jettison all classified material we have on board," the commander called to James.

"Into the water, sir?"

"Yes, lieutenant, into the fucking ocean! Where else?" Greeley roared. "We may only have a few minutes. Once that submarine crew confirms there's no active pursuit and no reinforcements on the way, they'll return."

Once they ditched all the paperwork and maps and any equipment they were able to remove, Greeley, James, Edward and the rigger darted into the chilly water. They clung to the side of the only life raft James and the rigger could inflate in time, as the other six men sat shivering against the edge, hugging their legs. They watched the gondola go down for good in the moonlight. The moon was no longer their friend.

Every crew member anticipated the slow creep of the returning sub.

"I'm sure they've heard the fading pulse of our engines," Greeley said.

Nobody uttered a word.

Using oars, arms and legs, the Americans paddled away from the wreckage. For six tense hours, they waited for either the enemy submarine or one of their own planes to find them.

Several U.S. aircraft were dispatched after first receiving the aircrew's Mayday. Finally, a single plane spotted the exhausted, shivering crew. The men were battling hypothermia, but they were alive.

"Remember boys," Greeley croaked when they saw the rescue helicopter coming. "I didn't lose one fucking crew member. Not one of you!"

CHAPTER 9

Edward and James sat in the captain's drab office at Moffett Field. Despite the lusterless matte gray walls, the room exuded an air of no-nonsense leadership. Maybe it was the American flag displayed next to the metal desk. Perhaps the framed portrait of Roosevelt hanging on the wall contributed to the atmosphere or, possibly, the charts and maps on the table next to the lieutenant sitting at his own desk. It could have been the teletype station in the corner or even the absence of the superior officer who was making them wait. Maybe it was all of those things combined.

When the silence and the waiting and nervous looking became almost too much to bear, the door swung open and the captain strode in.

The friends rose to attention and saluted.

"At ease," the captain said. He sat without looking at them and scanned the report in front of him.

"Heroic and harrowing mission, men," he said, looking up at one and then the other. "Still can't believe you all made it back alive. Lieutenant Greeley is a great commander, but he went against procedure in a rather aggressive manner. Still, he saw an immediate threat, a menacing peril, as his report puts it. Did you know your mission is only the second incident of a blimp attacking an enemy sub?"

"No, sir," they said in unison.

"Of course, you didn't. The other one is classified. It happened a few months earlier, in the Atlantic Ocean off the coast of Florida. One man was lost. Eaten by a shark. Imagine. The report says he was an awful swimmer. Hard to believe. The other seven came back alive and our forces were able to destroy the U-boat at a later time. The only reason I'm telling you any of this is to emphasize that that affair was classified, and so will yours be. You're burdened with these secrets now. These two battles, as valiant as they were, will never come to the light of day. Am I clear? Both missions, top secret. Do you understand?"

"Yessir," Edward and James said, again simultaneously.

"I'm not sure you understand the gravity of the situation. Let me draw attention to this key point: I do not want either of you to ever mention it again, not now, not two weeks from now, not five or ten years from now, not to your lovers or your kids or mother or father, or the boys at the local bar. When you leave this office, you forget about this entire firefight and how it went down and how it concluded. If we learn you disobeyed this order we will consider it a violation of military law and the military code of justice, a dereliction of duty and severe mishandling of classified information. We will track you down. Do you understand?"

"Absolutely, sir!"

"Sir, yes sir."

"Nevertheless, I know how distressing this battle was for you and your crew. Your valorous actions are not lost on me. Therefore, to reward your actions and acknowledging that you will handle the aftermath of this incident with great aplomb and regard for the armed services and the United States of America, I'm authorizing you both two weeks of rest and recuperation for you both. You may start as soon as you inform your immediate supervising officer and fill out the paperwork. I understand you are friends. You may take your leave together, concurrently, if you wish."

They took their R&R together and found themselves staying not far from their base, in a San Francisco hotel, hoping to make the most of their short-lived freedom.

Their time at first was a blur of drunken nights, in the company of unscrupulous, often undressed women and days spent dozing until midafternoon. When night returned, they started the cycle all over again.

On the fifth night, they cleaned up and took the elevator to the classy nineteenth-floor bar packed with sailors and soldiers. The Top of the Mark was packed with servicemen who were waiting with their wives and girlfriends for deployment to the Pacific theater. Edward and James were dressed in their pressed khaki uniforms and polished brown shoes. A few civilian male bar patrons were dressed in nice suits, and every woman wore elegant attire.

James noticed Edward had not looked up from his whiskey glass for five minutes. His left hand rested on a pack of cigarettes on the table.

"You're missing a fine view of the city and the Golden Gate," James said. "You can see Alcatraz right there. But you have to look up."

Edward said nothing, and James asked him if he was all right.

"Aren't you a little nervous?" Edward replied.

"Why?"

"About what the captain said. Do you think we're being watched?"

"Watched? By whom?"

"Command. Investigative Services. The Navy. I don't know."

Edward finally looked up and glanced around suspiciously.

"Why would they be watching us?" James asked.

"To see if we have loose lips. To see if we talk about the top-secret mission."

"That's nonsense. You're paranoid. Forget about that. Why would they have sent us on rest and recuperation if they didn't trust us? Come on, let's keep having a good time. We can't start thinking crazy now."

"They could easily get rid of us, if they wanted, you know. They could get rid of anyone who knows what we know."

"That's not how it works — let's talk about something else," James suggested, and tried to change the subject. "Do you want to go see your family? That might be good for you. We still have more than a week left. We could leave the city. Doesn't your father live nearby?"

"I don't want to see anybody. Especially him. His work with eugenics doesn't exactly sit well with me. It's discouraging, to say the least. We're basically fighting against the very ideas he's advanced."

"Come on, don't say that about your father."

"Maybe the Nazis do have it figured out."

"You really need to stop right there," James said, glancing around. "Hey, we could go up to Seattle. See your uncle and cousin."

Edward tossed back his whiskey and poured some more.

"I don't want to talk to Conrad. He's being groomed to run the company when he returns from service. I can't bear thinking about the family business anymore, or who will run the thing after the war. His father is a congressman, who will make sure he comes back from serving his country alive and in one piece. It's obvious from the letters Conrad has sent me that

Uncle Joseph plans a rapid succession for him. Joseph hasn't even sent me a note."

"He's a politician. He's busy with this war."

"Yeah, but I saw the writing on the wall before I left. James, did you know I'm adopted?"

"No, Edward, I didn't."

"I didn't find out until I was a teenager. What that means is I'm not quite here nor there. I don't quite have family, but I'm not completely alone. I'm an orphan, but I have parents. The fact that my parents told me I had a different mom and dad so late in my life means it's something they wanted hidden. Since that day, nothing about my relationships with any of my kin has ever felt the same. In the end, there's no reason for anybody to support me taking over the family company."

"Well, you'll be fine, either way. You're as deserving as Conrad, no matter what. This war has a way of messing with our thinking. It's hard to know how things are back home. Your father and his brothers — they all ran the company together. I'm sure eventually, the cousins will do the same."

"That's good of you to say, James. It's got me thinking, though. I should chart my own course. That's what I'll do, my friend. I'll take the money I have and go in another direction. I'm not that interested in the timber side of business anyway. Hey! Will you be my business partner, James?"

"Sure, what kind of business are we going into?"

"Travel. Did you know our family is heavily invested in Eddison Ocean Lines?"

"No. Who are they?"

"Before Pearl Harbor was attacked, they were bringing boatloads of tourists to Waikiki on these luxury boats. Hell, they practically invented the tourism trade in Hawaii. Then, December seventh happened and their liners were requisitioned by the government for the war."

"What does that have to do with your venture?"

"I'm just telling you to show that I have some idea about how the travel industry works and how we can have a real business advantage as soon as the war ends. If I play my cards right, I'll never have to go back to Seattle again. I'll live in sunny California, and vacation in beautiful Hawaii, and I won't see another fucking rainy day in my life if I don't want to."

Edward gently tapped his friend's glass and they drained their drinks again.

"Tell me how it works," James insisted.

"Look around. See all these seamen and soldiers. They all need some way to get to where they want to go. They all needed help getting here, and they will all need help getting somewhere else at some point. Some of these guys here probably would have gone somewhere else if it had been easy for them to grab an airplane ticket and just take off. The bartender told me tens of thousands of military personnel come through here every month. Every month! To this one hotel and bar. A million have left under that bridge and sailed out to the Pacific Ocean and gone into battle.

"There will be a lot of casualties over the next few years, but you know what? When the fighting is over I'd wager to guess more than half, five hundred thousand, maybe one million of them will come right back through this city. They will need help getting back home to Texas and Kansas City and New York."

"So exactly what kind of business are you talking about?"

"A travel agency. Stevens Family Investments already has a ticket office in San Francisco. It's not being run by anyone in our family, but it's on our books. Somebody else operates it. But we could take this ticket agency, expand it, set up shop on military bases, contract with the Navy and Eddison Ocean Lines and get first crack at all of these captive customers. Then we're in the catbird seat."

"Sounds like you've thought about it for a while."

"I have. We just have to get back here and start as soon as the war is over. Are you in?"

"Yes, yes. I'm in."

"Good. All right, partner, come on! Let's go to another bar. We can leave the whiskey bottle for the next garrison, for good luck."

They took one last swig and stood up. A little unsteady on their feet, they looked at each other and laughed. While standing there, a group of five sailors came over to their table.

"Are you guys leaving?"

"Yeah, and the bottle is yours," Edward told the group.

"Thanks, but we have a favor to ask. We aren't going to be able to use these theater tickets. If you don't have anywhere important to go, will you take them off our hands? There are five tickets here, so you can grab dates on your way to the show — one of you can take two girls."

Everybody laughed.

"What's the show?"

"Gilbert and Sullivan. At the Tivoli. It's just a mile from here, fifteen minutes by foot, but you'll have to talk fast if you want to bring somebody."

"Why is that?"

"The show starts in twenty minutes!"

Everybody laughed again.

"So you have to hurry. They might not let stragglers in until a break in the set."

"I appreciate it," Edward said. "That's what we'll do, James. We'll take them. Maybe we'll see you guys after the show. Come on, we gotta fly if we're going to find some dates and still catch the curtain going up. Thanks again, fellas."

"First, a quick toast to the Golden Gate Bridge," the sailor with the tickets insisted. "Cheers!"

They passed the bottle around, each taking a swig.

"If one is for good luck, two is better!" Edward announced and they all drank again and again until the bottle was empty.

"So much for leaving you anything for good luck!" James laughed.

"Come on, we have to fly!"

When they got into the elevator, the alcohol felt like a punch to the head. When they hit ground floor, they were unsteady but galvanized. They asked the first two women they saw if they wanted to see a show. To Edward and James's surprise, they said yes.

"Toasting the Golden Gate *does* work," James said, slightly slurring.

"But we have to walk fast. Can you run in those high heels?" James asked the women.

"We can sure try," one of them answered.

The friends took them by the hands, and they all scooted down Powell Street. The sidewalks and streets were crowded as workers were leaving their jobs for the day. People hung from every available bit of space on the cable cars that chimed along tracks in the middle of the streets. James and Edwards and their dates laughed as they held hands and darted between people and vehicles.

"I'm not fit. I'm going to pass out in my seat as soon as I get there and miss the show," James called out to the others.

"We'll toss some cold water on your face when we get there," Edward said above the city's din.

At Geary Street, the women abruptly stopped at the corner before crossing and their hands broke free of their impromptu dates. Still laughing, Edward kept running and followed his friend into the hectic intersection.

A sturdy GMC beer and ale delivery truck blindly passed a cable car that had stopped in order to turn onto Geary Street. The truck driver saw the airmen at the last second and tried to swerve to miss them. But the truck plowed into James head-on, and a corner of the bumper thumped Edward with devastating force, spinning and tossing him into the air. He landed in the street just a few feet from James. The truck slammed into a lamppost and stopped.

The uniformed men lay there motionless, shoeless, bloody, unconscious and mangled as if they had been gunned down on an asphalt battlefield.

PART II:

SHANE

CHAPTER 1

I am not an heir. I am not a Stevens. I have no claim to the family's money. I am just an observer, along for the ride. I've been living on the periphery of their 100-year-old dynasty by dint of my mother and my younger half-sister. And, because I love them both, I cannot disentangle from either, nor from the Stevens' lineage.

My half-sister, Sloane, is an heiress. Not only is she one of dozens of shareholders in the Stevens' companies, she is also sole beneficiary of a multi-million dollar trust fund her father created. This financial account is stuffed with old family money as well as new wealth he amassed through his own endeavors. I give him considerable credit for growing his own fortune through grit and tenacity, under less than ideal circumstances. As long as Sloane keeps mind, body and soul together, she is set for life.

I am her doting brother, solid friend, protector and steadfast supporter and was put on Earth to safeguard her mental and physical being. I am bound to her in good times and bad. I gave my word of honor to be by her side forever. I take that oath seriously, and I think she does, too. The task has been difficult, as you will see.

Sloane is my only sibling, and I am hers. We might as well have come out of our mother's womb together, for we are as inseparable as twins. We live large in each other's hearts and souls.

Let's begin our tale here.

I am sitting next to Sloane in the back seat of my stepfather's Cadillac Fleetwood. This time, I am literally along for the ride. He is driving and our mother is up front with him. Sloane is seven. I am twelve. We are coasting up Highway 99, vertically bisecting California.

I call my stepfather Eddy, sometimes E.S., rarely Edward, and never Dad — even though he would like me to do so. A cigarette dangles from his mouth. He is a heavy smoker, a chain smoker. Every minute or so, he inhales deeply from the cigarette, filling his nostrils, throat and lungs with thousands of chemicals. The act of exhaling is prolonged, too. All the car's windows are down, but thick smoke builds and lingers inside the car. We are riding in a fog of tar, nicotine, carbon monoxide, formaldehyde, benzene, arsenic, ammonia, lead — you name it. On top of smoking three packs a day, Eddy also is coffee addict, downing twelve cups daily. His big yellow teeth — the color of hard-boiled egg yolks — betray those habits.

Since we are on the subject of my stepfather's vices, he also drinks a bottle of Scotch a day. Perhaps that is an overused exaggeration; let's just say he is frequently under the influence, and when he is, his personality shifts from being as bright as a waxing full moon when sober to as dark as the waning crescent when drunk.

If I have learned anything about alcoholics over the years, it is that there are chronic, social and habitual drinkers. The chronic alcoholic you will find drunk out of his mind and passed out on the floor at the end of a night; the social drinker only gets inebriated at parties and other public events; and the habitual imbiber, his drinking is a measure of time, defining the hour of the day. Eddy was all three.

For the record, he treats me pretty well. Despite my biological distinction, I feel every bit a part of his nuclear family. Eddy told me when I was very young that he wanted to legally adopt me, just like how he was taken in and embraced by the Stevens family two generations ago. I told you before, he allows me to call him whatever diminutive I am comfortable with. But he does not tolerate anyone showing any disrespect or causing any suffering whatsoever for his miracle child.

The one-and-only Sloane was born five years after me. She is his most cherished treasure, his most precious asset. Her birthright is one of wealth and privilege. Mom and E.S. knew the delivering doctors personally. I remember the scene after my baby sister was brought through the door for the first time. Mom sat on the sofa in the living room with her new-born sleeping on her bosom. E.S. shuffled in on his wooden peg leg and surveyed the room. I sat in a chair ten feet from Mom and Sloane. Just five years old, I was so excited to have a little sister in my life that I was bursting with emotion. I got up and strolled over to see her, touch her, smell her.

"My baby, my baby," I cooed from above her.

You would have thought a bomb had gone off.

"Don't touch her!" Eddy shouted. "Get away from her! Don't even get close, Shane. Go back over to that chair, sit down and watch from there before I smack you!"

Regardless of what happens or what the truth might be, Sloane is the queen and Eddy will take her side ten out of ten times. His single-minded goal in life is to rectify the slightest injustice to his darling little legacy bearer.

If Sloane was crying, it naturally had to be my fault. He would chase me around the house on his crutches, those manifested extensions of his anger, taking swings when he was close, and I would hide under tables or chairs. One time I darted under the open drawers of a buffet table. He raised a crutch high and brought it down on the table, snapping the compartment in half.

Sloane embodies the power of hope, resiliency of spirit and triumph over adversity, and Eddy knows a thing or two about those qualities. Doctors told E.S. that he could never have children. Then, in 1958, lo and behold, Sloane was born. Ever since that day, you can tell by the glint in his eye whenever watches her, he has believed his daughter is a genuine blessing from God.

And lucky me, I am sitting next to this hallowed girl for the entire seven-hour drive north on Highway 99 from Sacramento to the Oregon border.

E.S. is the type of man who gives you the impression that his mind is a thousand miles away. In a single instant, though, he can snap back to the present and lock in on a conversation or activity that has been ongoing for an hour-and-a-half, and he will know, or thinks he knows, every detail of what has transpired. This is the scenario I have dealt with for the past three hours, because Sloane is bothering me to no end on this road trip. The pestering began a hundred miles ago, and I know she has been thinking of new and more innovative ways to annoy me. E.S. has already turned his body fully around three times to tell me to knock it off and shut up or he will pull the car over and leave us — well, me anyway — on the side of the road.

Ten minutes after his last threat, Sloane snatches from my hand the book I am reading. She hands it back after I ignore her, thereby avoiding any fight to get it back. Whenever she pulls something like that, I train one eye on the rearview mirror to see if Eddy is watching. This time, he is staring straight ahead at the road, inhaling the smoke from his Marlboro up his nose and into mouth and blowing it in any direction except at my mother.

Up front, Maureen is the picture of good etiquette and politeness. She is the fashionable wife, a very pretty woman whose looks appear to have staying power. With such allure, she will be attractive well into her sixties. Eddy has not said a word to her for miles and miles, and she does not seem to care if he ever speaks to her again.

I look up from the pages of my book and steal glances at my mother. I have sensed something going on between her and Eddy for a while. She sinks into these lugubrious moods that only I seem to notice. Is it resentment, regret, anger, forlornness, that percolates just below the surface? I watch her. She carries the mien of being too bored to give a shit about much of anything.

Sloane licks her finger and sticks it in my ear. That might be a little funny, but I know how this is going to end so I don't laugh. Instead. I give her a death stare and mouth the word "Stop."

Sloane has already finished the book she brought on the road trip. She is a voracious reader. We've played travel games, ad nauseam, like who can spot the most license plates from different states, and who can get a trucker to sound his horn first. Now Sloane is bored. And that spells trouble.

I see a Volkswagen bug out the window, and I whisper "Slug Bug" and hit her hard in the arm. Sloane is not ready for this, and I can tell my thump stings her pretty good. A minute later, she jabs me firmly in the rib with her elbow.

"Stop it, back there," E.S. growls.

Mom keeps staring straight ahead, expressionless.

Sloane and I take a break from harassing each other for a few miles. I pretend to be absorbed in my reading again but actually am waiting for a chance to get even. When she least expects it, I plan to pinch and twist the bare skin on her forearm until it stings. Something else happens while I bide my time; I actually become engrossed in my book again. I relax, and the story carries me far away.

Sloane puts her face out the open window to feel the wind on her skin and probably to get a blast of fresh air into her lungs. But before I know it, she seizes *Ribsy* from my grasp and tosses the book out of the car.

I am so red hot angry that I don't know what I'm going to do. I pay no heed to what E.S.'s reaction will be and I let out a primal scream. I yell that she is such a stupid idiot for ruining the best part of the book, the part when Henry gets to the dog show. I push one of my hands into her face, smashing her nose down hard with my palm, and ferociously rough up her thick, reddish-blond hair with my other hand. I end my attack with an assertive double-tug of her long locks.

I should have been ready for the counterattack. She takes hold of my right hand and sinks her teeth into my thumb. I scream-cry from the pain and lurch back in my seat and roll my shoulder against the door in anguish.

I take a side glance at the rearview mirror. My stepdad's fiendish eyes are fixed on me.

"That does it!" he proclaims.

He flicks his cigarette out of the window, whips the car over to the shoulder of the highway and slams on the brakes. The car fishtails. Rocks crunch under the tires and dirt, pebbles and dust fly. The big automobile skids to a stop, and E.S. slams the gear stick into park. He plants the strapped-on shoe of his wooden left leg into the floorboard and propels his body halfway over the front bench seat.

"I told you to stop! That was the last time! What's wrong with you?" he shouts at me.

Sloane turns her head to look out the window, emotionless. She knows she will not be touched.

I am not so lucky. Like the swing of an oar, the back side of Eddy's hand claps the side of my head so fast and hard that it sets my ear ringing and my eyes watering.

"Can't you act your age back there? You're gonna get us all killed! I can't even concentrate on driving with all your antics going on."

"But Sloane took..." I stutter and he cuts me off.

Mom shrieks and out of instinct grabs hold of her husband's arm. On impulse, he elbows her in the eye socket to free his arm, then instantly turns his attention back to me.

"How old are you? Older than her, right? Supposedly. You're the big brother. Do you understand? Or do I need to smack that information into your brain so it sticks? Are you OK, Sloane, sweetie?"

She does not answer.

Eddy's physical correction of my deviant behavior ends with a pair of palm knocks to the top of my skull. They hurt a bit but are mostly humiliating. He spins back around, glances at my mom to make sure she doesn't have anything to say on the matter (she doesn't). He shoves the shift lever into drive, and the car rolls onto the highway once again.

Without Ribsy, Henry, Larry and Mrs. Frawley to occupy my mind, I fume — until I feel Sloane's sweet, small, soft hand on top of mine, and she squeezes. I know there are tears in her eyes, and she is embarrassed for having caused the scene. I don't have to look at her to know this.

She is conflicted. She loves her father and strives to make him proud. She will try to emulate him her whole life to varying degrees of success. She is proud of him being a descendent of the venerable Stevens family despite not sharing that bloodline. It makes for a more exotic tale, in her mind. Also, he has proven his own to have a gift for entrepreneurship, an aptitude for making money through his own effort and for growing a business to achieve financial independence. He has overcome an obvious physical disability to succeed on his own. Why would she not use him as a role model?

On the other hand, Sloane does not like discord in our family. She dislikes any disunity and cannot tolerate any split in the seam of our immediate little clan. Sloane doesn't want the family divided two against two, or three against one. She just wants us as one, complete, intact. She regards the four of us as a special, unique and loving household and would never want to permanently break up our domestic unit, and certainly not to be the cause of our disintegration. She just cannot help herself sometimes.

"I'm sorry, Shane," she whispers to me. "I like our family best when we're all happy and together. I don't want to ruin everything. I don't want it ever to end."

I catch her eyes and smile. She grins at me benevolently, scoots close and leans her head on my shoulder.

Mom takes her iconic oversized sunglasses out of her leopard-fabric handbag with the gold-chain strap and slides them on. She will not remove them for the entire trip. Eddy has given her a shiner.

We proceed to a town north of the Oregon border because E.S. has arranged to pick up a Labrador retriever hunting dog, a purebred from a top breeder that has been professionally trained for the past six months. He paid two thousand dollars for the dog. That is a lot of money back in 1965.

I fully expect there to be fishing or hunting on this outing — there always is. But Eddy has something else in mind this time. It makes sense, looking back now, that outdoor adventures would not be part of this trip, because Mom is with us. Give her Hawaii, give her London, give her any glamorous spot — just do not make her participate in camping, hunting or fishing. Give her a book in front of a hearth or on a beach, or a dinner party conversation or an art museum. She and my father may have the money to travel anywhere, but that does not mean anywhere will do for her. No, getting the dog is the main reason for this excursion.

Sloane and I behave ourselves for the rest of the way. There are no more scrapes in the car. We pick up the new dog and an hour later we are heading back through Northern California. Sloane falls asleep on my shoulder, is soon stretching her legs across the seat and plops her head in my lap. The dog is up front, sitting like a good boy, between my mom and E.S.

Just before dusk, Eddy pulls into his father's old forest research facility near the small Sierra Nevada foothills town of Georgetown and stops the car. We have been driving for at least four hours and the stop is a surprise to all of us. Eddy's father, George, died a year earlier, in July 1964 (and his mother, Agnes, long before then). Before his death, George gifted the woodland property, called the Stevens Tree Station, to the federal government, and the U.S. Forest Service took over managing the research center.

"Why are we stopping here?" my mother asks, looking at her husband through her large, dark designer lenses. "There's no reason to stop here."

Eddy does not answer her. As we sit in the car, he tells us how his father put in a gazillion hours of his own time planning and supporting and toiling away at the institute.

"He invested half a million dollars of his own money to make this institute viable," he says, and then expounds on how many weeks his father spent away from home and his family as the research center's staff and reputation grew and grew.

Sloane and I nod as we listen to his story. Then Eddy reveals to us that he was invited here today to attend a ceremony hosted by The Men of the Great West Society and to say a few words on behalf of his father because the fraternal organization is dedicating a bronze plaque in honor of George, its founder. My stepfather shows us the invitation, which says the dedication and plaque will commemorate "the superb and brilliant work of George Stevens as a businessman, scientist, conservationist and pioneer of forest genetics."

My mother does not seem to want to look at the invitation. We sit in the dirt and pine-needle parking lot doing nothing for three or four minutes. None of us gets out of the car, which is now immersed in complete, uncomfortable silence. My mother looks more bored than uneasy. Sloane and I are uncertain why an underlying tension pervades and why nobody is moving or talking.

"What are we doing?" I finally ask.

"Yes, dear, tell the kids. What are we doing here?" my mother repeats, displeasure and disgust in her voice.

"My father is being honored by this organization," he says plainly, staring ahead.

"I know that. But do you think it's in good taste? Is it appropriate on this trip?" Mom asks from behind the dark glasses.

"It's for my father, and my family. An honor."

"We are not presentable, Edward," my mother says. "We have been traveling for hundreds of miles in these clothes. We are tired. And I have a headache."

"There is a space in the building to refresh our attire."

My mother does not respond for a minute, and we sit there as if Eddy knows more is coming. He is right.

"We talked about this. You thought that by surprising me like this, in front of the kids, that I would go right along. Now that we're here, you think I'm going to forget about everything, and put the past aside."

"You're putting me in an indelicate position with this."

"As you are, with me. If you feel you owe your father something after the years of absence in your life, or you want to make some kind of amends for what has happened in the past, then that's your issue to work through. One of many knots in a tangled mess that you, alone, need to unravel."

"Are we getting out, Mom?" I ask.

"*We* are not. I don't know about Edward."

"Why not, Mom?" Sloane asks.

"Because the organization presenting the plaque promotes exclusionary and white supremacist policies."

"What does that mean?" Sloane asks.

At the time, I was not sure if I knew, either.

"Time doesn't change the wrongs of the past," my mother says to her husband. "Typically not, anyway. Perhaps you feel differently about things now."

Eddy's hands grip the steering wheel like he is wringing out every last drop of water from a sponge. His knuckles are white. His face turns pale, then red. He snorts and then calmly turns the key over, and we are on our way home.

CHAPTER 2

To explain how we all got here, moving through space and time and emotions in the Fleetwood, I must take you back more than twenty years earlier.

It is 1944. Eddy no longer is the Italian baby boy dressed in a girlish smock who was taken aboard the Orphan Train in a rattan basket and then kidnapped. He is not that zealous boy armed with a powerful rifle and excellent aim who nearly got himself killed by a wounded bear that was playing dead. He's not the strapping teenager who freely embraced new experiences, sexual and otherwise, and testing conventional societal boundaries at his family's Lake Washington home during the long summer days and nights before college. The confident college student-athlete who rowed against the best oarsmen in the world also is gone.

In 1944, Edward Stevens lies in a military hospital ward facing a lifetime of struggles after surgeons amputated his left leg just below the knee. Recumbent next to him is his good friend — and double amputee — James Sizemore. James is suffering from the removal of his right lower leg and most of his left leg above the knee joint.

Surgeons tell the servicemen they tried to preserve as much of their limbs as possible — as if either young man cares about such immutable details at the moment, or can even comprehend anything positive about missing appendages. The doctors feel it is their duty to further explain to James that he suffered a compound fracture of his femur — where the broken bone came through the skin (he wished he hadn't asked what that meant) — and therefore was at a greater risk of contracting an infection, which is exactly what happened.

"Gangrene set in, and your left leg had to be amputated farther up the limb," the surgeon concluded.

Edward sees the vitality leave his friend's eyes at that moment. He wonders if his wounded comrade heard anything that the therapists said after that regarding artificial limbs. When the doctors exit the room, he tries to accurately repeat and convey to James what the medical staff told them: how their wooden legs would be shaped and how leather would be used for the straps and socket support; how the contraption might not be too uncomfortable; how the design for their prosthesis would allow them to stand and walk. Edward soon gives up. James' eyes have turned hollow as he gazes into a future abyss of ostracism, isolation, co-dependency, hardship and self-loathing for the rest of his life.

Edward hated two things about the hospital above all else, three if you include how damn long he had been there. One was the drab, jaundice-yellow paint on the walls and the sparse furnishings in every room in the ward. The second was the ridiculously small window across from his bed that showed only a patch of sky and nothing else — and none of the outdoor beauty of the flourishing Northern California landscape that surrounded the hospital. He could see no palms waving in the breeze, no sandstone cliffs, no sun-drenched ocean beaches. The ugly San Francisco infirmary was set amid the most beautiful environs of any city in the world, but Edward and James might as well have been on the barren moon. On the other hand, after being stuck inside a place like the Fort Miley hospital dealing with pain and setbacks and therapy for three months, Edward figured detesting only two or three things around him was a positive outlook.

The procession of military doctors and nurses, psychiatrists and therapists, nutritionists and orderlies coming around at all hours, and hundreds of patients and veterans roaming the halls and common areas no longer bothered him. They were just part of the scenery, and he soon preferred watching and talking to these people over staring at the austere walls and furnishings or his listless partner in the next bed. His earlier bitterness at nurses or volunteers for fussing over the stockings and bandages on his knee or droning on about blood flow and movement was gone.

As for visitors, he had none, on that he insisted. He did not want his big, proud, grand family coming up from the Pacific Northwest and trying to make his awful predicament better by throwing their advice and money around. They would be doing it for no other reason than to act like they could control the situation and put an end to such adversity of life in the same way they sought to manage markets, the environment and natural biology itself.

Hospital administrators asked if Edward wanted them to reach out to his family on his behalf and arrange a visit after his surgery. They explained that time together with loved ones can help the healing process. The hospital staff's tentative, bedside smiles vanished when they saw Edward's body go rigid. His jaw tightened and his eyes narrowed upon hearing the suggestion. His abrasive rejoinder began with a simple:

"You have no idea what you've just asked of me..."

Their words evoked strong emotions in him and he vented for a full five minutes. The staff recoiled at the retort, and afterward Edward felt satisfaction and very little regret.

He avoided writing letters to friends and family. He begged military advisers who came around to not let any correspondence, V-mail or traditional, come across his lap. Nobody from his past was going to see him less than whole.

James' depression was much deeper than Edward's. His identity reduced to ashes, he shuddered and screamed in terror from nightmares, never sleeping soundly. He woke every morning in a cold sweat. Edward worried his fellow lieutenant might be suicidal, and he stayed doubly vigilant over him.

One day, Edward's concerns were assuaged. His fears for his friend's mental state simply vanished after he broached a subject they had briefly talked about the night before their terrible beer-truck tragedy. Lying for weeks and weeks in the hospital, Edward had the time to shape and develop the idea into a robust plan before sharing his vision. As soon as he articulated his concept, he saw the inner light return to his friend's eyes and streaks of zestfulness come over his face.

They lay in their beds one evening, tired but not sleepy, when Edward first raised the subject. Both men's wounds were nearly healed. They had been measured for their prosthetics and counseled on how to use them.

They were far along in their rehabilitation exercise regimen.

"Do you remember what that bartender told us on the night of that accident?"

"You mean when we were maimed in front of our dates? Not really, Eddy. For fuck's sake, forgive me if I don't remember much from that humiliating day."

Eddy ignored his friend's sarcasm.

"He said thousands and thousands of military personnel came through his hotel and bar every month — that's more than a million boys arriving in the city during the course of the war. When the fighting is over, he said, they'll come right back through these military bases. A million people. Do you think the ODT can handle those huge numbers?"

"I don't know. I don't care."

Eddy stayed the course.

"Maybe some of them, over time. But not all of them. What do returning servicemen want to avoid the most in the whole world after four years of fighting overseas? Chaos. They've been through enough fucking chaos. They don't want any more uncertainty and madness in their lives. They don't want stress added to the excitement of seeing loved ones again. They don't want to worry about how they're going to get to from Point A to Point B. They just want to get to their homes and neighborhoods and see their loved ones. They don't want to sweat over getting the right tickets and making sure they have the right connections and train departure times or what jets are going where and when, and all that rigamarole. They just want to unwind. We can give them that luxury, that freedom.

"And then later, when they settle back into their daily routines, six months or a year from now, they're going to want to go on vacation somewhere fun, somewhere relaxing. And you know what they're going to do? They're going to call the people who first smoothed the way for them. They are going to remember. So let me reiterate my idea for you. The plan is to put together an itinerary, organize every detail of their travel schedule, and get them aboard that boat or plane so all they have to do is just relax and unwind."

"How will you do that?"

"I told you. My family already owns and operates a ticket office on the wharf here, and another one up in Seattle. We'll open another branch on the military base. We'll expand to other California military installations and spread out from there. Franchises up and down the coast and across the Central Valley."

"You think the Air Force is going to let us rent space at a military facility? Come on, Edward!"

"Do you think they'll deny us, an amputee and a bilateral amputee? Hell, they owe us. Plus, we're armed with a secret. Do you remember how worried they were that we might blab about the blimp going down? They sent us on leave, and ultimately to our fate here. They'll come to terms."

"Sounds like a lot of time and work, Edward."

"Not if we divide the labor. I'm going to make a call as soon as possible to get the ball rolling."

"I thought you didn't want to talk to family."

"The only person I'm going to talk to is Adam Eddison of Eddison Ocean Lines. Did I tell you about him? I saw his name in an article I read in the hometown newspaper. He said Eddison is ready to purchase airplanes to fly places in tandem with their ships. If we get access to private airplanes, we can carry out our plan way beyond what we imagined. We'll fill those damn planes for Eddison."

"How do we scale the business?"

"We contract with the United States Armed Forces, just like my uncle and father did when they were building ships before World War I. We don't need an office at every base, but we need to be on the ground floor at one or two of them. Some servicemen will make travel arrangements to get home through the usual military channels, and some will make individual arrangements, for whatever reason. The latter are the ones we'll be processing at first. They'll be customers for life. It's going to be very lucrative, James. What do you think, my friend? Will you be my partner?"

James didn't say a word for fifteen minutes, at least, so long that Eddy thought he had fallen asleep or back into a blank stupor.

"A few minutes ago," James finally blurted out. "I could have just shut my eyes and died right here and now. I didn't care. Death. That would have been fine with me. What is the point of living with no legs? What can a man looking like this do? Well, you know what he can do?"

"I think I do. But I want you to tell me anyway."

"Make lots of money. Maybe making money is all that matters now, Eddy."

"That's a fine revelation, lieutenant. But I've let you down by allowing you to languish here too long, doing nothing. I should have been more assertive in getting us out of this hospital and getting started on our new life. But I'm going to make it up to you. We are going to leave this hospital as fast as possible and get this partnership going."

⚓

Ten years after leaving the hospital, Edward spoke to his father for the first time in more than a decade. It is now 1954. I'm one year old. Sloane is still up in the starry sky. My mother has an engagement ring on her finger.

Even after losing a leg, Edward stands six feet tall, the same height he logged for the varsity rowing team at the University of Washington. His light reddish-brown hair is combed back with pomade, but it's thinning. He looks gaunt in the way excessively nervous people and tobacco addicts do. A chronic smoker ever since going off to war, he still sports big winsome white teeth. They have not turned yellow yet, but that is coming.

Ten years removed from service, he now owns five travel agency branches: one at Moffett Field, another at Travis Air Force Base, a third nearby in Vacaville, a fourth in a strip mall in Sacramento and a fifth overseas in the Philippines. His and James Sizemore's business is called S&S Travel. It is thriving. The partners' confidence is soaring.

Edward is newly engaged to my mother who is recently divorced from my real father. My dad is an outgoing blue-collar worker with a million buddies but no money. By his way of thinking, telling another good story is better than making another buck. He's destined to struggle financially forever. By the end of my mom and dad's time together, the only interest they share is a love for rhythm and blues music. Sometimes that was enough, but, eventually, not for Mom. Maureen only dreams of a better life — for her and me. When she finds herself single again at twenty-eight years old, her number-one goal is to get us out of poverty and never look back. She envisions a life of security, comfort and freedom from financial worries. Enter Eddy.

Mom is working in his Vacaville office, and they see each other almost every day. She not only sees Eddy every day, but she sees him at his best: responsible, confident, well dressed, assertive, wealthy, powerful. He has the comportment of a boss and distinguished leader. It is common office knowledge that he is a product of intergenerational wealth and his family is rich in resources and bathed in privilege. This backstory makes it very easy for my mom to overlook his character flaws, such as his excessive drinking and smoking, and his physical imperfections, such as his missing leg.

A confluence of factors creates an opportunity for my mother to step in.

Nobody in the office — nor in his family — knows that he was once married. That union lasted less than two years. They tied the knot simply and quickly in Las Vegas. They untied the knot just as fast and never saw each other again. He is too busy building a successful business to ever care or think about that marriage.

Over the next five years, Eddy carves out a pretty good life for himself in the world of profits and margins. He stands tall among his peers.

After his amputation and subsequent medical discharge, Edward avoided his Seattle relations and went about his own business, but his S&S Travel by now is prominent enough so that anybody who wants to can trace where he lives and works, which clubs he belongs to and where he loves to dine. His desire to maintain a distance from the Pacific Northwest family blows up in his face, though, when his mother, Agnes, dies. George's prosaic letter informing his son of her death arrives via carrier, and Eddy has no choice but to do the honorable thing and show up at her funeral.

He ignores all efforts to give him a role in the obsequies. He arrives at the church later than most other mourners so he won't be seated with family and close friends. He stands in the long queue to visit her open casket and avoids eye contact with everybody on his way to view the body. Kneeling, he whispers a few last words to her in prayer. He feels eyes locked upon him as he walks back to his spot against the wall at the side aisle. Head bowed, he listens as the bereaved share stories and memories from his mother's life. When the pallbearers start their solemn march from the altar to the hearse, he dashes out of the church ahead of them. At the burial, he wears dark sunglasses and observes the solemn proceedings from the back of the crowd. He flees when the first handful of dirt is tossed onto the casket.

Afterward, the shame from his antisocial behavior at his mother's funeral gnaws at him. He had always loved her and enjoyed her company even after she and his father revealed to him the astonishing fact that he was adopted. A lot changed after that day, but his love for her and their relationship remained harmonious. He felt he should have — and was expected to — say some words at her memorial.

When he returns to his home in Burlingame in the San Francisco Bay Area, Edward decides it is time to make amends and find his way back into the embrace of his Pacific Northwest family. It needs to be a slow process, if it is to happen at all. Two years later, he gets a chance at recompense by means of an invitation to a dinner banquet put on by the American Forestry Association. The organization says it is honoring his father with its highest award for service in recognition of George's twenty-five successful years working with plant genetics. He accepts. It seems as good a time as any to see his father again and rekindle their relationship before the next chapter of his life begins, his second and true marriage.

As the black-tie event's VIP, George is too busy most of the night to immerse himself in a meaningful heart-to-heart with Edward, but he makes sure his son knows what an honor it is to have him there. Every time they come together, however, a colleague or an acquaintance interrupts to congratulate and reminisce with George, or to pose for a picture with him or to talk about some lingering business matter.

Later, the crowd thins and father and son finally sit alone together at a table strewn with empty water and wine glasses, napkins, and plates with scraps of chocolate cake and frosting on them. They speak despondently about life after Agnes's death until the sadness dries up and fond, happy memories of her gush forward and flood their minds.

"Do you remember when Uncle Joseph, your mother and I took you and Conrad swimming in the Neptune Pool at Willie's castle?" George asks. "It was right before Willie became ill and moved to Los Angeles."

"That was the biggest, most opulent pool I'd ever seen."

"It sure was. Vermont marble, mosaic tiles, a hundred feet long if it's an inch."

"I remember Uncle Joseph swimming in the pool yelling, 'Watch me, everybody, I'm literally in the lap of luxury.'"

"That's right. And your mother next to those Roman statues, striking the same pose as each one them."

They laugh at the memories.

"How is Uncle Joseph?" Eddy asks.

"His health is failing. I'm not sure how long he'll be around. He's spending most of his time in Hawaii or San Diego, where the weather is warm."

Eddy feels aversion rise up in him. He did not expect it. He did not want to feel it. But there it was, triggered by some memory. Below his upper leg, a painful phantom sensation starts to pulse. He was mirthful a minute ago, and now he is galled. There is no warning for this. He is simply trying again to have a rapport with his family.

"Nobody called me, so I guess he left the company in good hands," Eddy remarks, but the words come out with a sarcastic bite.

"Are you still upset about Conrad being named president, Edward?"

"No, I understand. I was never part of the succession plan."

"You were absent, son."

"There were many reasons why it was never going to happen. I'm the non-biological male heir. No true bloodline. On top of that, I'm disabled, damaged goods. I've had trauma. One can't trust the future of a multi-million-dollar company to a battle-fatigued veteran, can one? It'd be an unstable situation. You can't have dozens of shareholders' future resting on me, can you? All the same, Uncle Joseph could have at least informed me of his intention first. We were once supposed to be co-presidents."

"It wasn't the sole decision of one man. And it wasn't decided in a day. The full board was involved. Beyond the full board, all adult family members were included at some level — and you weren't around. You never showed up. The hospital didn't know where you were. The military kept no records of an address. Telephone books were useless. If you had something to say, you should have shown up and spoken your mind at the annual meetings. Instead, you were like a ghost out there, never seen or heard from."

"Did you speak on my behalf, father? Did you voice any support for my leadership, even as co-president?"

"You're damn right I did. I put your name forth as a potential candidate, but the board had a timeline. We have bylaws, you know. I thought you might show up at the annual meeting for the formal approval of a successor and for the final announcement. I could have raised the issue."

"Why was it always Conrad over me, anyway?"

"Even if that were true, family dynamics changed in the war years, Edward. You made the choice to turn your back on Joseph, Conrad, me, the family business, your entire kin. We tried to visit you. We wanted to see you and help you in any way we could. We tried for three years after the war."

"How did those dynamics change, exactly?"

"Conrad traveled everywhere with my brother and learned the trade. He stuck around after V-J Day. He didn't disappear like you did. He was a steadfast presence."

"Of course, he was. Uncle Joe obtained for him an early release from service. That's not something I was able to get."

"Regardless, we still wanted you involved in running the business. You were a viable executive-level leader — until you went missing."

Edward understood his father's point — of course, he had sequestered himself. But that only gave them an excuse — he was never going to lead the powerful family business.

"But son, you are doing well. The business you started when you got out of the military — it's going gangbusters. You found all that success independent of the firm and despite your... your challenges."

"My challenges?"

"Your handicap. That is supposed to be a compliment, son."

Edward tries to quell the uneasiness that has unfastened and is spreading inside him. He pulls out a cigarette, lights it and takes a long drag. Stay calm, he tells himself.

"We're opening a fourth office in Sacramento," he boasts. "We are moving to the capital city after the wedding."

"Oh, that's fantastic news. A new beginning, if you will. I'm so happy you'll be close. I spend most of my time at my house in Foresthill. That's close to Sacramento, near my institute. Do you remember the institute? I'll be just a short drive up the hill from you. Do you and your fiancée plan on raising a family here? Sacramento is a great place for bringing up kids."

"We certainly do."

"Good. The Stevenses have always believed in strong, traditional family life. I'm just over the moon that you'll be living near me. I can't wait to meet your future wife — it's Maureen, isn't it?"

"Yes."

"And I look forward to another grandchild in the near future. No hurry, mind you — well, maybe just a little!"

George chuckles and his kind, close-set eyes twinkle. Eddy looks down at the carpet, not knowing what to say next.

"In that case," he starts. "I might as well tell you now. You won't have to wait for the future to welcome another grandchild."

"I don't understand. You just said..."

"Maureen already has a son. His name is Shane. And I plan on adopting him."

George is so speechless and dumbfounded that when he tries to cover up his feelings with a genuine smile, the futile exercise only causes one eye to twitch and his face to contort into a grimace.

"Look, father, it's not a sign of personal failure on anybody's part. The idea of a traditional family is changing, so get used to it. Don't be so judgmental. It's no different than when you adopted me."

"It's not that, son. It's not me. I'm very liberal. It's what others will think. You and your wife are going to face a powerful stigma. Society will call on you to account for your wife's virtue, not to mention her maturity. At best, polite society will be reprimanding in tone. I want you to be prepared — for the sake of her son."

"I've overcome worse from society," Edward says, patting his prosthesis. "And don't hold your breath, dad, if you're thinking that later you'll get a paternal grandson. Doctors say I can't have children. So the male bloodline ends here. It always has, really."

"How can they even know?"

Edward refuses to pump more friction into this reunion by telling his father that he first suspected he was sterile during his first marriage. Oh, how she tried and tried to get pregnant to no avail.

"It's complex," Eddy finally says.

"Stress from the war can't cause infertility, can it?"

"I don't know. I'm just telling you what I was told, that's all."

"It's not... not... I mean, it isn't because of your wound, is it? No, that can't be."

"No, dad, a leg amputation doesn't affect the ability to produce children. You should know that more than anybody."

"I just wonder how the medical establishment can say such a thing about a man so unconditionally."

"Look, there are physical examinations and anatomical examinations and medical evaluations. Like I said, it's complex. They wanted to prepare me for the probability."

"The... the... the loss, your loss, of the limb, must have been hard in many ways. I wish I could have been there to help you. But it doesn't matter now. You overcame the difficult challenges. You achieved success through your own efforts. You're a successful businessman — not just a rich kid spending his family's money. It's fantastic."

"Well, what else was I going to do?"

"Has it affected you in other ways? I'm curious. We haven't talked in so long."

"Did what affect me? Not being promoted to co-president?"

"No, your leg."

"This stump? How do you mean?"

The sudden aching pain and warmth in the space where his lower leg formerly existed makes him want to cry. But he's not going to cry here. Not in front of his father. He had not cried since the war.

"I don't know, like was it difficult to meet someone?"

"No. See, when you're the boss, any dish in the office is going to overlook your undesirable qualities," Edward sneers. "Look, can we stop talking about this? Please!"

"Of course. I'm sorry. I'm being insensitive and personal and prying when I just wanted to connect to you again, bridge the gap between us and become close once more."

"And I just came to say hello and congratulations, and see you accept the award. All your work paid off, and I'm glad somebody noticed. I truly am. I even feel like I have a small share in the award because of all the time I spent with you on our property, down in the nursery and the greenhouse, hauling mulch and manure and carrying pots and cuttings into the nursery and greenhouse. I didn't know everything you were doing back then — not a clue, really — but here we are. And you're being honored for it."

Since the war, rage and aversion lie tumultuously just below Eddy's skin. He always managed to harness the fervor — until now. Anger rises so fast in him again that he stands abruptly and pushes his chair hard against the table.

"I have to go. And don't worry about the 'stigma,' as you said. We're moving to Sacramento so I can grow my business. It has nothing to do with being close to you, dad, or with carrying on family tradition, or even any love I have to offer. But I don't have to explain anything to you. I'm not the one who needs to explain my actions."

"What does that mean?"

"It's not a secret what you did. Through your work you collaborated with the Nazis, the motherfuckers I was fighting against, along with the Japs."

"Is that what you've been so bitter about for so long? Well, you're wrong about that. My work in genetics only concerned plants. Others misinterpreted my efforts and conclusions. Badly misinterpreted it. They misappropriated the use and came up with their own conclusions. I traveled to many states to meet with these groups, to explain what I was doing."

"Yeah, well, I wonder what mom would have said about that," he says scathingly. "She either turned a blind eye or didn't know because you were working on your research somewhere else."

"I hid nothing."

"Goodbye, dad. Congratulations on the achievement."

George seizes his son by the arm. His grip is tight. Lingering attendees turn to look at them.

"No, we will not end on this note. I don't know what you want me to say to you, and I'm sorry if I made a mess out of our reunion here. Let's start over, please. Otherwise, we'll just get further and further away from each other, and further and further from the truth of what's been said and done. We need to face our past together, Edward. Please, come up to the old house. Bring Maureen up to Seattle so she can meet the family before the wedding. Please. I beg you. Will you do this for me? Set a date as soon as you get home. It will be wonderful."

"Look, I'll ask her. But don't count on it."

Maureen is overjoyed at the chance to meet the family she has heard so much about. She makes Eddy immediately set a date. They fly up in an Eddison-owned seaplane and land directly on Lake Washington practically in front of the house. Maureen is euphoric from the get-go. Just a year old, I am left home with a nanny and milk bottles.

As they settle into the vacation, the first thing Eddy notices about his cousin after fifteen years apart is that his role as head of the Stevens conglomerates had changed him. Conrad is authoritarian, tough and believes he is in complete control as president. At least that is the image he wants to project. To Eddy, he comes off as exploitive, threatened and insecure.

Maureen's experience from the very start of the visit is much different from Eddy's. She falls in love with the family's oneness and bigness, the dozens of sisters, brothers and cousins, aunts, uncles and grandparents. Eddy had miscalculated how big the reunion was going to be. He did not expect branches and branches of the family tree to be there. Their obvious wealth sweeps Maureen off her feet.

She happily bounces from group to group. Eddy sees her in the speed boat flying across the lake one minute, and playing croquet and other lawn games the next. First, she is in the swimming pool, next laughing in the hammock with his sisters. She giggles and chats the entire time while in the air when Eddy takes a couple of groups of five or six people for flights in his Grumman Goose twin-engine flying boat for an aerial view of Puget Sound.

She clings contentedly to the arm of the man she is going to marry as he pilots them home three days later.

"Your family is so... I don't know... regal," she tells her fiancé.

"I guess so," he responds.

"They have servants. And not just for cleaning and cooking. They have hired help to serve food, to drive their cars and boats, even to watch the children."

"Yes, they like to spend their free time in other ways."

"I never met a senator before, either. Your uncle must have been a force of nature when he was younger. I can see that in him still, even though his health is failing. But I hope he gets better soon."

Eddy thinks about letting Maureen enjoy her pleasing memories of the weekend in an unqualified way. She wonders why Eddy does not want to be more involved in the family enterprise and spend more time with this noble, interesting, amusing clan of his. He could eventually work his way into the role of co-president.

"Let me tell you something that happened," he started, but Maureen shushed him.

"Is it about how you got that fat lip and marks and bruises on your face?" she whispers.

"No. I already told you I had a mishap getting out of that damn speedboat with my wooden leg."

"The way you and your cousins were drinking, it's no wonder you ended up hurt."

"No, I was going to tell you about a conversation I had yesterday with Conrad."

Conrad and he had withdrawn to the old boxing gym on the third floor of Uncle Joseph's house — the one that often was used as a makeshift conference room.

"What do you want to do?' Eddy asked his cousin. "Spar?"

"I don't know. Do you?"

They sat at the old ringside table, a bottle of scotch between them and lit up cigars. At first, they said nothing. They hadn't seen each other since 1937, when Conrad left for Harvard, except for a couple weeks over a summer. That meant it had been seventeen or eighteen years since the two were bosom buddies, palookas, fellow hunters and oarsmen and skirt chasers. That was more time apart than any other two other family members ever had spent from each other.

Conrad studied business before the war in preparation for running the show, and his father hustled up a postgraduate finance job for him in Saginaw, Michigan, at one of the first banks Big Papa had founded. During the war, Conrad quickly worked his way up the ranks aboard a ship patrolling the Alaskan coastline. The promotions served solely to groom him for a leadership role in the family companies. He cared nothing about the higher pay each rank commanded; Conrad enjoyed being the voice of authority.

After his discharge, Conrad quickly married and was ready to gain first-hand knowledge of company operations. He acquired the skills to manage people, products and accounting books, and he picked up his father's social smoking and drinking habits, too.

In 1950, George assigned his nephew to an upper-management position in the timber and land management division that he controlled, but his nephew's real interest lay in the more tantalizing and dynamic real estate development field. Under George and Joseph, the firm had begun examining its land holdings at the edge of expanding cities. Their economic studies indicated timberland was still more profitable than selling tracts of wilderness for development. However, by the time Conrad was chosen successor, fortune reversed itself, and the Stevens-owned land around Bainbridge Island, Suquamish and as far east as Renton became more valuable as housing than as forest. Of course, Seattle was busting at the seams, too, and the family owned property throughout the city. Conrad foresaw more clearly than anybody did how an emerging post-World War II housing boom would reshape the landscape and demographics all over Washington and the entire United States. He teamed up with high-powered real estate companies to get out in front of the trend. In doing so, he made a name for himself within Stevens Family Investments.

Conrad did not give up on the company's still-profitable timber ventures, but he placed his real estate ambitions at the forefront. This initiative required thinking and action considered disruptive to many in the company. Conrad went behind George's back when he needed tacit consent from the board for ideas deemed too progressive for a conventional, stolid company. Joseph would approve of Conrad's idea and present it as his own vision in front of George and the board. Eventually, Conrad was forced to go around his own father to gain accruals to fulfill his ambitious desires. He found new hires who were intensely loyal to him, not the old regime, so eventually he did not even need Joseph's backing, let alone George's, to make things happen. The recruits then proved to be loyal supporters when Conrad finally assumed complete control.

By the time his cousin Eddy sat across from him at the table in the boxing hall, Conrad was in sole charge not only of the umbrella corporation and Port Seattle Timber, but all subsidiaries and sectors. His early days on the job were bolstered by soaring lumber exports to Japan and the need to provide more and more people with homes. With profits expanding, his reign was firmly established, his power consolidated, and corporate affairs left to his own devices. In just four short years, he held sway over all aspects of the robust parent company.

It did not hurt that his languishing father was spending less and less time in cold Seattle and more and more time in warm Hawaii. With Joseph away most of the time, Conrad consigned his Uncle George to a small, ground-floor office. George no longer had the enthusiasm for company matters, nor the stomach for corporate scheming, nor much ambition, so he took off to his home in the Northern California foothills for long stretches of time. When George or Joseph inquired from afar about business affairs, Conrad always told them the same thing: "Don't worry about business here — everything is running as smoothly and on course as a stream in the Cascades."

These were the circumstances at the time Eddy and Conrad sat at the table. Eddy wanted to hear it for himself.

"You've really established and secured your position as president. I hope the people you surround yourself with have the interest of the company in their hearts and are allowed to speak their mind. That's how our fathers ran things."

"My older brother Frank is my vice president, and you know he always lets me know what he thinks," Conrad retorted.

"Did he tell you I was a candidate to take over, along with you, after your father? Did anybody? From the start, it was supposed to be just you and me in line for the job. Did the board know I was in the running?"

"Did you want to be considered?"

"I would have liked to have been given serious thought, yes."

Conrad took a swig from the bottle and a big pull on his cigarette. As he exhaled, Eddy looked at his eyes and did not see any trace of the inborn kindness that was always present in his father and uncle's eyes.

"Listen to the elusive heir who was hiding just as duty called," Conrad sniggered. "Over the past few years, succession was talked about and planned in multiple stages and in scores of meetings and forums. You might have had your chance, had you been more welcoming and open to us and the possibility. Hell, even if you would had been present just once you might have a valid point. As it is, cousin, your suggestion is absolutely unreasonable."

"Any semi-competent leader of an enduring business would know there are ways to hold a top position open, or know when it's important to delay a final decision for the future good of the company — if only you cared. The two of us taking the helm together as the next generation of leaders is something we talked about from the time we were teens and young men."

Eddy needed a swig and took three gulps instead. The warmth from it spreading throughout his body soothed him.

"Edward — you are so fucking arrogant. You want it one way only — your way. I know you acquired great leadership qualities in the Navy. I know you've built a very successful travel business. But you know what? I'm not impressed. All I can think is that I should sue you for misappropriation of company resources and fraud. You used our hard-won connections and redirected clients to your own travel and ticketing business instead of ours. So while others might be impressed by your business acumen, I think it's the result of unethical practices at best."

"When did you become such a son-of-a-bitch, Conrad?"

"I'm actually being very fair to you. Do you know another reason we couldn't consider you for a senior leadership spot? And certainly not the president of this company? Reputation and public perception."

"What are you talking about?"

"Following the war, certain societal views became..."

A door opened and they turned to see whom the footsteps belonged to. George walked toward his son and nephew.

"I'll tell you what he's talking about," George said. "It's all my fault, Eddy. I'm sorry. There have been rumors, completely unsubstantiated, about my work as a geneticist, and there's been a substantial misappropriation of my work before, during and after the war. Even you had your opinions. We've talked about it. I know Americans continue to harbor suspicions about the enemy and Nazi sympathizers, but they have wrongly used my activity and my legitimacy in the field for their own advancement. It's caused people to associate me with that agenda."

"See, Edward? There's so much working against you!"

"Shut up, Conrad!" George thundered, interrupting his nephew. "Let me tell my son how it is. Conrad exploited this false background noise to his advantage to get more votes for the presidency, and certainly to wipe out any chance you might have had. I apologize for letting this get out of my control, to allow even the slightest suggestion of a connection between my work and their so-called applied biology..."

"For Christ sakes," Eddy exclaimed and rose. "I'm leaving. I'll keep my shares and my vote since it's all I have to exhibit any influence in this company, but I'm done with you people."

"Oh, come on!" Conrad roared disingenuously. "Don't say that, Eddy. I'll give you one more chance to prove to me that you deserve to run this company."

Edward knew he should not have stopped walking toward the door, but he did.

"Go to hell, cousin."

"Don't you want to hear the offer?"

Edward did not move, so Conrad carried on.

"We put on the gloves and get in the ring. If you knock me down just once or I throw in the towel and surrender, I'll step down as president and name you my successor."

Eddy said nothing.

"I'll give you all of my shares in the company, too."

"Don't do it, son," his father urged.

Eddy turned around and looked at his cousin.

"When did you become this insane?" he asked Conrad rhetorically. "Give me the fucking gloves."

Did Eddy think of all the disadvantages of boxing with a wooden leg as he threw off his shirt and grabbed some gloves and headgear off a hook on the wall? He must have known his balance and mobility would be compromised. I think my stepfather saw the drawbacks, but he had nothing to lose. At the same time, he had nothing to prove, either.

Conrad stood across the ring looking stout. Eddy looked skinny and pale.

"I'll give you a chance," Conrad said to his opponent. "I won't wear my headgear."

"You sure the hell will," George scolded. Even though he did not pull much weight around the office anymore, he was still their elder. Conrad shrugged and donned the protective gear.

Every peril you can imagine from having a peg leg and trying to brawl directly resulted in blows to Eddy's face or body. Slow footwork — Pow! Reduced stability — Smack! Snail-like reaction time — Wham! It happened over and over. Eddy was reeling.

He twisted, turned and awkwardly stood toe to toe trading jabs for a minute. Then he dipped at the waist, miraculously dodged a punch and came up in a position where he was set to wallop his cousin with an uppercut. But his wooden leg slipped in mid-blow. His punching power severely diminished, the punch amounted to nothing more than a slap from a young boy. Conrad's counterpunch found Eddy's jaw and he collapsed.

At that point of the ridiculous fight, George jumped through the ropes and into the ring. He ran between the two men, but his intervention did not stop the match. Conrad already had turned away as if ashamed — whether with Eddy or himself, I don't know. He shed his gloves and quickly left the room.

Eddy dropped his gloves on the ground and put his shirt back on. He wobbled slightly from the head blows. He did not say anything to George, who was sitting on the canvas with his head between his legs.

Eddy cleaned up and iced his face in his room that evening. He sent word to Maureen that he was feeling unwell and would not join her for dinner.

The next morning he rushed her from breakfast and out to the private dock where the seaplane waited. He attended to the bilge pump and other mechanisms and started the engine after a pre-flight systems check. Then, they flew off.

Joseph Stevens died a month later, but Edward didn't attend his funeral.

CHAPTER 3

As Sloane's storyteller, I assure you that I am particularly suited to the task. I was regularly present — usually front and center, but sometimes upstage and other times backstage — and constantly heard these real-life actors recite the lines of their real-life drama.

I am a peripheral member of this dynasty. From my vantage point, people talk without knowing I am paying attention. I know what I know, and I will share it with you. I know more about my stepfather, my mother, Sloane and the Stevenses than anybody else on this planet does. I saw, I heard, I was confided in and my questions were answered.

I am a first-hand witness to so much of this chronicle's unfolding. I put many of the stories down on paper. Recorded conversations with my sister, my mother and their friends are part of the evidence. Newspaper articles, business documents, board minutes and police reports corroborate much of what will unfold here. Personal journals and a surprising amount of letters still exist. Some affairs happened directly in front of me, raw and immediate, and other episodes I discussed at length with the participants afterward — an hour, days, months or even years later.

I have filed details personal of these experiences, dialogues and tête-à-têtes in my brain and can recall them with great clarity and precision (I think I have hyperthymesia). I have inherited legal papers, registers, logs and personal correspondences. Sometimes, I diverted documents and photos from heading to the dump and squirreled them away safely.

All of which is to say, dear readers, I vouch for the accuracy and the tone of this story. I sincerely wish I could alter the content, change decisions made in the past and amend history.

I cannot, so I will continue.

Life growing up with Eddy, my mother and Sloane amounted to a travelogue. My memory is an extensive inventory of vacations, stopovers, overnights, visits, camping and hunting excursions and boat trips. Outdoor activities are front and center, because the Pacific Northwest lifestyle runs deep in the Stevens men.

In our youth, there were long trips to Pocatello, Idaho, to hunt elk and waterfowl. There were expeditions to Alaska, where E.S. kept his thirty-foot fishing boat moored until it was time to hook some halibut. There were jaunts closer to home, too, like jet boating up and down the Russian River. I also remember laid-back, relaxing times spent on beaches in Southern California and Hawaii.

Whether flying, sailing, cruising or motoring, getting out and about was easy. In the 1960s and '70s, Eddy's business flourished like a sailboat catching the wind. His relationship with Eddison Shipping & Air deepened over the years, and the company's planes and ships seemingly were available to us on a moment's notice. There was easy money coming in and going out. Eddy and Maureen enjoyed an enormous amount of disposable income. Even into our young adult lives, Sloane and I purchased tickets and passes at big discounts on one of Eddy's credit cards that was tied to his S&S Travel bank account.

Our happy brood had become whole in 1958 when Sloane — Eddy's miracle baby — was born. He never expected to have his own child, and for a perfect little girl to enter his life was too good to be true. She was born four-and-a-half years after he reunited with his father at the American Forestry Association banquet and told him not to expect a grandchild of genetic relation. The joyous occasion marked four years since Eddy's encounter in the ring with Conrad at the family reunion.

Things were not perfect when Sloane entered the world. Our new nuclear family was fettered by prevailing social disapproval toward a gentleman choosing to wed a divorced woman with a child, the stigma George had warned his son about. But Sloane and I never felt any stain or shame, and E.S. deserves a lot of credit for that. He cared nothing for what others thought. Love for both of us gushed from Eddy inside and outside our home. He embraced all of us, counted us as a quantity of one, as close to a biological conjugal family as possible. Outsiders knew no different. Besides, by 1965, any hint of public disgrace over our situation had started to dissipate.

On that long 1965 trip to Oregon to get our purebred hunting dog, I noticed for the first time the numerous semi-trailers hauling Eddison cargo containers down the highway. I had noticed on long vacations we always took Eddison planes, embarked on Eddison ships and stayed at Eddison resorts, but I was interested in knowing more about the connection between this wealthy and powerful family to which my mother and I were now affixed and the ubiquitous Eddison Company.

When we returned home, I visited the library several times. There my reading soon made me aware that our family, or more precisely, Sloane's extended family, maintained a close, interdependent relationship with Eddison.

My research took me back to 1885 when Captain Eddison purchased two brigantines and greatly expanded his fleet's carrying capacity. One of the ships contained a refrigerated cargo area — and that changed everything. Eddison could send vast amounts of perishable food, especially meat, fish and tropical fruits, across the Pacific.

Jump ahead a quarter century and Stevens & Gibbs built Eddison's first six thousand-ton tanker, marking the beginning of their partnership. Stevens Investment Company provided the underwriting, and the shipping line's post-World War I cargo capacity surged.

Eddison's next huge fleet expansion coincided with an ever-swelling tide of tourists drawn irresistibly to Hawaii's shores and a robust commercial interest in establishing a reliable passage for transporting market goods to the islands.

But World War II broke out, and fifteen of Eddison's biggest, fastest, most modern ships now served the U.S. military. No stranger to government requisitions, the Stevens family took on an advisory role as Eddison directors watched most of its fleet converted to carrying troops and military cargo. The Navy paid Eddison handsomely to crew, provision and maintain the Pacific cargo fleet, and the shipping company was able to continue limited commercial routes to the islands. That was a victory for the shipping line.

Eddison's biggest move yet came after the war. It sold their Navy-requisitioned ships and used the money to build a new state-of-the art luxury liner, the swiftest in the world. Eddison constructed and launched another liner shortly afterward and was positioned as a major passenger and freight service to Hawaii.

Eddison's branding became synonymous with the islands' hospitality business. The moment vacationers arrived at the pier and stepped off Eddison ships, they were draped in leis and greeted by live Hawaiian music and dancing women in grass skirts, all courtesy of Eddison.

Fascinating me most was that Eddison's toehold on the islands just happened to align with Edward Stevens and James Sizemore's vision for S&S Travel, capitalizing on post-war travel trends. If you booked a trip through S&S Travel, you probably traveled on an Eddison vessel or plane.

A decade later, Eddison found its most profitable income stream yet, and achieved its highest level of success, with the invention of shipping containers. Those were transportation units I saw on dozens of big rigs as we hauled down the highway in the Fleetwood and provided the impetus for my research. By the time I was a teenager, the company had expanded into jet travel.

You can find dozens of references linking Eddison Shipping and Air to Port Seattle Timber and Stevens Investment Company and come up with your own conclusions, but afterward I had this epiphany: Sloane would forever be free of financial burden. Going into my little investigation, I thought little about how easily my sister's life might unfold.

Gap-toothed, spirited, mischievous little Sloane would never have to pay a dime of her own money to go anywhere in the world, if she chose. I guess that meant neither would my mother or I, but I was not sure.

I am looking at a picture of Sloane and me, in Pocatello, Idaho. She is probably eight years old, and I'm twelve or thirteen. Standing in front of a large canoe turned upside down on a pair of sawhorses, we are holding a string of fish that we caught. Sloane is the embodiment of a cute, gleeful, outdoorsy girl. Her plentiful auburn-hued hair is disordered, and her attitude is unselfconscious. Her partially toothless smile evokes a gentle aura of innocence. She will carry that fit, earthy, natural attractiveness into adulthood. I am just a tall, thin, awkward preteen in the photo.

The photo is remarkable for the surge of memories it evokes. I become choked up now thinking about the places to where we traveled and how we got there. A superb pilot, E.S. shuttled us up to Pocatello that summer in a Cessna 172 he chartered from Eddison. The passenger list was made up of only one of Eddy's business friends, Sloane and me. Again, my mother was not an outdoors enthusiast, and stayed behind.

Back then, that plain Pocatello hunting lodge the Stevens family had owned since the 1920s was so remote you could only get there by plane. As we approached the property's dirt landing strip, I heard Eddy tell his buddy sitting up front next to him that the crude runway was really just a small ribbon of cleared land bulldozed through the pine and dogwood forest. Yelling, Eddy communicated to his friend that the rudimentary airstrip was the exact minimum length and width required for a safe landing, not an inch more.

"And how much is that?" his friend asked loudly to be heard over the engine.

"Last time I was out here I think they told me it was fifteen-hundred feet long and fifty feet wide."

"And when was the last time you flew here?"

"About a year-and-a-half ago."

"Great," the buddy laughed nervously. "I'm sure the dimensions didn't get any smaller."

"I hope not, but those trees up on that hill at the southern end of the runway where we'll be landing have definitely grown a lot taller. Nobody is around to trim those."

"Is that going to be a problem?"

"They're getting to the point where we might have to make an adjustment to the flight path to get over them. We'll see. Normally, you want a stabilized approach and smooth descent. After the heavy winter rain we had, they may have grown so much we'll have to pull up and then back down, make sort of a dive approach. I don't like to pick up speed on my way down, as you can imagine."

Eddy laughed at his own words, but he was the only one.

"How tricky is that maneuver?"

"It's not too much of an impingement — as long as the downdraft isn't too bad."

He laughed again.

"What's a downdraft?" Sloane asked me. I repeated the question to Eddy, shouting it from the back.

"Just a strong downward current. It can happen in mountains."

Right then, the plane's altitude dropped. The descending aircraft suddenly felt heavier and our airspeed quickened. Why I looked up at the cockpit windscreen at that moment, I will never know, but I shouldn't have. Tall trees ahead, one hundred, twenty feet up from the ground, were rapidly increasing in size as we flew closer. I saw that they obscured a sizable portion of the airstrip approach.

Even at my young age, I noticed Eddy immediately recognized what was happening. He acted so decisively that I realized for the first time that he could function stably despite his daily abuse of alcohol. He applied full power to the plane and turned the yoke. The plane sped up, but in the next moment, the lift and thrust seemed to balance out.

"Speed over altitude," he yelled to nobody in particular, and then for some reason cried out, "Oh, for fuck's sake."

We all heard a knock below the fuselage and felt the aircraft roll and yaw as we approached the runway.

The flare occurred a little late and we hit the ground much harder than Eddy would have liked. He cursed at himself, then found his composure and asked if everybody was all right. When we assured him that we were all fine and safely exited from the plane, he peg-legged around the Cessna to inspect any immediate structural damage.

We waited for him on the grass and dirt runway with our luggage at our feet.

"I'll be damned," Eddy called out from the other side of the plane. "Look what I found in the landing gear.

He came around the tail holding a two-foot branch.

"Did it cause any damage?" his friend asked.

"It could have interfered with the full extension of the landing gear, or it could have locked up the wheels. We were lucky. The fuselage is fine, just a few scratches and there are no leaks. I'll inspect it again before we fly back. But, hey! We're here, safe and sound!"

Mother preferred trips to London, Paris and Honolulu. She liked fine restaurants and sunbathing over campfire meals and sitting in duck blinds. She would rather spend three hours in a museum than one minute standing in waders in a rushing river.

When she and Eddy flitted off to England, France or Hawaii, Sloane and I remained in the care of a nanny, particularly a Black woman named Genevieve Washington. She came highly recommended by the Eddison family. I remember overhearing my mother interviewing her.

"What is it, exactly, that sets you apart?" she asked.

"My former boss was very demanding and expected perfection," she answered.

"Your former boss?"

"Yes. Before I worked for the Eddisons."

Genevieve Washington retired after being employed as a maid at a hotel-casino owned by a notorious mobster who helped build the Las Vegas Strip. She worked for the gangster as his personal concierge until 1947, when he died in a hail of bullets at his girlfriend's house in Beverly Hills, and Genevieve was out of a job again. Shortly after the mob hit, she answered a newspaper ad placed by the Eddisons, who hired her as a nanny in their Los Angeles estate. The Eddison children grew up, left the house, and Genevieve retired again.

"Will you move to Sacramento?" my mother asked her.

"Yes. I have family there. I've wanted to move closer to them for a long time."

Eddy rented a home for Genevieve that was not too far from us. She would ride the bus to our house to take care of us during our parents' lengthy overseas travels. After Sloane went to bed, Genevieve would tell me stories about the mob while I smoked Eddy's cigarettes and drank a glass of his scotch in front her. I guess that after working for a gangster, you know when to turn a blind eye.

Later, when I was old enough to drive, I would take Sloane and a couple of friends over to Genevieve's house to hear her tell stories about the mob. For us, it was more entertaining than going on family trips.

By 1968, the frequency of Eddy and Maureen's couples retreats diminished. E.S. started going on vacations with his buddies or traveling alone for business. In his absence, mom was lighter in spirit and happier than usual. When he came home, she glared at him as he set down his bags in the entryway. He smelled like booze, looked tired, his thinning hair a mess, and a cigarette dangled from his lips.

Steadying himself on his wooden leg or his crutches if his artificial limb wasn't in place, he insisted that we all run to give him a hug. Sloane typically hurried over first, overjoyed that our family was complete again.

I waited for a nonverbal clue from my mother to see if everything was all right between her and Eddy, but she avoided my eyes. Left with no choice, I walked over and squeezed E.S. around the shoulders and muttered "hello." He always felt thinner and frailer to me after being away for a long time. Each time he returned home, his button-down shirt appeared to fit more loosely. Finally, it was Mom's turn to greet the man of the house. She walked slowly into the entryway and gave him a cursory embrace.

Although Mom and Eddy stopped going places together, he still took Sloane and me on wilderness escapes, at least until I became a senior in high school and only wanted to hang out with my friends.

Until I left the house at age 18, Eddy had insisted on adopting me, but he never did. The first time he mentioned it was during a hunting trip with our new dog. It was Char's first real hunting foray, and he failed badly.

By the time E.S. hitched his little jon boat and trailer to the car, it was late afternoon. I felt we were getting off to a very late start for this hunting trip. My stepfather apprised me that we were meeting three other hunters with their dogs at the clubhouse and staying overnight on the marsh.

"I don't think it's going to be a very good night to be outdoors," I told him.

"Don't worry, Shane. I've packed enough provisions and clothing for both of us. We'll be warm and cozy inside. The dogs will sleep outside under the porch. And in the morning, I'll introduce you to Duck Country!"

The acreage that makes up Suisun Marsh is an enormous expanse of natural tidal wetlands, seasonal ponds, sloughs and waterways now owned by the California Department of Fish and Game and some conservation groups. Back then, however, Eddy owned a private hunting club and lodge on a large tract of land there.

We launched the small boat into a barrage of high swells and made our way out to the island where the club's blinds were located. E.S was at the tiller of the motor pushing the little aluminum craft. Char sat in the middle, and I occupied the bow. On our way out, we saw tule elk and jackrabbits in the upland fields, river otters and beavers in the lagoons, and northern harriers, mallards, owls, pelicans and eagles taking to the sky. It was a blustery, overcast October day, past elk hunting season, so we were out to shoot ducks and geese.

The marshland waves were cresting at four feet, and I did not think we were going to make it very far. E.S. saw my fright but did not say a word. Several times on the way in he took a swig of Scotch from a bottle kept in his hunting pack.

I was looking down at the hull where more than two inches of water had accumulated. My stepfather motored on.

"I want to tell you something," E.S. shouted into the wind.

"What's that, sir?"

"I want to adopt you, Shane. You are as much my son as Sloane is my daughter, and you can't be more of a member of our family than you are right now. I love you. Sloane loves you. Of course, your mother loves you. But this will make everything official. No loose strings. What do you think of that?"

I had no idea what any of that meant. I wanted to remind him that I already had a father, a real one. But I didn't wish to upset E.S., so I just smiled. Sloane and the size of her inheritance crossed my mind briefly, and I wondered if formal adoption might make me rich one day, too. It seemed like a selfish thought, so I did not ask. Maybe Eddy wanted to tell me about his adoption plan while we were alone and that was why Sloane hadn't come along. But when he took another gulp of Scotch, I knew the main reason he didn't bring his little angel.

"It's nice," I finally said to answer his question, but Eddy had already dropped the subject, and we bounced our way toward the lodge without another word.

Most of the blinds accommodated two people, but a few of the larger ones could shelter four hunters. They were built on piers to sit above the marsh. The clubhouse was constructed the same way but larger, providing a kitchen, restroom and sleeping accommodations.

I might as well have slept out with the dogs on the small porch because I got little sleep inside. E.S. and his friends drank, played poker, drank some more, cussed, drank again, shared ribald jokes and bawdy stories, smoked cigarettes and cigars and drank some more. It was all loud balderdash to me. It turns out sleeping outside with the dogs would have been much, much worse.

In the morning, I watched the adult hunters, still drunk, open the door and stop in their tracks. Speechless, they slowly moved around the small deck groaning at what they saw. Groans turned to curses, and curses to shouts. I walked outside to look for myself.

Did you know every hunting dog has its own temperament? For Char, that meant he possessed no tolerance for an energetic young dog, and he needed to establish the hierarchy of a pack. The previous night, the drunken men put all four dogs outside and failed to supervise and consider the canines' interactions. Now, the most junior of the three dogs was bloodied and dead.

By the looks of Char's dominant behavior and attitude among the carnage, he seemed to be the leader of the pack.

"I think Char must have felt threatened by your pup there, Frank," Eddy said.

E.S. was not only hosting this outing, he owned the property, too. In addition, he was rich, and that status carried privileges, one of them being that if you wanted to continue being treated to nice hunting trips and fine drinks and cigars then you would not lay too much blame at his feet when something went wrong. Nobody knew what to say or how to act in the face of the carnage, so they just started drinking again. But I saw in my stepfather's visage and demeanor that the night's violent event seriously agitated him.

"Grab the bottles, the shotguns and your hip boots and let's head out to the duck flight, gentlemen," Eddy commanded.

He glanced at the mutilated dog in the corner of the porch where the hound must have been pinned by Char. The pup's throat and head were stained with an abundance of dry blood. The deck was spotted red from the fight.

"We'll clean this up later," Eddy said. "Let's go."

As the four of us and the two remaining dogs left the lodge to find the blind, I noticed a patch of hair missing from Char's neck and hind leg. He had not gotten away clean.

An earthy scent rose in the musty marsh air. Insects hummed, and frogs and minnows splashed around us. Ankle deep in mud, we squelched on in our boots. The men all carried Winchester Model 12 Heavy Duck guns, and I was toting a .410 bore. One of them sized up my shotgun.

"Eddy, your son isn't going to hit a damn thing unless it flies three feet in front of him."

The drunks laughed.

"Mind your own business, Bob," Eddy snapped back.

I realized that Eddy not only seemed flustered by what had happened with the dogs, but he also was nervous about how good of a hunting companion Char would actually turn out to be. He would be an expensive pet regardless of his retrieving skill, I thought.

We came to a permanent blind concealed by grass, reeds and branches and stepped inside. There was plenty of room for the four of us and the dogs.

"Wind direction here is good," one of the men said as we settled in. "Nice landing spot, too."

We waited patiently. There was not much talking among us. Two hours later, a flock of ducks flew overhead and cupped their wings to prepare for landing.

The birds dropped in front of our blind, making for clear shots. We flipped open the top, stood and fired. I cannot even remember if I pulled the trigger because Eddy and the other men were pumping shells as if they were pinned down by enemy fire. I believe to this day that a drunken volley of shots makes a different sound.

Then the men sent the retrievers out into the water, and that is when we discovered the quality of Char's retrieving skills.

The other dog that survived the melee back at the clubhouse showed his superior training and experience by gently carrying back the three birds he was signaled to retrieve. The ducks were all dead. I do not know if Char was distracted, lacked confidence as a young retriever, was poorly trained, or a product of fraud, but he returned to the blind with no duck in his jowls. Was his sense of smell and sight compromised?

Eddy was madder than hell and commanded Char to "Come." They headed into the bog together, man and hound, and I saw that Eddy's balance was quite impaired as he navigated his way through the water, reeds and submerged logs.

"Catch up, Shane. Help me find this fucking duck."

I tried to catch up, high stepping over obstacles and freeing my feet from the suctioning sludge. I followed Eddy's cursing. Despite the cool early morning air, I was sweating under my waders from the workout.

I saw Eddy and the dog stop ahead.

"Jesus Christ, you worthless beast!" he yelled at Char. "Dead or alive, you bring the son-of-a-bitch back. Do you hear? Do you fucking understand? Worthless piece of shit!"

As I reached them, I saw a wounded duck lying on weeds and moss at Eddy's feet. The duck was breathing slowly. Eddy kept yelling, and Char cowered.

"I paid two thousand fucking dollars for you. For what? You make me get out of the blind after one round. Piece of shit. Look! Look at me, Char! This is all you have to do! It's easy."

"No!" The word caught in my throat, half uttered.

Eddy reached down with his two hands and lifted up the duck. He stuck the duck's head in his mouth and crushed its skull between his big yellow teeth. I heard the skull crack, and then there was no more breath in that poor bird.

I wish I had not watched or followed him into the marsh. I wish I had stayed home with Sloane and mom.

"We need a new hunting dog, Shane!" Eddy declared. "God damn it."

Events stemming from that trip are so jarring that I did not mention them to anyone for a long time. To Sloane and my mother, I was tightlipped about our trip. I knew what transpired out there in the marshes did not fit my young sister's ideal of a happy nuclear family led by a strong, loving dad. My mom and I always tried to uphold Sloane's vision of her father as a paragon. If I described the hunting trip in detail to her, Sloane's vision of her father as a role model would forever be stained. For that matter, if I told my mother, her concept of how a family provider should act at all times, especially in front of his children, would be shattered.

In the end, my circumspection made little difference. Sloane overheard her father hissing loudly about Char's defects to my mother in their room. He tied in the mayhem from the night before and the aftermath on the deck. He swore he was going to take Char to the pound and find a new hunting dog.

As he droned on at full volume about the overpriced dog's performance and the embarrassment it caused him, I saw Sloane walk by my bedroom and slam her door shut.

That night I heard her screaming in her sleep. I ran to her bed and held her tight until she calmed down. It was her first panic attack.

Don't get me wrong. We took many happy, fun and relatively calm vacations. I am not lying. Not every family trip involved deadly dog attacks and narrow escapes in planes.

One of Sloane and my favorite getaways was going clam digging at Point Reyes and Tomales Bay, north of San Francisco. Eddy usually rented a home near the ocean in Inverness for a day or two. We would gather hoes, rakes and buckets from the backyard garden shed and toss them into the Fleetwood's trunk. Mom would get together a food basket for a picnic in the sand. After eating the meal, we would go explore the tidal flats.

Clam digging is best done at low tide, and we watched for small holes or depressions forming in the sand along the shore. We got to the clams below by raking or digging around the holes and putting the sand in buckets. We then sifted through the sand with a sieve. Sometimes we discovered hermit crabs and other tiny seashore life among our collection of clams.

Back at the house, we all shared in preparing the clams for dinner. Eddy always brought his vinyl records — jazz, swing and big bands — and a phonograph. One of his favorite songs, which he played repeatedly, was "The Girl from Ipanema." We danced in between rinsing the clams under cold water, scrubbing their shells and discarding the open ones. We gave the clams a good soaking before steaming them for ten or fifteen minutes. We ate them dipped in butter and garlic.

Carefree. That's the image I have of Sloane as she smiled and ran and skipped in the slightly hazy evening in front of a light-red sun on the golden beach — a perfect picture of blitheness and joy. One evening, I watched her from a driftwood seat on the upper beach, and her fresh-faced exuberance was indelibly sketched in my heart and mind. Eddy and Mom were nearby, also watching her, smiling at their miracle child, answering her singsong questions. Sloane's entire being was free and expansive in that moment.

Back in those days, we also spent time in the snowy Sierra Nevada, skiing and sledding around Lake Tahoe. I saw the same kind of spry cheerfulness in Sloane then, too, bundled up so that I could only see her rosy cheeks and greenish eyes.

She was a great natural skier, much better than I was. Her side-to-side movement coming down the mountain was effortless, efficient, fast, controlled. Sloane was the first skier on the lift in the morning. She never stopped for lunch, and she was the last person coming down the mountain in the early evening. The ski patrol sometimes had to go find her and tell her to come down off the mountain. I would be waiting with E.S. and Mom in the lodge when she finally unbuckled her boots and stomped inside. As she ate the sack lunch she had skipped, she regaled us with an enthusiastic, colorful account of every run and jump she took.

"Dad, how long do you think the face of the mountain is?" she asked rhetorically, "Like the distance down. Because I think it drops two thousand feet vertically into those moguls on Gunbarrel."

"It's a challenging run," Eddy assured her. "Very difficult. Double black diamond for sure."

"Well, I came down my fastest on the chute on Kellebrew. You saw me, Shane, didn't you?"

"I was behind you, trying to keep up. Just trying to not wipe out."

"When will we see cousin Ignacio?" Sloane asked.

"Tomorrow. We're going up to Olympic Village tomorrow to stay for a couple days," mother chimed in.

Ignacio Torres was Sloane's cousin by marriage, and a legendary downhill skier. Before Sloane was born, I met him in 1962 when he owned three ski shops around Lake Tahoe and was the premiere instructor for young expert skiers hoping to compete in the Olympics someday. He was riding a wave of admiration after training and coaching the U.S. Men's Olympic Ski Team during the run-up to the 1960 Winter Games. With his long, thick black hair, muscular thighs and cool language of a ski bum dashed with a Spanish accent, Ignacio Torres was the hippest dude I had ever seen. A few years later, when Sloane met Ignacio, she was similarly awestruck in his presence.

Squaw Valley was mother's favorite spot, although she never learned to ski. She took pleasure in all of the new motels, bars, restaurants and shops that had sprung up in the decade since the ski resort hosted the Olympics less than ten years earlier.

She loved to ice skate. I vividly remember her effortlessly gliding across the ice at the outdoor rink. Of course, Eddy was determined to try his luck at it, too, even though he had only one leg. Showing amazing ingenuity and adaptation, he custom-built his skates with a metal blade attached beneath a wooden footplate that he fastened on with leather straps. Mom guided him across the ice in a rare, unguarded moment of vulnerability and surrender for him. Her arm circled his waist to keep him steady, and his fingers clung to her shirt for balance as they skated with more bungling than finesse. They smiled and laughed as if nothing could get in the way of their love.

We spent a lot of time in Hawaii, either on the main island or in Lihue on Kauai where Eddison Shipping had constructed a major new deepwater port for its passenger and cargo ships. We roamed all over paradise so often it might as well have been our second backyard.

Those good times and trips rolled on until 1969 when I saw serious cracks in our concrete little family. Mother stopped traveling with E.S. altogether, which was ironic because he and a group of well-heeled partners had acquired Gold Wing Airlines that year. Based in Los Angeles, the commuter airline's main routes served Alaska, the Pacific Northwest and Hawaii. It seemed to us, though, that Gold Wing Airlines was nothing more than Eddy's own personal carrier, shuttling him to remote hunting and fishing spots on a moment's notice.

By then, I was sixteen and a junior in high school. My friends were now the most important thing in my life. I would rather spend every waking hour with my buddies than my own family. I did not care about my mom and Eddy's problems, and it did not bother me at all that E.S. was spending a lot of time away from the house. I was becoming independent, and my center of attention was shifting from "me and my family" to "me and my friends." My only concern was what my pals and I were doing next.

Then, the most exciting thing happened to me as a teenager. My mother recognized a deep sense of self-reliance growing in me, and she offered me the entire walkout basement. I jumped at the chance to graduate to a more grown-up space.

The basement not only had a bedroom, but a game room, a bathroom and a workshop down the hallway. This was not a dark, dank basement; there were many windows letting in natural light. Best of all, a sliding glass door provided direct access to the outside. I could come and go as I pleased through my private passage. It was the closest thing to having my own apartment. This was my kingdom and my kingdom alone.

CHAPTER 4

As I lived in my downstairs kingdom, 1970 was shaping up to be the best year of my life.

Sloane turned twelve that year. She was outgoing, charismatic and friendly with many people. She had a number of girlfriends — all popular, confident, pretty girls like herself. When I was feeling generous, I let her and her friends share my cool space. Sometimes I even allowed them to hang out in my big, bad room when I was not there.

Sloane's friends were daughters of dentists, judges, doctors, lawyers and company presidents, pretty typical of our neighborhood. Eddy and Mom planned to send her to the local public school, not a private institution but above average in most categories. Sloane and her public school friends fancied themselves a little more gritty than the girls enrolled in the expensive Catholic school five miles down the boulevard even though both sets were cut from the same socio-economic cloth. Sloane's group was just free from uniforms and praying. And they got to rub shoulders with boys all day long. They felt superior.

I, on the other hand, attended the all-boys Catholic preparatory high school just around the corner, which put me in what I thought was a distinctive position: I could mingle with students not only from the girls' campus during our joint mixers, but also at the broader, less-exclusive neighborhood public school parties. I played football in the fall, wrestled in the winter and joined the tennis club in the spring. I went to bed every evening figuring life was pretty good.

Through the natural progression of growing up, Sloane and I put some distance between our parents and us. Eddy and my mom's relationship was ripping apart at the seams, but Sloane did not notice. I saw but assigned little importance to the signs of marital dissolution, probably because I just did not care that much. I had survived one divorce already.

Still, when friends came over — slipping through the sliding patio door of my room to avoid any adults — my parents' discord was sometimes evident. Eddy often disrupted my life when he came home so intoxicated he raged at the slightest provocation. His shouting, cursing, arguing and thumping around reverberated through the planks and walls of the house and permeated every corner of my downstairs room. It was awkward and annoyed me, but I was also grateful to have my own space. I just turned the music up.

Sometimes I could not ignore or muffle the sound of Eddy's drunken aggression no matter how hard I tried. One evening he stormed unannounced into my room and caught Sloane sitting on a boyfriend's lap. Sloane was young but coquettish and had begun to test her budding charm and gently probe the edges of sensual awareness. Everybody found her doings innocent at the time — except Eddy.

That night I had drunk beer and smoked weed behind the house and was buzzed. At first, I laughed as the boyfriend wiggled out from under Sloane and scoured wild-eyed for an exit.

"Don't you run!" Eddy howled as he advanced on the poor kid.

Like a farm chicken being chased, he scrambled over and around furniture, this way and that, to elude Eddy.

"Come here, you son of a bitch!" Eddy demanded.

I doubled over in shrieking laughter — until I heard Eddy calling the boy a "kike" and a "laughing Jew." His bigoted outbursts had become more frequent, and I resented him using that language in my sacred space and in front of my friends.

But Eddy's target was cunning and intently focused on self-preservation. He saw his opening and bolted out the patio door. I thought Eddy would follow, but he stopped dead still in the middle of the room as if he had heard his name yelled. He turned to Sloane, who fidgeted nervously in her seat and avoided eye contact with everybody.

"If you ever marry a Jew I will disown you!" he bellowed.

Her face reddened as the heat of embarrassment gripped her. Eddy re-focused and glared at the record player, which was still spinning Otis Redding as if nothing had happened. We watched him in a hush. He stormed over to the turntable, ripped off disc and flung it, Frisbee-style. The vinyl shattered against the wall above me.

"I've had enough of that Negro music."

I cannot begin to keep track of all the bitter associations in that man's acerbic mind, so I have no idea how Otis Redding triggered such a repulsive reaction in him.

"Shane! You need to watch your sister like a hawk when I'm not here. What the hell is the matter with you?"

"I'm not her babysitter!" I blurted out.

Eddy took two angry strides at me. I expected to be punched, pushed or strangled. Anything was possible.

"I can't be everywhere watching you guys," he said, exasperated.

He appeared to be on the verge of saying something more, but instead angrily bolted from the room, punching a hole in my bedroom door as he departed.

Once he was gone, we commiserated with each other over my step-dad's galling behavior. We had all suffered from it. Soon, however, the old fun Sloane returned, and our little party resumed with one fewer of our friends in the room.

As I watched her recover, I thought how her father's overfondness made her feel safe most of the time, but her forbearance had limits. Most times, he gave his daughter unwavering support and encouragement. He hugged her, made her breakfast and often smiled at her. His wallet opened to her every desire. Someday the time might come when I would have to explain to her the entire, complex nature of this man, expose her to the unvarnished truth, the bad with the good. For now, I just put on another album, some good R&B to soothe the soul and something sure to throw Eddy into another fit if he returned.

The following Monday, I waited in the kitchen for Sloane to come downstairs so I could give her a ride to school, and the time to leave approached. Eddy was gone and my mother was in her bedroom getting ready to meet other Republican wives at a brunch and tea at California first lady Nancy Reagan's white Tudor Revival mansion on 45th Street in East Sacramento.

I waited and waited for my sister until a despairing caterwaul from her bedroom seared my ears. I flew up the stairs.

I heard my mother's shower running and the radio blaring in her room as the frightening lament carried on behind Sloane's closed door. I barged in and found her lying under the sheets in a fetal position.

"Sloane, are you OK? What is it?" I asked.

She rolled onto her back and slowly pulled the cover down under her eyes as if she did not recognize who had spoken from above the sheet. Her face was pale, her skin sticky.

"I'm OK. It was just a bad dream. I'm OK."

"Are you sure?"

"Yes."

I caressed her arm, until she asked meekly, "Shane, are you afraid of dying?"

"I... I don't know. I don't think about it much. Why?"

"I'm afraid I am going to die."

"You're fine. You're a healthy young girl."

"I don't mean now. Someday."

"Yes, but not for a very long time. You don't have to worry about that now."

"What do you think happens to us?"

"When we die?" I asked. "I don't know. Why are you worried about it?"

"I walked past the dog kennel yesterday..."

"Why? Where?"

"My friends and I took the bus downtown."

"To the animal shelter?"

"No, we were shopping but we walked by it. There was a dog that looked like Char there. He was standing all alone by the chain-link fence while the other dogs ran around the yard. He looked so sad. No dogs played with him. No dogs even sniffed him. I think it was the ghost of Char."

"What did you do?"

"Nothing. I just left him there and started walking to the bus stop to come home. On the way, we passed by the cathedral and the sun was setting and the light was shining on the stained glass windows and making the spires appear golden. I couldn't take the beauty anymore. It looked like heaven. I had to look away. It was in such contrast with death. On the bus, I started thinking Char should be in a more beautiful place than that stupid kennel, but..."

"But what?"

"I don't think my dad found him a home..."

"There are some things in life we just don't know. In a way, that's the beauty of it."

"But we will be together forever, right, Shane? You, me, Mom and Dad? I mean Mom and Dad for a long, long time — but you'll be with me forever, right?"

"What have I always told you? Yes. I'll always be there for you. Even if you can't see or hear me, I'll be standing next to you, right by your side."

I could not see her face, but her body quivered. She relapsed into heavy crying. I lay down beside her and held her tight until the sobbing stopped.

Even though she eventually calmed down, Sloane was in no condition to go to school. I downplayed the circumstances. I told my mom she woke up with really a bad stomach pain and that I would check on her again at lunchtime and after school."

"You're such a good boy!" my impeccably dressed mother told me.

When the lunch bell rang later that day, I darted to my car, avoiding any inquiries from friends or solicitations for rides. I wanted to get home quickly to check on Sloane. Outside her bedroom door, I knocked and then knocked again. When no answer came, I cracked the door open and looked inside. There was nobody in her bed, but I heard whimpering from inside the closet.

"Sloane? Sloane? Are you OK? Where are you? Are you in the closet?"

"Yes. Go away, Shane. I want to be alone. I want to stay in here. Don't get me or I'll scream. Please. Just let me be here alone"

I had managed to keep my mom at an arm's length from Sloane by telling her I had checked on her already and that Sloane said she did not need anything and just wanted to sleep.

E.S. didn't come home that night, so, thankfully I avoided lying to him about Sloane's predicament.

By the next morning, she was feeling better and actually beat me to the kitchen table, which she never did.

At some point, a kid gets bored of listening to his albums, no matter how extensive his collection is. I burned for some new music, maybe even an entirely new sound. One evening, I was looking through the albums I stored in a couple boxes in a hall closet with deep shelves. I was flipping through cover after cover forward with my finger when a cardboard container far at the back of one of the shelves caught my eye. I never had noticed this hidden box before, probably because the shelves were so long and narrow and obscured by darkness.

I knew nobody had been in the closet since the day I moved down to the basement because my mother had given me the only key so I could store my personal belongings without worrying about them. Somehow, I had failed to see this container. I set my two album cartons aside, reached way back and pulled out the mystery box and set it on my bed.

"I'll be damned," I said, looking inside.

There were a dozen albums in there, plus some sealed manila folders in the back of the box. The folders felt like they contained papers and photos. I set them aside because I wasn't interested in snooping into somebody else's business. But I was definitely interested in listening to newfound music. The box contained a veritable who's who of early, early R&B: Ray Charles, Fats Domino, The Drifters, Ruth Brown, Muddy Waters.

Maybe this was my mother's music. I did not know. But I had been listening to rhythm and blues greats at a friend's house, so I was excited at what I had stumbled upon. I carried the albums to my turntable and dropped the needle on one record, then another and another. I thumbed through the lineup of records and came to an Etta James album. There were two records inside one sleeve, which was odd. I rolled one of them out, set it on the turntable and placed the stylus on it.

I don't know how long I listened — thirty seconds, a minute? — before I figured out what I was hearing. There was no music, just a quiet conversation between a man and a woman. I turned the volume up as high as it went to try to make out what was being said. The audio quality was poor, but my ears fine-tuned themselves and adapted to the cadence and modulation. It was a recording of an intimate discussion. A woman was being seduced. The couple began giggling and moaning. The cooing and wet smacks got louder as if they were having...

My mother threw open the door and blasted into my bedroom. Her face was the whitest shade of pale; mine crimson. I had forgotten that in trying to decipher the content I had turned the volume up to the maximum.

"Shane, where did you get these?" she cried as she snatched the record from the turntable. "Where did you find them? Why are you listening to these?"

"From the locked closet," I said. "Remember? You gave me the key. What are they?"

"I gave you the key? Why would I give you the key?"

"I wanted a place for personal stuff, so you gave me a key. Why? What is this? I was trying to listen to some new music."

Mom did not answer, but tossed the record back into the box without bothering to slide it into the undercover sleeve. She piled the rest of the albums into the box and shoved it into the closet, slamming the door.

"Lock it! Lock it, Shane, God damn it."

I secured the hideaway.

"Give me the key."

"But you said..."

"Give me the key until we find another place for your stuff."

"Okay. Okay."

She pulled me by my shirt into my room and shouted that I must never mention this incident to Sloane or Eddy or anybody. She back-stepped to my couch and dropped into the cushions.

"What is this all about?" I asked desperately.

"It's my investigation. It's my evidence. It may save my — our — future."

Her life, my life, all of our lives were not the same from that moment forward.

She told me the whole story.

Mom had suspected E.S. of having an affair for years. About two years ago, she hired a private investigator to gather information on her husband based on her suspicions.

The detective she hired was the best that money could buy, she explained, and money was no object to her. He was well connected, creative and not afraid to take liberties with his target's privacy. His Rolodex was stuffed with the phone numbers and addresses of informants and other human resources cultivated in courthouses, police stations, county offices, law offices, restaurants, hotels, bars, taxies, photo labs, Fotomat kiosks, travel agencies, airlines, train stations, ship harbors and recording studios all over the state. His surveillance utilized the most modern and state-of-the-art methods. He broke down witnesses in interviews within minutes. He had a staff of six assistant PIs.

All of this was expensive, but if someday my mother needed proof of who was destroyed her marriage, she wanted to it to be irrefutable. She needed the evidence accessible to her and easy to hide. When the right time came, she needed to lock down a substantial alimony settlement to ensure our future.

When her well-paid sleuth summoned Maureen to his office to reveal what he had discovered, she was shocked.

"Are you telling me he has a girlfriend?" she asked.

"No. I'm saying he has five mistresses."

"He's sleeping with five other women?"

"At least two currently. Five since you hired me. At least."

Maureen took a deep breath.

"Where did these affairs take place?"

"Everywhere. Have you not looked at my itemized invoice of travel expenses? L.A., San Francisco, Oregon, Washington, Hawaii, Taiwan, Boise... here in Sacramento."

"That's eight places. You said he had five mistresses."

"Some liaisons overlapped geographical locations. He took some lovers on vacations. Believe me, it wasn't easy keeping tabs on his movements when he was flying his own plane all over the place and motoring off to sea on private yachts. You can view the material privately in our conference room."

"I've heard enough."

"You should look it over thoroughly until you are convinced."

"I'm convinced."

"What do you want me to do with the information?

"I don't know yet."

"Do you want to take possession of it?"

"Yes. I mean, can it be concealed until I need it?"

"Here's how we usually do it. And you've paid a premium for this. You told me you weren't sure when, if ever, you might, uh, present your case to your husband or to your lawyer or whomever. We, here at Scovin Personal Auditors, transfer all of our findings and any recorded conversations or material to vinyl records that can be discreetly stored, disguised as a regular music album and innocuously labeled. It's less suspicious than a tape reel, less likely to be tampered with and won't deteriorate. We keep our copies, and we give you yours. Photo negatives we can warehouse ourselves and present whenever needed. This transferring of audio to vinyl is complex, but we have the technology. It's expensive, but you expressed that money wasn't an issue."

"Fine," my mother said at the end of the conversation after her shock gave way to tears and then to anger, spewing forth in front of the head detective, who was accustomed to such reactions. "Give me the package, my marriage be damned."

At the end of her story, she was sobbing, and I felt and must have looked overwhelmed. I, too, was shaken from hearing that album's content. It was all too much for both of us.

Then Eddy walked in.

His eyes twitched from his wife to me, me to his wife, back and forth.

"What's going on here?"

Mom jumped off the couch, pushed him out of her way and ran upstairs. Eddy turned his gaze on me.

"Well? Do you need to tell me something?"

"No. I'm going to Sully's house."

I darted out the patio door.

Eddy did not know what had transpired, but he knew it wasn't good. He tried to figure it out with a million questions posed to Mom and me. We soft-pedaled the situation, underplayed its significance. He knew we weren't being forthright, especially when his wife kicked him out of their bedroom and down into the basement. Of course, that forced me to go back to my original bedroom. Whatever had transpired, he now knew how big of a nightmare this was. He wondered how long the fallout would last. I wondered how I ended up with the rawest deal of all.

We all spared Sloane the distress. What thirteen-year-old needs to worry about her parents' relationship? She believed their new sleeping arrangements and disengagement were temporary and in short order they would return to living together fully and equally, like they had before. We would all soon be eating together again at the dinner table.

Eddy's response was to be extra nice and stay as sober as possible. He tried to make amends by staying home at night, helping with meals and buying chocolate and flowers and bracelets for his wife. He stopped complaining about anything domestic and started suggesting outings we could take together. He wanted to buy Sloane a horse and board it near his father's land, but Mom blocked that idea. Instead, he bought Sloane the latest and best ski gear and private lessons. For me, I got a Wilson T2000 tennis racket, Adidas sweatsuits and any albums I wanted as soon as they were released.

Eddy's attempts to transform gnawed at him because, quite frankly, he was bad at change, he was not ready to become a different man and, like any human, he was scared to lose his innermost self, to have his very essence broken into crumbs. Yet, outwardly, he was more friendly and present than ever before. The sea change was noticeable.

In truth, he was riding a roller coaster. Every other week, he'd take a swig of Scotch, which led to another and another, and suddenly he was up and leaving for two or three days without so much as a handwritten note. During the time when he was on his best behavior, we would invite friends over for a backyard barbecue or to a dinner party, and he would throw back the single malts as if nothing had changed. At least we knew he wasn't indulging in extramarital dalliances when he was hard-drinking at home.

During this tempestuous, up-and-down period, Sloane and I learned some of how the world works. I remember the police brought Eddy home one night after he draped his car around a telephone pole. He was a businessman, a pillar of society, a contributor to law-and-order politicians. The police officers all knew him and lugged him upstairs and put him to bed themselves.

I sincerely believed he was trying to patch up a marriage gone awry and save his family from being torn apart. Drastic modification of lifestyle did not come easily for him. Yet, in the course of a year, I started believing he had changed forever — until one foul day.

CHAPTER 5

Months passed.

In the winter, Mother Nature unleashed a series of storms on California. Relentless rain, heavy snow and tumultuous winds deluged widespread areas of the state. The Sierra Nevada snowpack contained two hundred percent of average water content. Tens of thousands of acres of cropland were flooded to hold the eventual snowmelt. The roaring Sacramento and American rivers breached their levees and the weirs were opened up to ease the pressure.

Eddy watched the rain thrum against his office window. The restless, insistent, menacing storms were not calming any sooner than the tempest raging inside him. For months, he tried to show his family he was the perfect example of principled living, but Maureen's frostiness toward him persisted. He attempted to lead a life that completely revolved around the care and nurturing of his family only to find that his inner turmoil endured. He struggled to be the devoted husband and father but his true self pulled him from family and back to his old habits. The constant internal discord finally pushed him to the brink.

I knew something was wrong one day as I drove home from school at lunchtime and saw two black-and-white squad cars, a couple of unmarked police sedans, and a slick, black, civilian BMW motorcycle that I had never seen before, parked in front of the house. Detectives were interviewing Eddy in our living room when I walked through the door. He was sitting on the couch, wrapped in a blanket, his hair wet and head down, chin resting solemnly on his chest.

This is what happened on that squally day.

On the way to school, my friends and I drove to the state park to smoke a quick joint and watch the American River as it crested. Through our stoned gaze, we watched the tempestuous river's rapid flow. Debris and sediment swirled around in a turbulent current. The width of the murky brown river was twice as wide as normal and as loud as a locomotive. One of us suddenly realized we were going to be late for first period, so we bolted. As we pulled out, it appeared the brunt of the storm appeared to be passing.

Not in my wildest dreams did I think my mother and stepfather would be on their way to this very spot to fish.

Maureen came downstairs to start her day. Eddy surprised her. His mere presence in the kitchen at that time of day was startling. She asked him what was on his mind and why he was not at work.

"I have a favor I want to ask of you," he said. "It's just a small indulgence, if you don't mind. I know things have been tense between us, but hear me out."

She saw three wrapped presents on the kitchen table. Eddy told her to open them and he would explain.

"It's not my birthday."

"I know. Please, Maureen."

She removed the paper from the rectangle package first and opened the cardboard box. Inside was a pair of pink hip waders. She gave him a puzzled look.

"Wait. Now open the other one," he said, pointing to the gift concealed in a long box.

It was a new fishing rod and reel.

She looked perplexed.

"Now, before you say anything, let me explain. I'm just asking this one time — please go fishing with me on the river. Ever since you kicked me out of the bedroom, I've tried to be nicer. You never told me why you did that, but it doesn't matter. I know I need to drink less and not get so angry at stupid little things. But I want to show you how much I care about you. And how much I want us to be together. I'm ready to be understanding and supportive. It's been a very long time since we've done anything together as a couple. Well, I started thinking about that deep-sea fishing trip we took that time out of San Francisco Bay, and the hydro-jet excursions up the Rogue River. I was thinking maybe, just maybe, I could show you more of what I love to do, things I really enjoy, and maybe it's something you might grow to like. It's a way we could spend more time together. Afterward, I'll do or go wherever you want. We can start sharing our lives with each other again."

"You want me to go fishing with you today?" she asked incredulously. "Right now? In this weather?"

"I know. I know. It's crazy. But we need a little crazy right now. Let me explain. When I planned this I didn't know it'd be this wild outside. But the conditions are actually very beneficial for fishing. We'll probably catch a ton more. The fall salmon and steelhead will be in a feeding frenzy. They will be swimming into places they don't usually swim into. We'll cook them up for dinner, surprise the kids."

"Eddy! It's so cold."

"That's why I went out and bought that third gift. It's a down parka. Open it!"

He looked like a little child on Christmas Eve, she thought.

"Did you forget? I can't swim! I can barely dog paddle in a pool!"

"You'll have a life vest on, and I'll never take my eyes off you. Please, Maureen, I won't ask you to do another thing ever again. I'm just trying to rekindle some of the passion and togetherness we used to have. I want to find some common ground."

She ran out of excuses. She even laughed with him over the vision of being together in that small boat of his. His puerile mirth was infectious. She doubted this — of all things! — would be his path back to her heart, but she decided to extend the grace. Perhaps he deserves one last chance before I tell him it is over and I want a divorce, she thought. If she agreed to go, he could not blame her for not ever trying.

They drove to the launching area east of Sunrise Bridge and boarded the same ten-foot aluminum boat that we had taken out to Eddy's hunting clubhouse on that insane trip into the marsh. The parka did not fit over my mother's life vest, so he gave her one of his larger wading jackets. There appeared to be a break in the weather.

"See it's not too bad out here," he said. "We'll go up the river a little ways to find a spot. Once we're upstream, I'll cut the motor and we'll drop our lines."

"There's nobody out here. If these are such great conditions for fishing, where are all the fishermen, then?"

"It's their loss. We have the river — and the fish — all to ourselves. Come on, try to enjoy this," he said with a big grin.

The turbid, swift river current frightened her. She sat at the bow in her oversized jacket and bright pink hip waders. The dark skies to the north-east crept closer, and the wind picked up again. She was uncomfortable, a little confused and irritated for agreeing to this folly. At least I'm not frozen stiff, she thought, as some filtered sunshine showed through the clouds.

"The water level looks like it's two feet from the bottom of that bridge," she said. "We're going to hit our heads. And it looks like another storm is coming over there. See? This is crazy. Why did I come out here?"

"I know. It'll get better. Try to relax. Dip your head when we go under the bridge, OK?"

He adjusted the engine to a low trolling speed and pulled a bottle of Dom Pérignon from his backpack.

"Hey, look what I found?"

He sent the cork flying into the wind, took a swig and handed her the bottle.

"We have to drink out of the bottle? No glasses? These are steerage conditions," she retorted good-naturedly.

"Here's to us and, I sincerely hope, to second chances."

A twisted smiled widened across his face.

"At least somebody is having fun," she quipped, taking the bottle from him. She had come this far and might as well drink up.

Eddy set out his tackle box and rigged the bait.

"Maybe start with the sardine-wrapped plugs," he said. "When you're ready to cast, we'll have you stand up and toss it in that direction across the current so the bait drifts over there. You know, Maureen, this spot in the river is where Tiger Construction dug out its rock and granite, and then left. Fish are fond of those borrow pits they left behind. I'm going to troll a little closer to the shore — it looks like there's enough depth."

Nearer to the bank, he asked his wife if she were ready to cast. "Sure, why not?" she said unenthusiastically. "It's why we're here, isn't it?" She stood unsteadily.

"Whoa! I must be little wobbly from the bubbly."

"You don't have your sea legs, that's all."

Eddy cut the motor and the little boat carried them under the bridge just as the skies darkened overhead and the wind increased.

"It's getting pretty bad out here again," she said in a worried voice as they emerged from beneath the span, downstream.

"I'll tell you what. I'll cast too, and if nothing bites, we'll motor in. Keep your eye out there on your line."

She looked for her line in the water as he took glanced at the shore. The bank was about ten feet away. Fishing reel in hand and arms spread for balance, Eddy stepped onto the boat's low gunwale.

"Keep your eye on the line," he repeated.

He pressed his weight onto his artificial leg to gain a firmer hold on the boat's upper edge. His bulk plunged his side of the boat so far down that river water gushed over the side. Maureen turned to see what the hell he was doing and lost her balance. She tumbled to the deck and struck her head on the bench seat. As the boat righted, she looked up and caught a quick, woozy glimpse of Eddy on the gunwale, rising above her. She could not make any sense of what was happening.

She saw him pitch out of the boat and into the river, and he was gone. The starboard side shot upward and the boat flipped over on top of Maureen, pushing her face first into the icy-cold, roiling water.

The shocking chill made her muscles go rigid. Her heart pounded, and adrenaline surged through her. Panic and fear set in. She had no choice but to let go and permit the angry current to sweep her along. The torrent pulled her under, pushed and spun her, then dragged her down again. The hydrous beast took her wherever the hell it wanted to.

The river took her on an unstoppable, wild ride. Even if she had been a strong swimmer, it would not have mattered. When her face resurfaced for brief moments, she gasped for bits of air. Alarm seized her as she became conscious of the load of her water-laden waders and saturated clothing.

Pulled again by the violent flow into the river's depths, her body was jolted to an abrupt standstill. She was pinned underwater, the frigid, forceful undercurrent pushing against her but not carrying her away. She became tired and disoriented — and then indifferent to her ultimate fate. She did not care whether she lived or died.

Was that light she saw above her? She stretched her arm toward the gossamer brightness overhead. Something squeezed her hand. Something snatched her arm. She was jerked and jarred loose from the lethal tree limbs and branches holding her below the surface. She kicked her legs as she was tugged upward. In the next moment, she was being dragged along sand and soot.

They were fishing buddies. One was a car mechanic and the other a butcher from the McClellan Air Force Base commissary. They loved casting a rod in this type of weather. The inclemency imparted an energy and exuberance to their fishing. Their fishing lines had been stretched into the water when they saw something moving rapidly downstream — some type of large debris, a small, capsized boat.

Moments later, something smaller, more compact in the water danced erratically toward them. It came to a jarring stop underwater several yards upstream. A human hand appearing from below the surface initially made them jump back but then spurred them into action.

The butcher braced himself in a wide stance as far out from the shore as he could manage to try to seize this hand — clearly a woman's — without being swept away himself. Behind him, the mechanic hung tightly onto his friend's jacket, his legs splayed.

"A little more!" the butcher shouted.

The mechanic inched closer to the water until his friend got a firm hold of the hand.

"Closer!"

The mechanic broadened his footing and lowered his stance. The butcher snatched the woman's forearm.

"Her hand is small, but she's heavy," he yelled. "Why is she so heavy?"

He secured a firm grip on her jacket, and the body budged, then it separated from whatever held it below the water. The men fell onto the sandy shoreline and dragged her higher up the riverbank. Face down, the woman choked and spit up dirty water. The friends gasped for air while lying on their backs and looking up at a sliver of blue sky splitting the heavy dark clouds and growing wider.

Her vision was still blurry when she rolled onto her back and discerned two men hovering over her, apparently searching for signs of distress or hidden wounds. They asked her several questions. Why was she out here? With whom? Why was she dressed like that? Was that her boat they saw go by? She did not answer. She searched for the reason why she had ended up fighting for her life in a frothing river. She wanted to shout at the men to leave her alone and give her space to compose herself.

She saw one of them look away.

"Flag him down," his friend ordered.

He leapt up to chase down a park ranger in a pickup cruising atop the wet levy road.

The butcher stayed next to her. He told her to take deep breaths, to try to relax, and that she would be all right. He asked again if there was somebody with her when the river swept her away. Had she been fishing with somebody? He asked again about the capsized boat.

The mechanic returned with the ranger.

"Let's get her up to the pickup," the ranger said. "We have accounts of a man whose boat capsized up the river. He reported his wife might have drowned. I'll radio for some help down here, and then let's get her home."

The butcher offered to stay with Maureen until the authorities sorted out the ordeal.

Maureen was thinking clearly and practically now. She resolved not to talk to anybody and hardened into silence. Had she not always navigated her adult life mindful of a better tomorrow, always searching out a brighter future? Her destiny might have been shrouded in uncertainty this morning, but what lay ahead suddenly presented itself with unequivocal clarity.

My mom arrived home shortly after Eddy.

The detective headed me off at the door to my own house.

"What's going on here?" I asked.

"Everybody's fine, but there's been an accident down at the river. We're sorting out what happened."

"An accident at the river?"

"It appears your father and mother were fishing..."

I laughed. The detective was nonplussed by my odd reaction.

"Fishing? My mother? I don't think so."

"That's what they say."

"Voluntarily fishing?"

"That's what she says."

"Can I talk to her?"

"We're interviewing them in separate rooms. It's standard. Come along."

Eddy spotted me.

"Shane! Shane! Come here! Come over here real quick!"

Sitting on the sofa wrapped up in an afghan, he looked terrible. He was chain smoking and lit a new cigarette as thin smoke swirled up from one recently crushed out in an ashtray on the coffee table that was crammed full with butts. His thin arm protruded out from under the blanket. It looked to me as if his skin was hanging off bone. His balding pate looked even sparser because his thin hair remained plastered to his head from having been wet. When he called to me, I saw his teeth were dulled to a washed-out yellow color. His entire visage signaled weariness.

"Ed!" the detective called to my stepfather from the stairs. "You can talk to your son later, OK?"

Upstairs, I saw a strange man sitting on my bed. He watched me walk past my bedroom.

"Who's that guy? And what's he doing in my room?"

"He's the one who saved your mother's life," the cop said. "I thought Ed was the only one crazy enough to go fishing in a storm. Turns out that guy also likes riding his motorcycle and fishing in the rain, fortunately for Maureen."

I figured the nice R 69S out front was his bike.

I opened my mom's door, and she ran over to give me a big hug.

"Mom, what's going on? They said you were fishing with Eddy. That can't be right. That's crazy. You and Eddy? Fishing? In this weather? None of it makes any sense."

"Could we have some privacy?" she asked the detective, and he and a uniformed officer left the room, closing the door behind them.

My mother then told me her side of the story, starting all the way back to the moment she realized Eddy knew that she was going to leave him. A few weeks ago, she said, Eddy found a letter in an envelope addressed to a high-powered divorce attorney and, of course, suspected the worst. When mother realized she had left the letter in plain sight on top of her vanity, she ran upstairs to grab it. She found that envelope had been moved and the letter lying open on the bed.

Two days later, thinking Eddy was gone, she called from the kitchen telephone to confide in a good friend. Midway through the call, she heard a faint click on the line, like a handset being quietly replaced in another room. The moment she hung up, Eddy appeared in the kitchen, seemingly out of nowhere. The look on his face said it all: He had been listening. Eddy knew a split was imminent, but he did not say a word.

"He mentioned nothing about the letter, or the divorce attorney, or the conversation on the phone," my mom said. "He knows a divorce will get messy. He knows it will be expensive. He knows the family will see it as a failure, his failure, and his reputation will be damaged if I publicly, in court, bring up the issue of his infidelity, his drinking and his abuse. Today, he made up his mind that he wants to keep his money and his good name intact while avoiding an expensive divorce — at all costs! But that's not happening"

"At all costs? What do you mean? What are you saying?"

"He coerced me to go fishing on a stormy day, in a swollen river, dressed in heavy gear — even though I can't swim. Figure it out, Shane."

"Jesus! Are you saying he intentionally tried to drown you?"

She put her hand over my mouth, then walked over to the door and peeked out to make sure nobody was nearby listening. She then quickly closed it again.

"That would be a very easy way out for him, don't you think? He would keep his fortune and his social status and go back to all his mistresses. Nobody would be the wiser."

"Do the police know? Did you tell the police?"

"No, Shane. It was an accident," she said sardonically. "I refuse to give the cops a statement stating otherwise."

"What? Why? What are you talking about? You just told me he tried to kill you!"

"It's my ace in the hole."

"If you are telling me the truth, you need press charges. Now."

"No."

"Why not? He needs to be punished. This is insane! It's attempted murder. Do you want Sloane and me to live under the same roof as a deranged killer! None of us are safe."

"Shane, keep your voice down," my mother said, staring intensely into my eyes. "I gave the detective my statement. I said I agreed to go fishing with Eddy today because he wanted to rekindle our bond and bridge the chasm in our relationship. I was more than willing to get dressed up in all the new gear he bought me and try one last time to salvage our marriage. But then the accident happened, and I fell into the raging river."

"Did they believe you?"

"I don't know. They all know him. They drink together. They call him 'old buddy.' They gave him a blanket and let me shiver while they interviewed us. Remember that time he was drunk and crashed his car into the telephone pole? They didn't care. They brought him directly home and put him to bed without a report. They protect his reputation, and he offers them free trips. I know that. But the police shouldn't even be here. If it weren't for that guy with the motorcycle and his friend suspecting foul play, nobody would have called the police."

"What made them think it was foul play?"

"Somehow they got it in their mind."

"He did save your life so..."

"Well, now he needs to get out of my life."

"What did Eddy tell the cops? What's his story?"

"The same."

"This is serious, mom. You can't let this go."

"Stop making a big deal out of it, Shane! Tell me you understand! Say it! It was all just a silly, embarrassing accident."

"Why should I?"

"Because I know how I'm going to punish Eddy in the end...."

"It sure doesn't sound like you do."

"...And it's *not* by trying to send him to prison for attempted murder."

"How then?"

"If I tell the police what Eddy tried to do, maybe they believe me. Maybe they don't. They're all good old boys. They owe him. And it's not just the cops. The district attorney is indebted to him from the last election. Those two golf once a month together. I think they'd make me sound crazy before he ever saw a jail cell, but I'd lay bare all the facts."

"You can't just let him walk away. What, you're going to drop it?"

"No, I'm no dropping it," my mom said, oddly with a complacent smile. "I'm leveraging it. Now, he has a reason to make this divorce quiet, quick and to give me everything I ask for. By denying anything criminal happened and keeping my mouth shut, I have something he badly needs: my silence. I have the power to destroy his reputation. It's all I have."

"Blackmail — that's the path you're going to take? You just said..."

"Call it whatever you want, but I'm going to walk away with my life, your life, Sloane's life, all intact — and a ton of money as a settlement. I'm not going to allow him to twist the story and drag the case out for years. A quiet dissolution sweeps everything under the rug. I get what I need. He gets what he ultimately wants. And we all get out of here safe and rich."

"You said he's protected."

"In the end, the possibility of jail scares him more than a mutually agreed-upon divorce."

"What about Sloane? What do you tell her?"

"She doesn't need to know anything about this. Everybody will be gone by the time she comes home from school today. If you love me, you won't say a word about this."

"What are you going to tell her when you kick her father out of the house and divorce him?"

"I know two things. One, Sloane must never know about what happened today. Do you hear me? Promise me!"

"I promise. I promise"

"And two, she must never know the real reason why I am divorcing her father. He cheated on me multiple times throughout our marriage. He has terrible anger issues. I've been a victim of his verbal and physical abuse, just like you have. He has a heavy, heavy drinking problem. But Sloane is young. She is only thirteen. She's innocent. She loves her father, worships him, and I will not let her go through life disillusioned. All of this would screw her up so badly if she found out. She can come to her own conclusions when she's older."

"You have to tell her *something*."

"I will tell her that her father and I are taking a break and spending some time away from each other in order to find some space to patch up our relationship and move toward a better future."

"If it sounds like bullshit to me, mom, Sloane will know it's bullshit. She's too smart. She'll know you two are splitting up for good."

"Eventually, yes. When she can handle it. But that's all she'll know. None of the other stuff."

"She'll catch wind of it at some point. It's a tight-knit neighborhood, people talk, especially with our family."

"So be it. I won't be the one to drive a wedge between my daughter and her father. My way is the cleanest way."

"She'll blame you for the divorce, not Eddy. She might never talk to you again. You know that, right?"

"One day, she'll be able to deal with all the fallout from the divorce, but she would never be able to cope with the heinous details about her father and what he's capable of. I will continue to make life as normal and comfortable as possible for her. I love her too much."

"Then don't you think she deserves to know the real reason?"

"I — we — cannot burden her with that, Shane. Don't you get it? Trust me on this. Promise me, Shane. Before I let those cops back into this room, promise me you're on my side. Eddy played his cards. I'm holding mine."

"Yes. Yes. Of course, I'm on your side. Your secrets are safe with me, Mom. I'll watch out for Sloane. I'll always be here for her and for you. I promise."

CHAPTER 6

Life changed for all of us in 1971.

Eddy moved out. He lived with his longtime business partner for two months before buying a big house up in Granite Bay, east of Sacramento, with a covered equestrian riding arena, barn, paddocks and tack room.

Mom was now twice divorced, a single mother on her own again, but the three thousand-dollar alimony check E.S. faithfully wrote to her each month unquestionably took the sting out of her situation. She remained a member of the tennis club and the National Federation of Republican Women.

I graduated from high school, enrolled in the nearby community college and moved back into the basement, my nearly-the-real-thing apartment. Like the light seeping beneath my closed bedroom door, adulthood crept into my life.

In the fall, Sloane started high school and two weekends a month stayed with her father at his house and rode her new horse. She joined the ski club and tennis team.

Eddy remained kind and decent to me whenever our paths crossed, but I did not plan to forgive him. I did not talk to him for a year-and-a-half. But I lived in a space where anger gave way to questions, and the questions grew into to a tired acceptance of how things stood. Whenever I drove

Sloane to her riding lessons, Eddy would invite me inside and ask her to remain outside, and one day, I took him up on his offer.

In time, it became possible to speak with him as if nothing had happened, but at first the air was thick with silence and unasked questions. He wanted to know how my life was going and what I had been doing lately. He wanted me to be certain that if I needed anything — money, tickets for traveling, a place to stay, whatever — that he would make sure I received it. He even said he still considered me his son.

One particular Sunday evening when I was picking up Sloane, he answered the door and engaged me in a superficial conversation. Sloane was not present. After we exchanged banalities, he took hold of my hand and placed a MasterCharge credit card in my palm. He told me the revolving line of credit was tied to an S&S Travel expense account and would provide financial means that I should not hesitate to use if I ever needed it. With me, Eddy always struggled to verbalize his feelings into words, and he found it was easier to offer gifts than apologies. For an eighteen-year-old boy on his own — just beginning to cross the threshold into a big new world — this single act of generosity on Eddy's part could go a long way toward fostering forgiveness toward him.

"You never know when you'll need it," he said, holding onto my hand a little longer. "But it gives you freedom. I'll give Sloane one when she turns eighteen, too."

"May I ask you a question?" I asked after a short, awkward silence. "How is Sloane when she's around you? Does she show any resentment over the divorce? Does she ever get angry or lash out when she's with you?"

"Why? Is your mom asking?"

"No, I am."

"How is she at home with you and your mother?"

"Mostly fine. Growing up fast, really fast. Wants to stay out later and that kind of thing. When she's not getting her way, she uses the divorce to lash out at mom. But that's all normal for a teenage girl, right? But I was wondering what you see? How she behaves when she's not at home."

"She blames Maureen for everything that's happened, even though I don't fan those flames. We never told her the truth about anything. We never even talked about it with her. Maureen thought Sloane wouldn't understand. That's how your mom wanted it."

"And you? How would you have handled it?"

"Hell, I don't even understand all that transpired between your mom and me after the boating accident. She was so bitter afterward. But your mother and I agreed that, with Sloane, this was the best solution possible. I'm making the most out of the situation."

I thanked him for the credit card and asked where Sloane was. He told me she was in back of the house, probably packing her suitcase. I left him in the kitchen and walked down the hall toward her room, but I heard Sloane in Eddy's office and library. She was standing in front of his extensive book collection displayed on built-in custom shelves. She placed a finger on the spine of one of the books.

"Have you seen my father's library?" she asked without turning to look at me.

"Yes. I remember it was quite an impressive collection."

"Have you read some of these titles?" she asked incredulously. "There is a lot here about World War II, the Sovietization of America, Zionism, even the occult. Here's one, *Elders of Zion*. What's that? Next to it is this 1921 book by an author named Nesta Helen Webster. It's about the Illuminati. Over here, he has *Mein Kampf,* and shelf full of *Signal* magazines. Have you read any of these?"

"No."

"I haven't either, but every time I'm up here I skim through them, enough to get an idea of what they're about. They don't seem to be books normal people would have in their collections. What do you think?"

"Eddy was an officer in the Navy in World War II, so I could see why he might be engaged with ideas popular at the time. He inherited a lot of books and periodicals from your grandfather. Why are you so interested?"

"I don't know, but some men came over to see him on Friday. I think they were sailors on the USS Liberty a few years ago. He showed them the library. I eavesdropped on them and heard the men ask if he wanted to invest in a movie they were making about the ship and how Israel attacked it with fighter jets and torpedoes. A lot of Americans died."

"What did your father say?"

Sloane's eyes shifted to the doorway, and I knew Eddy was standing there.

"I told those sailors that the attack on the Liberty was a dark spot in our history, and I'm only too happy to help them with their project," Eddy said. "I told them it was a shameful act and that we should have cut off all ties with Israel."

"Did you give them money for their movie?" I asked.

"Yes."

"Is it going to get made?"

"I don't know, but I don't care if I ever get my investment back. It's a noble endeavor. If you or Sloane want to read more about the USS Liberty, you know you can find all kinds of books and magazines on the subject right on these shelves."

On our drive back to Sacramento, I asked Sloane how many of Eddy's books on Zionists and the occult had she read. Even if she was casually interested in the titles, she was a fast, voracious reader and could consume a lot of the material in a short amount of time.

"None, really. Like I said, I glanced at some. Who has time to read that old, outdated stuff?"

I wanted to gauge her mood. Her father remained her hero, mentor and one of the most inspiring people in her life, but mom and I had witnessed his personal demons at play. I looked at her again, but her mind had drifted away from our conversation and me. She was staring out the window at the cars on the freeway.

I swallowed my concern that day, but a couple decades later Sloane would immerse herself in Eddy's historical books.

In 1972, Sloane turned fourteen. She had grown to be a slender, five-foot, seven-inch beauty. She wore her thick auburn hair loose and messy and let it fall over her shoulders. She was blossoming physically, her gangling, angular limbs now strong and tan, her once-androgynous silhouette now curvy. Her gawky gait transformed into a confident strut.

An engrossing charisma supplanted her low-key demeanor. By her junior year, she was chatty with everybody. Unlike most of her peers, she was capable of expressing her rapid-fire thoughts clearly. Teens in every corner of campus found it difficult to articulate and communicate their thoughts and emotions, but not Sloane. Words sluiced from her mouth at breakneck speed. She splashed in a joke or two, along with a sweet laugh just to be even more engaging. Boys and girls all found themselves drawn to her.

My own friends told me she was gorgeous and was probably the hottest freshman in the school. I said I did not care for their unsolicited opinions and told them to shut up. Before long, my mother was pestering me about Sloane, too. She prodded me to talk with her about the virtues and advantages of being a demure young lady — of which I could think of few at the time.

"Why me?" I asked.

"You're her older brother. You're in college. She respects you. She trusts you more than anybody, and definitely more than me. I just want her to act her age and try not to show off around those upperclassmen who have their eyes on her."

"I have my own life, Mom, and she has hers."

Our two lives intersected one night in her sophomore year. I was the cool college-age guy showing up at a high school kegger, feeling mature and special, respected like a celebrity. It was the first time I saw Sloane drinking.

"Looks like your sister knows her way around senior parties," one of my friends said after spotting her. We were standing by the kegs.

"She doesn't look like a sophomore, that's for sure," my other friend noted.

"Shut up and fill up my cup," I said.

"Does Sloane party a lot?"

"Yeah, didn't your mom tell you to keep an eye on her?"

"As long she keeps her grades up, it doesn't matter," I said.

I came home earlier than Sloane that night but was asleep before I saw her. When I started paying more attention, I realized she regularly snuck into the house after being out, usually around dawn. Late-night adventures became the norm for Sloane, even on school nights, but Mom did not find out for a long time.

Mom was right. I should look after my sister, since she wasn't. I should probably step up and say something. But first I needed a plan first. I did not want to impinge on Sloane's fun because nobody ever did that to me. And I didn't want to drive a wedge between us. So when the time came, I simply suggested that she tell me where she was going at night, who she was hanging out with and when she honestly thought she might be home.

"That way, you know, it will just be better. You can call me if you get in trouble or need a ride. No questions asked. I can better manage our parents this way."

I don't know how she avoided bumping into mom after her all-night revelries. When Sloane entered the house in the early morning hours, she was not quiet. I usually heard her walking around in the kitchen, unsuccessfully trying to be noiseless. Often, it sounded like she was running and jumping upstairs. Mom never heard a thing. I typically ignored the racket and fell back to sleep.

One morning as I was waking up, I heard Sloane screaming, like that time when she was seven or eight years old. I ran up the stairs. Outside Sloane's bedroom, I could hear Mom's radio playing in her room down the hall.

I opened Sloane's door, stepped inside and shut it behind me.

"Sloane? Are you OK?"

"It was just a nightmare, Shane."

"Why are you still dressed from last night?"

"Who gives a shit, Shane?"

"Do you need anything?"

"Go away."

On my way out, I found Mom standing in the hallway wearing a white tennis skirt and top.

"Was that a scream I heard?"

"Yes."

"Was it Sloane?"

"Yes. A bad dream is all."

"Is she OK?"

"Yes."

Mom thought about going in to check on her daughter, but she did not want to miss her tennis reservation at the club. She kissed me goodbye, shot downstairs, grabbed her tennis tote and car keys, and was gone.

I don't blame Mom for focusing on her own life and personal activities after the divorce. She was still young, fit and rich. Her behavior seemed normal and healthy. A time came, however, when I wondered if she were blind to — or ignoring — little signs of trouble regarding her daughter.

Sloane was navigating a complex landscape of female adolescence just like any other young teenage girl out there. She was trying to fit in with her peers, worrying a bit too much over body image, asserting her independence. She craved friendship and high social status. I believed it was better than the alternative: withdrawing from the world.

Sloane's eating habits troubled me more than anything else did. Her diet appeared to consist solely of Diet Pepsi, beer and coffee. I noticed that she was losing weight. As her older sibling, I asked her several times a week if I could buy her lunch just to make sure she was eating healthy once in a while.

It was not the worst thing in the world for a single mom to be preoccupied with herself and not notice obvious changes in her teen daughter. Such obliviousness had resulted in household harmony for us. I say this because sparks flew in our house like a surge from an electrical overload on the day Mom decided to take on Sloane's developing sense of identity — the entire tangled mix of her moods, style and struggles.

Sloane walked right into the fire in the wee hours of the morning when Mom, unable to sleep, arose early from bed. She was sipping coffee at the kitchen table when Sloane tiptoed in. I awoke up to their loud arguing and lay in bed wondering what had taken so long for this clash of wills to happen.

I sneaked upstairs from my basement quarters to the dining room to furtively watch the fireworks. Mom was standing in front of the sink with her arms crossed tightly against her chest. The window above her revealed dawn's arrival. Sloane's back was to me as she defiantly stood by the breakfast table. They must have circled each other once or twice before I arrived.

"I will not put up with you staying out all night," Mom said, struggling not to yell. "I did so for too long with your father, and look what happened."

"Who cares?" Sloane shot back with indignation, tossing her beautiful hair over her shoulder. "You really don't care, do you?"

"I gave you a curfew, because I love you, and I expect you to keep it."

"Midnight is too early of a curfew, mom. Nobody comes home at midnight. I can decide for myself."

"No, you can't."

"Why not?"

"Because you might get a reputation as being a..."

"Really? A what?"

"A slut."

"You're one to talk."

Amazingly, Mom kept her composure with that clapback.

"Nothing good can come of staying out all night, sweetheart."

"Don't sweetheart me. You don't trust me. You know, not everybody is doing bad things out there. Me and my friends — we just hang out. That's all. I can take care of myself, so don't treat me like a baby. I'm not in junior high anymore!"

"It's dangerous, Sloane. The world isn't what it used to be. What if you get in trouble and need help?"

"Need your help? Now? Now you're concerned? Now you want to be there for me? You kicked dad out of the house, so guess what: You have to deal with my shit alone. You're stuck with me. You have to cope with who

I am all by yourself. I'm not sure you can handle it."

"Leave your father out of this. Even if he were here, he wouldn't give a damn about what you are doing. So either way, you were always going to be my responsibility. He was always out drinking somewhere, every night, just like you — oh, yes, I can smell alcohol on you — or he was passed out on the couch or on his office floor. I've handled everything by myself for a very long time."

"Don't worry. You don't have to burden yourself anymore. I can make my own choices. You see, you'll never understand, mom. You've never been independent enough to understand. You always needed a man to define who you are. You always needed a husband to support you."

"I'm pretty damn independent now, aren't I?"

"Yeah! It's easy now. Dad pays for everything. And while we're on the subject, why did you divorce dad? I've heard people talking. If you want me to follow your rules, tell me how we got into this situation in the first place. What broke up your marriage?"

"We just grew apart," Mom said, quieter now, her voice trembling. "And I don't want you and I to grow apart."

"Too late!"

I wanted to hear nothing more so I tip-toed back to my room. I know Sloane's words stung my Mom, and every time she had to lie to Sloane about why she kicked Eddy out of the house, another sharp pain stabbed her deep in her heart.

No truce was coming for Sloane and Mom anytime soon. It never came. There was just an uneasy mother trying to do the best she could for her daughter; and there was an uninhibited child trying to shape her own identity and experience new, wonderful, unbridled freedom, while the forces of biology and society pulled her in different directions.

Any chance of peace was shattered the day Mom finally noticed that Sloane was hardly eating and losing too much weight, and handled it all wrong. Against my advice and her better judgment, Mom tried to solve the problem by shaming her daughter.

"Sweetheart, I see you're hardly eating anything lately. What's wrong with you?"

"I'm not your sweetheart. I'm not five. And I said I was fine."

"You're wasting away. I just want you to feel strong and be happy. But all you do is push me away."

"Maybe I'm tired of your constant nagging — like Dad was. That's why he left, isn't it? Well, I'm tired of it, too."

"That's enough, Sloane! Don't you dare bring your father into this! You have no idea what that man put me through. I just care about your health."

"And the way your daughter looks so you can brag about me to your friends."

"I only care about how you're feeling inside, sweetheart."

"Don't!"

"Prom is coming up. Don't you want to look and feel good? That dress we bought you is going to slip right off your bones. What will your date think?"

"He'll love it. Less work for him in the end."

"Sloane!"

"Why are you obsessing over me, Mom? Why do you care? You can go to hell for all I care!"

"I'm not trying to obsess. I love you, and I'm concerned. You sound like a spoiled brat who can't handle a little scrutiny or take advice without growling and gnashing your teeth."

"A brat?" Sloane howled. "Keep calling me that and I'll lose what little respect I have for you as a mom. Just leave me alone. I swear to God, Dad's lucky he doesn't have to deal with you anymore!"

I don't know what drove Mom to say such hurtful words when I know she didn't mean them or intend to say them with such spite. She must have been masking her pain.

All I know is that I needed to leave after that cruel exchange, escape the air in the house, thick with poison. I grabbed my coat, slammed the door, got in my car and drove away from the war zone.

As I cruised around without a destination, I realized Sloane lived in binary worlds. On one hand, there was the tense environment at home, where the air was always thick with simmering frustrations and lingering anger; and on the other, there was this wonderful life with friends, the warm embrace of easy conversations, silly jokes and shared youthful experiences in a social setting. When Sloane was away from home and her mother, she felt the icy friction of their strained interactions evaporate, as ephemeral as mist, and she simply reverted back to a typical adolescence. In eleventh grade, though, Sloane no longer could balance the scales of her duality. The milieu was not built to last, and a breaking point was inevitable. Either her friends or her mother would have to take the fall.

There always was that third ingredient tossed into their relationship — Eddy. Even if he was not physically present, E.S. contributed to the flavor and balance of our family life. Sloane held Mom accountable for the family's breakup, even though years later she confided to me that she deserved just as much blame as Mom.

The flash point was near.

"I'm done with you," Mom yelled at Sloane one day. "It's like your father is living here again. The drinking. The yelling. Vanishing for days. If you can't abide by my rules — go live with that overindulgent man you love so much. Let's see how he does raising you alone. I can't take this behavior. You aren't welcome here any more."

Mom picked up the phone and started dialing.

"Are you calling Dad?"

"Yes. He can come get you. So go upstairs and pack your bags."

"You'll regret destroying the last scraps of our family, Mom. You cast Dad off, then you rip me away from Shane. This is all your fault, and you can't even see that."

Mom hung up the phone before Eddy answered. She was unable to send her only daughter away to live with an alcoholic philanderer — for the time being. One day, however, she didn't end the call and carried through with her threat.

I was absent from that scene, but it must have been brutal. The actual tipping point for Mom came after I left. Where was I? I was gone. I had moved out of the basement and left the house and the entire city. I took up life as an impecunious ski bum working at a Lake Tahoe resort. I was 21, armed with a useless associate's degree from junior college and possessed little patience for continuing my formal education. I decided to educate horizontally, not vertically. What else was I going to do? I was having a blast, but I heard all about what led to Mom's terminal decision.

She got a call from the school's vice principal regarding an altercation between Sloane and another student on a bus during a school-sponsored event. The high school sponsored snow trips up every weekend that were open to the entire student body. Sloane was a member of the ski club, but she joined the recreational weekend ski group, too.

Sloane's infectious spirit usually made the two-hour bus trip to Squaw Valley go by a lot faster for everybody aboard. Her stories could absorb an entire busload of passengers in a quick minute. Then she was hopping from one small chattering confab to the other. Sloane was either standing in the aisle or sitting on somebody's lap, but she never remained in her own seat.

If you are prone to rambling at a blistering pace, as my sister was, truth sometimes becomes a casualty. Tales grow taller from row to row, seat to seat. Nine out of ten times, people laughed off her cock-and-bull stories. On this fateful day, a student named Jim Bollinger reached the limits of his endurance for Sloane's whirlwind energy, nonstop animation and loud laughing that pealed like a bell.

Jim was trying to finish math homework that was due the following Monday, and his semester grade depended on it. He would have preferred to be socializing with his classmates, but there was no wiggle room for him in this class. Unfortunately, he could not drown out Sloane's incessant chatter. Her voice suffocated his every thought.

He might have shut his trigonometry book and given in to the social overtone, except Sloane happened to have snubbed him the previous week when he asked to hang out with her at the football game and go to the post-game dance together. He had not gotten over the affront, but Sloane seemed to have forgotten the slight and Jim altogether. Her exuberance grated on him like a rusty hinge on a gate blown by a wind.

"...and, after that," Sloane recounted, "he took my pencil without asking and flung it at the ceiling and it got stuck up there with all the rest of the pencils. Mr. Henderson turned around right at that moment, and he ended up in detention instead of me!"

The bus erupted in laughter. Everybody anticipated more.

"But wait!" she continued loudly. "I started thinking, 'Now he's all alone in the vice principal's office and I'm stuck here in class.' That's not fair! So I walk right up to Mr. Henderson and confess that I was the one who flung all the other pencils up there, you know, just so I could get sent to the office, too. But he didn't believe me. So I see a pencil lying on his desk and I grab it and fling it up to the ceiling right in front of him. He loses his cookies and sends me right out. So I get to the office, and I see Johnny. We're both sitting there — and that's when I ask Johnny to go to the prom with me! The vice principal walks out of his office, and we're kissing, totally making out!"

The ski bus was in hysterics. Jim Bollinger grimaced. Sloane kept talking.

"We're forbidden to go to the prom now, but we're going to go out that night and meet up with you guys at the parties!"

Jim's jaw clenched. She prattled on.

His frustration finally bubbled over, and he slammed his book closed and stood up.

"How about giving it a rest, Sloane," he said, meeting her sparkling eyes dead on. "Just shut your mouth for once, huh?"

"Oh come on. You're not serious. It's a field trip, Jim. We're supposed to be having fun. What are you doing up there, homework? Or are you, you know?" Sloane closed her fist loosely and moved it up and down rapidly.

The kids laughed even harder than before. Jim, shaking his head, rose from his seat. He strode down the center aisle to the row of seats where Sloane was standing and pushed her forcefully against window of the bus. The back of her head hit the glass with a nasty thud. The other students gasped in surprise. They knew Sloane and collectively thought, "Now, she is going to kill him."

Sloane had gained back a lot of the weight she had lost before I left home. She was healthy. She was taller, too. And she was as tenacious as always. Jim must have forgotten with whom he was dealing, as well as failing to remember that there are always negative consequences for pushing or hitting a girl. Ongoing hostilities toward her mother fueled Sloane's retaliation and aroused a raw fury in her. She flew at Jim, lowering her shoulder into his flank and driving him all the way into the seats across the aisle. She jumped on top of him and reached back with her fist and slugged him twice, then three more times with her other fist before the adult chaperones on the bus rushed in to break up the fight.

Neither Sloane nor Jim were allowed to ski that day, or do anything else but sit in the lodge under supervision. It was complete torture for somebody as full of beans as Sloane. It got worse. When the ski trip organizers searched her backpack, they found a half pint of whiskey, a bota bag full of wine and weed inside a plastic bag. They reported that violation of conduct to the school, and the vice principal told Mom. I never heard the details of the row Sloane and Mom got into when Sloane returned home that evening, but it must have been a full-blown brawl.

Sloane called me a few weeks later to tell me she had "broken the camel's back one too many times." Mom finally made good on her threat of booting her out of the house and forcing her to move in with her father. By the time Sloane called me, I had already heard the news from Mom and from Eddy, but I was glad to hear her voice and noticed her mood was very upbeat.

Why wouldn't she be cheerful? She had her very own horse stabled at Eddy's and was taking private riding lessons there. She said she still hung out with her old friends from the neighborhood, but she was getting along with the kids at her new school, too. I told her she ought to stay with me on weekends during the winter season. She liked that idea.

At the end of our conversation, I asked if she had spoken to Mom since being kicked out of the house.

"No."

"Maybe you should call her. You know, just to say hi."

"Mom deserves nothing from me," Sloane hissed bitterly and hung up. "She ruined our family."

CHAPTER 7

Sloane accepted my offer. She visited Lake Tahoe several times at the beginning of her senior year to ski with me. Sometimes her cousin Ignacio hit the slopes with us, offering us tips to make us better skiers. He outfitted Sloane and me in brand new gear from his ski shop, and we swooshed down the mountain in our stylish attire. After we came off the mountain, he typically treated us to dinner and a hot tub soaking at his eight thousand-square-foot lakeside chalet. Ignacio always complimented my skiing ability, but he sang Sloane's praises to no end.

"Sloane, you have this extra quality that I've only seen in the top professional skiers," he said in his Argentinean accent. "It's like, I don't know, you and your skis become one with the snow, one with the mountain, with the moguls."

After January, I did not speak with Sloane for five months. In June, I saw her briefly at her high school graduation and the following weekend at various parties and celebrations.

Since then, she had traveled widely. Sloane and her father took a business trip to New Zealand in April to visit a land tract of two hundred-thousand acres of old-growth timber that Port Seattle Timber Company had recently acquired. The company's business associates in the Southern

Hemisphere insisted that Edward Stevens make the trip in honor of his father, whom they had admired so much over the years. Eddy agreed after making sure his cousin Conrad would not be joining them. As a major shareholder, E.S. led the contingent of Port Seattle executives, bringing Sloane along as a fellow stakeholder.

The North American delegation inspected vast tracts of New Zealand forest land worth millions of dollars on the company books. The group evaluated the health of the trees to determine their market value and identified where logging operations should take place. They surveyed new roads to extract timber and transport it to mills and shipyards. Sloane especially liked sitting in on the talks about land acquisition, tax benefit opportunities and future market decisions.

She recounted the trip in detail, from the food and drinks she consumed to the people and customs she observed. She told me about scuba diving and snorkeling and described the manta rays, sunfish and other interesting sea life she had seen up close. Her tales of safaris where she had seen large parrots, striking blue-and-green birds called takahe and a reptile known as tuatara were nothing short of bizarre.

After an hour of recounting the journey to the Southern Hemisphere, Sloane switched gears and caught me off guard with her next great plan. She was moving to Lake Tahoe in the fall to train for a spot on the U.S. women's ski team. Disbelief washed over me.

"When I got back from New Zealand, Ignacio called. He's going to train me and introduce me to the coaches of the men's and women's teams."

"How did this all come about? What motivated you to do this?"

"He just asked me if I wanted to do it, and I said sure. Ignacio says moguls are the newest trend in racing. They're the most exciting new free-style race to come around in a long time, he said. Popularity is skyrocketing, and he said my approach to skiing fits the event perfectly."

"Really?" I asked. "And when do you start?"

"In the fall. And don't worry about making room for me at your little place up there. I've found a room to rent in this big house. There's something like ten or twelve bedrooms. One big kitchen. It's communal living, but everyone living there is a like-minded athlete. Some are skiers, some are marathoners, some like to climb mountains. And with you — my big brother — living right down the road, if there is anything I need, you'll be there for me. It's perfect!"

In my mind, it seemed far from perfect. To have any shot at making the national ski team, she needed to be focused, rested and fit. Living with a dozen people in one house did not seem conducive to those goals. At the same time, Ignacio was mentoring her, so she would be under the eye of someone she trusted and held in high regard. She would listen to him. Her aspiration and doggedness to secure a place on the team might curtail her tendency to party. Maybe Ignacio would get her to eat more nutritionally. Still, that was a big house full of people and temptations.

"I'm not sure you're going to get the sleep you need to be sharp the next day," I argued. "You're one hundred percent sure you want to do this? You're entirely ready for this? It's going to be by far the hardest thing you've ever tried to do."

"It's my dream, Shane. I've never been more excited in my life. I'm bursting at the seams. It's the only thing I want in the entire world. I'm not interested in college right now, or starting a career. And it's not like I can stay in Sacramento, either"

"Why not?"

"Didn't you hear? Mom put the house up for sale. There's already a sign out front. And Dad is either buried up to his neck at the office or working nonstop on getting Grandpa's property up in Foresthill ready to be his main residence. The timing couldn't be better. I feel good about this all around."

Sloane told me two of her friends from high school agreed to come to Tahoe with her, and that raised more alarms with me. All of her friends that I knew liked to indulge in long nights of unrestrained revelry. They surrendered to the intoxicating allure of excess without a fight. They were hedonists.

"Sloane, do you think that's a good idea? What will they do while you're training and preparing to make the team twenty-four hours a day, seven days a week? The last thing you need is more people crammed inside that house distracting you. I don't care how big the property is."

"We'll be fine," she said, her tone clearly dismissing my apprehension. "Besides, you know one of the girls."

"Who?"

"Heather McClellan."

Hearing that name, I stopped thinking about the pros and cons of her decision. Warning signs stopped flashing, and I no longer cared what was good or bad for Sloane. This was great for me. I had had a crush on Heather McClellan ever since she walked into my basement room with Sloane years before. Sure, she was four years younger than me, but I didn't care then and I didn't care now.

Sloane did not tell her father or mother where she was staying, or with whom, or any of the circumstances. I am certain Ignacio talked to them, but it was possible Mom and Eddy were too busy to care about the details. He probably withheld some specifics anyway, to keep from jeopardizing his chance to train his hot new skiing prospect. Regardless of the level of disclosure, Ignacio's distinguished stature and maturity allowed Mom and Eddy to believe their baby girl was in good hands.

I talked to Sloane the night before she left to start her new life on the mountain. She harbored no doubts about what was required for her to earn a place on the U.S. ski team. Eddy gave her more assurance, sliding an American Express card into her hand and telling her if she ever ran into difficulties that required money then she should not hesitate to use the card.

"Will Heather drive up with you tomorrow?" I asked her.

"Shane, you horndog!" she teased. "I'm going to tell her you are inquiring about her."

It turned out that I did not see Sloane or Heather for the first few months after they had settled into the house on a hill off Olympic Valley Road. My summer job had turned into a full-time gig. I had transitioned from being a carefree chair lift attendant to a more serious person working for the Tahoe Regional Planning Agency in a job that asked more of me.

One of my assignments at the agency was to visit rest stops and gas stations along the highway and ask travelers to complete a questionnaire. We covered territory from Applegate to Reno, Meyers to Markleeville. We wanted to know where folks were from and where they were going, and what was their final destination. We asked them how long they were staying, which services and facilities they planned to use, how often they came to Lake Tahoe and several other questions.

One afternoon, a female co-worker and I decided to take a more scenic lunch break than usual and stretch our legs. The winter air was fresh and invigorating, and the sun was out, so we grabbed our bag lunches and walked up a gentle hill off Interstate 80 to where we could see a panorama of snowy mountains and valleys.

Near the top of the hill, we heard a dog whimpering. The mewling came from the other side of the ridge. We crept forward so we would not disturb the animal. We peered over the rise and saw a single puppy shivering in the snow below. We figured it had been left behind by the rest of the pack. Dozens of paw prints of different sizes led into the dense woods below, but only one dog from the litter had been left stranded, forgotten and alone.

"She's a wolf dog," I said to my co-worker, taking off my coat and wrapping the pup in its warmth. "See, she looks like German shepherd and wolf combined."

"How do you know?" my co-worker asked.

"My stepfather was into dog breeds. A wolf-dog hybrid has large pointy ears like this, not floppy ones. And look at the shape of the eyes, and the tail is not curved. Maybe they were turned loose on the side of the road because the owner couldn't handle them."

"What are you going to do with it?"

"She's probably going to be a pretty social little thing," I said. "I think I'll give it to my sister. She loves dogs and misses her old one. She lives in a house with a bunch people who can watch her and play with her."

"She needs a name."

"I have the perfect name: Zara."

After driving to Sloane's commodious ski house that evening in my four-wheel drive pickup to drop off Zara, my life got busy. I could not pass up free ski tickets, so I went back to operating the lifts, working two jobs. I did not see Sloane or Heather for a few weeks. When I finally visited, there were so many cars on the street that I had to park my four-wheel drive up on a snowbank to avoid a half-mile walk to the house.

Zara bounded to the front door to greet me with unrestrained joy. Her expressive blue eyes and happy bark momentarily distracted me from Heather, who had opened the door. That is how adorable the dog was. An unleashed bundle of energy, Zara darted in between our legs and around and through us and as we walked into the great room. A lively fire was burning in the large floor-to-ceiling stone fireplace. The room was crowded, wall to wall, with young people. I was not expecting such a large gathering.

"Aren't you skiing early tomorrow?" I asked Sloane.

"Of course. I ski every day."

"Who are all these people? Where'd you meet them?"

She knew some of their names.

"That's Mark over there — he was hitchhiking with some people along 89 a few days ago and didn't have anywhere to stay so I offered up the couch. Jenny and Billy, we met them in the ski shop. They're going back home tomorrow or the next day, or maybe never. That's how carefree they are. That guy over there, we call him Snake, but his real name is Jake. He lived two doors down but just got kicked out of his place, so he's flopping here until something comes up."

Jake was a handsome guy with flowing locks of blond hair who was apparently warm enough in front of the fire to have his shirt off. I glanced at Heather; I never expected competition. She caught my eye, but misinterpreted my playful concern.

"I just live here," she said, raising her arms in mock exasperation at the crush of people and the continual party atmosphere of the place. "Don't ask me who anybody is."

"Can we talk?" I asked Sloane.

"No, Shane, we can't talk, because I know what you're going to say. Just relax. Grab a beer if you want, and shut up if you're going to judge people."

"I just know this is your dream. You said making the ski team means everything to you..."

"Yeah, my dream, not yours. You're not living my life. If you want to know how it's going with me, don't come here and pass judgment. Wake up at four in the morning and head to the mountain with me, and then tell me if you have any concerns about not keeping my eyes on the prize."

"I will, God damn it. When?"

"How about tomorrow?"

"Great."

It was not great. I was incredibly tired the next morning. But I showed up at the base of Squaw Valley before dawn. The darkness hid the mountain's steep cliffs, slick chutes and cavernous bowls lurking above me. Gloved and enveloped in a down-filled parka, I followed Sloane to the gym for her warmup, a workout with weights and flexibility training with a coach. Back at the slope, I strapped on my skis and mounted the lift with her and Ignacio. We were out on the runs before any other soul, so I could see how my little sister was doing.

When I ski, I hit the bumps sixty to seventy percent of the time. When not working or sleeping, I am usually on the mountain. I ski damn well and very fast. But the first day I headed out early with Sloane and Ignacio, her mentor and our cousin, I was unprepared for just how much better and faster a competitive-level skier can be. I learned how much I did not know about mogul skiing techniques.

I joined their private coaching sessions two or three times a week. Under Ignacio's tutelage, Sloane's progress and advancing skill utterly astonished me.

"The best mogul skiers get their weight over the new downhill ski very quickly," Ignacio said as we caught our breath halfway down a run.

The rising sun peeked over the ridge.

"Got it, got it," Sloane responded.

"This allows you to initiate the turns efficiently. Let's try it."

He skied a short distance down the hill to better observe her technique.

"Quicker on the transfer!" he shouted.

I skittered down after Sloane's turn but received no advice from the master.

"Let's go again," Ignacio barked, and they tore down the remaining section of mountain paying no heed to me.

Next time I snuck in a hurried run ahead of Sloane. Ignacio waited impatiently for me to finish and shouted for my sister to "Go!"

Sloane shot down the line.

"Too late on the downhill ski," he said under his breath.

Sloane hit one, two, three more moguls before her feet were gone from under her. She crashed and rolled past us. Self-reproach consumed her, and she flung her poles down the mountainside.

Ignacio and I traversed over to her. She was covered in powder.

"I can't go any faster or this shit happens!" she cursed. "Look at me! I thought I was a goddamned good skier."

"Listen," Ignacio said. "Back in my Olympic days, I was skiing pretty well, hitting top-three finishes, a first place here and there, but I didn't have full mastery of the moguls. So I started working with this German coach, and he told me to do the same thing we're going to go do now. We're heading into the lodge to watch film of the best mogul skiers. I have some good reels ready to play for you. Let's go in and watch."

"Inside? I need to be out here, cousin. I'm only going to get better if I'm on skis, you know, skiing!"

"Call me coach, damn it!" Ignacio corrected her harshly. "And listen up. Everyone has a different style. Jack Taylor is compact, controlled. Bob Salerno, loose, high and fast. Wayne Wong — flamboyant. Kathy Kearney has precision and grace. Guess what? You have your own style, too. But one thing they all did in common: They stacked themselves over their downhill ski and when they went to make the new turn they quickly got their weight to the new downhill ski, in a split second."

He turned his skis across the fall line and stepped sideways up the hill to demonstrate.

"Watch. The great ones go from here to here extremely fast," he said, demonstrating the maneuver in slow motion. "The idea is you want to get your ski on the back side of the bump. You want to have purchase on the inside edge of the downhill ski. Otherwise, you're riding the ski all the way and don't start making the turn, don't start putting pressure on the downhill stick, until you're fully in the rut. And if you miss this part of the mogul, and you land here, your skis shoot out. And you know what that feels like? Of course you do. It just happened to you. You made three turns and — bam — you blew out."

Sloane's lessons kicked into overdrive after that day.

Another time as I watched, Ignacio told my sister that she needed to master matching the angle of the mogul.

"Bend the tip of the inside ski into the ground as you go over the back," he explained. "It will force you to fall down the backside and initiate the turn. Go! Go! Pull your heel towards your butt over the bump!"

With Ignacio's attention bearing down on Sloane, I got lost and could not keep up. The deeper the moguls got, the faster she whipped down them, and the more intense Ignacio's shouted instructions got.

"Heel back! Tip in the ground! Heel to your butt! Heel to your butt! Force it! Force yourself to fall down on the backside!"

The tutorials bounced from pole planting ("Cock your wrist! Float the basket out!"); to edges ("Don't lift that tip!"); to body position ("Fall down! Fall down the backside!"); to initiating turns ("Are you feeling it in the hamstrings?").

One evening after I had stopped joining the pair for the early morning sessions, Sloane came home from training and flopped down onto the sofa in the family room of her giant chalet. Heather and I were cuddling in the love seat. I had tried to thin out the crowd at Sloane's house. Mark the hitchhiker was back on the road. Jenny and Billy from the ski shop took off. Jake the Snake left, too, but came back a few weeks later when his new accommodations fell through.

The legitimate paying residents had dwindled to five. Heather and I mostly cared for the wolf-dog Zara on a daily basis when Sloane was skiing. We fed her in the evening, walked her in the afternoon. But when Sloane walked through that front door, Zara loved nobody more than her. She slept in her bed and followed her everywhere from the moment she got up.

"Are you OK?" I asked Sloane as Heather straightened up and scooted over in the love seat.

"I race Thursday."

"As in a competition? With other skiers?"

"Yes. For team points. They need to know where we rank in the world. It begins now, brother. Air, speed, turns. Air, speed, turns."

"This calls for a celebration," I said, and jumped up to grab a bottle of champagne we stored in the fridge in anticipation of New Year's Eve. "Or maybe you need to take it easy?"

I was standing with the refrigerator open, gripping the champagne bottle's neck and waiting for her answer.

"It's a day off tomorrow," Sloane shouted back. "Bring some glasses."

We saluted Sloane's great fortune and hard work. She told us that she would be traveling with the team for the next month or so, maybe even to Europe. The conversation quickly trailed off. Sloane gazed off into space. Heather and I looked at one another, puzzled.

"I'm so physically exhausted, so fatigued," she softly chanted. "So physically exhausted. I'm going to bed."

Just like that, she and Zara were gone, and Heather and I were left with a nearly full bottle of bubbly.

Heather called me the next day to tell me Sloane had hardly stirred in her bed. She did not want to talk or eat. She demanded her bedroom door stay closed and the lights out. I was busy and could not check on her, but promised I would come by as soon as I could.

On Monday, Sloane still had not left her room. Heather called me early and told me Sloane missed her early workout with the team. I called Ignacio, apologized on behalf of my sister, and then drove to her house. She needed to be on the team bus to get to the Colorado ski championship by Wednesday for practice runs.

Sloane missed the bus. I knew she did, because I drove to the loading zone to make sure she was with the team. I had given Ignacio my word she would be there.

"She's just not feeling well, but we'll get here there. We'll fly. Eddy and I will make sure she's there."

If Ignacio had not been family, Sloane's dream might have crashed down around her then and there. He covered for her. He vouched for her. And it was ready to pay off for both of them.

Eddy requisitioned one of the planes of Gold Wings Airlines and flew the three of us and all of Sloane's ski equipment to Colorado the next day. She was lively again, talkative, and showed no signs of illness or fatigue.

For Sloane, Ignacio, the women's ski team and Eddy, the next three months proved exhilarating. It was a revolutionary time for freestyle skiing. Its popularity elevated just as the Freestyle World Cup circuit began to take shape.

Eddy told Sloane he was happy for the first time since his marriage blew up four years before. He never had been so joyful and proud of his cherished little treasure. Sloane was his gift from heaven, his sun, moon and stars illuminating everything in and around him. He felt like he was going to explode from jubilation.

Sloane displayed mastery of the bumps. She ascended the rankings, beginning with her breakthrough winning performance in Colorado and a second victory notched in New Hampshire. Beyond gaining wide notice, her style of precise turns and physical prowess was not only noticed but was setting the standard. She was caught in a head-spinning ascension in the realm of competitive mogul skiing, showing the finesse of an artist at the peak of her craft. Physically, she was a marvel of strength and endurance. Skiers admired her not just for racking up consecutive top-three finishes but also for the elegance and grit she brought to the new women's sport.

And that's how the 1976 ski season ended.

Sloane and I spent the summer in Lake Tahoe. I tried to call or stop by her house every day to make sure she was staying disciplined, but also happy, in the offseason.

"Shane, damn it. I'm OK. This is my calling. This is my dream. My career. I'm not going to fuck it up. Relax."

She spent the spring focused mostly on recovery. Her emphasis was making sure her muscles and joints were healthy after winter's extreme physical demands. In the summer, Sloane hiked and cycled to keep up her conditioning. The team regularly trained at the Squaw Valley gym. But Ignacio recognized the importance of balancing intense training and competition with purely fun activities and downtime.

I have a picture in front of me right now as I write. There are five women sunbathing on towels on a large wooden deck overlooking Olympic Valley. The pair in the foreground are reclining and propped on their elbows. They are smiling widely at the camera. The second one is Sloane. A girl in the middle is supine and absorbed in her book. The other two in the background are lying on their stomachs and looking back at the photographer with big easygoing grins. They are robust, youthful, tan, happy. That's how I will always picture Sloane during that summer and fall at Squaw Valley before winter arrived.

At the U.S. Ski Team's first orientation of the season, Ignacio strongly advised Sloane that she should move into the comfortable and newly built dorms at Squaw Valley, so she could live, mingle and share camaraderie with her teammates. But the idea sent shock waves of panic through her, and she refused his suggestion without saying exactly why.

She disclosed to me that she could not explain her resistance to moving into the dorms; she just knew how she felt. She was content with where she was. She started the ski season where she had left off: in top form. She was skiing too damn well for any of the coaches to push her to do anything she did not want to do.

Through December and January, she emerged as one of the top five female mogul racers in the world. Experts and analysts talked about her boundless potential and what lay ahead. All eyes were upon her in Lake Placid in late February.

Sloane took a deep breath at the top of the mogul run and the crisp mountain air filled her lungs. The sun flooded the snow below in sparkling light. She was poised at the starting gate, gloved hands lightly squeezing and releasing her poles. Brain focused, muscles activated, heart throbbing, soul calm, sounds fading into the background. The fellow competitor next to her stopped existing in her world, in this intense zone of hers. The white waves of evenly spaced moguls down her fall line looked like clouds in heaven. She identified the flat spots. It was all committed to memory.

Her descent began, and the landscape became a constant shifting blur of moguls rising and falling in her vision. Snow sprayed. Skis carved. Her legs moved powerfully in unison like pistons. Shush. Shush. Thump. Shush. Shush. Thump. Limbs flexed, extended. Her muscles burned.

Midway down the line, Sloane knew it was all over. She knew it by the faintest whisper in her head. She knew it in a microsecond.

Her weight shifted too far inward and the mountain snatched her ski. Grace detonated into chaos. Snow and sky turned over and over and blurred together. Solid terrain disintegrated into a bumpy sea of rolling white.

When Sloane's body finally came to a rest, the white-hot pain in her knee was the worst agony she had ever felt.

Eddy tried to coax her into returning to Sacramento. The suggestion sent her into a rage. She cursed him until he was left dumbfounded over why his angel was behaving so violently toward him. She threw chairs and tossed lamps and flung books around the ski house as her roommates took cover. She screamed obscenities at them.

The team found an orthopedist who gave her pain pills, and forbade her to drink alcohol until a clinical examination and X-ray imaging revealed the extent of her injury.

Heather remained at Sloane's place, but was not a great help or a very positive influence. A haywire party atmosphere enveloped the grand home like never before. Sloane was supposed to rest, ice her knee, elevate it and stay off her feet as much as possible. Instead, she hobbled around with a drink in one hand, crutches in the other. She never slept. Friends with friends came by, unexpected guests never left, and new and old connections streamed in and vanished without a word.

I did not visit her for two weeks after the day she arrived home following the accident. I feared what I might witness from what Heather told me. When I finally went to see for myself, the filthy disorder of the house shocked me. Heather decided it was time for her to flee. I did not dissuade her.

The orthopedic surgeon's interpretation of the injury came in, and we all held our breath, even though we knew the findings would be bad. The anterior cruciate ligament in Sloane's knee was compromised, probably torn. Nobody had the guts to tell my sister that her ski career most likely was over, her dream unraveled on the cold hush of a mountain.

Things for Sloane got worse. One morning, her wolf dog Zara escaped from the house unnoticed and a pickup truck ran her over. A neighbor who knew where Zara lived wrapped her bloody corpse in a blanket and left the remains on the porch step. The neighbor later told me that she tried knocking on the door, but nobody answered, even though she heard loud music and people shouting inside.

The next morning, with everyone else conked out from alcohol, Sloane walked Heather to the door to say good-bye and stumbled upon poor, beautiful Zara. Sloane immediately fell into despondency. Heather stayed and called me to tell me what happened. She said my sister had not left her bed for days since discovering the dog's fate.

"She'll snap out of it," I told her unsympathetically.

"Shane! Don't be mean."

"I'm sorry. But I think I've had enough of Tahoe."

"If I'm still here, you have to stay, too!"

"Fair enough."

Two days later, Heather called again. It was early evening.

"She's gone," she said.

"What do you mean, she's gone?"

"Sloane's missing. The front door was left wide open. Her crutches aren't here."

"Jesus, Heather, it's snowing hard out there. Are you sure she's not somewhere in the house, or that somebody picked her up in a car?"

"She's gone off the rail, Shane, completely off kilter. This injury has really fucked her up. She thought this was going to be her career. This was her Olympic dream. She's not that far out of high school and thinks this injury is the end of the world. Booze and that hyper-jet personality of hers are not a good mix."

"I thought she was practically comatose in bed?"

"Well, now she's not, Shane. She got up, started drinking, and now she's missing."

"OK, let me think. Did you check the snow for any footprints?"

"Not yet."

"Well, shit. Go look for her footprints and tell me what you find, where they lead to."

Heather returned to the phone.

"Prints in the snow lead out to the street, then they disappear."

"Fuck. I'm coming over. Stay there."

We decided to drive slowly along the snow-covered roads, down one, up another. Visibility was poor. In the glow of the headlights, snow flurries tossed about in the biting wind. After twenty minutes of driving over white streets in the steady snowfall, we found what looked like footprints next to small but deep holes along the roadside about a half mile from their house.

We bustled out of the car to look closer. The tracks led up and over a hill to a thicket of evergreen trees. At the top of a hillock, we saw snowy prints and those indentations, probably from her crutches, but no Sloane. We called out and looked all around the area. Finally, we went home feeling melancholic and fatigued.

The police called the house an hour after we got back.

"Good evening, this is Officer Kelly. I'm calling about Sloane Stevens. She's fine. But we picked her up earlier this evening for public intoxication. She was hitchhiking and wandering into traffic and acting crazy. We felt she was a danger to herself and others, and the way she reacted when we found her... well, let's just say she fled from us and ended up in a neighbor's yard. We brought her in for her safety, and so she could sober up. She's calmed down now and seems to be in decent shape, so we want to release her to a responsible party."

"This is her brother. Is she being charged with a crime?" I asked.

"No, that's not what this is about. Like I said, we didn't want her causing any trouble while being intoxicated in public. Several officers know Sloane pretty well. We wanted to do what's best for her. As her brother, can you come down to the station and take her home?"

I hung up and told Heather what the officer said.

"She's no more of an alcoholic than any of us," Heather said, "but when she drinks, she's like Doctor Jekyll and Mister Hyde."

I drove to the station alone. An officer ushered my subdued sister into the lobby after I had signed some paperwork. I told Sloane to sit still and wait for me while I used the restroom. When I came out of the men's room, nobody was in the lobby, not even a clerk at the desk. Sloane had bolted back into the snowstorm.

I headed out into the frigid night air and got back into my truck to search for my sister again. I found her a half mile down the road, hitchhiking — in the opposite direction of the house.

The next day, more bad news slapped Sloane in the face. The devastating blow came in the form of a final diagnosis of an ACL tear. The team doctor gave Sloane his recommendation for treatment and suggested a pain management plan. He prescribed direct repair of the torn ligament by opening the knee and suturing the tear. He explained that long-term results might be unsatisfactory even for an athlete of her stature. Sloane spiraled into a storm of despair and trashed the doctor's office. She knocked from the walls down pictures, framed diplomas and certificates and shredded the paper covering the exam table.

I could not stay with Sloane around the clock and neither could Heather, who ultimately gave up on managing the mayhem swirling around her friend and got the hell out of Lake Tahoe. I had skipped a lot of work to deal with Sloane's escapades, but when I returned to my job every scrap of motivation was gone. I went straight into my supervisor's office and quit. The charm of Lake Tahoe had faded. My patience had waned. I could find no enthusiasm for staying. I needed a break so I severed my Tahoe ties and returned to Sacramento. It was time to get on the ball by enrolling in college.

Despite my enduring promises to Sloane, I wasn't there the next time she melted down.

She was drinking heavily at a casino in South Lake Tahoe and blacked out. The cops picked her up along scenic Highway 50 near Harrah's after they responded to calls about an irate female throwing rocks into windows at several businesses.

This time, Eddy had to drive up and bail his princess out of jail.

CHAPTER 8

At Eddy's quiet horse property in the foothill countryside, Sloane's motor stopped racing. Her big mood swings became fewer and milder. The unrestrained peaks of elation and plunging valleys of gloom flattened out. She experienced short periods of sadness when recalling the exhilaration of her competitive skiing days, but that was when she mounted her horse and took long, invigorating rides through the countryside.

In the evenings, she and her father held gentle conversations during which he encouraged her to explore possible next steps in her life might be. Their talks sometimes circled back to what Eddy had been doing at her age. She thought undertaking some type of business venture sounded exciting.

His stories about the heady days of rowing at the University of Washington especially intrigued her, and they began paddling their kayaks on Sugar Pine Reservoir a couple days every week. They shared memories of about their achievements when each of them were dominating athletes in their sports, about building strength and endurance, and of the thrill competing at the highest levels brought them.

"That's when I feel my best, my happiest, and most content," Sloane revealed to her father one day when kayaking on the lake.

"Of course, you do," Eddy agreed. He extracted a cigarette from the old military surplus bag that he liked to bring along and lit it.

"Really, Dad?" Sloane laughed. "We're out on a beautiful lake, talking about achieving great physical health, and you light up a cigarette?"

"For me, those days are over. But for you, I was thinking that maybe you should look into studying sports medicine, kinesiology or something."

"I like the sound of that."

She took her father's advice and signed on for a summer internship in the sports medicine department at Sierra College in the nearby town of Rocklin. Both the junior college's football team and the professional San Francisco 49ers squad held training camps there in July.

Excitement buzzed around the campus and little town when the Niners showed up and took over the practice fields. Family Day alone drew nine thousand fans to the facility. Sloane even got a chance to meet a couple of the NFL players while she went about her apprenticeship.

When the drills stopped, the grunts and whistles fell silent and field maintenance crews turned their attention to repairing the worn-out grass on the practice fields, Sloane went back to long horseback rides and conversations with her father about the past, present and future.

As they reminisced one day about idyllic family trips to Hawaii back when Sloane and I were kids, talk veered onto the topic of Sloane continuing her education. Discussion followed about her possibly attending the University of Hawaii on the island of Oahu. They explored how perfect that setting would be to allow Sloane to stay fit, partaking in her new favorite pastime of rowing, and to dive into the study of kinesiology.

Eddy retrieved her high school transcripts and SAT scores from a file in his garage. Her GPA was 3.9 and her combined standardized test score was 1450. The marks almost guaranteed that the university would accept her if she applied.

E.S. loved the idea in every way, especially how getting Sloane to Hawaii and back would be a breeze and how visiting the island himself would be convenient for him. He was enraptured when the college accepted her. They talked about living situations. Sloane said she was averse to living in a dormitory or sharing an apartment or house with anybody else after the lodging chaos in Lake Tahoe. Eddy called real estate agents he knew, as well as the Eddison family. They found a vacant condominium in an oceanside apartment building owned by the Eddisons that was only four miles from the university. Eddy gladly offered to pay the kingsized rent for his queenly daughter.

When Sloane moved to Hawaii in 1978, at age twenty-one, she struck a statuesque figure. Her chestnut hair tumbled down her back like a roaring chestnut waterfall. Rowing had sculpted her arms, back, legs and shoulders.

Before she boarded the passenger ship for the voyage — a free excursion except for taxes and gratuities on food and services — to her next land of opportunity, she begged me to go with her.

"You can find a job there, Shane," she encouraged. "Or transfer to the University of Hawaii with me. You need to finish your degree anyway."

"I'm almost finished at Sac State, Sloane. Why would I do that?"

"For me! Do it for me!"

I promised her that I would think about it, and at the very least hop over to Hawaii during my break. She came home to the mainland for a short holiday in 1979, but my first visit to see her in Oahu happened in 1980.

Sloane felt like she could conquer the world — and she looked the part. Her condo was spectacular. The moment I walked through the nine-foot tall, white front door to her penthouse, I stopped in disbelief. I floated across the living room and stood in front of the wall of glass that over-looked the vast azure ocean. The shimmering sandy coastline stretched for as far as I could see out the window to my left and right. Dramatic, thick clouds skittered toward me from the direction of Kaalawai Beach. I dropped my bags at my feet and walked, as if on air, out to the breezy, humid lanai and stood awed by the towering Kuilei Cliffs to my left. Sloane's penthouse merged earth, ocean and sky in sublime harmony. I did not think I would ever leave.

"And you live here alone?" I asked feebly, as if that was all that could be uttered about this home. "How do you get anything done?"

One of those dramatic gray clouds suddenly seemed to have covered her face. I did not know how my questions could have saddened my sister, but they obviously did.

"I... I just can't tolerate people right now," she said, the warm breeze on the balcony whipping strands of her reddish-brown hair. "I mean, I can't tolerate anyone living with me, always being around. I'm fine when I'm at school or the gym or out on the ocean on the outriggers, or on the beach. But in this space... I don't need anybody upsetting my apple cart. Hell, I can't put my finger on it — you know what I mean, Shane?"

Tears flooded her eyes. I rushed over to hold her and searched for something to say that would be uplifting.

"Come on now, that's fine. Perfectly fine. I know exactly what you mean. Let's just grab a couple beers and enjoy this view. I mean, you enjoy it all the time, so it's probably no big deal — but let me take it in for a while!"

We talked about her schooling, and we talked about her outrigger canoeing. We talked about what she did on her days off and about her impressive physical fitness routines.

"It's very lively and diverse down on Waikiki Beach," she said. "The energy, the vibe, the whole fitness culture around here, on the beach or in the gyms, is awesome. I've been working on bodybuilding with some of the best in the business."

"I can tell."

"Look."

She flexed her bicep. The tight knob was impressive.

"I hope you find time to just be mellow, too," I laughed.

"Absolutely. I mean the outriggers are great exercise, but more than that they give me a sense of belonging and connection here."

"A connection to what, exactly?" I asked, feeling as if I could reach out and touch the thick verdant canopy of the Diamond Head mountains. The dense foliage appeared to press up against us.

"A connection to the water, the community, local tradition, the Kama'āina," she said.

"Did you declare a major yet? Is it business, like your father, and his father and so on? Like all of the Stevenses?"

"Marketing."

"Oh. Cool. Why?"

"It fits my plan. If I stay with bodybuilding, I can market my own business as a certified athletic trainer, and the contests, my whole career. It's a versatile discipline. If I want to go in another direction and, say, become involved in the family business, that works, too."

"You would never go work for your uncle, would you?"

"Probably not. But I enjoyed the business trip I took with Dad to New Zealand. That part of the job was cool."

"I can't see it."

"Why not?" she challenged, but returned to the topic that really warmed her heart. "I mean, I guess not, because I really like the people I've met in the fitness world, and I like the way pumping iron makes me feel."

On Sloane's insistence, I returned to Hawaii in the summer of 1982 to see her. She was now on target to graduate the following year, on the dean's list with a GPA of 3.9. That was no surprise.

By then, her goal was to become a recognized figure in bodybuilding and fitness training and was making impressive progress. She wore bright-colored bikini tops and cutoff shorts everywhere, around her house, in town, and pretty much all the time. She was more fit and well defined than ever before, so I could see why.

She was dating many young men — local outrigger paddlers, police officers and professional body builders. Our family had Portuguese roots, and many of Sloane's new friends and classmates hailed from families who had immigrated from the Azores and Madeira islands to work on sugarcane plantations in Hawaii. She became particularly close to a tight-knit group of Portuguese police officers who worked out at her gym. The relationship with them turned benefited her. I found out later she had had a few scrapes with the law — public drunkenness, vandalism, fights, a shoplifting incident — that her cop connections straightened out before formal charges came down and, more importantly, ahead of Eddy finding out. Ironically, the relationship with law enforcement resembled the one enjoyed by her father.

By flourishing in the world of professional bodybuilding and fitness training, Sloane developed deep connections with various accomplished athletes and a few celebrities, especially ones notable for their physical fitness and rugged handsomeness. She was invited to VIP parties hosted by these superstars of the big screen and playing fields. She was given sideline tickets to the NFL Pro Bowl, and introduced to NFL quarterbacks and wide receivers and large linemen. In February, she lost herself in the vibrant pageantry of the weeklong all-star extravaganza.

"My career is so ready to take off, Shane," she told me excitedly. "You have to come with me to the gym tomorrow, and I'll show you what I mean."

So I did.

Gold's Gym in Waikiki buzzed with a vibrant energy, hubbub and rhythmic motion. The interior was dimly lit and tightly packed. Beautiful bodies pulsated, grunts emanated, sweat glistened, veins bulged. Sloane, wearing a red Lycra leotard and white Adidas running shoes, walked me through the gym.

"So that's it," she said when we finished the short tour. "Let's get a sweat going."

She left my side quickly to immerse herself in the free weights along the back wall. I stood by the Nautilus machines but mostly just watched the scene. Sloane repeatedly came over to introduce people to me.

She asked one of her pals if he had seen "Lamont" at the gym today.

"He hasn't left the island yet, has he?" she probed.

"No. I think he's here for one or two more days before flying back to L.A. He's probably working out down at the beach. Why?"

"I just need to talk to him before he goes back to the mainland. Let's go find him, Shane."

The beach near the gym was a lively, fun, communal atmosphere. Against a backdrop of golden sand and clear blue water, large, diverse crowds — equal numbers of locals and tourists — engaged in aerobics classes and rhythmic dancing. Loud reggae music blared from boom boxes. Tan, robust people shimmied in colorful swimsuits.

Sloane scanned each face seeking this Lamont guy. When she spotted him, she gave out a quick, high-pitched scream and waved her hands to get his attention. I could not tell who specifically she was looking for among the hordes. But when this one chiseled young, handsome man with long black hair looked up and recognized her I almost fell over in disbelief.

I seized her arm above the elbow to stop her from running over to him.

"Wait! Is that Lamont Stone?" I asked. "The action film star?"

"That's right, silly brother. Try to act normal."

We walked over to him. They did not embrace, but shook hands. We stepped out of the center of the throngs to talk more privately. Sloane never formally introduced me to Lamont Stone, so I stood there surprised and listened in with growing astonishment.

"God, I'm glad you haven't left the island yet," she told Lamont. "I need to give you my portfolio. You told me to get it to you, remember."

"Of course. It's OK, though. I'll give you my agent's address. Send your talent portfolio and comp card there."

"No, no, it's ready now. I'm going to run home and get it."

"Come on, Sloane, relax. I told you, I'm not going to abandon you. You can send me the portfolio."

"But it's ready. I'm getting it."

"Just so you know, there's no rush. Ideas for the movie are being brainstormed, and there's not even a script yet."

"But I want my name to get out there."

Lamont laughed, and I stood more dumbfounded than ever. Music and people swirled around us.

"I understand that," Lamont chuckled as if placating a child. "The development stage can take a lot of time, though."

I broke in. "What film are you guys talking about?"

Lamont looked at me as if I had just dropped down to earth from a spaceship.

"It's a Marvel comic book movie based on the character She-Ra," my sister informed me.

"Oh, yeah, I see it now," I said excitedly. "Tall, flowing red hair..."

"Well, there's a lot to do to get to the next level," Lamont said, cutting me off before I got too aroused. Then he uttered in anguish, "Oh, shit."

My face grew hot and red from my uneasiness. I thought I had made a gaffe until I realized Lamont had noticed someone approaching our little confab. I turned and recognized Klaus Wagner. I instantly put two and two together and remembered reading in the Variety magazine at Sloane's apartment that these two Macho Men did not like each other at all. They were lionhearted rivals — and their paths were about to cross in front of me.

Wagner nodded to Sloane and greeted her by name before turning to face Stone.

"Why aren't you in L.A., Lamont?" Wagner asked. "I thought you might be pouring through scripts in search of something that might rival my last movie. The one you turned down."

The tension turned concrete, and I made it worse by exclaiming "Earthquake King!"

That was the name of the latest Wagner film.

"I saw it!" I blurted out. "You were great."

Wagner smiled. Stone rolled his eyes. Sloane shot me a venomous look.

"It broke box office records," Wagner said.

Sloane gazed at me with eyes wide in a tempest of panic, as if her big chance for a Hollywood career was going down in flames, and I was largely responsible for it. I took a step back, not understanding what was happening.

"If I do pore through scripts, they won't be recycled plots like *Earthquake King*," Stone quipped. "Even if our young friend here liked it."

"What are you working on?" Wagner asked scornfully. "I haven't heard your name mentioned in certain circles lately."

"When I find something that piques my interest, Klaus, at least I'll be brave enough to do my own stunt work."

"I intended to do the stunts, but my agent wrote it out of my contract. He said I'm getting to be too big of a star to risk..."

"We should wager. Let's see who can pull off the bigger stunt in their next film! We'll get a movie critic to judge."

"We're leaving," Sloane interrupted, turning to Lamont. "I'll send my resume and visuals to your agent. You two enjoy your pissing contest."

Her parting smile was intoxicating. Both men laughed.

When we got home, Sloane poured herself a straight vodka and, to my surprise, cut three lines of cocaine on her glass dining room table and hoovered them up. She did not bother to ask me if I wanted a drink, a snort or anything else, partly because she never stopped yelling at me for being such a "rube" and embarrassing myself and being so starstruck that I was unable to hold a conversation with famous people. I was dumbstruck at both her actions and words.

That evening, she left the house alone without saying a word to me, slamming the front door on her way out. She did not return for three days.

I had plane tickets for a flight home the next day when she walked into the penthouse apartment at ten in the morning with an air of nonchalance as if she had just gone for a stroll around the block. She struck up a conversation with casual grace. We did not talk about what happened at the beach, or where she had been for the past seventy-two hours, what she had done, whether she was safe or in trouble, or how rude it was for her to suddenly leave me like that.

"I've got to show you something," she said excitedly in the middle of making a pot of coffee. In high spirits, eyes crackling, she rushed downstairs to show me a shiny, new black convertible Fiat 124 Spider parked in her reserved spot.

"I bought it and drove it all over the island, Shane," she said, laughing playfully. "I met a boy on the north shore and we hung out. You have to meet him. He's a big guy. He's from a Polynesian canoe family who's been on the island for a very long time."

"I'm leaving tomorrow, you know?"

The news seemed to hit her like a jolt. She didn't offer an explanation or apology for her behavior, but insisted that I should come back in January to visit her.

"I'll take you to the Pro Bowl! Promise me!"

"I don't know, Sloane, we'll see."

"You have to promise. Promise to God, Shane. Say you will, right now."

"The last thing you want is me tagging along with your celebrity friends to Pro Bowl parties."

"I do. Promise me you'll visit in January! When I moved here, you said you'd come see me regularly. Don't you remember? Don't you understand? You must."

"OK, I promise on a couple of conditions."

"Always the big brother. What are they?"

"One, you have to come home over the holidays and see Mom..."

"I can't, Shane," she blurted out in distress.

"Why not? She deserves to see her daughter more often."

"But I broke up our family. Not you. Not Dad. Not Mom. It was all my fault. I caused a lot of trouble. I can't face her right now."

"No, it wasn't your fault. Believe me."

"You're wrong. I drove them apart."

"Sloane, they were completely incompatible. They get along better now that they're separated than ever before."

"How do you know? Do you spend any time with either of them?"

"I see Eddy for short periods. I've worked on that. And Mom? Yes, I visit her regularly."

"How do you know they're on good terms now?"

"I wouldn't say good terms, but they've bumped into each other while working for Reagan's presidential campaign. They told me they've hung out a bit at rallies and at campaign headquarters in Sacramento."

"It's almost intolerable to do so, but OK, I promise I'll fly home to see her — if you keep your word to come back in January."

"I have another stipulation. Next time I'm here..."

"In January, Shane! The next time you're here is in January. Mark your calendar"

"But I'm going to book a place of my own to stay, just to give you a little space."

"Fine. It's a deal, then."

Sloane called my hotel room not even an hour after I landed in late January at Honolulu International Airport.

"We're coming to pick you up in the limo," she said.

"Who? When?"

"Joe, Dwight, Jesse, me."

"As in..."

"Yes. Montana, Clarke and Sapolu."

"The five of us?"

"And probably a couple other women. Dates, I think."

"Uh-huh. OK. Where are we going?"

"Tom Selleck's birthday party."

I laughed incredulously.

"Tom Selleck's birthday party? The actor? Come on Sloane!"

"No, really. Be in the lobby at five o'clock. Don't be late."

I knew Sloane was charismatic, confident, pretty and fit as a mare, but her plans to hang out with A-list celebrities and highly regarded athletes blindsided me nevertheless. Fate had aligned harmoniously for her. She moves to Hawaii to study sports medicine and she's soon training alongside bodybuilders and action film stars. She settles down in Oahu and the NFL decides to permanently change the Pro Bowl game venue to Aloha Stadium. Now she travels in the orbit of superstars.

I dipped my head into the darkened limousine, with white ambient lighting, still expecting this all to be a joke. But there they were, the elite of the NFL's elite, Super Bowl champions and MVPs. Their physical stature dwarfed me even though I'm six-foot-two. They exuded the confidence and swagger of five-star generals, but they did not have to say a word or do a thing for their matchless beauty and superior achievements to fill the air. Even the three stunningly radiant women next to them in the car, including Sloane, possessed unwavering self-assurance. The stretch limo could seat fifteen people, but still did not seem big enough.

"Oh, shit," one of the players exclaimed as soon as I sat down. "You're right, Sloane. He is a dead ringer for Tom."

This doppelgänger stuff has happened to me before, especially since my growing a substantial mustache. I have a mirror, so I know I look a little bit like the actor, but it did not seem that obvious to me. Still, in the company of these ruggedly handsome blokes I was happy to play along.

"Here's what we'll do!" Joe said with a wide grin, calling the play as usual. "We shield Tom, this Tom here, just a little bit as we walk in and get him into a place where the light is a dimmer, like the corner of the living room, and then we'll try to make everybody believe he's the real Tom Selleck. Let's see how long we can pull it off."

Everybody fell into hysterics. I smiled but didn't find it that funny. Still, I was on board if that was what they wanted to do.

"Sounds like a Hail Mary," I wisecracked. Everybody laughed again, and I felt pretty good about it.

Sloane passed the champagne bottle to me, and the night started.

"But how are we going to keep the two Toms away from each other?" asked one of the girlfriends or wives or whoever the enchantresses were.

"Tom Selleck is not going to be there," Joe said.

"He's missing his own birthday party?" Dwight asked.

"Yeah, he's filming *High Road to China*."

"I thought *Magnum P.I.* is shot here in Hawaii," I said.

"Just don't mention *Indiana Jones*," Sloane said.

I didn't get the joke, but everybody else laughed.

"He doesn't regret that one bit," one of the other women informed us.

"Anyway," Joe continued. "He's involved in both productions. They had to shoot a couple scenes for *High Road* in mainland China, and he missed his flight to get back here in time for his birthday. But he called and said he didn't want to cancel the party and that everybody should go to his house anyway and have fun and celebrate on his behalf."

"What a guy," Dwight said.

"I mean the party was all set to go, so why not?"

"To not have the real Tom Selleck there makes it easier to pull off the prank," Jesse said. Everybody laughed.

"It will be perfect," Joe concluded.

We drove down Oahu's rugged southern coast. Black Point rose before us like a fortress of luxury, waves crashing on the black lava rocks at the base of the prominent knoll. Somebody rolled down the window and asked if others thought the air smelled like salt.

"Salt *and* money!" Dwight said.

He was not wrong.

In the twilight behind us, the lights of Honolulu twinkled in the distance. Ahead lay a topography of darkened rock, from the island's fiery birth, and whispering palm fronds. Heading down a narrow road past a private gate, the black limousine wound past several charming bungalows until we reached Selleck's oceanfront house.

"Savage beauty," somebody shouted as we climbed out of the stretch, and I assumed it was a reference to the ocean or maybe to a line from a Tom Selleck movie.

We entered the white, country manor-style house via a lush courtyard with palm trees swaying above us.

Our little ruse worked right away on several people — if only for a second or two. Some party guests were fooled for several minutes. We quickly grew tired of our silly ploy and abandoned the trick.

After that, Sloane talked to Jesse for a long time. I tried to engage with them but felt like a shadow next to their vibrant connection and soon drifted away and tried to mingle with other guests.

Two hours later, I wanted to check in with Sloane and see how much longer she planned to stay. I had not seen her since the beginning of the night when she and Jesse were chatting. I got the feeling she and her athlete friends were going to stick around for a while longer. At one point, the party grew very crowded and the house soon sweltered. Even out by the pool and on the balcony, the number of revelers swelled. Soon, men, women, singles and couples, were jumping into the pool. I watched them dunk and splash each other and dive into the water until I needed some space. I slipped out of the property's side gate onto the sidewalk that led to the beach.

I was walking along the access road when I heard a car approaching from behind me. The man and woman in the car were carrying on gaily. I knew it was a convertible before I even turned to look. I did not expect to see a new black Fiat Spider.

Jesse was driving, and Sloane was in the passenger seat. They stopped alongside me. The champagne I drank in the limo and the mai tais I consumed at the party must have been toying with my mind because the man with Sloane definitely had broad shoulders, a powerful torso and rich mahogany skin that appeared burnished by the Polynesian sun. But the driver was not Jesse Sapolu. I did not recognize this hulking figure stuffed into my sister's sports car was at all.

"Shane, this is my boyfriend, Tui Alano," Sloane sang out.

I didn't care who he was; I couldn't believe they were going to leave me at the party. If they hadn't seen me walking, they were gone.

"Where are you going?" I asked my sister.

"To another party."

"And another one after that!" Tui imparted to me.

"Were you going to tell me, Sloane?"

"I couldn't find you."

"How am I supposed to get home?"

"The limousine, obviously."

"Or hop on the back and come with," Tui said, laughing.

"Screw you," I said, suddenly in a bad mood, but I don't think Tui heard me.

"I'll come by your hotel room tomorrow," Sloane shouted as the Fiat sped down the street with Tui at the wheel.

I did not see Sloane the next day or the day after that. She called two days later to tell me to meet her at the gate of Aloha Stadium for the Pro Bowl game, but she was not there when I arrived. I was not troubled by thoughts of her safety because I knew Sloane too well.

The next time I saw her was when she visited the mainland. Mom showed me a letter she had written before flying home. In it, she mentioned she was dating a boy, but did not reveal his name. I assumed it was Tui.

I always have found that when Sloane talked about liking a guy, the relationship unquestionably fizzled in three or four months. She stayed on the hunt, but never prevailed in the long run. I naturally expected the worst.

Nevertheless, her tone was upbeat:

Well, by now you should know how happy I am. I can't wait to see you. I've missed you so much. I never really did appreciate you and Dad til now. I love you more than you know.
— Forever yours, Sloane

When she arrived, she was excited about the future and talked incessantly about her plans after graduating in a year. She appeared to be at peace with herself, and with others.

"Do you know what goal I'm going to pursue when I start my fitness training career after graduation?" she asked me one day while we were lounging in my apartment.

Words failed me. It could be anything, really.

"I'm going to be the first female athletic trainer for the 49ers."

"Don't you need more training for that?"

"Yes. I'm graduating with a business degree, but to get on the sideline, I'll need to strengthen my resume. I'll enroll at San Diego State for a bachelor's in kinesiology, then head up to Venice Beach to train with Stone and Wagner — separately, since they still can't stand each other — for the She-Ra role. This will get me in the best shape of my life, keep me connected with famous people, and give me a deep understanding of anatomy, physiology, exercise prescriptions and knowledge of rehabilitation. What do you think?"

"It's a fabulous plan," I said — and it was.

But the road to success was never easy with Sloane.

⚓

I got the heart-thumping phone call around 2 a.m. Pacific Time.

I jumped out of bed in the dark of night, and by noon I had landed in Hawaii.

During her two-month visit to see us in California, Sloane let Tui Alano use her Fiat and her penthouse. When she returned to Hawaii, the condo was a mess — trash strewn about, walls smudged, floors scuffed, furniture askew, fixtures broken — and her new car gone. Calls to her boyfriend went unanswered.

Tui lived somewhere on the North Shore on a property behind a gate with four or five homes and a bunch of cousins living there. During their relationship, Sloane had never visited, nor did she know the address.

My sister never took disrespectful treatment of her and her belongings in stride. This insult was worse than a slap to her face, more than a punch in the gut. After two weeks of silence from Tui and no sighting of her car, the affront ate at her brain like a parasitic roundworm.

She had recourse. As I witnessed first-hand, Sloane was blessed with many friends on the island. Most were strong, muscular men who would do anything for her, but she would never think of asking them to clean up her mess or do something she would not or could not do herself.

She was not, however, averse to calling in a favor from her Portuguese friends in the Honolulu Police Department. It was a start. They quickly zeroed in on the address of her ex-boyfriend.

The muscle men and police officers on her side offered to help as much as she wanted, but when she declined their assistance they warned her against going halfway across the island alone to settle a score against a big native boy with a large family.

In the 1980s, the North Shore of Oahu was rugged, undeveloped and distinctly local. Sloane rented a Jeep and revved onto the scenic Kamehameha Highway. She wound along the coastline, rehearsing in her head how she would retrieve her car and give the one-time flame a piece of her mind. The narratives playing out in her head made her blind to the charming towns, sweeping mountain and valley views, lush cropland and pristine beaches she sped past.

A map, held down in the passenger seat by her beach bag, flapped in the wind. Taped to the map were hand-written directions telling her when to exit the main road and what natural landmarks to look for to help her find the Alano property. After an hour's drive, she pulled up to a gate and parked. Riotous tropical vegetation concealed any view of an estate beyond the fence.

The gate and fence were wrought iron, but she easily circumvented the barrier by getting out of the Jeep and slipping under a rail. On the other side of the gate, the driveway was long and lined with palm trees. Verdant ferns, fruit trees, flowers, shrubs and creeping groundcover grew dense on both sides of the dirt road.

After fifty yards, the countryside opened up and she saw a plantation-style main residence elevated on posts. A wide lanai and overhanging eaves wrapped around the structure. There were at least two other houses behind it. A couple of hammocks were strung between trees in front, and laundry was drying on a clothesline. Sloane later remembered the atmosphere as secluded and peaceful, a faint scent of plumeria hanging in the air and the consistent crashing of ocean waves in the distance. I'm surprised she remembered anything.

My sister walked up three broad steps to the main house and a powerfully elegant woman — even bigger than Tui — opened the front door and stepped out. Another adult female, similar in size, followed her onto the porch.

They stood only five foot, four inches on powerfully built legs, but were broad-shouldered and a little shy of two hundred pounds. Sloane froze two steps below.

"You have some nerve, *haole*. Nobody invited you onto our land," the first woman said. "You are trespassing."

"Did you see the gate?" said the second one. "Or are you blind and stupid?"

"The gate is there for a reason," the first woman pointed out, "so why don't you turn around right now and leave — before we grab you and throw you off our property?

"Yes. Go back to where you came from, haole."

"Oh, I see," Sloane said with composure. "Tui is being protected by girls. Are you his sisters? Yeah? Well, go back inside and tell him not to be a pussy and that I need to talk to him. Go! Now!"

Sloane ascended another step, and told the sisters, "Or, you can get out of the way, and I can go get him myself."

"Turn around now, haole, and don't say another word if you want to live to tell about this!"

"First, show me where my Fiat is. I won't stay another minute if you just show me where my car is parked. I won't even stay long enough to tell your brother or cousin or bitch dog — whoever the hell he is to you — that he's nothing more than a common asshole and a thief."

"I'm tossing you off this land headfirst," one of the sisters snarled.

Sloane walked down the steps, but felt the woman descending upon her. Sloane did not go toward the gate where she had parked, but headed in the opposite direction toward one of the other houses, deeper onto the Alano property.

"I'll look for the car myself," she declared.

The immense women stomped down the porch steps quickly and followed her. Sloane expected they would, and turned to confront them.

How Sloane got to the hospital after fighting those Herculean sisters, we will never know. A medical staff member believed somebody anonymously dropped her off like a damaged package, crumbled, broken and bruised on a bench outside, until a paramedic spotted her.

I still have the doctor's medical report specifying the injuries Sloane sustained in the brawl:

- Closed fracture of right radius, requiring surgical intervention and immobilization. X-rays confirm. Grade III concussion, headache and dizziness.
- Multiple lacerations to the face and scalp, largest of 5cm requiring sutures.
- Contusions and abrasions to the torso.
- CT scan shows no intracranial hemorrhage.

The doctor called for a treatment plan consisting of surgical reduction and internal fixation of right radial fracture, neurological monitoring of concussion symptoms, wound care and sutures for lacerations, and pain management and anti-inflammatory medication.

Sloane experienced short-term disability after the hospitalization, but the recovery period was estimated to be six to eight weeks and the prognosis for a full recovery was considered good with proper adherence to physical therapy.

I spent the next two weeks at her side, first at the hospital and then in her penthouse in front of the floor-to-ceiling windows overlooking the ocean. I never had heard Sloane say so few words over such a long period.

Her wounds were well on their way to healing, and her spirits had lifted some by the time I had to leave. My anxiety and unease for her physical and mental health obliged me to return a half dozen times over the remainder of the school year.

Over time, Sloane regained her impressive physique and retained her status among the academic elite at the university. When she graduated, she still graced the dean's list. Her heart and vision did not stray from the lofty goals of earning her kinesiology degree, auditioning for the She-Ra role and becoming the first female athletic trainer on the 49ers bench.

At this point in our lives, I lost regular contact with my sister simply because I was putting in serious hours and long weeks to make my commercial real estate business a success, but that summer Mom reestablished regular contact with her daughter. I was happy and content to hear she was calling Sloane at least twice a week. They often talked for hours at a time.

Sloane moved to San Diego and enrolled at San Diego State University to complete the prerequisite courses for her national fitness training certificate. She studied anatomy, physiology, biology, nutrition and all the other courses essential to her earning a kinesiology degree.

In her second semester there, she received a surprise phone call from Lamont Stone.

"Hey, it's the Honolulu Kid!" he exclaimed when she answered, using the nickname he had given her in Hawaii.

The call complicated matters and disrupted her immediate objectives, but Stone's plan appeared to dovetail with her own ultimate goals.

"Gold's Motion Pictures is going forward with the making of a live-action movie based on the *Masters of the Universe* character She-Ra," Lamont spelled out for her. "And I can't stop seeing you — with your strong, chiseled body and that mane of red hair — as the She-Ra character. You are She-Ra embodied in the flesh. Simply put, you're perfect. There's nobody else."

"What does this entail?" Sloane asked, flipping closed her anatomy textbook.

"You need to come down here to audition in front of the director, producers and casting executive. I'm going to get you bulked up for the part and put you on a strict diet."

"You really think I'm a perfect fit? In your words, how would you describe this character?"

"She-Ra is a powerful heroine fighting against evil hordes. In the *Masters of the Universe* franchise, she is a prominent character, the princess of power. She's the twin sister of He-Man."

"He-Man?" Sloane laughed. "Good God, Lamont!"

"I saw the producers' animated mark-up of *She-Ra*, and wait till you see it. You're a dead ringer for the role."

"Let me guess. Judging by your enthusiasm, I'd say you are backing this production with your money."

"Not just me, but Wagner is aboard."

"Excuse me? Get out of here! You're collaborating with Klaus Wagner?" Sloane asked skeptically.

"I know. Will miracles never cease? So what do you say?"

"This acting gig isn't part of my long-term career plan. I'm trying to get my kinesiology degree and national fitness training certificate."

"We talked about this in Honolulu. It most definitely should be part of the plan. It fits perfectly: bodybuilder, trainer, action-hero figure, spokeswoman for Gold's Gym. We can start building you a client list while you're down here. Klaus and I can give you referrals for your marketing. We'll get you the most elite clientele of any trainer around. Affluent people. Serious people. Famous people. They'll pay top money for your personalized program. Klause and I will give you recommendations."

"What about my degree?"

"UCLA extension offers the same thing as San Diego State. Let's get you enrolled right away."

"This is all happening very fast."

"You deserve it. I know you want it, and I know you can handle it."

"What do you want me to do?"

"An official invitation letter to audition will arrive in a couple days. Read it and make your final decision. Then, let me know."

After receiving Gold's Motion Pictures' invitation in the mail, Sloane agreed to the audition and wrote back to the company. She also called, just to make sure they would be expecting her. She finished her San Diego State courses and applied to UCLA.

In the meantime, communication with Stone and Gold's Gym slowed. She received no more phone calls and was sent just one general letter over the next six months. She was accepted into UCLA's extension program but might already have earned her national trainer's certificate by now had she kept on track in San Diego. Regardless, she didn't slow down and didn't look back.

Her energy was boundless. In addition to her studies, she started a month's training regimen so she could pass the rigorous physical test required of applicants to the Los Angeles Fire Department. Sloane passed the challenging upper-body strength tests, such as dragging a one hundred, sixty-five-pound dummy in full gear, and endurance trials. Then came written exams, agility assessments and interviews. She held her breath as the fire department took two weeks to conduct a background check. Finally, the chief called Sloane into his office to offer a job and congratulations, making her a trailblazer there, too, one of a small handful of female firefighters in the city. It was a Friday.

"There's just one more thing to get done," the chief said. "No big deal. But you need to cut off that big mane of red hair, per department policy."

"Oh, no. How short?"

"Women and men must have military-style, short haircuts for safety reasons," the chief answered, and when he saw her unenthusiastic response, he emphasized, "Sloane, the first woman we hired as a firefighter was in 1983. That was just a couple of years ago. We have a total of three women on staff. You're going to make history. You've blown right through our physical standards, no accommodations needed or offered."

"I need to talk to someone first, chief. I'm sorry. I'll just need a couple days."

"You can have until Monday."

That weekend, Stone called her frantically.

"You're getting your national certificate, right?" he asked.

"I've transferred to UCLA to finish."

"Fine. That's not what's important. Just wanted to check, because we need you to move to Venice Beach right away. I want you to keep up with the training service, but focus on the Los Angeles area. It will be part of the persona we are building. Keep growing that client list. In a few weeks, we can start getting you ready for auditions."

"I haven't heard anything about auditions."

"You will. Trust me. Listen, I know this is starting to move quickly. Just be ready. Get plenty of rest and keep working out and eating healthy. You'll be getting cut for the part. Klaus and I came up with a diet for you that aligns with the nutritional strategy bodybuilders implement to prepare for competition. You'll soon be more than the embodiment of She-Ra. You'll be the warrior -princess. How does that sound?"

"Fast and scary... but exciting."

"Is that a 'yes'?"

"Sure. Where should I look for a place?"

"Start with West Hollywood, because there's a gym, Matrix One in Beverly Hills, where you'll want to split your time with Gold's to get the most work in with clients. If you can't find something you like in West Hollywood, I can get you closer to Venice Beach. Do you need help with rent and down payment and all of that?"

"No, Lamont. I'm an heiress."

"I almost forgot," he laughed. "Soon to be an actress."

"Lamont, I need to ask you something."

"Sure, anything."

"I'm on the last leg of this journey to get on with the L.A. Fire Department. I like to challenge myself and want to keep all my options open, while making some good money myself."

"OK. And?"

"The department requires women to cut their hair as short as men, military style."

"No way! That's a deal breaker, Sloane. You know it. You are She-Ra, the embodiment of a superhero. You can't wear a wig on set and while you're out doing publicity events — what would people think? That auburn mane, those locks, they must stay if you want the part."

My sister was devastated. She liked the idea of being a feminist trail-blazer in all aspects of her life. But she grasped the truth, the Hollywood truth, and turned down the firefighter job.

Not long after she moved to West Hollywood, Sloane called me in Sacramento, excited again. She had launched Sloane's Training Service, and already had signed four big clients.

"My top-tier client list is growing every day," she told me.

She was particularly thrilled about signing up what she called her "best client ever," a woman who lived, worked and played among the glitterati of Los Angeles. Her name was Christie.

"What does she do for a living?" I asked.

"What does anybody do down here? People just seem to have money and want to spend it. I think she was married to a movie director, or some-thing, and is now dating somebody who plays for the Dodgers. She wants to get into bodybuilding and acting. It's important to her to stay in shape and look good. She's willing to pay a lot for it."

"Where are you living now?"

"That's the only thing in my life that I'm disappointed with. I'm going to be moving, though, because the place I'm renting, well, the physical condition of the apartment building is unacceptable. It's actually a nightmare. The front door doesn't close properly, the interior painting isn't finished, there are exterior lights that aren't working. And the tenants in apartment five have made living conditions intolerable. Two guys moved in and they play loud music and turn the TV up to full volume. They fight and use foul language. They're always slamming doors and crashing objects. I have to sleep on my sofa so I don't share a wall. The landlords are going to have to compensate me for reupholstering the sofa because of the wear and tear."

"That's terrible. Why did you move in?"

"I made a mistake. There isn't much choice in living accommodations down here. Besides, I've never really looked for a house or apartment by myself."

"How long has this noise and stuff been going on?"

"Months. I've tried to talk to the neighbors and was subjected to violent physical threats when I was only reasonably trying to correct the situation. Shane, I'm so incredibly stressed out by all of this."

"Did you tell management?"

"Of course. And we've called the police on several occasions. I'm talking to a lawyer about filing a lawsuit."

"Maybe you should move right away. Didn't you say Lamont Stone or Klaus Wagner could help?"

"I don't really want to ask them. And I'm too busy to look for another place right now, anyway. I pretty much come home, eat and try to fall asleep."

Despite the troubles with the neighbors and landlord, good news multiplied for Sloane. Three weeks later, she called and told me a date was set for her screen test. Lamont and Klaus were certain she would receive a callback, she gushed.

Sloane talked fast, and I listened joyfully to her account of the accomplishments. She described her new workout routine and the protein diet the action film stars had rolled out for her.

"What's the diet?" I asked, remembering when she experimented with different eating patterns back in high school.

"I eat like six or seven times a day. It's mostly egg whites, lentils and whey protein for muscle repair and growth. Very little fat. I'll slowly reduce my water intake, too, as the audition gets close."

"Are you sure that's healthy?"

"I've never looked so good or been so fit in my life, Shane"

"Is must be hard to maintain with all that's going on with you. How's school?"

"Great. And don't worry, I'm in good hands. You should come down and see for yourself. I've been talking to Mom every day, and she wants to visit."

"I'm proud of you, little sis. Are you staying away from the drugs, too? I know there's a lot of pressure in your sport and with the whole Hollywood lifestyle. I read about this new growth hormone, HGH, that's becoming more and more attractive to bodybuilders and athletes for achieving permanent muscle gains and increasing tendon and ligament strength."

"Christie was just asking me about that, too, because some guys down at the gym are pushing us to take synthetic drugs, but I told her to stay away from all anabolic steroids. We're building healthy bodies *and* self-respect. We don't want to destroy our chances. Weight training is dear to our hearts and has brought many of us through our darkest times. This isn't a multiple-choice answer for me — I'm opposed to all drugs, except marijuana. And when in athletic competition, I think all drugs including cannabis must be banned. I can go on and on about this subject because I have trained hard and want to compete. I'm hungry. Christie is hungry, too. But we're not insane enough to destroy our chances at having a healthy baby someday. We're women. We know how to endure pain. I'm a completely natural bodybuilder and will continue to be, no matter what the cost."

"Sounds like you're staying the course."

"I am. I'm studying physiology at UCLA, so I'm well versed in organic chemistry, Shane. Besides, those drugs are illegal. I told Christie that, if it comes down to it, I'll even testify in court on behalf of my fellow athletes, just to bring justice for all. I'll step on toes and make enemies, I don't care, because that's the passion I have for organic bodybuilding."

Sloane kept chattering.

"You might like to know, brother, that Heather lives close to me. With her, I have a safe space for expressing my thoughts. Somebody to uplift my spirits and validate my feelings. And when things get really bad with those asshole tenants next door, I can go stay with her. Why don't you drive down here with Mom? Maybe you can stay at Heather's."

"Very funny."

"Look, Mom calls me every day, but I need to see you guys. I need to see family. You're so far away. You could come for my She-Ra tryout."

"OK, I'll check with Mom and find a good time," I said.

But we didn't make it to Southern California to see Sloane — at least not then. The steady rhythm of her communication with Mom and me ceased. A spectral quiet replaced our warm exchanges.

"I'm worried, Shane," Mom said to me one day. "I've talked to her every day for the past year. If I left a message, she'd called me right back."

"How long has it been since you spoke to her?"

"More than a week, I think."

"Have you tried the gyms where she works?"

"Yes. They haven't seen her."

"I'll call Heather and see if she's seen or heard from Sloane in a while."

Heather said she had not. Normally, she also talked to my sister daily every day. She even dropped by once or twice a week.

"I admit I've been busy lately, but now that you mention it, yeah, this feels strange," Heather said. "Let me see.... I stopped by her apartment two, no three days ago, and nobody answered the door. I'll see if I can get a key to get inside and check on her there."

On Valentine's Day, Heather connected with the property manager, who let into the apartment. The scene inside made her feel like she had been punched in the gut. Every room was in a state of disarray. Clothes were strewn about the living room, haphazardly heaped on the back of the couch, the floor, even hanging off lamps. Notepad pages covered in writing littered the carpet and were scattered across furniture. Several random stacks of fitness books and magazines sat as barriers in the middle of the room.

Heather saw piles of unwashed dishes in the kitchen sink and encrusted food cartons on adjacent counters. On a wall, broken eggshells were stuck to hardened yellow and brown smears. The egg carton and plastic bag containing some kind of beans littered the floor below, apparently where they came to rest after being hurled across the room. Receipts for clothing and food supplements were scattered on coffee and end tables and all over the floor. Several fist-sized holes marred the walls.

One spot on the kitchen table seemed deliberately cleared off, a place to write. There, Heather saw a diary or journal opened to a page that was blank except for one line. The preceding pages of the notebook were filled with reports and commentary leading up to this single sentence, but the journal contained no entries on any pages afterward. This one brief line said:

"Feb. 14: From this day until death."

Across the table, Heather saw a yellow legal pad with words scribbled under a title: "Rough draft first will and testament." The handwritten document was dated Feb. 13.

Heather sat and collected her thoughts before calling me from the apartment.

"Shane, I'm so scared."

"Everything will be fine. Who is named in the will? Maybe she informed someone about it, somebody we haven't thought to call."

"Oh, Shane. It's you!"

Heather's details set the three of us on a frantic search. Mom and I immediately flew down to Los Angeles and stayed in Sloane's apartment while we began our hunt. We called all the hospitals and visited the LAPD and Los Angeles County Sheriff's Office. We telephoned Sloane's friends for whom we had numbers and sifted through the disorder of the apartment to find any receipts or bank statements that might offer clues. In the end, we uncovered no hints to her whereabouts. We could not find her. Nobody knew where she was. There was no paper trail.

The beloved child had disappeared.

"When do we tell Eddy?" I asked my mother a week or so after our search began.

"Now," she said, decisively but with apprehension.

Eddy bore the news with composure. He told us he knew a retired FBI agent working as a private detective for an agency in Beverly Hills. The former fed located Sloane within a half hour.

Eddy called us with quick news. Mom grabbed the phone in Sloane's now-tidied kitchen, and I picked up the receiver in her bedroom.

"She's in L.A. County jail," he told my mom.

"Where? Why? Since when?"

"She's been at the Sybil Brand Institute. I don't know exactly how or when she got there. The detective said officials there were acting a bit cagey, and it's unclear as to why she was taken into custody in the first place."

"We're going over there now," I announced.

"I'll fly down," Eddy said. "Hopefully, you'll have her out of there by the time I land."

Sybil Brand Institute is a four-story hulking mass of concrete, a monstrosity of brutalist architecture looming over a residential landscape. As Mom and I drove to the women's correctional facility, we tried not to speculate on how and why Sloane had ended up there. The parking lot and main entrance to the institute were bustling, and we knew we faced a significant wait before being helped. We were part of the system now. One hundred female inmates a day were processed here, but we only cared about one.

We filled out the blue property release forms and other paperwork and handed it back to the custody staff. Then, we waited.

After an hour-and-a-half, a female sergeant approached us with a gloomy look.

"I'm sorry, but I can't release her to you," the sergeant said. "She needs to get to the hospital right away."

"What? Can we at least go inside and see her?" I asked. "We haven't talked to her in two weeks."

"We need to know what's going on?" my mother beseeched.

"No, we are in the process of expediting her transfer. Staff is preparing to take her to UCLA Med Center now. You can go and await her arrival there. Do you know how to get there?"

The Medical center's reception area provided little comfort for waiting families, but we remained as patient as possible. Biding our time, Mom and I swallowed our multitude of questions about Sloane's health and welfare: Why was she being relocated now? what was the final destination? Who was in charge? How long was this nightmare going to last?

Mom was sitting with her back to the front door and windows. I sat across from her looking out at the hospital's circular driveway and porte-cochère where patients came and departed. We sat and waited for a long time until I saw an unmarked Econoline van with a long wheel base and blacked-out windows pull up and stop. I sensed that Sloane was inside the van.

"Mom," I said, trying to conceal my dismay and the gravity and urgency of what was taking place in front of me. "Why don't you go get us something to drink from the vending machine down the hall there? I'll wait here and make sure we don't miss Sloane's arrival."

Mom left on her errand and I bounded to the window to get a better look. The van's sliding door swung open, and a sheriff's deputy stepped out with a pump shotgun. He took four or five paces and turned around. Then Sloane stepped out, bound in leather handcuffs and wearing a thin, sleeveless hopsack dress. She was barefoot and wore no underwear. Deputies on each side held her arms.

Her typically beautiful, groomed hair was a grotesque mass of greasy, wet, uncombed and tangled locks. Remnants of past meals and tossed drinks made her tresses stick together in clumps. I saw cuts on her hands and bruises on her arms and legs. I teared up at seeing the cruel neglect and mockery of my sister and ran outside to get as close to her as possible.

I did not know what to say or how to act, but the guards felt no threat from me. They must have known I had been waiting to see her, in her miserable state. My sister stood just a few feet away, and I wanted to reach out and gently touch her arm, but I did not. I smiled weakly, barely able to conceal my inner turmoil. She stopped and blankly stared at me in a catatonic stupor.

With as much energy as she could muster, Sloane remarked rather blandly:

"Oh, it's Tom Selleck."

Then, deputies hastened her away.

"Where are they taking my sister?" I asked as they departed.

A man standing behind me and wearing a physician's coat answered.

"Sloane is going to get cleaned up and then checked into the psych ward at Cedars-Sinai," he said.

"Sloane!" I called out. "Mother and I are here now. We're here for you. You're going to be all right, sweetheart. We're going to get you cleaned up and find a good doctor, OK? Sloane, I'm here for you. Always. As I promised. From now until forever."

I did not foresee how hard it would be to fulfill my promise.

PART III:

SLOANE

CHAPTER 1

Two weeks earlier.

Pounding heart. Racing thoughts. So difficult to write down what's jammed in my head. Late winter storms rage. Pacific Coast Highway inundated with flooding, road closures and mudslides. Boulders the size of cars crash down from above without warning. High winds batter the granite coastal cliffs. Monster waves crash onto sandy shorelines up and down the Southern California coastline. My overburdened heart strains as if struggling to contain dark clouds and swift ocean currents. A thunderous, unyielding drumbeat, so much like the turbulent weather, hurtles me forward day after day, night after night, and makes me unstoppable. I am unstoppable, that's what I am. Unstoppable.

Nature's tempests are mere whispers compared to the swirling vortex of plans, dates and schedules and flurry of activities I must juggle. Endless demands — work, social, financial, familial, physical, nutritional — splinter any continuity of thought... but just for a second. Then, each concept in my head expands and becomes more brilliant than the last. A kaleidoscope of bright pulsating colors paints its way across the universe before me. Monday, Wednesday and Friday pulse purple; that's when I take classes at UCLA. Tuesday and Saturday, when I see my best client, flash pinkish red. She's up in Malibu. I have built a client list of four regulars — all great women — but she's at the top. I'll pick her up and drive to Gold's or Matrix One, where we work on weights and doing resistance exercises. This client's voice nibbles in my ear. She's fabulously wealthy, but wants more from life, to push her body to the limit. She craves to be the best female bodybuilder ever, and I will make that happen for her. She's incredibly excited about the goals we've set and the system we've built so she can reach the moon and beyond. She purrs, sotto voce, "I want greatness."

And so do I. Our desires interlock. We're each other's destiny. Our arcanum is encoded in to-do lists and postures and form and a torrent of goals and deadlines and procedures that denote a fabulous regimen, an interstellar map revealing our physical journey across the galaxy together. Enthusiasm and eagerness has been building in me for two days like a pressure cooker.

I don't know which outfit to wear tomorrow morning, and which one I should bring for Christie. Maybe she prefers blue. Maybe she's in a black mood, or a neon frame of mind. I like these pink leotards, and I also like the sheer. The green is nice, the black with sequins is sexy, and yellow is sunny and warm. I'll bring them all and buy a few more to make sure we have all the right combinations. I laugh at the laugh that bubbles up from deep inside me. The laughing sounds feverish, but the joy electrifies me, and all of a sudden I am twitching with energy, my skin tingling like bells ringing throughout my body.

I know how prophets, gods, geniuses feel.

To think they wanted me to take synthetic drugs to be like She-Ra. Why did my brother even have to ask me about it? Doesn't he know me? Do they know who I am? I am a supreme being. I don't need that shit, or anything else.

Paranoia shakes me for a second, a thunderbolt moment of frozen pain. The ticking of a clock slows down. Away dread. Away dread. Away mediocrity, base feelings. The ticking speeds up until that knock-knock sound is a blur and has no meaning or limitations. A flood of ideas and a volley of sounds and voices in the fatherly cadence of Lamont and Klaus cascade upon me. I'm no mere mortal, it's clear, so I push aside the panic and voices. Nagging doubts disappear. It's clear. I can do it all.

After I take my client to her home, I will rehearse with my acting coach for the She-Ra role. I'm ready. I look the part. I speak the part. I am the part. I am She-Ra. Princess. Goddess. Warrior. I've reshaped myself, because I can shape anything in the world. I possess the powerful body and mind of a heroine. Have you seen the studio mock-ups of the She-Ra character? It's me! From head to toe. I embody superhuman strength and agility. I was cast in that role because nothing can stop me. That role was made for me. I was made for it. The fire department's requirements still seem overly ridiculous, unkind and petty, but it worked out for the best, didn't it? The move to L.A. may have been fraught with stress, and my family and friends may be far away, but fear will never hold me back. Fear is weak and I cannot be abide it now that I'm so close to understanding and achieving everything and anything. I've earned second and third academic degrees, diplomas, certificates and honors. I've started a thriving business. I've built a preeminent clientele list. I'm going to star in a motion picture. All dualism has ended. I am one with my work, one in space, not emotional, just deep and spacious. Trust builds, love is everywhere.

Standing translucent, I turn on the radio and dance to the music. This body of mine is too chiseled and sun-kissed to keep clothes on. I undress. I'm naked and free and dancing, and the music is wonderful. I run to the window and shout every word to every lyric.

Nothing can stop me now. I run to my albums on a shelf and throw on the record "Jazz." Energetic, I entwine myself with the melody. I lose myself in the musical embrace. I leave the music on and drift out my front door like the breeze and walk into apartment three. I strip the boy next door and push him into the warm shower where we make love passionately under warm droplets like so many times before. He can't get enough of me. In the afterglow and post-coital euphoria, I go home and grab a catalogue selling workout attire and gear and order five more sets of neon-colored leotards, as well as leg warmers, headbands, sweatbands and four more tracksuits of various colors. The vibrant combinations are a perfect blend of practicality and flamboyance for my client. She'll love them, and so will everybody else, because we are all, like one big congregation, following a selfless deity that is fitness and health consciousness. Do you feel it, too?

I fell asleep. Or did I? I dozed off, but I don't know for how long. It was a disturbed, interrupted shut-eye of some sort, I guess. It's still the early morning hours. I'm awake. Four in the morning. I have to be at my client's house in Malibu by eight. I need to make sure I get there with plenty of time to spare since she's my newest and most important follower. She is very punctual. I'll leave at seven at the latest.

I need to eat but can't and don't want to. I go to the fridge and take out a carton of eggs and a plastic bag of lentils and I heave them across the room because I'm sick of this diet that I am supposed to be enduring based on the recommendation of Lamont and Klaus, but I don't need it anymore.

I'm cut as fuck already. Fuck lentils and beans, fuck amino acids and protein, and fuck carbohydrates and fiber and iron. This shit is disagreeing with me. I don't need anything from Lamont and Klaus anymore.

Do I hear music next door? Is that what woke me up? Why do my neighbors have no respect for my schedule, my life? Dick heads. Dick heads in apartment five. All of them are dick heads. Shallow pieces of floating shit. They have been a nightmare since moving in. Why do they conspire against me? I'll make them pay. I'll get them evicted. The poor Farmer family next door to them had to move their young daughter to another part of the house because of apartment five's sexual preoccupations in the adjoining bedroom. Windows and curtains open for all to see and hear. And the noise levels, loud music, cursing all through the night until sunrise. She's seven years old, for Christ sake. I find my baseball bat and beat it against the wall. Again. Again. And again. Now there are several holes in the sheetrock, but I don't think I hear the music anymore. I'm not paying for the repairs. So there goes your absurd plot to ruin my career starting with my number one client who I must see tomorrow, you dickheads in apartment five. You sons of bitches, sabotaging my audition. I know what you're doing.

I'm calming down. The noise has stopped. Do my thoughts seem fragmented? No, no, no. They're more genius and solid than your typical smattering of little ideas that go nowhere. I will reshape this world. Nothing will stop me. I'm so pumped up for this session with her. I understand with great lucidity how this all fits together in the grand, longterm scheme. Forever. Forever. Forever.

I need to get to her house on time. Christie demands a lot. Her schedule and mine are crazy. Checklist before I go: workout outfits for client; notepad; thermos of hot coffee; Gatorade bottle from fridge; niacin tablets; gym keys; car keys. Let's see, what to wear? I'm going to throw on — what? I pull jeans over my neoprene pants and step into my slouchy boots. I grab my brown suede jacket and am ready. The sun is just coming up. Nothing can stop me. A new day dawns.

Before I leave, I write:

Feb. 14. From this day until death.

CHAPTER 2

Steep cliffs to the right, crashing waves to the left, highway winding down the middle along the coastline's natural contours. Beachside houses hug the PCH. The roadway wet and slippery, muddy from yesterday's rains. The morning sun rising over the mountains, painting sheets of clouds in orange, yellow and red.

I'm driving my blue V-8 Dodge Ram van to my number one client's house, but I hit a standstill of automobiles and slam my brakes hard to avoid a rear-ending the car in front of me. We are going nowhere. Twenty vehicles at a dead stop in the two northbound lanes. I look at my watch. Seven-thirty in the morning. I've reached the Sunset Boulevard exit, but I should have left the house earlier, six-thirty at the latest, like I said I would, for fuck's sake. I lay on the horn. More horns answer back, but nobody is moving. My heart races, adrenaline, agitation, fear course through my body. I shift to park and repeatedly stomp on the floorboard, my fingers drum madly on the steering wheel, then I punch it. This delay is catastrophic, career-ending, life altering. I disengage from park, reengage, then take it out again. Should I get out and run to my appointment? I'm fucking She-Ra. Damn right, I'll run. No, I'll fly.

But I don't. I just sit. I stomp and tap and punch. Fuck it. I slowly edge out of the line of cars into the center divider to get a good look up the road. A rockslide must have blocked the Pacific Coast Highway. There is nowhere to go on Highway 1.

Up ahead, I see California Highway Patrol officers telling me I can go, signaling me through. They understand. They're here exactly for this type of situation. Nobody is coming southbound that I can see, so I drive forward, fast. They probably know me, these CHP officers. A bunch of them work out at Gold's, so they'll recognize me. Of all people, they understand I need to get somewhere important. It's imperative that I see my client. With a CHP escort, I will be at her house on time. I veer into the narrow center dividing lane and pass ten vehicles. It's a tight squeeze as I try to avoid driving into the oncoming lane. I pass a few more idle cars, and everybody is shouting at me through their windows. They don't understand my predicament.

Two officers are frantically waving. See? Look! They know me. Come on through, come on through! Let her through. They're waving wildly. They want me go through, but I'll have to speed up to beat the police motorcade coming in the other direction. I get back to my side for the oncoming traffic. I don't see a vehicle anywhere on the road behind the wildly gesturing officers, at least as far as the blind turn up ahead. It's a little hair-raising, but this is working out perfectly. I will make it to Christie's on time. The officers are madly crossing their arms above their heads. I can't hear them as I gain speed in the center lane and whoosh by.

A quarter-mile down the road a cop car comes up fast behind me, lights flashing. They're saying something through the vehicle's speaker. Pull over to the side of the road? Get somewhere safe? Why? That's not the plan. Oh, I get it now. It's a joke. I get the joke. I'm laughing hard. Fine, I'll pull over. The joke is on me. Santiago Barcellos is playing a prank on me. He got me. Santiago is always fooling around. It's all for a charitable cause, so fine, I'll play along. I'll pay the money to charity to get out of the fake jail they'll take me to. Santi always loved a joke. He's fully acting this one out in a very real way. With real officers. I have to say, though, not great timing, Santi. Not great timing at all. I will have to hurry and pay the fake judge, because I cannot leave my client stranded. I'm getting angry now thinking about how Santi has inconvenienced me. I'll let you know, Barcellos, how inappropriate all of this is the next time I see you. It's not funny anymore.

I approach the avalanche. It's spread across both northbound lanes. Boulders and sludge piled as high as the roof of a car. On the other side of the highway, southbound, a flashing patrol car escorts another column of vehicles past the landslide, another unit holds up the end of the motor-cade. After that, there is nobody — no cars, no police vehicles — in those southbound lanes. This is fantastic. What luck. An open road. I can go again. I head off course onto the other side of the highway. The officers keep tailing me, though, lights flashing. I'm going fast, so they probably ought to knock off the jest.

In front of me, I see a lot of cars stopped. More patrol units wait up there. They're blocking the road. They need to move so I can get through. I swerve back to the northbound lane and pull over. Let's get this asinine practical joke over. I'm not very happy.

Stopped on the side of the road, I watch through my rear-view mirror as the so-called officers get out of their cars and approach my vehicle. Hands on holstered guns is a bit much, isn't it Santi? I check the time and take another glance up the road. Shit. I'm late. Go? No. I'll wait. Go? No. I'll wait.

An officer taps on my window. I see another cop coming up to my passenger-side door. I'm smiling — what else can I do at this point? — but the officer violently throws open my car door and yells at me to get out. He's scaring the shit out of me. I try to move, but I can't. I'm stuck. Stuck and smiling like an idiot. Caught in this stupid charade of Santi's.

"What the hell are you laughing at?" the man in uniform shouts. He grabs and tugs my arm, but I can't get out of the driver's seat. I'm stuck. "Get out of the car! Get out of the car now!"

I'm fearful, afraid and distraught. I don't know why I can't get out of my seat. The other officer comes around, and he's pulling and jerking me, too. Two minutes later they stop tugging and heaving, because they figure out I'm wearing a seatbelt. One of them unbuckles me. Now a third uniformed man shows up, and they all drag me roughly out of the car. My arm hurts. My knee hurts. They hold my arms so I can't move and then brace me against the van. I try to wiggle and shake loose. This doesn't feel like a joke anymore. It doesn't feel right at all. I struggle to get free. I break away from their grasp, and finally I am running to my client's house, like fucking She-Ra. I run down the center of the highway, and they follow me. Just let me get to Christie's, I scream. Let me see her so she'll know I'm OK. I'll explain everything when we get there. You'll see. You'll see your mistake. I'm a goddess. I'm a heroine. I'm saving planets. I'm bestowing dreams on people.

I lose my balance and tumble to the concrete, my desperate flight over. I look down and see that my knees and elbows are scraped. Now I'm on the ground and an officer pushes on my head, smearing my face into the gravel. I elbow him in the ear. The other cops kick, hit and scratch at me. I'm handcuffed and thrown in the back of a squad car. Nobody asks to see my driver's license or registration. I hear them trying to figure out what to do with my van and where to leave it. I'm being driven a long distance handcuffed in the back seat, bleeding and in so much pain. The steel shackles are crushing my wrists.

The restraint is unbearable, and I scream, my mind ready to explode. My back hurts, knee swollen and cut raw. I thrash, convulse and shout with all the power my diaphragm can generate. My captors in the front seat look back at me and say nothing.

"Who dressed me like this?" I shout. "Who put me in these bizarre clothes? Where is my proper workout gear? Did you do this, you sons of bitches? I have a fitness training session starting in a couple minutes. Get me out of these boots and jeans and this coat. Get me out of here. I'm fucking She-Ra! Santi! Santi! Bail me out! I have to go get a client and bring her to the gym. Fuck this charity fundraiser bullshit!"

We stop, and the men force me into a concrete building. I am still yelling, trying to make sense of what is happening. Somebody please tell me, somebody please explain.

I'm locked in a jail cell, a hard bench its only furniture. Why am I still shackled, confined alone in a dark place? I lie on my side on the bench and sing. I sing to soothe my mind. A guard rattles open the cell door and orders me to remove my boots. I pull one off and heave it at his head.

"You want my boots? Pervert. Eat my boots!" I shout, casting the second one at him.

My thoughts race. I talk. I shout. I pace back and forth in the cell. I knock a tin cup against the wall. I sing and sing and sing.

In the morning, the guards burst in while I'm lying on the bench, facing the wall. They pull me up, pin my arms behind my back and frog march me in my stocking feet down a corridor. Euphoria and combativeness mix together and gush over me as never before in my life. I'm summoned into a courtroom and made to stand before a judge.

My bombastic mood contrasts sharply with the quiet of this courtroom. I silently look around and listen. Soft murmurs. Creaking of wooden benches. Shuffling of papers. It's so creepy in here, and I can't bear it, my irritation recognizing no boundaries. Unable to contain the raging disquiet, I belt out a full-throated version of the song "The Girl From Ipanema."

"Tall and tan and young and lovely, the girl from Ipanema goes walking.

And when she passes, each one she passes goes, 'Ah.' "

While I sing, I look at the judge and recognize him. I know he knows me, too. And now, I am aware that my life is in danger.

"You're that big Hawaii crime boss," I shout at him. "You're Teamsters mafia. I need to get out of here."

The judge raps his gavel and turns his stern gaze to me, the tall, hand-cuffed redhead sandwiched between two deputies. I fall silent and stare at the mobster judge. He takes advantage of the sudden hush in the room to declare:

"After careful consideration of the recommendations from the court-appointed psychiatrist and the obvious evidence of your current mental state, I find it in your best interest to receive appropriate mental health care rather than incarceration in a jail facility."

"I wasn't finished," I interrupt, and start singing the second verse of "The Girl From Ipanema."

"When she walks, she's like a samba, swings so cool and sways so gentle that when she passes, each one she passes goes, 'Ooh.' "

The judge slams the gavel so hard the handle breaks off in his hand.

Where's Santi? I need to know. Santiago is going to bail me out. Wait for Santiago, your honor. We'll pay the charity to get out of jail.

"I hereby order you remanded to the USC Medical Center for comprehensive evaluation and treatment with the hope that you receive..." the judge shouts over me.

I scream back, "You told me your needs, and now I must amplify mine. Let me explain. I'm only going to tell you once. My client is waiting for this freaky sideshow to end. She needs me. I'm going to advance her career. And I need her. She's going to advance my career. Where are my rings? Who stole my rings? Where are my boots?"

The judge finishes his order and with dramatic flair exits the court-room for his chambers.

"Where are you going, fucking Jew judge?" I call out, but the deputies drag me away to a waiting van.

For an hour-and-a-half, we drive — and all the while, I'm in the back of the van complaining how these goddamn handcuffs are mutilating my wrists. I'm lonely, sore, stiff, shoeless.

When we arrive at the second facility, they drag me to a cold, concrete, rectangle room with fluorescent lights humming overhead and a slick gray floor beneath me. There, my captors strip me and search my cavities and push me completely naked into a desolate communal shower room. The cold water stings my skin. Everybody is watching. You want a show? I yell, I'll give you a fucking show, you shithead assholes. I shout that this fucking humiliation must end, but they keep watching. Fucking perverts. The cold water suddenly stops pelting me, and a towel is thrown at me. At the dry edge of the shower, they drop a hospital gown and some sneakers that look like tennis shoes without the laces.

I put on the gown and shoes, and they take me down a corridor and run me into a cell. They pin me face down on the mattress and a big man pulls my arms behind my back. I don't know what they're going to do, so I resist, kicking and biting at them. The big man scrapes three rings off my fingers on both my hands, cutting and bruising me. I scream for someone to get me out of this charnel house before I die.

I don't know how long I'm in there before they bring me food. Poison! Poison. Poison! I shout, but nobody comes. Nobody cares.

"I won't eat this shit, because you're trying to poison me!" I yell.

I toss the tray of food in the air and wait for the guards to come back. I fling the tray and remnants at the bars. The guards walk away. I feel food in my hair, and I rub it in real good to break down the deadly toxins that are in it.

The first night behind the steel grating never ends. Voices don't stop. Visions don't stop. I can't distinguish what's real and what's imaginary. I know that Satan is standing here with me, blood dripping from his lips as he stands there in the corner of the cell in the flickering shadows with snakes entwined and slithering at his claw feet. He stands just four feet tall and two feet wide, solid as a boulder and white as a ghost.

The devil whispers:

Stop, priest, sprinkling of holy water.

And what you entreat.

No, priest, Satan does not retreat!

I say, "Reign, Satan!"

I stand by the demon's side. Together, we are wielding the scepter over executions during the Inquisition. Priests cut open pregnant women with chainsaws. Pools of dirt, pieces of flesh and blood are everywhere. Horrific screams of red-hot pain sound out until vocal cords snap. A hundred thousand snakes slither out of the doors of a marble mausoleum and slide along the ground, but the earth is just a long, flat, burnt expanse of terrain. But Santiago and I will find the victims. I leave Satan and go inside the mausoleum where I hear phantom cries of distant battles and guerrilla warfare. We come to a jungle in the Philippines, and there are bugs and snakes everywhere. I hear explosions on the horizon, as if the end of the world is approaching. I feel the crushing weight of guilt in the form of my M-16, my combat boots, my rucksack and my helmet. I tear my clothes off.

As I stand naked, Satan and his evil watchers take a cold grip of my wrists and ankles. I slip free and run from them, but they grab my extremities and spread me out like a sacrificial animal and strap my limbs to four pillars and all at once they pummel me and spit on me, pull my hair and twist my nipples.

They leave me naked on a bed of nails for hours. Satan visits in the form of an owl sitting on a high marble pedestal in the middle of the cell. From its perch, the night bird's big eyes stare down at me.

"Go to hell, Satan! Go straight to hell and leave me alone!"

It's silent once again. Somebody put folded sheets on my bed. The sheets transform into a boa that slithers between my legs. I squeeze and rub that boa as if I'll ride the evil out of him, fuck the life out of him.

The camera-like eyes of the owl watch me the entire time.

CHAPTER 3

Sloane," the woman crouching next to my cot said softly. "They've asked me to come and talk to you about how you're feeling. It looks like you're calmer this morning. Would you like to take a warm shower and clean up before I ask you a few questions?"

I stopped breathing for a moment and shook my head emphatically. I was lying on my back, but turned my head to see her better.

"I understand," she said. "It's OK. I'm going to ask you some questions, OK? A few days ago, when you were taken to that second jail, not the first one, do you remember appearing before a commissioner or judge?"

"No," I whispered.

"Do you know why or how you ended up in a second jail, instead of a hospital?"

"The Hawaiian mob boss sent me there."

"Let me ask you a question, Sloane. Have you ever experienced delusions or schizophrenia in the past?"

"When?"

"Before you were taken to jail back on the fourteenth."

"I don't know what day it is."

"Let me limit the question to ten years before you were taken to the second jail. Did you experience delusions or schizophrenia in that timeframe?

"No."

"Sloane, how would you describe your mood right now, at this moment? Energetic? Maybe irritable?"

"Yes."

"Do you feel a need to sleep more?"

"No."

"Can you concentrate, or are your thoughts racing?"

"Racing."

"Do you have family living or staying nearby in the area?"

"Who's that?" I asked. It was a dark shape, but I could see the outline of a man standing by the iron barrier at the end of the room.

"He accompanied me here. It's OK. Can you answer my question?"

"What?"

I sat up straight as a pole and watched the figure in the dark background.

"Do you have family nearby?"

"I don't know where I am."

"I have some good news," the woman said. "You are going to get cleaned up, and afterward..."

"No! They'll watch. They stand there and leer."

"No, this time will be different. Everything is different, now. After we talk, your family is coming to get you. Do you remember your family?"

"My brother? My mom?"

"Yes. In just a little while. Your name is Sloane Stevens, right? And you are a member of the Stevens family? The timber and real estate family from Seattle?"

"Yes."

I pointed to the man near the door. The woman sent him away with a nod of her head.

"I just want to tell you, Sloane, that we'd like to correct, or adjust, your court-ordered placement, so I'm here to ask you some questions. I'm a doctor, Sloane, and you're going to be all right."

"Where'd he go?"

I stood up and looked around.

"Please, Sloane, sit down. He left. We're alone now."

I went to the iron door and didn't see anybody. I plopped back onto the cot, scooted my back against the wall, brought my knees to my chest, and wrapped my arms around my shins. The doctor resumed her inquiry while

I watched the door, in case the man returned.

"Do you recall going to court on or around the fourteenth or fifteenth of February?"

"No."

"Do you recall at any time being seen by a nurse or psychiatrist on or around the fourteenth or fifteenth of February?"

"No."

"Do you recall being given a hearing of any kind while you've been here?"

"No."

"Do you recall anybody telling you that you were going to be placed with other inmates here?"

"No."

"Did anybody tell you or give you any form or piece of paper indicating you should go someplace else, like the USC Medical Center?"

"I don't remember."

Two men dressed like guards and a man in a white coat appeared. I stood on my cot and started jumping up and down.

"Sloane! Sloane! Listen to me. I am going to walk over there and get a glass of water for you, so I want you to calm down. I have two pills you need to take. They'll make you feel better. These round white capsules are nothing stronger than Tylenol, really. Can we do that?"

After I took the pills, and the woman and the guards left, a physical and mental stillness spread over me. My limbs felt like leaves drifting on the surface of a lake in a slight breeze.

Emotions absent, time distorted, I was only aware of being transported somewhere across space and time. They did not try to strip me again, nor did they force me to shower in front of anyone. They did not lock me up in a cell with Satan. Instead, they brought me to a light, open, beautiful place.

I remember having a vision of Tom Selleck, one of my favorite people in the world, greeting me when I arrived. But I could recollect little else.

At Cedars-Sinai, my hallucinations stopped and I started to come around to the normal side to things. People my age were at this hospital, including guys. It had a kitchen and eating area, a family room and TV rooms. The grounds surrounding the medical center were meticulously landscaped, and I found it an oasis of tranquility. The large yard was sectioned into what were called "healing gardens," each with its own name. I met and talked with my doctor in one of the gardens, and there were benches, walkways, and table with seats under umbrellas.

I stayed there for two weeks and never wanted to leave. The sharp edges of the world around me softened. My breathing slowed and steadied as a tranquil haze washed over me. I willingly received medication, and they let me exercise.

My brother visited. My mom and dad came to see me, too. They weren't getting along any better than usual, but I didn't have to bear the weight of guilt over their discordant relationship, like I did when they first divorced. Their words to each other, even if uncivil, entered my eardrums like wisps of a cloud, instead of the clap of thunder.

My mother was consumed by a fervent yearning to sue Los Angeles County to compensate for my shock and distress caused by my incarceration. Dad, always the prudent businessman, didn't want to pay for an arduous lawsuit where a favorable outcome was improbable. I heard him repeatedly tell Mom how expensive my care was at Cedars-Sinai, and how costly my ongoing medical treatment would be. If I could, I would gladly pay whatever the cost to stay here forever. The respite felt good.

"She's going to have to live with this nightmare for the rest of her life," Mom whispered to my father as I pretended to be sleeping in my shaded garden chair. "It's something that's going to affect her ability to work, her relationships, her health, everything. I'm not a doctor, but I can tell you what the permeating aftereffects are going to be."

"A lawsuit won't change the past," Dad said.

My parents agreed on one thing: After Cedars-Sinai, it was time for me to move back to slower-paced Sacramento. Even so, they were at loggerheads over whether I should stay at my father's house with therapeutic access to horses and equestrian trails or at my mother's place (which entailed living with her third husband, a surgeon this time around) on the bluffs overlooking the peaceful American River.

"What do you think I should do?" I asked Shane.

"See if E.S. will buy you a house with some acreage near his spread in Foresthill. You'll have your own space, but he'll be nearby. I won't be far either."

"I like your thinking, Shane! That sounds perfect."

During those weeks at the hospital, I found myself looking forward to the times I talked one-on-one with my psychiatrist, Dr. Ryan — even when we probed the haunting memories of those dark days in jail, those still-vivid demonic visions, the physical abuse, harsh lights, poisoned food and the humiliation and stress of constantly being watched.

Our talks soothed me. He was gentle in his prodding, and I no longer fell to pieces when I recounted the injustices I endured. Dr. Ryan's gentleness opened up a therapeutic space where I could examine the whole awful experience with a soft self-care.

"I don't, nor will I ever, understand why this whole thing happened to me," I told him. "How did I end up in this predicament? Nothing can justify it. But I guess I am beginning to accept what occurred. It's just a story now, my story."

"Accepting it isn't the same as approving of it," he said. "The stories we remember of our past are not real, they are no longer happening. With time — and lots of support — we can change how we relate to it."

"Why is everybody here so kind? Why would anybody have sympathy for me? Why is my family not ashamed of what happened? I can't even love myself right now."

Dr. Ryan's gentle smile unfurled, soft and warm.

"You are still sorting it all out, Sloane. Have you heard of Stephen Levine?" he asked. "Stephen Levine once said, 'Healing comes when we meet our wounded places with compassion.' "

That's how my treatment — immersed in compassion and tenderness — proceeded. Dr. Ryan led me gently and carefully through our dialogues and interviews about the humiliation and terror of my incarceration. His voice was untroubled, his touch warm. Wounded, healed or somewhere in between, I cried a lot, especially the first time we talked about my diagnosis.

"I don't know how I feel, or *if* I feel anything," I explained to him. "I know I've never felt whatever this is."

One day, he talked about the medication that I was taking, then he explained his diagnosis and finally my therapy.

"You are taking six hundred milligrams of lithium carbonate three times a day and two hundred milligrams of Desyrel at bedtime," Dr. Ryan told me. "We will continue to monitor your levels to make sure we have the right dosage and the medication is working for you. How are you feeling right now?"

"Balanced. Less agitated. I don't feel as hopeless. But I detest some of the physical side effects, like this taste in my mouth, and I'm always thirsty."

"Lithium is effective, but it's not a cure. That's why you're here. But if you take your medicine, you can get on with living again. You are a fortunate young woman. It's now up to you."

But when he told me the diagnosis, his words fell on me like the closing of a coffin lid: bipolar disorder with psychotic features.

When my sobbing subsided, I breathed deeply and asked him for what seemed like the millionth time: "What happened to me?"

"You deserve to know. I think it's as good of a time as any to tell you. I carefully reviewed the history and records from your arrest and incarceration at Sybil Brand, as well as notes from our private conversations, so I can say without a doubt you suffered from an acute manic phase at the time of your arrest. Here's what really went wrong. The judge ordered you to undergo a complete examination and treatment at USC Medical Center, but a clerical error resulted in you being mistakenly remanded to the Sybil Brand Institute, a women's jail, instead. You were supposed to be committed to the mental health hospital to receive care, not subject to the harsh realities of mass incarceration in an overcrowded facility. I've asked officials at the courthouse and the authorities at Sybil Brand how this happened, and so has your mother. And all they can say is, it's a busy courthouse and miscommunication and misfiling happen occasionally. Regardless, it should never have happened, and it should never happen again."

"I fell through the cracks," I said.

"Yes. You fell through the cracks of justice. Instead of receiving the psychiatric care you needed, they put you in an isolation tank where you remained in a catatonic excitement state with acute manic symptoms for several days afterward — just how long is disputed. During your incarceration, you were subjected to the humiliation of being stripped and searched and physically abused to the point of sustaining bruises and cuts. On top of all that, you were actively hallucinating. I'm sorry you had to deal with this travesty of justice, especially as a young lady who is only twenty-seven years old."

"Is there anything I could have done differently?"

"No. The ordeal you went through was prolonged. Had there been timely intervention and medical treatment, you would not have experienced such an episode. Do you remember what they originally charged you with, Sloane?"

"Driving under the influence."

"Yet, you had no alcohol or drugs in your system," Dr. Ryan said, shaking his head. "They added reckless driving later."

"Yes."

"Sloane, do you recall, when you were at the second jail, Sybil Brand, anybody examining or evaluating you?"

"I don't remember."

"What's the next thing you remember after being released from the second jail?"

"Seeing my brother, who apparently I thought was Tom Selleck..."

Dr. Ryan and I both laughed at this.

"Well, your brother does resemble him a little," he said.

I laughed again. I couldn't remember the last time I felt sane enough to laugh.

"He's always there for me," I said about Shane.

"And after that? What do you remember?"

"Just memories from here, Cedars-Sinai."

"In evaluating the records, it appears to me that no real attempt was made to check your identity even though your car and all the necessary documents were available. Your father had to hire a private investigator to find you. If he hadn't done that, this nightmare would have gone on even longer without adequate psychiatric care."

"I'm so embarrassed at how I appeared when my brother and mom showed up. My hair was matted, I had lost twenty pounds in jail. I wasn't making any sense at all."

Dr. Ryan said my grandiose delusions and hallucinations continued up until our first session together.

"Look, the clinical picture shows you had delirium mania — that's a life-threatening condition," he said leaning in toward me. "We just don't see that anymore in modern psychiatric practice, not since the introduction of potent psychiatric medications."

"Why did this happen to me?"

"I know, you keep asking that. And it's all right. Your condition is primarily due to a chemical imbalance over which you have no control. It was triggered and exacerbated by this absolutely horrible experience in jail, where no medical treatment was available to you."

"Could it have happened to me anywhere, at any time?"

"I find it hard to predict what, if any, degree of stress could have precipitated such a severe manic episode at this stage of your life. You're twenty-seven years old and have not had clear-cut evidence of manic-depressive disorder. Yet, it is possible that you could have gone a long time without experiencing such an episode."

"It sounds like a ticking time bomb."

"The symptoms could have — perhaps should have — been picked up much earlier, given your intellectual, socio-economic and educational background. But our society is still coming to terms with diagnosing bipolar, manic-depressive and schizophrenia and the stigma. I hope we can change that somehow. Maybe you can help more people understand because of what you went through."

"Do you think I'm crazy, doctor?" I asked.

"No. This is a process. There's nothing wrong with the intellectual part of your brain. But to get benefits from our therapy, we have to fix the chemical imbalance through medication first. That's where we are. It's stabilized, and therefore we can make sense of all this through talking."

"Is this diagnosis forever?"

"I believe prolonged therapy will not be necessary."

"But what happened was so frightening and real that..."

"It doesn't matter what has happened, Sloane, because in this moment you can start anew. It doesn't matter what you did, or said, or thought, or who hurt you or who you hurt, or even why. We are not our pasts if — if — we start anew. We are starting anew, Sloane, in this moment and every moment. We are free.

"Let's end today on that note. Is there anything you'd like to say before we depart?"

"I want you to know how much my brother's love and concern for my happiness means to me, especially through all of this. And I wouldn't have survived without my mom and dad's unconditional support. I hope I will have the time and place to properly tell them how I feel and try to return the favor."

"I'm glad you feel that way. And you will, Sloane."

"As for you, Dr. Ryan, I wouldn't have recovered without your care and tenderness, either. I thank you so much, as well."

CHAPTER 4

After my two-week in-patient stay at Cedars-Sinai, Shane convinced me to live near him in Sacramento until I settled into my new life. I rented an apartment in the city while my father searched for a house for me in the foothills near him.

I looked for work, too, tailoring my résumé for fitness and marketing jobs and using the services of an employment agency. But job hunting turned out to be deeply stressful. I answered some ads by phone, but I wasn't confidence enough to do in-person interviews. My brain felt foggy, and the knee I injured skiing hurt if I stood or walked on it for too long. I couldn't imagine working on my feet all day. After a day of interviews with four or five potential employers, I was so tired that I usually slept for two days straight. A persistent exhaustion in the morning made me sleep late, and long afternoon naps threw off my rhythm.

At least my depression did not feel as deep as it had the preceding two or three months, but I cried frequently. Time and again, I became nauseous and lightheaded for no apparent reason. The worst problem I faced by far was diarrhea, a result of taking too many stool softeners and laxatives in an attempt to relieve the severe constipation caused by my anti-depressants.

Finally, after a few months, I was close to landing a job at a branch office of AAA insurance. They strung me along and ultimately hired someone for the position from within the company. A similar outcome a week later at another firm made me wonder if my driving record was the actual reason I wasn't being hired. It seemed to me that documentation from the traffic incident was the issue. My trust in government was as low as possible, considering deeply troubling machinations that entangled me in Los Angeles County. How many times was I to be punished for what happened while I was in the grip of an acute manic episode? I thought all the charges, including reckless driving and driving under the influence, were dropped. My brother and mother believed all that remained was an "unsafe lane change." If incorrect information on my driving record could raise concerns, who knew how much a curious prospective employer could uncover about the entire ugly altercation? I did not need the additional stress.

Eventually, I took low-level sales jobs, but work relationships gave me high anxiety. I was constantly on edge about possibly slipping into another manic episode. I thanked God that my support system resided close to me. Without Shane, Mom and Dad, I would not be writing any of this. I'd be dead or, worse, existing in an unending, nebulous, torturous mental state.

They constantly reassured me that my main job was to rest, keep up on my medication and therapy regimen and slowly acclimate to my new surroundings. I knew I could never live in Los Angeles again. I lacked the courage to survive in that indifferent, hostile and chaotic environment, where I encountered the complete disregard for human life and justice. Mom persuaded me to wait until after the settlement of our lawsuit or the conclusion of the trial to pursue a serious career.

Not having Dr. Ryan in my life and helping ease my fears made some days feel wretched. I was thankful, though, that I found a wonderful psychiatrist in Sacramento to continue my care. I liked Dr. Vivek Kapoor almost as much as Dr. Ryan.

"Here's the thing I want you to remember most," Dr. Kapoor said on my first visit. "Those little beige pills you're taking in the morning and at night with water, they'll keep everything on an even keel. But it's just as important for you — for us — to continue therapy. Therapy cleans up all that debris left behind in your life. We'll work on this together. Can we do that? Is that OK with you, Sloane?"

That sounded fine to me, but the detritus in my head was piled high, and it continued to accumulate faster than the doctor and I could shovel it away. Putting aside my need to return to work eventually, I worried about so many other things. My biggest concern revolved around my desire to someday have children and the accompanying fear of not being able to sustain a fetus because I was taking lithium. But how could I cope with a lithium-free pregnancy?

With great enthusiasm, Mom set about cleaning up the legal mess and finding justice for me. She fixated on our lawsuit against the County of Los Angeles, flooding our attorney with voluminous notes, reports and opinions on the matter. She called me five or six times a day about various aspects of the litigation. She wanted me to call our attorney to request copies of all the reports so she could find out everything she needed to about the case.

"Mom is just avoiding dealing with husband number three," Shane said. "If she keeps busy enough, she doesn't have to talk to him or go anywhere with him."

"I thought she was doing it out of love and concern for me!" I said, my voice heavy with condemnation.

"I'm sorry," he apologized. "I didn't mean it that way."

For Mom, I called the attorney. I didn't tell him it was my mother pushing these demands on him, but he saw right through the pretense. His response sent me into a mild depression.

"This is completely off-base," the lawyer said, his anger undisguised. "The fact that in making such a request you are probably reiterating an appeal by your father, or probably your mother, is very disquieting to me. It serves no useful purpose for you to review reports concerning the facts surrounding this incident, since that will obligate you to be cross-examined on the contents of those reports, when such cross-examination would never take place if you hadn't read the reports. And furthermore, the reports contain matters that are best explained by a medical doctor and might cause great grief or concern if you read them cold turkey!"

As for Father, I remained the radiant sun that flooded his life with color and banished the dark shadows. He fully supported anything that might benefit me. When Mom convinced him how traumatized I was from my mistreatment, he opened his checkbook to bankroll her legal crusade. Supporting the same cause, however, did not stop them from bickering as if they were still married and taking every opportunity to zap each other. Even though Eddy helped because of his love for me, Mom shut him out. Their long-suppressed aversions spewed forth in hot words and fiery accusations.

The pressure mounted, news spread, and the extended family heard rumors. Dad brooded about how the trial might bring bad publicity to his Pacific Northwest family. Shane told me Eddy was unreasonable, but there were signs that he wasn't imagining things. Conrad and the Family Council summoned him to Seattle. After decades of trying to minimize his interaction with the family, he traveled to the place he grew up to answer their questions. Mom joined him. She was not going to be persuaded or intimidated or quieted by their money, power and prestige.

"How dare you talk about how the mental health of a direct heir, our daughter, might harm the family business," she screamed at the gathered members of the Family Council. "Foremost, this is a young woman. She is a human being, not a product on the market. This is a human rights case, not an economic report. If anybody understands government infringing upon the basic rights and freedoms of private individuals or corporations, it should be this family. You all should still remember how much Joseph and George hated Franklin D. Roosevelt. When government oversteps, holding the office accountable is a human obligation and a priority for capitalists like you! Los Angeles County failed to administer reasonable care and should be made to pay. A great family should support a direct scion. She handled all the costs incurred for her medical treatment. All she asks in return from any of us is family support."

Dad was aghast at Mom's independence in front of the council, but the family never said another word.

Afterward, my parents' relationship fractured completely, but for another reason. Mom got back from Seattle and insisted on bringing our lawyer into a landlord-tenant problem I had encountered down in Los Angeles. Mother was determined to settle all my past entanglements. Even Dad said she was going too far on my behalf

"While we're at it, why shouldn't we try to settle that mess, since that's where it all stemmed from?" she shouted at him while I listened from the other room.

Dad said nothing, but it was the breaking point for our lawyer.

"This doesn't serve you very well," my attorney wrote to me. "I told your parents when I met with them that I would tolerate no interference on their behalf where that interference was to your detriment. Add to that the fact that your mother considered me to be a legal advisor for all regards, including your trouble with those apartment managers and neighbors. All of the foregoing factors have led me to the irrevocable conclusion that I must withdraw as your attorney. I don't think my intercession on your behalf would be of any benefit to you when you consider all the static that is going on from all different sources."

We found another attorney, but by 1991 — five long years after my arrest and wrongful incarceration, and long since going on serious medication and beginning continual psychotherapy — I needed to move on. I needed a job, to finish courses for my national fitness training certificate, and to get down to living my best life again.

Marketing, fitness training and sales were the vocations I once loved, and at which I know I'm good — and I needed to pursue them again. I also decided to look into the field of emergency medicine, because fixing acute problems coming at you fast and raw sounded appealing to me.

In 1992, the wrongful imprisonment lawsuit was adjudicated in favor of Los Angeles County. Mom was devastated, but my case had lost far too much steam after the withdrawal of the first counsel. Our new legal representation said she felt the lawsuit was too much of an uphill battle from the start, and she told my mother as much. By any measure, the lawyer didn't go into court with guns blazing, even though Mom believed she should have done so.

Did that stop Mom's pursuit of justice? Her anger frothed, and she became as unhinged from reality as I had been. She insisted the county had suppressed information, falsified claims and participated in character assassination. She found a new lawyer and filed a two million-dollar claim for damages in the appellate court.

"This is now my life's calling," she said.

I agreed with her premise. I was held unjustly against my own wishes and rights and my life was endangered. I underwent extreme mental anguish, which will stay with me until I die. My body was in such terrible shape that a witness said a Sybil Brand nurse told her I looked "as white as a ghost," and she could not pull herself together afterward. I was administered so many drugs, heavyweight serotonin receptor antagonists and re-uptake inhibitors, to save my life. The long-term effects of them have never been studied.

But now, I was trying to go in a new direction in Northern California. I was moving forward, and Dr. Ryan said that was imperative: "We are not our pasts, *if* we start anew."

To make a fresh start, I wrote this letter to the new attorney and thanked him for all of his hard work on my behalf:

The outcome of the case really doesn't surprise me. The result was a combination of suppressed information by the court, falsified claims and character assassination. Placing blame at this point, however, seems futile. It appears that justice simply does not exist in this world. As far as the county of L.A. is concerned, this matter is over. For me, though, this matter is just in the beginning stage — a small snowball. There are many loose ends to tie up before I depart this earth. Emotionally, I have moved from depressed to angry. And this is a wonderful state of mind for a call to action. You know what they say: Hell hath no fury like a woman scorned. The sons of bitches at that jail didn't kill me, they just made me stronger. I guess I didn't realize just how much more.

I wrote to Dr. Ryan one last time, too:

This whole ordeal has not affected me in a vacuum. People have suffered, particularly my family. Financially, my father has footed the majority of the cost of my hospital care and treatment, and I shudder to think where I would be without his support. My mother has weathered the brunt of my stormy ups and downs for too long. The pain she felt for me, I feel the same for her, because she has been reliving this entire sordid mess repeatedly. And next to these two stands my brother — the anchor I cling to as we cross a sea of hell, hoping I'll emerge from the fire and ashes, whole again.

After sending the letters, I was ready to return to a stable, productive life.

CHAPTER 5

Rebuilding my life started with quiet days and little strain. I moved out of my apartment near Shane's because I hardly ever saw him. I knew he'd drop everything if I needed him to set things right with a word or an action or a hug or just listening, but he was working eighteen-hour days and, from what I heard, exponentially expanding his real estate business. He spent most of his time socializing with peers and networking with professional acquaintances. In his free hours, he liked to meet women and go on dates.

Mother empathized with me, as she always had, but now she was remarried to the chief surgeon of a very large regional hospital, and I could not cope with that living situation. He spoke four languages fluently and played violin, bass and piano. The Sacramento Symphony called him to fill for absent musicians. He and Mom stayed active in the Republican Party and frequently traveled abroad, most often to his native Germany. One time in Rome, they were invited to a diplomatic lunch with the United States ambassador to the Vatican.

For some reason, he and I locked horns. If we were in the same room, we quickly became confrontational, probably because he constantly jockeyed for Mom's love and affection and paraded his abilities with theatrical flair. He required her constant admiration like he needed air. I stayed away.

That consigned me to Dad's place, and he was overjoyed that I lived with him for a while. Since the day I was born, he was my most ardent admirer and devoted supporter. Everything required for my resurgence he provided — quiet shelter, plenty of space if I needed to be alone and unconditional love. He surrendered to all my needs and became the best person to shepherd me along at this point of my healing journey. He buttressed my self-worth (not to mention my net worth).

His vast property was a sanctuary I had practically all to myself, a place to hide from all the hurt, if necessary. It's where I started seeing clearly and came out of the thick, heavy, cold fog that enveloped me all through the late 1980s. It's where I regained a small degree of independence. This was exactly what I needed — along with the lithium and valproate. Fresh country air, peaceful surroundings and mood stabilizers gave me a sense of calm and effortlessness I hadn't known for a long time. The simple act of choosing something to wear or going to the store or fixing dinner again became easy.

For more than a year, I lay low at Dad's large but modest home. I stitched together a new résumé and set my intention on finding a job. I wasn't looking for the type of work where I could transform the world and leave an indelible mark on mankind. Before my escalation into that full manic episode with delusions in Los Angeles, I handled a heavy college course load, four or five classes, worked full time, exercised daily in the gym, golfed, rowed, traveled and enjoyed a full social life. I trained elite bodybuilders in the fitness capital of the world. I came close to being a star in a big Hollywood film production, for Christ's sake. Those heady days were gone, but certainly, I could manage one routine job, couldn't I?

I finished my curriculum vitae, and Dad agreed that my education and work history looked strong:

Education

Certified Athletic Trainer
Bachelor of Business Administration, University of Hawaii.
Dean's List May 20, 1984
G.P.A. 3.8

Work Experience

Student Athletic Trainer

Independent Contractor
Administrative Assistant
Personal Trainer

The résumé landed me a job as an administrative assistant for the regional director of sales at Red Lion Inn. I handled the benefit needs of a staff of sixty employees who reported to my boss. The position lit a fire under me and gave me confidence to assume more responsibility and self-improvement in my life. I applied to Chapman College so I could finish my health sciences education. I aligned myself with a couple of gyms, which agreed to allow me to bring my clients in for personal training. My National Athletic Trainers Association certificate arrived in November 1992.

Dad liked what I was doing and told me he was proud of me. He encouraged and empowered me to plant a flag in Foresthill.

At home one evening after working at his travel agency's main office in Sacramento, he asked what I needed to help me develop greater self-reliance.

"What do you mean?" I answered.

"I mean, if you want to stay here at the house, you know I would love that, and you're welcome to live here for as long as you want. But, say you were ready to get into your own home, and have enough financial resources to sustain you until you started earning a really good living — I mean, what dollar figure would you put on that?"

"I have my own money, Dad. I don't need any extra help."

"I know. I know."

"And you've been so generous in getting me to stand on my own two feet again. Just opening up your house and your heart, that's all I need and want. It's enough to get back on track."

"My loving support for you is unlimited, Sloane. But visualize being on your own again. What would that take in a monetary sense? I mean, without touching your own personal nest egg? Tell me how much?"

I paused to absorb the question. I admitted to myself it wasn't the first time I had examined this scenario, so a dollar figure was ready in my head. My attorney had posed a similar question so we could arrive at a feasible settlement sum in my lawsuit.

"I would have to say a million dollars," I told Dad.

Within one business day, my bank account swelled by a million bucks. Within a month, as Shane availed me of his real estate experience and connections, I found, purchased and moved into a new house in Foresthill. I could even walk or ride a horse to Dad's place. I still had half a million to live on without even touching my own money.

This is how my recovery took shape. This is what returning to health looked like for me. I slowly found the former cadence of my life. I inched toward the independent lifestyle I used to enjoy. I knew how fortunate I was to be surrounded by comfort and did not dare take it for granted.

I rode horses on equestrian trails around my property in Placer County and walked my dogs along the ridges and in the valleys across the Sierra Nevada foothills. I volunteered in search-and-rescue missions to recover animals lost in floods and wildfires. I opened my home for free so these dogs, cats and horses could have the shelter and care they needed while being rehabilitated. I happily paid the veterinarian bills for all of these sweet animals.

I traveled to see old friends, too, in Canada, Utah and Texas. Heather had married, moved to a ranch outside San Antonio and brought a baby boy and girl into the world. Over the years, she let me drop in unannounced whenever I needed to regroup. I even ventured back to Los Angeles once or twice, trips that made me realize I could never go back to the stress of living in that enormous, bustling, unforgiving city. Besides, the City of Angels was too far from my family. But up here in Foresthill, in the fresh air of gold country, I thrived — or at least, I saw how I might thrive again.

I gathered referrals to get Sloane's Training Services up and running again. The grind was much harder than when celebrities such as Klaus Wagner, Jesse Sapolu and Lamont Stone stood by and promoted me with unwavering loyalty, and the powerhouse Gold's Gym in Venice let me use its influential name and reputation in my marketing. Regardless, on my own — little by little, one by one — I signed up a handful of clients.

In 1994, seven years after my wrongful incarceration, I was maid of honor in my brother's wedding at his bride's request. I made a wonderful speech and at the reception remembered how much I liked to dance. I kept my footing and was swept into neither euphoria nor despair throughout the day. I went straight home after the celebration ended.

For two years, I prevailed as normalcy held sway. Stability guided me; no crises, only calm. I governed my emotions with supreme purpose, health and mental balance serving as my vivid signposts.

But hidden fault lines, seemingly dormant, can shift abruptly. Stable ground can give way in an instant.

One cold winter day in 1996, the reflection I saw in my full-length mirror depicted a cruel parody of my former self, seriously bloated and wearing clothes tightly stretched over my skin. The weight gain was significant. How long had I put up with this appearance? I seemed to have become twenty-five pounds heavier without even noticing. My legs looked like tree stumps. How dreadful and awkward for my fitness clients to witness this. I was ashamed. In the corporate office and in sales meetings, my outward condition clearly was unacceptable. Is that why I wasn't being asked to represent the company at functions or present reports to staff? How had I not seen my true self before this?

Worse than my physical appearance, my thinking slowed to the pace of dripping molasses and my energy was sapped. The pain in my surgically repaired knee crippled me daily. I couldn't stand for more than ten minutes. I felt disconnected from my previously ardent self. I lost track of my workload, was unprepared for meetings and fell behind on virtually everything. I panicked at the smallest office issues and dropped into an unsustainable pattern: After a few days in the office, I went home, collapsed and slept for two days, stayed in bed, and called in sick. I yearned for the euphoria I had known but suddenly had lost.

One day at work, I called Shane. I was lying in my office under my desk, crying hysterically.

"I can't do this," I screamed through my tears. "I can't handle this. It's not me, Shane!"

"Sloane, you're not being clear," Shane said. "You're OK. Just tell me why you think you can't handle this, so I understand."

"My knees and my back hurt so much that I can't concentrate. I'm scared. I'm listless. I need Dr. Kapoor to take me off the meds. I don't feel like myself on them. I'm disconnected from body and mind."

"Don't go noncompliant on your own, Sloane. You have to keep up the medication and adhere to the therapy. Dr. Kapoor will adjust the dosage. You'll be fine."

"I don't want Dr. Kapoor to adjust the goddamned dosage!"

"Fine. We'll talk about it later. Right now, though, I'm coming to get you and take you home. Stay where you are. You can tell me how you're feeling when we get to your place."

"I don't need to talk. I don't feel a need for anything. I don't feel, I don't think, I just breathe. I barely exist, Shane."

I knew Shane was concerned about me because he started coming around my house much more often after that episode. He tried to convince me to see Dr. Kapoor, but I flatly refused. I didn't want to be judged by the doctor, so I ended our sessions. I cried and cried. In an intellectual daze, I quit the Red Lion job. I stopped scheduling gym sessions for my clients. I couldn't even muster the creativity to do a single personalized workout routine.

Soon, I had no energy to resist Shane's demands that I resume professional crisis intervention, and I returned to Dr. Kapoor. I endured the visits to my psychiatrist by telling myself that it was just a fifty-minute session, an hour of mental torture. I can handle a short hour, anybody can. I dutifully picked up the prescribed meds, as I was told to do, so there'd be no questions asked, and then swiftly locked them away unopened in my safe at home. If I was to get better, I needed to do it my way.

Within a couple of months, my energy skyrocketed and ambition filled every cell in my body. My self-esteem swelled, too. I craved new adventures like a daredevil searching for the next boundary-defying thrill. Colors all around me intensified and sounds sharpened. My thoughts raced again, but in an orderly way. I bought a rental property in Sacramento to generate extra income and purchased another home in Roseville so I'd have a place to stay when I came to the city to see Shane.

Dad spent most of his time at a home he owned on the Pacific Coast in Nehalem, Oregon, where he fished rivers and crystal-clear streams for coho salmon and sturgeon and hunted blacktail deer and quail in coastal emerald forests. I couldn't walk or ride my horse to his house in the foothills anymore, because he was never there, and that angered me. So, in 1998, I acquired a huge tract of undeveloped acreage next to his beautiful Nehalem property overlooking the river.

The lot already had utilities, and I immediately hired architects and interior designers to model and build my Nehalem home. I chartered private flights to Oregon every couple of weeks so I could supervise the construction. Without thinking about the cost or reason, I instructed the pilots to keep the plane waiting and the meter running — sometimes for several days — until I was ready to fly back to Sacramento.

Dad and I agreed that plans for the house were spectacular — rock masonry siding, custom chandeliers, Italian marble countertops and exotic hardwoods. Seeing the progress in the construction was exhilarating, but underlying my elation was an irritability that caused my temper to flare whenever my ideas clashed with those of the designers and builders. I fired two or three of them on the spot for refusing to see things my way or for not finishing certain parts of the project on time.

Days and nights during this time blurred together. When I wasn't flying up to Portland, I took off on whims to South America, London and Portugal. I could not stay still. I needed to move. I needed fresh experiences. Months and months peeled away like minutes.

One week in the year 2000, I returned from an RV trip to Texas, where, on impulse, I had visited Heather. Shane was parked in my driveway, waiting for me. He told me that Mom had quit the legal fight she had sworn to wage on my behalf until justice was served, even if it took the rest of her life.

"Mom said by the time my case reaches the appellate court any jury they seated would be fully knowledgeable of the laws protecting the mentally ill and society as a whole," I complained to Shane. "She said that we would win, and that's why she'd never give up. Her whole cause was to educate more and more people about mental illness and manic depression, on my behalf. What happens now? Who fills the void, Shane? The mentally ill in this country need advocates. Why is Mom quitting?"

"You were never alone in this, Sloane. I saw what you went through, too. I am one hundred percent behind the cause to get proper help for people with mental disabilities. But, now, we have to fight for the cause outside the courtroom. And we'll continue to do whatever we can."

"But what did she tell you? Why is she dropping out of the fight?"

Shane looked away, so I badgered him some more for the answer.

"She's got a lot going on..."

"Like what?"

"She left her husband. The mental and physical abuse he put her through was too much for her to handle. Now, she needs to take care of herself and tend to her own health."

"And you agreed?"

"Her doctor told her."

"What about the appeal?"

"I suggested she drop the appeal, yes, and move out of that house. She's found a nice place in Sun City Roseville."

"I knew it was you! Mom wouldn't have abandoned the cause. You didn't like how much money it was costing her."

"I'm only interested in her health. That's the bottom line."

"How bad was the abuse, then?"

"I don't know. Bad enough to leave him and just get out."

"You know, Shane. How bad was it?"

"Mom said they pulled guns on each other one day."

"Jesus Christ!"

"The cops came. And that's when she knew it was over."

I dropped the subject and left the room because I felt my body getting tense. Irritation squeezed my shoulders and back. Fury sparked in my chest and flashed into my eyes and temples. I heard Shane walk out the front door and start his car.

I ran outside and down the driveway to try to catch him, but I didn't know what I was going to say or do. My restless mind jumped to something else, and I ended up at the rural mailbox on the road at the edge of my property. The box was full, but I managed to carry all the letters and small packages back to the house.

I opened up an envelope sent from Stevens Family Investments. It was an invitation to the annual shareholder meeting. The timing could not have been better. After receiving a proxy statement a few months earlier, I started paying attention to the strategic moves being made at Stevens Family Investments, Port Seattle Timber and the company's growing real estate division.

A keen desire to delve deeper into the company's performance tugged at me. I wanted to know more. Dad wouldn't live forever, so I felt obliged to educate myself about our pecuniary affairs. Considering how much I was spending on my Oregon home, my own accounts required scrutiny, too. I scoured annual reports, tax returns and shareholder correspondence to see how decisions were affecting my father's portfolios, as well as my own.

If I still had been groggy from lithium and other medications or toiling away at that dull, brain-numbing servant's job at Red Lion, I could not have taken on this consequential task of delving into board minutes and requesting additional records and public disclosures. My now-lucid mind propelled me.

I seized the opportunity to call cousins and uncles and suppliers and buyers — the entire ecosystem of the company. I asked them about the meaning, outcome and perceptions of our business strategies. In my former state of mind, I would not have uncovered deeply troubling decisions being made by Conrad and other leaders at our Pacific Northwest headquarters.

While this was going on, construction was completed on my Oregon coast home, though I had not been back to the site in a long time and had not seen the finished product. Now my research into the family business brought me back to Nehalem in order to talk to Dad about my concerns. It had been months since I had seen him, too, and the annual shareholder meeting was fast approaching.

On the flight north, with my yellow legal pad covered in questions, I became peeved while thinking how much time Dad spent in Nehalem instead of near me in Foresthill. Why did I have to make the effort to get on a plane to see him? Why did he abandon me and move up there in the first place? I didn't run away from him; he walked out on me. He never once said he was grateful that I was building a home near his or stopped by while it was under construction.

My irascibility grew into a maelstrom of anger, and my heart fluttered as fast as my thoughts. I plugged into the in-flight entertainment system and listened to talk radio. Passengers and flight attendants interrupted several times to ask me to quiet down because I was loudly repeating the words of the talk show host. I was verbalizing everything as fast as I was hearing it, astonishingly in sync with the speaker. God, I thought, I knew the words before they left his mouth, transformed into electrical signals carried by radio waves and reconstituted through my in-ear headphones. The duration of the flight sped by. I was relieved when we touched down on the runway. I felt like I hadn't taken a breath during the entire flight.

The trip to elucidate my worries and ask Father face to face about his interpretation of certain financial judgments was ill-timed. He did not answer the door, so I entered with my own key and called his name. I checked the kitchen, family room and television room, but he wasn't there. I walked farther back into the house to his bedroom.

I wasn't prepared for the shock upon seeing him lying in bed with a thin cover over his rigid barrel chest. I instantly knew he was in bad health. His lips and tips of his fingers displayed a bluish tinge, and his eyes looked weary. His hands trembled slightly, and his voice was soft but hoarse.

"Dad! What's going on? Are you OK?"

"Honey, you caught me at a bad time. I'm fine, really. I didn't hear you come in. I was feeling a little tired and under the weather, so I took a nap. I'll get up in a minute and fix us something to eat, all right? Come over here first. Pull up that chair there. "

I sat next to him, and he insisted he was just suffering from a cold.

"And old age," he joked.

I let him believe I accepted his lie and changed the topic.

"You need to come back down to Sacramento, Dad, where I can keep an eye on you. What do you think you're doing up here all alone?"

"I want to be closer to my roots. This place reminds me of where it all began. In the great Pacific Northwest. It draws me back like an old song. I can fish and hunt to my heart's content, just like we used to."

"You're spending too much time up here all alone. You should be more connected to me and Shane. There's a new active adult community called Del Webb. We can get you a place there, something smaller that you can keep up with."

"Did you drive all the way up here to tell me that?"

"I flew. And, no, that's not the only reason. I have some concerns with some of the family's business decisions that I wanted to run by you before the annual meeting. Let's fly to Arizona and attend together. We'll be united."

"What are you so worried about, sweetheart?"

"Protecting our stake."

"The company is on solid financial ground."

"They won't be much longer if they keep selling real estate at a loss and talking about steward ownership of our land assets and all this socialist stuff. Conrad is putting societal benefit over our personal gain. He has a fiduciary responsibility to us, to all of the shareholders. I need to protect you, as my father, and your stockpile of money, as well as my own, and ensure that the family still intends to adhere to their mission of providing wealth for generations to come. The importance of asking hard questions at the meeting and digging to the bottom for answers to their actions never seemed greater."

"There are clear valuation methods for our shares. Your grandfather wrote the company bylaws and made sure family control and harmony is maintained."

"Bullshit. You know it can all be rewritten. Come with me and let's take action. Let's assume some control before it's too late."

"Look at my girl, all fired up about the family business. I can't make that trip, though, sweetheart. Not right now."

"Fine. I'll handle it myself. But will you at least consider moving back to be closer to me? The elk and bear and trout around here aren't going to look after you."

"I'll think about it," he said with a chuckle, swinging his good leg and his stump over the edge of the bed. It required a great effort. "Let's go in the kitchen and find something for us to eat. How's your mom, by the way?"

"She's fine, why?"

"It's just that I haven't talked to her for a very long time."

"Shane said she stopped her legal fight against L.A. County."

"Well, it's been fifteen years. Maybe it's about time. Shane didn't think she'd be able to keep that up with her health issues."

"What health issues?"

"Nothing. I mean, she's just getting older like all of us, that's all."

"When I talked to Shane, he acted like he wasn't telling me everything. Is there something wrong with her?" I asked while watching Dad fit his stump into the socket of his prosthetic limb. "Why am I the last one to know? Why do you and Shane think you need to protect me? What is it, Dad?"

"You're overreacting, Sloane. I haven't seen or talked to your mother for a very long time. We're all getting older and can't do what we used to. I certainly can't. Come on, I'm up! Let's grab something to eat, since you came all the way up here."

CHAPTER 6

The annual family gathering took place at Rancho de los Ojos in Wick-enburg, Arizona. After packing the night before my flight, I rewrote in a notepad each grievance I wanted to address. I began each item in capital letters with phrases such as: "THIS REALLY WORRIES ME" and "THIS REQUIRES SERIOUS EXPLANATION." At the airport and on the flight, I reread my notes and confidential files I had acquired about distributions, redemptions and growth, and went over my notes again.

My knee throbbed and stiffened throughout the flight. After deplaning, an airport passenger assistant provided crutches for me, and I hobbled to the ground transportation area to rent a pickup truck. I took pain pills for my knee and drove an hour out to the ranch.

Sun-baked saguaros and rocky untamed wilderness surrounded Rancho de los Ojos. On the distant horizon, mountains rose from the desert floor like fortress walls, colored burnt orange and deep purple. On my way to the rustic little guest casitas, I encountered nobody. I watched the vibrant desert sunset from the porch, then went to the nearby cantina.

I nearly missed the next morning's general meeting after going on a morning hike and losing track of time. When I hurriedly entered the meeting room, a singer was just finishing an entertainment interlude be-tween speakers. The door banged open a little too loudly, and the racket echoed across the room. Heads turned around to see who had caused the commotion.

I wore the same outfit I had gone hiking in four hours earlier and was profusely sweating under my old baggy corduroy breeches. My leather boots, wet from crossing streams, squeaked on the floor as I walked to my seat. My hair was falling out of my ponytail.

The seated shareholders were part of a company whose origins hearkened back to blue-collar stevedores laboring on noisy, bustling docks, and lumbermen swinging axes in dense forests, so more people wore flannel than tailored, navy and charcoal suits at this corporate meeting. Even so, my attire set me apart.

I settled into a seat about four rows back from the stage in a conference hall filled with about one hundred and fifty people. I felt an electric tension in the hall. The southwest sunlight streaming through the windows splashed across the burnished wood floor, rustic chandeliers shined overhead and a subtle aroma of leather, cologne and coffee blended in the air. Lunch-pail workers built Port Seattle Timber and Stevens Investments, but we were all owners of a good, old-fashioned, for-profit American company.

I spotted Conrad sitting with the executives on stage. He wore a dignified, tailored gray suit, a model of controlled confidence in front all these people who looked on with calculated interest and polite scrutiny. He had aged significantly since I last saw him. He was older than Dad, perhaps eighty-three. His son sat next to him and was going to be named the next chief executive at this retreat.

After the break, I waited for the question-and-answer period to address the board and everybody in the hall. My foot tapped impatiently as Conrad reported on real estate ventures and moved on to the Investor's Briefing segment. I could no longer wait and stood in the middle of his presentation.

I don't remember how I started my broadside, but words erupted from my mouth. I recall a microphone being shoved into my hand and thinking, do they really want to amplify my fulminations? OK, then. They did not know what was coming next.

My personal, scathing, uncontrollable, rapid-fire tirade is on record. You can read my rants about the board's questionable investment decisions anytime. Nobody interrupted. Nobody could — or would.

This is how I began:

"Your bloated egos and country club Jewish connections and petty power trips are steering us to disaster. You all — yes, you and you and you — know what I mean; don't pretend you don't. I see your faces. You ignore blunder after blunder after — after all, why change now? Well, I won't stay silent anymore. My father is a direct descendent of Big Papa Conrad and Joseph and George Stevens, the past and last great leaders of what is now a carcass of a company, its blood and raw flesh dripping off the lips of our CEO."

My eyes were intense and wild as my arms gestured frantically. Everybody was stunned into silence, paralyzed, unable even to summon security.

"You can't silence the truth. It rises above all. Now you must hear it. Your disastrous decisions, your retarded brainchildren are costing me millions of dollars, costing dozens of others in here the millions of dollars they were promised through our company's touchstone of generational growth. We've led our lives, planned our future and overseen our phil-anthropic initiatives based upon Big Papa's idea of long-term family prosperity.

"But now, what? Stupid choices that a child wouldn't even make if he were at the helm of this company are costing us all money, but these unintelligent decisions may literally kill my father, who is dying as we speak and could not be here today, because he may not be able to afford the safety net that would prolong his life or at least make his last days upon Earth comfortable and worth living."

The board exchanged furtive glances. I heard someone shuffling papers. I faltered for a microsecond, and my hands trembled. Was I making sense? Did any of them see what I saw? The truth?

Conrad started to move his microphone closer as if he wanted to say something, but he slowed his reaction. I glared at him, pointing an accusing finger at the board of directors, and resumed.

"Don't you dare try to defend yourself, Uncle. You sent an email out to everybody here stating that my Dad and I would not be attending because of his failing health. Well, surprise, you fucking communist. I'm here and you better listen up. This isn't your own Bilderberg Group or your own Anti-Defamation League or some New World Order. You need to listen to somebody other than the outsiders who you've allowed into the family to ruin everything. You let a Zionist marry your own daughter, my cousin, and get a toehold in the family business.

"Now what? Don't you know they want to take over the United States? Why are we selling off assets now? Because Conrad says it's best for the stewardship of the land and the environment? Or is it because someone wants us less profitable, to weaken the family so outsiders — yes, the same ones you let onto the board — can seize control? You say debt is low, but who benefits? Not us, not the people who built this company. The Russians and the Jews and all the gypsies. If any of you want proof, just take a look at our measly cash distributions. The company yielded a shitty net profit of fifteen million dollars last year. During the last quarter, we sold one hundred and eight million dollars of real estate. One hundred and eight million! That represents ten percent of the asset value of the company. Net profit on land sales was about three million, representing a return of two percent, but inflation is nearly three percent. This return represents a loss to the company. A loss that you think we all should shoulder. Who's in charge? I haven't seen the numbers add up for months, but nobody will answer for it. Suddenly the family has no voice. Where's the strategy?"

I drifted into the center aisle to have more room to move and breathe and continued pointing out the company's egregious errors. Conrad, gripping his armrest tighter, tried again to answer my accusations, but I drowned out his feeble attempts.

"Port Seattle's cost of debt is supposedly very low, in fact, so low that I'm wondering why the company would retire debt by selling land at a loss when the prospects of a huge profit from our investment is impending with the interchange opening up on August eighth. It's a growth corridor, for Christ's sake. Why would you choose to liquidate this much asset base at this time? And at a loss? Why? It's idiotic. It's communistic. It's socialistic. The trend shows we're not profitable and we carry a lot of debt, leaving nothing for unit holders. We need to be profitable again, like in the days when Joseph and George led the company's strategy. I understand the Zionists have purchased this country lock, stock and barrel and are in cahoots with the communists, but the reinvestment between forestry and real estate divisions is nearly a fifty-fifty split, yet you want us to be satisfied with losses on one side and..."

I saw the vice chairman mouth something to an aide. I had paused for effect, and now Conrad pounced.

"That's enough Sloane. You're out of line. You're out of order. We have business to conduct and you are wasting people's time, not to mention slandering us. You need to stop your racist rant, leave this hall and this gathering altogether and get back on the road and get back on your medication. Security! Center aisle! Security!"

"We all just want what my grandmother and grandfather wished for and worked so hard to achieve, living their good lives. They insulated themselves from suffering and..."

"I can assure you, Sloane, that George and Agnes suffered a hell of a lot on a very personal level," Conrad answered back. "They bore more than their fair share of heartbreak — which is something you would do well to remember."

Security guards closed in on me so I sped up my words to get them out before being hauled away.

"You love communist Russia too much, Conrad. I see what you're doing with this company. And you have the audacity to poll the family and skew the results on whether we want investor-ownership or steward ownership? You want to prioritize long-term purpose over profits, reinvest gains for societal benefit rather than wealth for generations to come — which Big Papa wanted. You've made it so ownership of our land cannot be sold or inherited in order to ensure an alignment with the new mission of social justice pandering, shareholder theft and profit masking. My father will die sick and penniless after being forced to sell his home because you want to reinvest profits for the good of society instead of personal gain for those of us whose predecessors worked so hard to provide for. This company is crumbling under your misguided leadership. Crumbling! Everybody in this hall, mark my words: This is a circus of incompetence!"

Guards grabbed my arms and forcefully led me out of the building and down the flagstone pathway to my casita. They waited at the door for me to pack up and watched as I drove away in my rented pickup.

On the way to the airport, an idea struck me. I should record my internal dialogues. Journaling was always my habit, but lately my thoughts rushed past, relentless and too swiftly to catch on paper. Keeping a true record — a running log — might help if anything were to happen to me. Someone might care to know.

I pulled into a shopping mall and bought twelve cassette recorders and dozens of batteries from an electronics store. Now I could catch my train of thought — once too wild, relentless and impossible to hold.

The letters of admonishment from the Family Council arrived within fourteen days after I returned from Arizona.

I still hadn't talked to my father about the meeting because something didn't sit right with me about the trip. I needed to figure out what it was, but I remember little from the family gathering. I felt a vague sense of shame and regret but was unsure why, so how the hell could I accurately explain the meeting to him?

Afterward, I recorded a few hours of my own reflections on the cassettes, but I didn't have time to review them. I know I asked sharp questions of the board. After reading the Family Counsel's disciplinary letters, I recalled some of what happened. The correspondence was addressed to my father and me.

Sloane,

Your outburst prematurely ended what I thought was a very informative investor briefing last Saturday. I was embarrassed for you and your father, as well as for the family members who had to endure the total lack of respect that you personally displayed to us all.

Sloane, this is just the type of behavior that the Family Council has been trying to determine how to manage, as it is very corrosive to the fabric of a healthy family.

I should have known better than to try to answer your questions at that time for that only seemed to further enrage you. When I observed that your questions had turned into personal and group insults, I became very concerned about the damage that was being inflicted on the people who have labored tirelessly for your family for decades and who more appropriately should have been thanked for their excellent performance.

While there is really no way for you to retrieve the very damaging words that you said at the meeting, I believe that you can restore some respect by promptly apologizing in writing to the Family Council. I suggest that you copy those attending the meeting as well.

It is also imperative that you respond similarly in writing to the Board of Directors and to me personally with direction that I pass your letter on to our officers - all of whom you insulted with your disparaging remarks about their qualifications, loyalty and character.

In closing, I suggest that at some point in the future you take the time to write me a letter describing exactly what it is that you really want. There must be something behind your anger that I cannot discern.

As we discussed after the meeting, if you and your father continue to be frustrated with our economic or other performance you should submit your personal units for redemption.

Conrad Stevens
Chairman and CEO

And then the second letter arrived.

Dear Eddy and Sloane,

As fellow Stevens family members, and in some cases persons who have known you and enjoyed your company for years, we appreciate and applaud your interest in the family company. And we all note and are grateful, Sloane, for the personal care and assistance you afford to you father, to enable and facilitate his continued active involvement as a unitholder and family member.

However, as Family Council members bearing the responsibility to foster constructive communication within the family, and between the family and the Board we are profoundly disappointed at the style, tone, and inferences of your comments and questions at the end of that Investor Briefing. There is ample room for factual questions, and for the expression of disagreement with particular decisions or plans of company management, of the Board, or of the Family Council. And there is ample room for articulating the reasons for that disagreement. But in every case this communication must be characterized by decency and respect for other individuals and their integrity. Your comments and questions were often characterized by attack, insult, and implications of lack of integrity. As such they were and are destructive of healthy relationships and therefore unacceptable. We cannot allow room for such comments at family gatherings.

We have reviewed the letter to you regarding your behavior at the meeting, and support his conclusion that an apology is both necessary for and would go a long way toward restoring your dignity and respectability as caring unitholders and family members.

This letter is written out of care for the well-being of the whole family, including yourselves, and of the company, and we trust that you will hear it in that vein.

Stevens Family Council

As I finished reading the last letter, Shane drove up to my Foresthill home. I was physically and emotionally exhausted before I even read the letters. I must have slept a lot the night before, because I did not know what time or day it was when my brother unexpectedly showed up. My head was reeling.

"Tell me about the family gathering," he said as I bumbled around, fixing coffee for us. Until he asked about the trip, I hadn't said more than a few words to him because of the vortex between my ears. My jaw tightened and pressure pushed against my heavy eyelids from the inside

"My general impression is there was an air of unhappiness with everything, among everybody," I told my brother, releasing a long breath as I struggled to contain my annoyance. "I don't know why."

"Did something bad happen?"

"It's all kind of unclear to me."

"Unclear? Did you talk to anybody there to find out if they shared your feelings?"

"I left early."

"Did you talk to people when you got back? Did it defuse the situation?"

"I don't know."

"What have you been doing since you got back?"

"Sleeping. Resting. The traveling exhausted me."

"Are you taking your medication?"

"I told you I was done with that, Shane. I wouldn't have been able to go to Arizona and address the board if I had been on the meds. I'm stable now — balanced. Getting things done for once, you know."

"You don't seem very balanced to me. It doesn't look like you've slept or showered in days. You need to continue taking the lithium and valproate. And go back to seeing Dr. Kapoor regularly."

"You're not inside my body and mind, Shane. You have no idea what it's like. Do you like being mentally sound, coherent and steady? Do you like feeling normal? Feeling something? Anything? Well, so do I. That's what being unmedicated is like for me."

"Have you talked to your father since you got back?"

"I tried, but didn't reach him. I should get back up there. He didn't look too good last time I visited. I think he should move back down here to be closer to us, to me."

"That's a good idea."

Suspicious, I studied my brother.

"Why do you say it like that? What do you know, Shane? Is he all right?"

"Just try calling him again. I'm sure he'd love to hear from you. He probably wants to know all about the trip."

I felt my voice tighten.

"Last time I was in Nehalem, he asked about Mom. Did I tell you that? He sounded like he was very concerned about her. But there was something else. I felt like he knew something and wasn't telling me. Is mom all right, Shane?"

My brother shifted, avoiding my eyes. I asked again, my voice rising. He stayed quiet.

"I'm feeling tense like the last time we spoke about Mom. Since you won't tell me what's going on, I'm going to go over to her place right now and see her myself."

I grabbed my car keys.

"Sloane, wait," Shane said. "I didn't know when — or how, really — to tell you..."

"Tell me what?"

"Sloane, I don't want to worry you and get you all worked up," Shane said, softer.

"What is it, damn it?"

"Look, Mom's not getting along too well."

"She just left that abusive husband of hers, right? It's going to take her some time to heal, don't you think?"

"That's not whole picture."

"What do you mean?"

Shane hesitated.

"Several weeks ago I became very concerned about her behavior..." he began again.

"What kind of behavior?"

"Sometimes she can't find the words for simple things."

"For example?"

"She'll call the dog 'that thing,' or she'll ask me the name of common everyday items, like kitchen utensils. She held up a fork the other day and asked what it was."

"It happens with old age."

"I took her to the store and she was commenting loudly about how other shoppers looked, you know, their appearance, and what they were buying and how they were walking. She was just blurting out her biases and opinions. She didn't even bat an eye, like she didn't even realize what she had was saying."

"Oh, hell, we all do that," I reasoned with an anxious laugh.

"But what really disturbs me is she's neglecting basic hygiene. Lately, I've been going over there and she will not have showered or bathed or combed her hair or even changed clothes for several days."

My heart stuttered.

"Jesus, Shane! Did you do anything? Did you take her to see a doctor?"

"You won't even go to the doctor, Sloane."

"Well, did you?"

"Yes, in fact."

"And?"

"She's diagnosed with frontotemporal dementia."

"What the fuck is that?"

"It's a progressive condition."

"Like Alzheimer's?"

"No, it primarily affects behavior and personality rather than memory."

Guilt, panic, anger — something tightened in my chest.

"Why didn't you tell me? This seems pretty fucking important, Shane. You couldn't call me, for Christ's sake?"

"You've been busy, Sloane. You haven't been home very much in the last few months. How was I supposed to call? I drove over here, didn't I?"

"Dad knows, too, right?"

"Yes."

A wave of indignation spilled over me.

"I knew it. You told Dad before you told me. And you don't even give a shit about Dad. You never like talking to him. Do you think I can't handle bad news? Are you trying to protect me, you little shit? He and Mom couldn't get along, not even when I needed them the most after I was hospitalized, and you thought it was good idea to tell him about Mom's illness before me? Don't you know how Dad complicates things, especially when it comes to Mom. She needs our unconditional love and support. Yours and mine, not Dad's. Dad doesn't offer her love and support. He gives her the opposite. Do you think you're the only one who can give her strength and respect? Not me?"

Anguish flickered inside my body, but I continued.

"I'm sure you just want the best care for Mother, but you're egotistical. And it pisses me off when you keep things from me. When were you going to tell me about any of this? You think I can't handle it, didn't you? You thought if you told Dad that he might let his little angel down easier. Poor, fragile, Sloane — she needs protection. Is that what you thought?"

"No... I..." Shane stammered.

I heard my voice shaking, my anger boiling over.

"Well fuck it. Cat's out of the bag, and I'm going to go see Mom. Alone this time!"

"Wait! I thought it was best to bring Eddy back into the fold. I believed he'd make his way back down here if he knew everything that was going on. Despite his flaws, he might want to help out. I told your father how upset you've been because he spends all of his time in Oregon. I told him not everything centers on his needs. I told him he can't re-live his youth up there and ignore everybody else. He needs to find his way back down here, at least until we figure out Mom's care and you get back to therapy. He can't just check out and go back to living like he's a child again. Isn't this, ultimately, what you wanted? "

"How did he take the news?"

"He said it was all his fault. I told him there's nobody to blame here."

"But there's always somebody to blame, Shane," I said, quieter now. "Always. Even when they don't mean to, they exacerbate the problem, never knowing what damage their actions, their inattention, their apathy can cause."

I kept my glare fixed on the floor.

He reached for my hand, but I pulled away.

"Do you know what I mean?"

"I do."

I nodded, fighting the urge to scream or sob, and turned to leave.

We found out there are no cures for FTD. You cannot alter the course of the disease.

At first, Shane, Dad and I came together as one to provide the best care for our mother. We didn't want Mom institutionalized, so we let her stay at her own home. We came up with a personalized approach to go along with the antidepressant and antipsychotic medication. We arranged for language and occupational therapy. We took her to support groups. We set up regular massages and took her to coffee shops to meet friends. We were being comprehensive in our approach. When her medication needed to be professionally administered, we hired a nurse to stay at her home during the day — at a cost of six thousand dollars per month.

Once she was diagnosed, observable signs of the disease manifested quickly. As her symptoms multiplied, I feared Shane again was withholding information from me. For example, he didn't tell me why he had confiscated her car keys. He also never explained how the authorities ended up suspending her driver's license after she had caused several fender benders. I didn't know he had received an emergency call from Sun City after she wandered off across the community's golf course in one hundred and five degree heat dressed in a sheer chiffon dress with no underwear, high heels, a sun hat and umbrella. He found her dancing and twirling across the fairways.

I was dating a boy I really liked named Pat, but all of the drama around Mom was stressing me out and straining our relationship. Suddenly it seemed as if I didn't exist to Shane, or to Mom. He never called me. He never stopped by. He never provided any news about Mom. I never knew whether I should cancel a date or cut short a road trip with Pat to lend a hand in dealing with Mom's condition and her changing personality.

One day, I summoned the courage to leave my house, even though I was experiencing a lot of anxiety. I drove to Mom's apartment unannounced. Shane was there, and Mom was so happy to see us together that she insisted on making scrambled eggs and toast for all of us for lunch. As she wished, Shane and I visited in another room while she cooked. When I walked into the kitchen to offer her help, I found Mom cooking the eggs directly on the electric stovetop — without a pan.

After that, we decided to provide Mom with round-the-clock home health care.

"That's going to double the cost to twelve thousand dollars per month," Shane said reluctantly. "I'm already cutting checks from my personal accounts to pay for Mom's care."

"Why don't we work together to get hold of her trust," I suggested.

"I thought you knew. Mom has already made me successor trustee."

I was mystified.

"What? When? No. She would never make you the sole trustee. She would either have you and I do it together or bring in an institutional group, like a bank, or trust company to handle her affairs, but not you. Everybody knows you're a spendthrift."

"A judge has already signed off on it. You have to understand how important it is for me to be able to quickly make decisions on behalf of Mom in all sorts of matters."

"I don't believe you. Show me the trust!"

"No. But from now on, I'll inform you of all decisions, OK?"

"Who was your attorney?"

"Nina Schwartz."

"A Jew!"

"Sloane! What the hell?"

"This is horrible. I am going to get an attorney myself and get that trust."

"What has gotten into you, Sloane? You're being unreasonable. Let's work together on Mom's behalf."

"I never expected to get anything from her, financially. I don't want any of her belongings, either. You can have them. I just don't believe she'd make you sole successor trustee."

Two weeks later, I was talking to my dad by phone and he told me Shane relocated Mom from her home to an assisted living facility. I ripped the cord off the phone set and drove directly to Shane's house.

At his door, I nudged his wife aside and bulldozed my way in. He was on the couch, watching a football game.

"How out of touch are you?" I yelled, standing in front of him. "How utterly unaware? You knowingly made a unilateral decision on Mom's care against my wishes and against her will."

"I needed to make a financial decision so I placed her in a facility with a good nursing staff. It's close, in Citrus Heights. What's the problem?"

"What's the nurse-to-patient ratio?"

"One to fifteen."

"Jesus, Shane! That's terrible! You're tactless. Your decision crosses the line. This is emotional and physical mistreatment. She would rather die than be ripped from her old, familiar surroundings and shut in a group home like that. That's what she told me. I don't know what you were thinking. All I ask, she said, is to die at home after living a most wonderful, remarkable life. After she told me this she broke down and cried for hours thinking about it."

"We can keep looking for a better living situation — I have no problem with that. Maybe we can find a place with more staffing. But she cannot stay at home. Paying for twenty-four hour home health care is unsustainable. "

"Why? She's got money. I have money. Maybe I need to gain temporary conservatorship so you're not making stupid, biased decisions all the time. It's true; males have no business dealing with this type of end-of-life decision making for their parents."

"That's out of line, Sloane. I'm doing what I think is right."

"You know what all of this has done for me? Driven away another boyfriend. Another good one, gone. He said he couldn't handle the emotions you and Mom put me through."

"I'm sorry. Look, together we can get temporary co-conservatorship of Mom. It'll take a formal court process, but I'll get Nina Schwartz on it right away."

"Not her!"

"What is your problem with her? That's the compromise, Sloane, take it or leave it. You can have equal say in health-care decisions, but my attorney will handle the petition. She's already intimate with the details."

"I bet she is. But I want the power to make health-care and financial management decisions."

"Fine, we'll get Nina to sort out the financial management part, too."

I should have seen it was a deceptive arrangement. Ten minutes into the meeting in the law office of Nina Schwartz, I was humiliated. She was privy to my very private struggles with manic depression and acute bouts of schizophrenia. Her eyes bore into me in judgment, and shame washed over me in waves and my cheeks started burning.

"Your battles with mental health still reverberate in everything you do, Sloane," she said. "No judge is going to entrust you with the stewardship of your mother's affairs. It'd be like a ship in the middle of repairing its sails heading out to sea to face a storm. It's not wise and it's not fair."

I stood up and stormed out of the office.

There was only one way the Zionist attorney could have found out about my past. My brother was supposed to be my valiant champion in life, forever, but he was willing to resort to ruthlessness to gain ultimate control over Mom's money and health — to the point of holding the sensitive nature of my medical history and the pain it continues to cause me in contempt.

I vowed not to utter another word to him ever again.

Shortly after the day at Nina Schwarz's office, Shane showed up without notice at my house in Foresthill.

"You have some fucking nerve to come up here," I yelled, cutting him off on the path up to my front door.

"I just wanted to tell you the court approved a third-party fiduciary to serve as conservator," he said. "Nina thought that'd be in our best interest to relinquish control of direct-decision making. It's fair. See, she isn't that bad, is she?"

I thought about this for a few minutes as Shane waited uncomfortably for my response.

"You are the lowest," I said. "Your actions are so demeaning. Is it the money, or the prospect of money, that prompted you to be such an asshole? Have you grown tired of living on the fringes of great wealth all around you, while never actually being able to enjoy such affluence? Or are you just a control freak — the strong older brother who gets to be sole successor trustee?"

"What are you talking about?"

"I've hired my own attorney and we're going to sue you over the trust. I don't know if we'll ever recover from the irreparable damage you've done to our relationship."

"You said you didn't care about the money, Sloane. Neither do I. You didn't let me finish. The fiduciary has already found a Sacramento home for Mom with one nurse for every two patients. It's what you wanted! It's the best case scenario."

I went inside without another word to Shane and locked the door. Mom lived out her remaining years there, and Shane and I never talked again before she died.

For years, I staggered from loneliness. I choked on gloom. I would never be able to recapture precious time lost. I could have been at her bedside comforting her, but instead I stayed away out of fear of encountering Shane face to face. If we ever met by chance at her residence, I didn't know how I'd react. So I played it safe.

Instead of spending her precious final days at her side, I spent hours talking to attorneys and appearing before judges because I knew Mother would never have made my brother sole successor of her trust on her own. I set out to prove myself right. After all, Mom was undergoing chemotherapy treatment at the time she put the trust together. She was vulnerable and easily persuaded and manipulated. When I first learned Mom was terminally ill, she told me that she had signed an amendment making Shane and I co-trustees — but Shane and that horrible, Jewish attorney of his, secreted that document from me.

One day, I called Nina Schwartz and bitched at her over the phone.

"Why was I never shown the amended trust?" I demanded. "Where is it?"

"It doesn't exist," she lied.

"We'll see. I'm going to have you deposed," I told her.

"No judge will ever depose me!" she responded emphatically, egotistically.

In the middle of my legal dispute with her and Shane, a higher power intervened.

Mom died.

I wish I could erase her last days from my memory, when she was just a fragment of the person she once was. When I last saw her alive, she showed no vitality. Her cognition sputtered, and any language was a distant memory inside her cerebral cortex. Her body stiffened, her limbs went rigid. A large part of my soul dried up, too, and blew away in the wind.

Mom sent me a vision from heaven. A truth was revealed. Even at my most wretched, I now clearly understood that my brother was one of them. He was gypsy. He was against me. He was one of my enemies, part of a vast problem and a component of the worst global criminal conspiracy.

We avoided each other when Mom was ill, and we didn't speak to each other at her funeral. Shane planned everything: the services, the guests to invite, the type of casket, the grave marker and headstone inscription, the cemetery and burial plot. But I paid my respects.

Dad was too sick to attend the funeral. Months earlier, I had finally talked him into leaving Oregon and moving close to me, but he, too, deteriorated quickly. He died a year after Mom of chronic obstructive pulmonary disease and malnutrition.

In his final moments, I looked at his sunken eyes and his incurved cheeks. With my finger, I touched his lips, colored with cyanosis, and watched his lucidness fade. Soon his long, busy, imperfect, bittersweet life ebbed away.

Crushing sadness and despair pervaded my entire being, but somehow I managed all the details for Dad's funeral and burial. We held services in Seattle. The attendees swelled with Stevens family members, and I guess that made me proud, although I was mostly numb to any feelings other than fatigue and sorrow.

My world, once anchored by the presence of Mom and Dad, spun recklessly out of control after his funeral. The rapid succession of deaths of the two people I loved most in life dragged me into a cavernous depression.

I emerged from this unrelenting, bone-deep blackness two months later. And I missed Dad even more after such exhaustive, pointless grief.

Shane tried to talk to me at Dad's funeral and apologize for how acrimonious our relationship had become.

"Sloane, I'm sorry. Words are hard to form after the silence that has existed between us for so long, but I want to tell you that if you need anything, any kind of support, I'm here for you. It would mean a lot to me if we could be close again."

"Just give me space, a lot of space right now, thank you," I said tersely, and turned abruptly away as another guest approached me.

I ached to see Dad one more time. I missed him even more than I missed Mom. He always saw my potential. His confidence in my intellect and abilities never wavered. He championed my growth and objectives.

Every day I regret that I never got a chance to tell him about the plot I saw developing against me. I never had an opportunity to point out to him how the conspirators were trying to eliminate me. He would have understood when nobody else did.

He would have watched the tendrils of suspicion grow into this irrefutable reality I wrestle with every day. I would have convinced him beyond a doubt that certain groups of people were chasing me, closing in on me. He'd have been highly alarmed by the evidence I have gathered, and will share with you shortly.

Together, Dad and I would have gazed into a world unseen by most people, but it was as real as the wind howling through the trees.

CHAPTER 7

After Mom and Dad's deaths, my heart raced incessantly. Suspicion and dread pressed against my chest. Shadows and voices drifted through my house as if conjured from nowhere. Intervals of peace and quiet provided relief, but the mental maelstrom lasted for years.

At age forty-seven, a decade of severe menopause began, bringing with it hot flashes, night sweats, palpitations, insomnia, weight gain and vaginal discomfort.

Had these been the only problems I faced, I would have felt blessed. A much bigger worry was the consortium of groups relentlessly stalking and wanting to harm, silence or kill me. These evil people sensed my new vulnerability and my isolation from family and friends. They zealously wanted to test their psychological and technological weapons on me. They would not stop until wrongs that I and others like me caused were put to rights.

When Shane invited me to dinner at his home — let's call it an overture of reconciliation — he did not know the scope and scale of this wild, dangerous, weird and diabolical ragtag mob intent on destroying me.

At the time of the dinner, Shane wasn't partnered with the politicians, FBI, Bureau of Alcohol, Tobacco, Firearms and Explosives, the federal Drug Enforcement Agency, the Jewish Anti-Defamation League, Russian communists, or Placer County employees and neighbors who all wanted to torture me. But he wasn't trying to stop them, either. And he certainly didn't listen to what I had to say.

I accepted his invitation with hesitation, trepidation and lingering suspicions. His wife and two children, ages eight and three at the time, were present. I was cordial, even though I certainly had other ideas about how I would raise those kids. The eldest child, a boy, should have been sent to a therapeutic boarding school or wilderness therapy program. The little girl was sweet enough, but I think I would have hired a nanny right away to handle the obvious emotional and cognitive challenges she faced.

I expected Shane to offer an olive branch, but he didn't care about my difficulties, which I had explained started four months after I filed my lawsuit against Placer County in February of 2009.

"I am being barraged by these thugs of Placer County," I told Shane and his wife, while their son blankly stared at me. "My next-door neighbor is trying to destroy the serenity of my home and damage the value of my property."

I described the strange people who came into my house under the guise of workmen and repairmen.

"All my communications are being intercepted, Shane. My security system was dismantled, and these imposters, representing the cable company or the utilities or pest control, arrive unexpectedly at my house. Contractors I've hired repeat things back to me that I had said the night before on the telephone to friends and family who live far away."

I told him about the hundreds of legal documents and handwritten notes I pinned to the walls of my house, each tracking what the conspirators had done. I also had dozens of audiotapes locked in my safe, all recording the details of their plot against me. Shane dismissed everything as hallucinations brought on by the trauma of losing my mother and father. Was he lending a hand to the other side?

"These thugs want to break into my home and steal and ransack what they can," I continued. "I only leave my property to go to the post office or haul my garbage to the dump so the wild animals won't get into it. Your house is the only other place I've visited in the past two months."

"Why, Sloane?" my sister-in-law asked. "Why? Have you asked yourself why they would want to do this?"

"Because of my political beliefs," I said simply. "And because I have means and resources. They want to take it all away from me. They have a large network here — and I have shown the audacity to take on one of their own. The hearing for my lawsuit against my neighbor is scheduled in two weeks. I expect the harassment will get worse. I live by myself on eighty-eight acres and have no immediate family. My friends have all run for cover. One of my best friends told me over the phone that he thinks it's all mafia who is after me."

Shane and his wife either didn't believe me — or they were part of this deadly game. That's the only conclusion I could reach. I left my brother's spacious, elegant home feeling more suspicious of him than ever.

I also felt a little strange upon leaving. There was pressure on my eye sockets from inside my skull. A bit wobbly, I walked to my car and rested in the driver's seat until the sensation eased.

Shane had asked me why they would do this to me. Another answer came to mind: to test their energy weapons.

The enemy is everywhere, even next door.

Like I said, it all started after my neighbor began constructing a large building, and what appeared to be a massive fuel tank, right at the lot line we shared. He was clearly encroaching on my property by building within twenty feet of the lot line when the approved setback is ninety feet. The intrusion enabled his surveillance camera to capture my driveway and record the front of my house so they all knew my comings and goings. No records of a building permit exist for these structures, another clear violation of county zoning ordinances and my rights as a neighbor and landowner.

He owned a communications, security, electronics and computer repair company and worked for the county's special investigative unit.

I wrote to the county about how all this activity was adversely affecting the value and development potential of my parcel. I hired an attorney who knew exactly how to deal with issues like this. I could not have fathomed how my world would start to unravel three years later. I never imagined how far the illegal and unethical activities of large groups of bad people and state-sponsored terrorism reached until the stalking began in 2009.

Sabotage, sleep deprivation, food tampering, medical malpractice and community ostracism were the tactics they used at first. Then, the warfare escalated.

My complaint against my neighbor started in the zoning division and worked its way through the planning department. Finally, the board of supervisors took up my grievance. At every turn, I was defeated. My neighbor had intentionally and willfully violated the county's own code — and the county now was complicit.

Next, I took my case before a Placer County Superior Court judge. Again, I was defeated.

"You can't really expect justice until you get to the appellate court," my attorney told me. "That's why they call them justices in the appellate court and not judges. You'll get justice there."

We filed a notice of appeal in the appellate court, but the justices did not rule in my favor.

I remained undaunted and appealed my case to the California Supreme Court.

Though seeking redress of grievance against the government and my neighbors for damaging the value of my property was a draining uphill battle, I also endured so many others coming after me in the most malicious ways. My life began to fall apart.

A judge signed an order for me to stay away from my neighbor's home — not the other way around — until county officials and legal counsel could make their determinations. I continued to document and observe everything going on around me, because my life depended on it.

My audiotapes are my most important possession. The gun collection I inherited from my father is the second most important. The firearms — Winchesters, Rugers, Mausers, Brownings — were worth one hundred thousand dollars, but moreover, they held great historical significance. They were built with fine craftsmanship, and gave me a piece of mind.

When I was alone doing chores on my property, I usually carried one of the weapons in case I came across a mountain lion or a trespasser I needed to scare off.

One day I was working on my property with my new puppy, Josie, at my feet. I was building burn piles on the front twenty acres near my driveway. Josie took off running and barking down to the edge of the driveway, so I went after him. I saw a sports car parked adjacent to the entrance to my property on the other side of the road. A man sat inside the vehicle. From behind my electric gate, I watched for a long time but I did not approach or say anything. The trees and brush I crouched behind were thick enough to conceal my presence.

The man exited the car carrying a sizable laptop and what appeared to be a computer tower and walked around to the side of my house where a ravine ran along the property line. Nobody was supposed to be down there. He returned to his car without the high-tech, military-style sensor equipment I had seen him carrying and caught me writing down his license plate from the roadside

"Is there a problem?" he asked me.

"Yes," I said.

"Do you want to talk about it?"

I put the paper with the license plate number into my pocket, and he just stared at me as if I were waving my Winchester in the air.

"You're as wacko as they say you are," he yelled in a frightened voice, and then hurried back into his car and sped away.

Twenty minutes later, two sheriff's vehicles came down the road and drove by my property. I walked back past the gate and waited for them to come back. The deputies soon returned and stopped at my house. One of them got out of the patrol car. It was Deputy Glenn McNamara.

"Sloane, did you just pull a gun on someone?" McNamara asked. "He said you waved it around and were threatening him."

"No, but I did take his license plate. Would you like it?"

McNamara laughed.

"No, we know who he is."

"I'm sure you do," I told him. "And if you're involved with what's going on at my neighbor's house, God knows I'll take you down with all the rest"

That was my first encounter with whom I later learned was Mitchell Jackson, the guy in the sports car. I found out he was a BATFE agent. My neighbor brought him in to cook something up against me, to discredit my case on the variance. That's what communists do in their rigid adherence to Marxism. You've read Aleksandr Solzhenitsyn's book The Gulag Archipelago, haven't you? It's essential for communists to discredit anyone who goes against them, to assassinate their character, turn them into villains. They go after people, and they use federal agents like Mitchell Jackson to get it done.

I told you everything began to come apart when I filed my appeal in the Supreme Court. Next, my renters in the Roseville house I own moved for no valid reason. They called me the day after my encounter with Mitchell Jackson to say they wanted to move out. This was a big surprise. I never raised their rent on them, took immediate care of any maintenance issues, and the house was tidy and comfortable. They loved it there. Last Christmas, they even bought me a Christmas present and gave it to me when I delivered some home-baked cookies.

I found it very unusual that they would want to leave, so I called to ask them why. They told me they had found another property that was bigger, better suited to their needs and was fifty dollars per month cheaper.

"How much bigger is the house?" I asked.

"One hundred and fifty square feet."

"That's it? One hundred and fifty? That's hardly any more space than you have here," I said.

But they remained resolute in their decision to relocate. When I returned later to put up a rental sign to attract new tenants, a strange-acting man approached me. He wasn't interested in renting, but he told me he was in law enforcement and worked with the Placer County Sheriff's Office and some federal agencies. He gave the impression that he was just fishing for information about me and my property. I was unable to rent the Roseville house ever again.

After that episode, the property where I lived was vandalized. The expensive electric gate I installed was damaged. The repairman told me a screwdriver had been jammed into the gate's mechanism to render it inoperable and unrepairable. The panel that controls the electronics was fouled up, too.

A week later, somebody ripped down several hundred feet of fence around my property. I saw small tennis shoe prints going to and from the house where the air vents are located. I immediately closed off the vents with cellophane and heavy masking tape.

Next, my vehicles were sabotaged and windows broken. I put in a security system, but my protection was quickly compromised by the people who installed it. I don't think they worked for the security company; they were likely BATFE sheriff and FBI.

Even though I had avoided speaking to my brother after that strange dinner at his house, I needed to tell somebody about the devious events. I called him. I cried when I described what I was going through. Shane characterized it all as coincidences. His dismissal infuriated me, and I hung up.

Several other things happened after that. There was traffic on the road late at night and early morning that didn't correspond with anybody's normal work schedules. My home was bugged, and my dog and I were being psychologically terrorized with high-frequency devices that woke me up at one-thirty and three in the morning. The attack caused Josie to act very aggressive around eight-thirty at night when I'm usually lying on the sofa, watching TV and relaxing.

Unfamiliar people kept came into my house. I noticed things moved from one place to another. Food items were tainted. One day I drank a cup of tea and immediately felt sleepy. I thought, "Oh, my God, they put a sedative in this tea. This usually wakes me up." There was no explanation for that.

A year-and-a-half after these goings-on had started, I came home one night and poured a glass of white wine from a bottle I opened the night before. It did not taste right to me, but since there was only one glass left, I finished it off. The next morning I woke up with a heavy metallic taste filling my mouth and my body tingling from head to toe, all the way into my extremities. It felt like Alka-Seltzer was running through my veins. I had no clue what poisoned me. I felt awful, but I at least I wasn't throwing up, and my breathing was OK.

I possess a large clinical library from my days of studying sports medicine, so I looked at my emergency medical books but couldn't figure out the symptoms. I needed to find out what was causing this unusual tingling symptom. I left the house to see a doctor.

I was forced to drive an hour into Sacramento because my regular doctor was gone for the Thanksgiving holiday, or so they said. On my way to the clinic, I figured out how this poisoning had occurred and what these hostile people were doing to me. There are so many involved.

There's a gypsy in Foresthill who is originally from Hungary, and he came into my house at the behest of the Bureau of Alcohol Tobacco and Firearms to put the concoction into the wine. He breached my home security and my centrally monitored alarm system and bumped my Schlage locks, obviously with the help of Mitchell Jackson and a woman whose son is in the corrections department. I believe it was the BATFE agent who got the security company to turn off the alarm system. It all made sense.

The weather was terrible that day. And nobody will ever convince me that God doesn't exist because I saw His hand at work. I saw the Holy Ghost in action. God was not keen on having that lawyer, Nina Schwartz, reach the doctor's office and the lab before I did.

It was stormy, windy and wet when God sent that truck up the Penryn on-ramp and onto the freeway. The semi-truck and trailer lost control, hydroplaned, crossed the center divider and was coming straight at me and Josie, who was in the back of my SUV. I gunned the Expedition and narrowly escaped being clobbered. The big rig passed my vehicle and crashed head on into the car behind me. Every single vehicle behind me could not get through. It was a huge pileup, closing all lanes of traffic. I'm sure that Jewish lawyer got stuck in the mess and was unable to get to the lab to poison me.

I walked into the doctor's waiting room, and it felt haunted. Patients and staff looked shocked when I came through those doors, as if I weren't supposed to be there. In the small examination room, I realized that I was not being attended by my regular physician. I had never seen him before. Based on his behavior, I asked him if he were Jewish.

"Because if you're Jewish, I can't trust you," I said.

I waited several seconds for his response, but said nothing.

"Are you Jewish?" I asked again.

"We'll talk about this later. You can trust me, Sloane."

"Fine," I said before enumerating the series of strange occurrences culminating in my clinical visit. He said little until I exhausted the list of all that had transpired in Foresthill.

"Well, Miss Stevens, what can I do for you today?" he asked.

I was shocked.

"I just told you, I've been poisoned and need to find out what this is in my body so I can get it out of my system. I don't know — what do you do? A blood test?"

He looked like the proverbial cat that swallowed the canary when I told him I inquired about a blood test.

"The lab has been moved to different area," the doctor said. "It's not here. It's not where it used to be."

He summoned a woman to make sure I got to the supposedly new clinical laboratory for the phlebotomy. The lab room was down a long hallway. It felt surreal when I walked in. The man at the desk looked worried, his lips pressed together, brow grooved and lower jaw jutting as if something bad was about to happen. The phlebotomist appeared, chatty and cheerful. Her name was Beverly, and she appeared to be of Mexican descent. I told her about how I almost hadn't made it in to see the doctor because of a bad accident on Interstate 80. Beverly appeared thunderstruck and stared at me for a minute.

"I almost didn't make it either," she said, and pointed to a woman standing behind me.

I will never forget the look of shock on the patient's face when I glanced back.

Without a hint, Beverly plunged the needle into my arm.

I walked out of the lab thinking, "What did I just let them do to me?"

I believe now the woman behind me was exposed to poison through the needle prick, too. But when my blood test results came back, the doctor told me nothing was there.

I knew he was wrong — or worse, conspiring with my neighbor, Mitchell Jackson, the sheriff and all of them. I knew from my research that some hazardous chemical had been injected in me, and it was likely barium.

I hired a man who had started an environmental lab testing service in Sacramento after leaving the Department of Defense. He came to the house to investigate potential environmental contamination in my wells and in the ambient air. I told him I was sick and had been poisoned, wanted to find out where it was coming from and hoped he could rule out certain things.

He opened his vest up and revealed two large, holstered firearms. They looked as big as cannons. I knew this was some kind of psychological warfare tactic, but I ignored it.

"I'm just sick with this and want to know how I got it," I repeated. "I may have no choice but to go back for another doctor's visit if you don't find anything."

"Well, I wouldn't let them do anything to me, if I were you," he said. "Did they?"

"Yes, they stuck a needle in me, and I think they made me sick with something else."

"Then maybe it's already too late," he said. Then he started his testing of my water and air.

A point in my life came when the harassment campaign—the tampering, the intrusion, the persecution and the intimidation — crashed down on me like an avalanche and I had no other choice but to take matters into my own hands. I would tolerate no further interference in my life.

They knew I was serious the next time Mitchell Jackson parked his sports car near my property. I saw him by my gate, so I took my chainsaw from the shed and pulled the starter cord. The chain whirred into action as I ran down the driveway. Holding the chainsaw high over my head, I reached the car and was about to bring its buzzing teeth down on the shiny hood when Mitchell Jackson punched the Corvette into drive and peeled away.

The road was clear after he left, and I wanted to keep it that way. I crossed the street and walked to the point on the road where my property line begins. I took the chainsaw to a hundred-foot-tall liquid amber and dropped that enormous tree right across the road. Then I walked in the other direction just past my driveway and felled a large live oak, which slammed onto the roadway. My property effectively was cut off from through traffic.

An hour later, I looked out my window and saw that the fallen trees were causing a big commotion. Cars and trucks had stopped on the far side of the blockage, and I could hear people loudly discussing what to do about it.

In the middle of this, I saw my neighbor and others snooping around at the edge of my property where he was illegally building his structure, apparently trying to figure out something. I opened my gun cabinet and grabbed my father's powerful goose gun, a heavy-gauge shotgun with a thirty-six-inch barrel and full choke that looked intimidating even from a distance.

I walked around to the side of my house where the neighbor and his friends snooped and fired two booming rounds in their general direction — just to let them know I was aware of what they were doing. I aimed wide, but all hell broke loose.

Adding to the clamor along the road, distant but oncoming sirens screamed louder and louder by the second. Here they come, I thought — for me. This is how it is. They start something, I respond, and the communists want to throw me in the nut house. I'm physically sick. I'm spitting up stuff. There's a cyst in my neck, and fluid is coming out of my sinuses and teeth. But the Jews and the communists and the sheriff are still coming for me and my guns.

I needed to talk to somebody who might take my side before the cops got there. I called Shane. It dawned on me that if he had not gone over to their side yet, he'd help me now. We'll see.

Shane agreed to come and see out where things stood, but the cops pulled up before he arrived. They were joined by two different tree service trucks, at least five sheriff's vehicles and two tow trucks. When Shane finally showed up, I watched him talk his way through the gauntlet and make his way to my house.

"They say you were waving a chainsaw at cars, cut down trees to block the road and then fired shots at the neighbors and their kids," Shane recounted, shaking his head. Tears shone in his eyes and his voice was shaky.

"They deserve this, Shane!"

"What the hell, Sloane? This is serious shit. They consider this a very dangerous, hostile situation. They're setting up a command station to coordinate some kind of action. They'll probably storm the house if we don't convince them otherwise. They say you've barricaded yourself, that you're armed and dangerous."

"See, liars and manipulators. Why'd they let you through, then?"

"Because they know you, and they know I'm your brother. They are giving you the benefit of the doubt for the time being. I still had to talk my way through. Tell me what's happening."

"I'm sure they've dropped plenty of trees that have gone across roads, or maybe they don't even know how to use chainsaws because they're so stupid. It's not like I shot at anybody."

"But you did. What the fuck is that shotgun doing there by the door?"

"I don't know, Shane. I just feel sick, sick in my body, all over. That's all. I want it to stop. And nobody can help me. Nobody can make it go away."

"We need to unwind all of this somehow, Sloane. They gave me twenty minutes to talk to you."

"This is absolutely ridiculous. They're communists. They're paranoid about the gun thing because they don't want anybody to be able to fight back."

"What are you talking about, Sloane? You're not going to fight the law."

"If somebody is torturing you — and that's what they're doing to me — you have two choices: You can flee or you can fight. People are torturing me, doing horrible things to me. But when I fight back, they don't like it. I'm suddenly the thug?"

"First, we're going to calm down and defuse this situation. You shot at a neighbor..."

"I did not!"

"Fine. You shot in the direction of the neighbor's house. You cut trees down on a public road to block people from getting to your property. Now, we need to figure out how to get out of here without anybody getting any madder, without anybody getting hurt and without anyone getting killed."

"I learned martial arts, Shane, did you know that?"

"What does that have to do with anything? I don't care. You can't karate chop your way out of here."

"I'm not a thug. They're the thugs. But I am a fighter. I learned in martial arts that you try to flee, but when you are completely cornered, you must be prepared to stand and fight. That's what martial arts are for, to defend yourself. Self-defense. This is not an aggressive action on my part. This is self-defense."

Shane was pacing in my living room, running his hands through his thick hair and stroking his mustache. Beads of sweat broke out on his temple and forehead.

"Sloane, you have to listen to me. You called me, right? I didn't come up here on my own. I came out of love and concern for you. You called me to help, so I'm trying to help you."

"You see, the whole thing that the Jews have done is to try to get me to fight. But, fortunately I have money, so I've been running instead."

"Then let's reduce the pressure here, and maybe you can go somewhere nice and pleasant for a while. Just get away from your tormentors."

"The communists need chaos to take over. I posted that on the Internet, you know, and the response I got back can be summed up in one word: 'precisely.' Everybody agreed. And that's what they are trying to do here. Communists need to foment unrest, and there is no better way to instill hysteria and panic in people than using explosions and gun blasts."

"I'll tell you what we'll do. And you have to listen to me here. We need to buy some time, and get you to a place where you can calm down."

"This is their plan, Shane. They're beaming the crap down, running the poison into my house. They're provoking me."

"Remember, I'm here to help. But we're running out of time. I'll tell you what; let's agree to have them take you into custody on the condition that you go back into the psychiatric hospital for assessment. What's so bad about that? They'll put you on a fifty-two fifty hold, and you can go unwind at a nice facility and get better. You can go to a place like Cedars-Sinai. You can get back on your meds, if you'd like, and talk to a doctor. Remember Doctor Ryan? Your life will be normal again."

"If I go on an involuntary psychiatric hold, Shane, they'll take my dog and cat away. They'll take my guns away. They'll confiscate Dad's firearms collection. That's what they want. They're doing it so they can take my guns — my only protection — and take my pets, which are my only support system."

"I don't think so."

"Don't be naive. A fifty-two fifty hold is pretext for taking my arsenal. The sheriff will take my arsenal at the behest of the Jews, Shane! They want my guns for the Jews and the communists."

"They're waiting down there, and they are going to take you out of here one way or the other, Sloane. Guns or no guns. Let me talk to them. I'll get them to come to some kind of agreement that you will support. Have I ever let you down?"

I watched Shane walk down to the end of my property line where the sheriff and his deputies were waiting. He talked to them a long time, and then he jogged back up to the house. He asked me to give him a moment to catch his breath.

"What did you tell them?" I asked.

"I told them that if the goal is for you not to use the guns anymore, to cause no more harm, then they can come up and we'll have them unloaded, with the chambers open. I'll stand outside with you while they search the house for any other ammunition or loaded guns. You'll keep your guns, but you'll have no ammo."

"They're going to throw me in the nuthouse and give my arsenal to the Jews."

Shane grabbed my shoulders, gave me a bear hug and then looked me straight in the eyes while bookending my upper arms with his strong hands.

"Sloane, this is the best scenario. I pulled this idea right out of my ass. But somehow the plan gave them a high level of comfort. I think they see how quietly this can all go away if you just agree to get rid of all the ammunition, make the firearms temporarily inoperable and get yourself into a facility for professional assessment."

"I don't trust them. What exactly did they say about seizing the guns?"

"The sheriff said it's not his intention to completely disarm you. If we agree to this plan, he's willing to take you in and get you evaluated before that happens."

"So they are going to whisk me away instead of whisking the trees off the road. They're going to whisk me down to the nut house and whisk my father's guns away while I'm gone."

"You'll have them; you just won't be able to shoot them. I didn't have to tell them about the whole arms cache up here, but they were glad I did. That led to our compromise. Because this kind of behavior you resorted to — sawing down trees along a public road, shooting in the vicinity of a neighbor — can get you sent away for a very long time."

"They are paranoid sons of bitches, brother. They don't want anybody to ever fight back."

"Probably, sister."

For Shane, I didn't fight back this time.

We stood outside while they seized the bullets, birdshot, buckshot and slugs and searched house's interior. Afterward, they took me away, and I took a long breather at the Center for Psychiatry.

Making promises to the devil always proves hollow, though. Placer County made me pay for sparring with my neighbors, quarreling with other townsfolk and getting into a standoff with the sheriff.

While I was in the nuthouse, the cops and their lawyers went into my house and took my guns, just like I knew they would. People testified that they knew me well and distrusted me. Some said I scared them. They convinced a judge that it was in the interest of public safety to take possession of a hundred thousand dollars' worth of a citizen's vintage firearms.

Shane went before a judge on my behalf and tried to reason with law enforcement. He came to the psych ward to tell me about the court order.

"I told you it was the sheriff's intention all along to fully disarm me and give them to the communists and Jews," I scolded. "This is all born out of their Old Testament, Shane. The Old Testament is a horrible book. If they burned every single Bible, I wouldn't care. It is no longer a holy book. I was brought up believing it is the word of God, blah, blah, blah. No. These are words written by Jews who think they are as God, passing on some parts of history and leaving some out. And it's the same for Muslims. I realize that they will go after people and kill them for humiliating Muhammad, or defaming the Quran, but these are just books..."

Shane stopped me right there.

"Enough, Sloane! Write it in your journal, record it on your cassette tapes, but I don't need to hear it right now. I came here to tell you that the sheriff's department seized those weapons, but they assured me they are sending them to a gun shop to be sold, and the proceeds will be returned to you."

Shane is unworldly. They sold my guns, and I never saw a dime in return.

CHAPTER 8

After being released from several months confinement in the mental hospital, I decided to not return to my Foresthill house for a while. I drove up to Oregon and prepared Dad's Nehalem home for sale. Money from the sale would be nice to have because my legal fees were adding up and I was uncertain what might happen to my shares in Port Seattle Timber and Stevens Family Investments.

The first few days in Oregon were relaxing. I took tranquil beach walks and looked for unique shells and driftwood. I hiked through Nehalem Bay State Park and shopped in Lincoln City.

Suddenly, I didn't feel right. On the fourth day in Oregon, my arms and legs grew weak and I had a shortness of breath. There were times when anxiety and nausea simultaneously welled up in me.

One day, I became aware of a guy stalking me. He followed me to the beach, where I was exploring the freshly exposed wet sand after high tide. I stopped and sat on a log that had washed ashore. When the man walked past, I headed in the opposite direction to my truck in the parking lot.

I had parked at an odd angle and plowed into the car next to me when I hurriedly backed up. The damage to the side of the car was considerable. I left the driver a note, and he called me later. He took his car to an auto repair shop, and we arranged for me to come by and pay for the work.

The shop owner was sitting behind the counter when I walked in, and he smiled at me. Another man was sitting in a chair in the waiting area pretending to read the newspaper. Right away, I knew he was some kind of fed. The shop owner went into the back to see about the progress of the repair, and the federal agent and I struck up a conversation about the required work, the bill and some other issues. As I bided my time, he tapped the newspaper he was reading and looked up at me.

"They don't like it when you say or write things even, though they're true," he commented.

There was that word: "they."

I didn't notice a woman had joined us in the repair shop, suddenly materializing in a nearby chair. She looked excited and happy, but demonic, and she couldn't sit still. She had heard us chatting.

"When you're the target, you can't say or write anything," she told me, fidgeting in her seat.

I didn't respond, but I was familiar with their code words: "when you're the target." This was proof that the entire Sayanim know that I'm the target, their target.

I remember that, a while ago, security expert Ari Levine came up to my house to put in a new surveillance system. When we finished reviewing what needed to be done around the house, I told him all the things that were happening to me. As he gathered his paperwork and tools, preparing to leave, he said:

"You're going to be a target for the next seven years."

Seven years. That is the number of gods, a recurring theme in ancient cultures and religious traditions. That's when I knew he was Jewish and part of the Jewish mafia, and at the top of it all is Sayanim. They're the ones perpetrating these horrendous crimes against me.

There is something in our bodies called a blood-brain barrier. There's no doubt in my mind that when the chemicals distributed by the flow tube they've inserted in my nose that it is crossing this highly selective semiper-meable border of endothelial cells. Even when I plug my nose, squeezing as hard as I can, the tube is still disseminating deep into my bloodstream

and crossing the blood-brain barrier.

I can track several instances where and when I've been infected. They've loaded me up with heavy metals, and I feel them bubbling in my head all the time.

Before going to Oregon to see about selling my property, I talked my doctor in Sacramento into giving me a urine test, and I secretly sent a sample to Doctor's Data on the East Coast. A positive result came back from the private company's specialty testing lab, and it indicated there was barium and cesium in my system. My regular doctor obliged me and ran a further analysis. It came back negative. I now knew there was a lot of lying going on at my medical center.

Another time, I went to retrieve my medical records from the center and they supplied me with only one of my blood tests, the negative one, not the two draws that I had done. I believe they were protecting that Russian conspirator who jabbed me with the needle.

These contaminations not only happen by way of needles. The first time I was exposed to direct energy weapons occurred in a courtroom in 2010. An appellate court justice was hearing motions in my lawsuit against my neighbor. Three women were sitting a few rows behind me, and I felt an odd sensation. I turned and looked at them, wondering why they were in the appellate courtroom, which was very small. Typically, only parties to the case being heard are present, which in this instance meant my neighbor, his wife, their attorney, a county official, my attorney and me. I felt sick, so I moved, but there wasn't a lot of space, so I couldn't move far. The sensation continued, and I grew sicker.

The second time I remember being tortured like this was at my Oregon home. My neighbors, Ken and Brianna, with whom I had been friends, did it that time. Brianna is Jewish. Ken, I believe, is a gypsy. I sensed an uncomfortable feeling while inside my house and became sick.

They call these directed energy weapons "non-lethal." They can go through the walls of a house or a car. They'll even go through the walls of a bank. I've never actually seen them, but I've read about them. There's a Rand Corporation research report that's over six hundred pages long

addressing this subject. The document was published in 2003, if you'd like to check.

The mafia — and when I say mafia I mean the Teamsters Union — infected me with what it calls the "gill" or "spy sac." It starts in your neck as a lump. I've had one in me for about five years, and every day it causes a general feeling of malaise to sweep over me. The gill has mushroomed into what's called a "Dutch oven" — in other words, a slow cooker. The fluid-filled sac works like a pressure cooker. The fluid is forced into my cranium, causing an abnormal buildup within the ventricles. This condition is essentially like water on the brain, or hydrocephalus.

When I was sixteen years old, I was injured in a tail-end collision with a drunken driver and found out the hard way that water on the brain is our body's response to an emergency. I was in the hospital for two weeks, so I know the importance of releasing cranial pressure before brain tissue becomes damaged.

Fluid from the bursa, the spy sac, travels through your whole body. It certainly has reached down into my lower back and spine. It's extremely uncomfortable. My hands often go numb and turn white.

You probably are asking yourself, why would anybody do this to me? What would motivate somebody to actually poison me? Well, have you been listening to my recordings? The vandalism, sabotage and retaliation stem from people who wanted me to drop my lawsuit before I shed too much light on particular people, properties and issues. There is lot of marijuana grown in Placer County; therefore, a lot of cash is moving around. People are unhappy with me because I am not afraid to illuminate dark, forbidden areas.

Just before I started experiencing these acts of aggression against me — driven by anger and resentment — I started reading books from my father's extensive library and giant heritage. His collection was comprised of tomes about World War II, the Sovietization of America, Zionism and even the occult. I began to see the problem with this country was a Jewish mindset based and rooted in Judaism, the Talmud and, of course, Cabala. The Talmud is a bad book, but I was more horrified when I read the Rev. Dr. Ted Pike's book.

I soon learned and understood what was happening all around me. Yet, ignorance kept the truth hidden from most people.

I sought medical help from all over the western United States. I received recommendations for treatment from friends in Washington, Oregon, Utah, Texas, Arizona and Northern and Southern California.

In Utah, the directed energy weapons cooking me from the inside out like a microwave for the past six to eight months made me so sick I had to take cover at my friend John's house. It was the summer of 2014.

I stayed at John's for two weeks, and after that visit, we were no longer friends. His wife, I believe, is Jewish and she was very unhappy with me for figuring things out, particularly the chem trails, and being unafraid to voice my opinion. The Jewish network utilized their underground pipeline to get word to Kristin about what I was doing and what I was sorting out.

On my last day at John and Kristen's house, I was examining myself in the guest bathroom. Directed energy weapons can cause you to bleed out. I had blood in my stool and blood in my urine. I knew I might end up with septic shock if my colon became infected and perforated. Suddenly, Kristen barged in screaming and swearing, calling me an ungrateful bitch and a lowlife motherfucker who deserves what I get. In the middle of her tirade, I calmly collected my stool and then continued my journey to the Pacific Northwest.

I found a doctor in Redmond, Washington, who is the only one who ever really helped me. He had been treating me for the past few years and was the same physician who found through urine testing that I had been poisoned with barium and cesium. During my previous visit, he determined that I also had been poisoned with thallium. He discovered I had been spiked with uranium — and everybody knows that's Russian handiwork because it's so strictly regulated.

But that discovery took place after the BATFE had me jailed in Washington.

After my awful Salt Lake City stay with John and Kristin, I was approaching Redmond in my new 2014 truck with the old travel trailer attached. I was sick at the wheel, and the temperature was climbing to a hundred degrees when I crossed from Idaho into Washington.

On Interstate 90, a pair of Washington state troopers stopped me on the pretense that my trailer registration was unreadable because it was old and extremely weathered. Someone had installed a GPS tracking device on my vehicle. The BATFE orchestrated the whole setup.

The feds sent their Jewish cop after me. I saw the red lights flashing in my rearview mirror and pulled over. Instantly, I jumped out of the pickup and briskly walked toward the trooper.

"You sons of bitches will go after anybody anywhere, won't you?" I shouted. "You rat shits from hell — anybody you want to put down, you will try to."

The trooper's nervous partner exited the passenger's side of the patrol unit.

"Stop right there and move safely off the roadway, ma'am," the trooper ordered, quickly coming at me. "Don't walk on the fog line. Get over!"

"I'm not taking commands from you," I screamed, pivoting back to my truck.

I needed to get out of there quickly. Everything about this traffic stop pointed to torturers sent by Mitchell Jackson. The trooper ordered me to stop, but I kept walking. I'd be safe once I reached Seattle.

The cops came up from behind me, one on each side, and grabbed my arms and wrists. They yanked me around and dragged me back to their patrol car, bracing me against the hood and putting wrist restraints on me. I fought to get loose, struggling to pull my hands free from the restraints.

"You're under arrest," one officer said.

They forcibly escorted me toward the back of the patrol vehicle, but I broke free from their grip. I kicked one of those compulsive deviants hard in the groin. He gasped and doubled over. Both were infuriated, but I was sick and needed to stay out of their poisoned vehicle at all costs.

As the one trooper clutched himself and tried to regain composure, the other one seized me by the wrist with his left hand and struck the back of my right arm just above the elbow. The blow brought me to the ground in a fierce instant. He held me down with a knee on my upper back, my ear scraping against the gravel, until his partner recovered enough to assist him. They applied maximum restraint straps to my ankles and linked them to the wrist cords before carrying me, hogtied, to their vehicle and tossing me into the back seat.

"Josie! Josie! Josie!" I called.

"Who the fuck's Josie, you nut job?"

"My dog. I need him. He's in my truck!"

"We'll get him if you shut the fuck up."

"Stinky! Stinky!"

"Who's that? Another dog?"

"My cat."

"You're traveling with a cat? Go crack the window for her pets, partner."

"It's too hot!" I warned. "They won't survive."

"Shut up. Your animals will be fine."

As we headed for jail, I began to tingle and panicked. I smelled it — the cops were poisoning me in the back of the patrol car with barium. This entire plot was heinous.

On the way to the holding cell, the troopers took me to the intake room, and the cop behind the counter who was processing me asked if I had any enemies.

"Yeah, the Jews and all the other communists," I said.

It was obvious he knew who I was and when I would be arriving at the station. I saw a big smile come across his face.

They left me in the holding cell across from the guard station, where everybody coming and going could look right in. There was no privacy. I felt like I was suffocating. I was sure these cells were rigged to emit toxic stuff. They used a poison called Zionist Zombie. They've tried all kinds of different substances, chemicals, metals, poisons on me, but Zionist Zombie is the most horrible. It makes you feel like you're suffocating. I was held for two weeks, every second wondering if I were going to be asphyxiated.

Interesting things happened in that jail cell. I crossed paths with an incarcerated informant, a woman who called herself by her middle name — Jane. A deputy gave her poison to slip into my milk at suppertime. As soon as I took a sip, my mouth went numb. I immediately emptied one of the Ziploc storage bags the guards give inmates that contain a toothbrush, toothpaste and comb. I poured the rest of the milk into the resealable container and put it into another baggie. I asked for a manila envelope and put the sealed bags inside it. I secured the envelope and wrote my initials over the adhesive flap so it would be obvious if the seal was broken. I carried that envelope with me for an entire day, even taking it into the bathroom when I needed to go.

The sheriff rolled the inmates that night. His deputies rooted through the cells looking for contraband, as they did from time to time. I told him I was poisoned by somebody in the cell and wanted to give him an envelope, which hadn't been out of my sight, that contained the evidence. He looked at me with an expression of shock. I swore to him I'd sign a chain of custody form to document that the property was within my possession the entire time until that night. He took the package, but I never found out what happened afterward. I never ascertained whether the woman who helped the jail staff poison me or the deputies who roughed me up during my arrest were disciplined, but I hope the authorities nailed them. They both deserved to be arrested on second-degree felony charges.

I met another person in jail, a Jewish woman with whom I became friends. She was originally put in my cell to try to provoke me into an altercation to get me locked up longer. This was one of the ideas Jews had for dealing with me: Keep me in custody for as long as possible. The woman had been arrested for being high on meth and creating a huge scene on the freeway when she stopped her car and got out in the middle of four lanes of traffic. In the fracas, she sprayed a trooper in the face with Lysol. That type of poisoning is a second-degree felony in Washington, so that's how I knew how much trouble the other woman and the deputies faced for trying to poison me.

I didn't want to involve Shane or anybody else in my business, so I didn't call to ask for help with bail or in finding an attorney or anything else. But I am part of a huge family up here in the Pacific Northwest with a half dozen cousins scattered all over Washington state and high-powered attorneys on retainer. They all talk to each another. They have connections in every industry, police headquarters and courthouse in the region. They often know when I'm driving up here. Whenever I do, they ask me to dinner. Because I am suspicious of the activity around their houses, I leave as early as possible. That's why I didn't call any of them either.

Shane found out anyway when my cousin Conrad Stevens, who succeeded his father, also Conrad, as CEO after the fateful Arizona meeting, learned of my arrest and told my brother. The situation concerned the family so much that Conrad called me. I told him that I'd rather rot in my jail cell than have Shane, the family or anybody else become involved. Nonetheless, he rallied around my cause, bringing the full force of the family's influential law firm — arguably the most powerful group of attorneys on the West Coast. These top legal minds followed every trail, no matter how small, to the very end. They even located Josie and Stinky at an animal shelter and reunited us.

A Superior Court judge granted me a medical furlough, and I spent two weeks in a Washington state mental health hospital. He suspended all criminal proceedings.

My Seattle family bailed me out, but I remorse overwhelmed me for treating Shane so badly. After all, he was just trying to help his sister and stay true to his long-ago promise. I vowed to reconcile with him.

Conrad and a few of my other cousins said I could repay them by having dinner with them. I would rather have paid them a million dollars instead, because the timing was terrible.

While at the psychiatric hospital I felt the Dutch oven growing inside my neck. It started in the base of my skull but clearly had traveled into my cranium. The fluid from the cyst was building up and cooking my brain. Because there was no place for the watery, viscous substance to go, it flowed out of my nasal passages and drained through my jaw and teeth — a yellowish, slimy, bubbly, yucky and horrendous juice.

And, God, they insisted on taking me out to dinner.

"Sloane, we have reservations at your father's favorite restaurant in Seattle, really the entire world," Conrad enthusiastically told me. "He and the Eddison clan met the restaurant's owner in Waikiki when he opened his first eatery after the war. He moved to Seattle and now his kids run the place. They are excited to meet you."

I obliged but did not tell them about my health issue.

This was top-tier dining with multiple courses. We sat at a table in front of large windows and looked at the city lights sparkling around Lake Union. Luxurious granite and glass elements surrounded us.

Everything was unfolding in serene elegance — until the servers presented a dish of prawns sautéed in butter and garlic, the plates sizzling fragrantly. I looked down at the bubbling, creamy white-and-yellow sauce and swallowed a belch.

"Fuck," I said aloud without realizing it. "This looks like the stuff I'm spitting up and is coming out my nose."

I looked around the table at saw mortified faces staring back.

"I don't see anything, Sloane," my cousin Marie said, maintaining her composure.

"I know. I know it sounds crazy," I said.

Miraculously, I didn't run out of the restaurant. But as the night went on, I realized that was exactly what the prawn dish was prepared to look like.

The Jews think this type of intimidation is funny. They are extremely demonic. That evening they also put barium, or maybe tin, into my water. I doubt they did anything to Conrad or my other cousins, but I noticed heavy metals were baked into the cream brûlée.

I needed to get out of Seattle quickly, distance myself from the family, and stay ahead of the Sayanim, the Russians and all of the dirty cops and torturers who were using Stinky, Josie and me as their moving targets.

My immediate counteraction to neutralize the terror was to find a safe destination. The attorney in Washington, who the family had provided, told me in private, "You need to go where these people tormenting you are hated." I liked the way he put that: Go where they are hated. That way, they won't be around to bother me.

I returned to my house in Foresthill with the hope of starting fresh and experience no more dangerous meddling in my life. I was wrong.

It became more urgent than ever that I keep moving while attempting to vanquish all threats — or at least die trying. I decided to leave the country. I ditched my dirty pickup and travel trailer and bought a recreational vehicle for thirty-five thousand dollars. I wrote a check for it and took off.

Josie, Stinky and I first went to Canada, but after a week, I realized being in Vancouver and even as far out as Vancouver Island was futile. Betrayals by every East Indian motel and gas station manager and other informants I encountered let BATFE agents always know where I was. I drove east on the freeway out of Vancouver, but Josie, Stinky and I were assaulted by energy weapons aimed at my car. The RV was clean, but we were moving targets.

After a month on the road, it became apparent the motorhome wasn't big or sturdy enough for this trip, so I found an RV dealership in Utah and traded it in for a new, forty-foot model that cost me eighty-five thousand dollars. I lost a lot of money on the trade-in, but this rig was twice as big. I insured the vehicle at full value — as I did for all my homes, cars and trucks.

If anybody needs to piece together my whereabouts during these months, all the dates and times can be verified with credit card receipts.

I drove the motorhome south to Aubrey, Texas, near Dallas, where my friend Heather and her husband lived on a large horse ranch. She never begrudged my popping in unannounced. This time, though, was different.

A Russian man followed me up to her electric gate. She had given me the key code, and as I was entering it, I turned and saw the Russian sitting in his big white car. I scrambled onto her property and closed the gate before he could get any closer. The unsettling encounter left my nerves raw. My visit with Heather turned disastrous because she would not believe how far my enemies would go to afflict me.

"You're scaring my children with your ridiculous stories, Sloane," Heather said.

"I just want somebody to help me. I think their discomfort from over-hearing the truth is insignificant compared to my need to tell my best friend about this horrendous ordeal I've lived through for the past five or six years."

"Sloane, all this talk about conspiracies and the Jews and communists waging technological warfare on you is bizarre. You never stop. Nobody has ever been able to help you, Sloane, because you don't actually want people to help you."

Our talk escalated, and soon I was throwing things to jolt her into seeing what I saw.

"You think I want this? Do you think I like never feeling safe?"

"I don't know how to reach you, Sloane!"

I broke a lamp, statues and other furnishings before Heather's husband intervened, demanding I leave and not return. He followed me down to the gate in his pickup to make sure I departed into the black night.

My journey with my pets to find safe ground didn't stop in Texas. We crossed the border into Mexico. About an hour-and-a-half south of Nogales, I pulled the RV into a modern new gas station and convenience store, and the Russian appeared again. He stood behind me while I waited in line in the store to buy water and snacks. When I turned around, he laughed in my face.

"I know who you are," he whispered loudly in my ear. "And we know where you are. All the time — no matter how far you try to go to get away. So I think you better go back to the U.S."

CHAPTER 9

I spent most of 2015 abroad, traveling to twelve countries. People told me to escape the poisoned atmosphere by going "up." I didn't know what they meant or how to interpret "up?" Up a mountain? Up into the troposphere? Up above the layers of filthy air? Was I supposed to board an airplane and fly somewhere? That's eventually what I did — took to the skies.

The one lawyer in Washington told me that to find safety I should go where people trying to harm me are hated. Accordingly, I set off for Iran.

While in line at London Heathrow Airport waiting to purchase a ticket to Egypt connecting to Iran, I smelled stale tobacco. No one near me was smoking, so no plausible explanation for the smell existed except for it being a premonition. It was a portent telling me that Bureau of Alcohol Tobacco Firearms and Explosives agents awaited me in Egypt. I stepped out of line immediately.

Shortly after that auspicious day, a Russian airplane blew up, killing two hundred, twenty-four people on board. Evidence pointed to a bomb.

I know how BATFE likes to blow things up. My theory is this: BATFE

sent the Russians a message on behalf of the CIA — kaboooom! — to not fuck with changing the reserve currency from U.S. dollars to something else, even if the Fed is broke. After that attack, China backed off the currency idea, too.

It was a conspiracy to commit murder and a soft kill on the international stage. Why wouldn't they take me out, too? We all know conspiracy is not a theory; conspiracy is a crime.

In the end, there was no getting away, regardless of mode of transportation or how far the trip. I left my poisoned house and my poisoned vehicle and got to the poisoned airport. I sat in the poisoned terminal waiting for my plane, which also was poisoned. I traveled across the country to get to my destination, and the next terminal always was worse than the one before. The taxis and rental cars were poisoned. I made my drivers take me all around the cities until I found places where I would feel safe and could breathe. Each sojourn, seeking decent locations cost me over three hundred U.S. dollars. Then I got to the hotels, and they were poisoned. The whole chore of traveling was no good for me.

In addition to London, I journeyed to Ireland, Scotland, Australia and New Zealand but always found the Mossad secretly following me. Sayanim's underground intelligence, as evidenced by their Nogales appearance when I traveled to Mexico, always knew where I was. They declared they had "a belly full" of my incessant roaming all

Still, I kept moving, to Finland, Sweden, Italy, Spain, Germany, even to Costa Rica and the Philippines. A cop named Benedict B. Tiu intercepted me at every customs check.

Think about that name for a second — it's code for Traitors Beat You. Well, no they haven't. Not yet, goddamn it.

It was Sunday Jan. 3, 2016. Somehow, I had made it to 2016. I was back from a full year abroad and now roamed around Foresthill, Roseville and Loomis on wheels. I was always on the go.

Life was getting harder. My little house in Roseville, which I never was able to rent again, was no good. My big garage was contaminated. I had all but abandoned my Foresthill property.

Zionists had inundated all of Placer County, and destructive forces were everywhere. It was all related — from the chem trails and elements they had disbursed into the air, to the radio frequencies bombarding me and satellites keeping watch. I know it was done through technology, but I don't know how.

I'm sure somebody can explain it to Congress, which ought to be arresting these poisoners left and right, starting with the sheriff. I don't care if they wear badges and carry guns, they're poisoners. Lock them up behind chain-linked fences in the desert for all I care.

President Obama didn't even know about these weapons until I wrote him an email about what was going on and how I had been hurt and tortured by these weapons, primarily orchestrated by the Jews and the Russians. A presidential briefing informed him. So I taught the president something about armaments.

I bought a new forty-five-foot RV — modern and shiny — loaded up my pets and took off to find a good place to sleep. I took the motorhome to an oil stop on Sunrise Boulevard, but they loaded the vehicle with Zionist Zombie. It was filling up my feet. It was filling up my lungs. It was making me sick.

The whole damn ordeal is so hard to believe. There is Sayanim everywhere. They come out of their houses, and they're sporting colors. It's just disgusting. It's like the Stepford wives, like living in the Twilight Zone. The whole chemical warfare being waged on me by Senator Dianne Feinstein and the rest of the pigs — it's so hard to believe. I mean what the hell does the FBI do? Why are we paying the FBI? What does anybody do? What does the sheriff do? Nothing. BATFE agents are chasing me around in their fucking white trucks all over the place. I can't even stop to sleep.

These depraved monsters must be locked up. We don't want them running around the country. We certainly don't want to be paying their salaries.

People say, "You need to go to the doctor, Sloane." Oh, right, the fucking Jews will murder me on the operating table. Nobody's going to sue the fucking doctor for medical malpractice. Nobody cares. Nobody gives a damn. You're all tripping.

These goddamned cars on Sunrise with their bright lights came up behind me to let the people watching the satellite know where I was. Josie got riled up. She started running around the RV. Cyberstalkers drove by with their dog barking out their window and hit me with their energy weapons. I was dizzy. One minute I was fine, and then I wasn't. This was not a good spot, and I had to leave again.

I found a decent place to sleep in the RV, out in the 'hood where I never go. I felt better there than I did in Roseville — "Ritzville" — where the Zionists were. The gypsies, the Russians, control these weapons, so I slept better there than I did in a lot of places.

I woke up feeling good and made my way over to the DMV office in Rocklin. It's all mafia in there. Russians, Jews, gypsies and union mafia, of course, because the railroad is centered there. By the time I got to the office, I wasn't feeling too hot.

At the DMV, I scored a hundred percent on my written driver's exam, but the woman administering the test was Russian. Radov was her last name, and she was torturing me inside the examination room. It was all a. setup. The cop who wrote the ticket was obviously part of the ploy to take my driver's license away.

This is what the communists do. They poison and torture you to create a problem, and then this country and you, basically, are fucked. That's how they think.

A gypsy in Roseville told me they want to make an example out of me, and then he told me I am a tester for them. This is being done to me because obviously they want to see how the weapons and poison works so they can use it on other Americans. To be a target, all you have to be is a real Christian, a political dissident, an American, someone who abhors communism and somebody who owns private property. If you have no debt, then you're even more desirable. If you have any sort of an estate, you're an extremely desirable target. Needless to say, I'm a big target.

The woman at the DMV office demanded that I see a doctor, which is a joke because there are no good doctors in this area. Inside the DMV office, this woman was giving me dirty looks. She told me to close the exam door as though I was the problem.

They're all communists. You can't trust them. They'll hurt you. They'll do something to you to cause you to become even sicker. I need to have my neck operated on to get this Dutch oven removed. What am I supposed to do? I'm not the problem.

The people who did this to me are the problem. What do you want me to do about it? Go down to Sutter General and let the doctors murder me tonight? Would that make everybody happy? I'm sure it would. Well, I'm not ready to die yet, if that's what she meant by closing the door. Commit suicide? It ain't going to happen. And if you think I'm going to walk away from my properties, that ain't going to happen, either. So I don't know what you door slammers think you're going to get out of all of this. I am not going to give up my property. I'm not going to continue to let you terrorize me.

Never forget, this whole thing started seven years ago with my neighbor and the lawsuit.

The Federal Reserve is a private corporation with Class A stock owned by eight Jewish families. They're the ones who have raided and looted this country, and they have done it for their tribe, their criminal tribe.

No, I won't close the door. You'll have to hear me out. Out in the open.

I've been told that the JDL, the Jewish Defense League, is also

involved — one hundred percent — with terrorizing me. Warfare on U.S. soil I believe is imminent. War is coming unless the enemy and the technology available to them are headed off at the pass. I learned about their chem trails, which started in the 1960s, from a little magazine called Spotlight, now the American Free Press. I read that in my father's library in 2001, and the article talked about the U.S. Air Force up in the air spraying barium, salts, aluminum oxide and strontium. This is essentially chemical warfare waged by the U.S. Government on the American citizens.

In the summer, I was pacing under the fluorescent lights of the Public Civil Investigation Office in downtown Sacramento, waiting to speak with an attorney about stopping the terrorizers. Maybe I appeared to harbor my last hope, which was true, but people beheld me with stunned looks, as if seeing and feeling the storm raging within me. Their faces froze. If they really wanted to know, I would tell them. My story was credible, and I think they comprehended that. I proceeded to tell them everything, from the beginning.

I don't really know what you people expect me to say or what you should do, because every state in the country is wired up. There isn't a state that isn't infested with communists. I mean, one out of two people in the country are communists. Every other person you look at is a communist. This is what Joe McCarthy was trying to put a stop to, and the communists assassinated his reputation. Those who try to do something to better the country and get the communists out are either murdered like Congressman Larry McDonald or their characters are assassinated like Joe McCarthy's.

Do people know they are ending up with a country that's going to look like Kosovo, nothing but mafia? Nothing but drug dealers and whorehouses. No businesses. It's going to be nothing but propped-up money laundries. It's going to literally be a facade of a country. There's going to be nothing holding it up. It's a house of cards. It's nothing but a structure built on sand. There's no foundation. That is what the country essentially is, so you can go on and terrorize me, but there is no substance to this country. None. It's gone. It is virtually gone. The Jews and other communists have stripped your country of all moral and cultural integrity. It used to have that. It no longer does. It's gone, period.

So you might as well get used to that idea, or start to do something else to change it. I don't know how much longer I'm going to be able to go on. There's a reason I won't close the door.

Inside the Public Civil Investigation Office, the clerk approached me in midsentence with a delicate smile but maintained a respectful distance.

"Hello there," she said in a soothing voice that was like a healing balm to me; then quieter, so only I could hear, she continued:

"It looks like a lot is troubling you, but there may be a physical element to your problems where we could provide some relief. We have some wonderful attorneys who work with doctors specializing in managing pain. Would you like to talk to someone now?"

An openness washed over my body from crown to sole. Where before was suffering, now was a tender embrace. Where before was division, now was unity. I puzzled: Is this how a clean environment truly feels? I hesitated, too, even though this wonderful woman had given me a flicker of hope. In the next moment, I was silently nodding. Yes, I'd like to talk to somebody.

"I've been living in my car with my dog and my cat," I told her, and she placed a reassuring hand on my arm. "It's a horrible experience. No person should be expected to drive around like this just to get out of the virulent air. A Dutch oven has invaded my cranium. My insides are bubbling. They've used those weapons on me in too many places to count.

"These dog parks that I try to take Josie to so she can get out and run around, she can't. Satellites beam these weapons down. I'm trying to let her have some kind of normal life, but we're living in an RV. They spoil it for the poor animal every time. I'm not at the dog park for me; I'm at the dog park for her. It wasn't good enough that they separated us, Josie and me, several times. They're not going to be happy until she's in their hands, basically. And Stinky, too. But they're my only support system, and they don't want me to have any pleasure."

While I'm saying all of this, the kind woman led me into a bright, expansive, clean-smelling room where an equally pleasant man in a suit rose from his chair and came around the table to introduce himself.

They must have had heightened awareness, because they found me a non-Jewish doctor uninvolved in the underground who performed a complete physical exam. The only catch was his practice was in San Francisco, but it was worth the trip. The doctor ordered blood tests, and I watched the phlebotomist bring the entire package out in plain view and open everything in front of me. I was so relieved at her honesty. We moved on to imaging tests and finally a biopsy.

"How is your diet since you've felt you were poisoned?" my doctor asked.

"It's been hard to eat well with being on the road for so long," I answered. "It's actually been difficult ever since I started feeling sick after they poisoned me with the heavy metals and stuck those needles in me."

"I want you to do something before we get all your results back," the doctor said gently, "and that is clearing, or chelating, the heavy metal out of your system. It's a more holistic approach, but I've seen it help. This first step will not be a difficult thing to do. We will have you only eat the right foods. Apples, pears, bananas, spinach — these are good chelators. Eating plenty of greens is great. Let's consider homeopathic remedies and adding charcoal and bentonite clay, both of which can help you detoxify, in support with your body's natural processes. Just make sure you take vitamins while doing this to replace the minerals drained by detoxing. You should begin to feel better, and then we'll look at more medical-grade therapies."

I was so optimistic afterward that I regularly called Shane on my cell phone. I still mostly lived in my RV on the road with Josie and Stinky, and as I drove, I had long conversations with my brother about growing up together

We laughed when we recounting stories of our past. We swapped memories of nearly crashing on that primitive airstrip in Washington, dancing to Dad's music in our beach house while Mom steamed the clams, and telling all the guests at that party in Hawaii that Shane was Tom Selleck.

We cried while reliving Mom and Dad's and when I had to leave our home and the family broke apart. One time I called him from an airport where I had parked far away from the terminal and nobody could spy on me, and Shane became emotional over my predicament. He implored me to drive away, so he could get off the phone.

He always took my calls, even when he was busy at work.

"Sloane," he reproved me mildly when he was occupied. "I'm in the middle of an important meeting. We are about to close this huge deal."

Then we'd talk for an hour anyway.

We yelled at each other, too. Sometimes I wished he would just listen without a word of judgment when I explained how effectively I was being tortured and how keenly I felt the omnipresence of the terrorizers and their technological weapons.

"This is what I've been thrust into, Shane! You don't see the stuff that I see; you don't know the stuff I know, unless I tell you. See? Right here is a good example: Some kind of vehicle just drove by me with big letters on its side — P-I-C-K-S. Do you know what that means? Pink Communist Kills Stevens, or Pink Communist Kills Sloane. One of them."

"You have to stop associating bad things with what you see."

"But that's part of the communication in their world. That's what I'm telling you. You just aren't aware."

"It's probably just a regular business car, like a tax consultant or home computer repair guy might drive."

"That's how the world works, Shane. I tried to email Congressman McClintock this morning and tell him about Joseph Stalin because in the representative's recent letter to his constituents, of which I am one, he talked about Governor Jerry Brown having passed legislation that's going to open the door for votes that are corrupt, or from dead people or illegal aliens or, I don't know what, somebody who should not be voting or double voting. Joseph Stalin basically said that it doesn't matter who casts the vote; it only matters who counts the vote."

I told my brother many things about the way I was generally feeling physically and about being a target of Zionists, communists, gypsies and the mafia, but I didn't inform him about my latest health problems. I didn't want him to worry, too.

But test results that came back from the lab left me reeling.

The good news was they found a non-cancerous tumor in the cartilage around my knee that had been surgically repaired years before. That explained a lot about the knee pain I had suffered for years.

The bad news? Melanoma and a recommendation to undergo surgery to remove the malignancy.

I traveled regularly to San Francisco for appointments with my orthopedic surgeon and various oncology specialists. I also saw a psychiatrist as my health care team worked to manage my preoperative medication based on my psychiatric history. Advocates at the Public Civil Investigation Office found a friendly driver to take me to my appointments.

My entire medical and legal team inspired a deep sense of assurance within me. Somehow, they did not allow my enemies to intrude, relieving much of my anxiety.

At this time, I needed to hear Shane's voice more than ever. Feelings of safety and calm came over me when I talked to him — even though I did not share all my medical issues.

"Where are you right now?" he asked me one day. "Are you in the car?"

"I'm going shopping, Shane."

"Where?"

"San Francisco. I love to shop in San Francisco."

"You're not driving that RV into the city, are you?"

"No, silly. I have a driver. She's a really nice lady."

"You have a driver? Well, that sounds good. I should go with you sometime."

"You? Shopping? I don't think so. I'll tell you what I want to do with you instead. I want to come to your house for Christmas. I want to see the kids, get them nice presents, catch up with everybody."

"Then come. You're more than welcome. That will be great. In fact, I'm having a little party on Christmas Eve, mostly family. I'll send you the invitation."

Shane, his wife, Vicki, and their children, Michael and Isabelle, live in a gated home with a seventy-foot driveway leading to a stone portico. I parked my RV by the gate and walked up the driveway to the front door.

Inside, the tiled foyer is large and formal, and the living room ceilings are twenty-one feet high — which accommodates the tall Christmas tree the family erects every year. Shane always positions a noble fir in the corner of the room adjacent to the fireplace.

When I walked in, a fire was roaring, crystal ornaments and glass snowflakes sparkled, fairy lights twinkled, handcrafted garland arrangements and candles adorned the gracious home, and traditional holiday songs resonated throughout. There wasn't room for another present under the tree.

We played charades and a game where players reach into a stocking filled with random items and guess what they've taken hold of, without looking.

Michael and Isabelle loved hearing my bowdlerized telling of stories about growing up with their father and our escapades in Lake Tahoe and

Hawaii.

"You knew so many celebrities, Aunt Sloane," Isabelle said. "Of all the famous people you met, who did you like the most?"

Immediately, I thought of Tom Selleck.

"I met him very briefly while on the set of *Magnum P.I.*," I responded. "Tom's bodyguard happened to be the nephew of my landlord in Kahului. We exchanged pleasantries, then he went into his trailer to study his lines. He's one of the few actors who rose above the smut of Hollywood. He's Quigley, for crying out loud, a real American we can be proud of."

"What about Joe Montana?" Shane asked, smiling by the fireplace where he stood with a whiskey in his hand. "How'd you two meet for the first time?"

"I met Joe while I was an intern in sports medicine at Sierra College, where the 49ers used to hold their preseason training. The 49ers and the Wolverines overlapped their schedules, so we all shared the campus at the same time, which was pretty cool.

"I was waiting in the breezeway to put towels in the dryer when Joe walked out of the locker room. There wasn't a soul in sight except for him and me. We talked for a while, and then off he went. I thought my father was going to disinherit me for not getting down on one knee and proposing to him. But we saw him later in Hawaii, didn't we Shane?"

"Yes, we did!"

"Joe, Tom Selleck and Lyle Alzado — they were all class acts," Sloane continued, looking happy and relaxed. "Joe and Tom were brief encounters, but Lyle, on the other hand, trained at Gold's Gym in Venice where I worked out. I tell people all the time that he is the only man who ever called me 'sweetheart' every day for a year-and-a-half. I certainly didn't know him in the biblical sense — do you kids know that phrase? Lyle just called me sweetheart because he was a warm, embracing man. I greatly respect the courage he showed in admitting his abuse of anabolic steroids. He changed my mind about them. I'm sure they caused the brain tumor he died from."

"What about Rod Stewart?" Michael asked, remembering my stories from the past.

"I met him while I was backstage at Hughes Stadium around 1974. Do you remember that concert, Shane?"

"Yes. Loggins and Messina and Peter Frampton played that day, too."

"Well, Rod was finishing his set and walking down the steps and saw me sitting at a table where some, um, uh, extracurricular activities were occurring. He looked at the guy I was sitting with and told him, 'Get her out of here, she's too damn young.' But I was starstruck and tongue tied."

"How old were you Aunt Sloane?"

"Only fifteen, but looking back I am really appreciative of Rod Stewart's candor. Whether he put his foot down to protect himself or me or both, I still respect him for his stern assertion."

We all laughed.

"But who did you like the best?" Isabelle asked.

"I can't really say. I met them at the top of their game in their chosen fields, but they all acknowledged me and were professional. I just feel privileged to have crossed their paths."

Reminiscing became bittersweet. Encroaching thoughts of my impending surgery caused intense anxiety to sweep over me. The sweet children looked at me with happy, sparkling eyes in anticipation of more fun tales, but I couldn't go on. My energy plummeted, and I felt worthless for having talked about brushing elbows with such great people, men who today would not recognize or even notice me. I came close to fame and fortune when I was young, but the right conditions never came together for me to pull it off. Fate? Bad luck? Uncertainty? I don't know why my hard work and aspirations never carried me to the pinnacle. I looked at the others mingling in the big living room, mumbled that I needed to use the bathroom, and ran off.

I stayed in the bathroom for twenty minutes, finally concluding that I had only one way to counter this rising despondency: Get the hell out of there. I quietly approached Michael and Isabelle as they sat before the Christmas tree and told them to follow me. We walked into Isabelle's bedroom, where I took my checkbook from my purse, wrote each of the children a five hundred-dollar check for Christmas gifts and fled the party without further goodbyes.

In January 2017, I underwent surgery to remove the melanoma and non-cancerous tumor in my knee cartilage. I let no family or friends visit me in the hospital. I only allowed visits from my doctors and Public Civil Investigation Office support staff who had stood by me. Once I returned home from the hospital, I couldn't sleep or eat — and my tormentors sensed my weakness and came after me again with a vengeance.

There was no precipitation the day I returned home from the San

Francisco hospital, but the weather was extremely cold. It was thirty-nine degrees that afternoon. Josie started acting strangely, scratching and rubbing her ear so obsessively that I knew something was in her. They'd again attacked her and me with satellite weaponry. The very next day, Josie, Stinky and I got in the RV and departed my Foresthill property for good.

Listen to me. There is some sort of receiver on top of my vehicle. I am all wired up from it. This is outright torture. My head hurts. All these fucking communists. Communists. Communists. Communists. Fucking pieces of shit. I want them all executed when I finally die from the torture campaign they've waged against me now for a decade.

My vehicle is bugged. They listen to every single word I say. Every single word. This is Dianne Feinstein. This is the Anti Defamation League. This is the Bureau of Alcohol, Tobacco, Firearms and Explosives.

By the way, they're the ones who did 9/11. They did 9/11. They did 9/11 — so wake up America! There are no laws left in this country. Their maroon vehicles follow me around. They're gypsy mafia. They're setting me up. These goddamn pigs at the Department of Justice. What the hell are you people doing? What the hell?

It was February 2017 and I was driving all over Roseville with my pets. The Syanim and the mafia all had their vehicles rigged up to do a number of things, and one of them was to design their headlights to operate independently. The bright one indicated to someone observing the satellite that I was over on one side of the road or the other. They wiggled the light. They dimmed it. They brightened it. They operated the lights independently or at the same time to convey various information.

And right on cue, there the fuck they were. They came up behind me, bright lights glaring. I could not see anything in my rear-view mirror. The white flashes blinded me and I could not see my lane.

I was at the intersection of Cirby Way and Vernon Street when — shit! — I struck the car next to me. The other driver began yelling something at me through his lowered window. I threw open the RV door to see if he was BATFE.

"What the hell, lady?"

"Is this how you're going to end it?" I demanded. "Murder me in broad daylight on the street in the dead cold of winter?"

"What? End what? You swerved into me. Pull over. We need to pull to the side."

"The fuck if I'm going to follow you to the side of the road."

"I just need to check your insurance. Exchange information. Come on!"

"You have everything you need on me. Don't pretend otherwise. I expected you to have your shit together. Amateur! You're an amateur. What are you? A new recruit? Mafia? Mossad?"

"Calm down. Just calm down. Let's just get safely to the side of the road and..."

I heard a chirp, chirp — the unmistakable short, sharp burst from a police vehicle announcing its approach. I saw the cop car coming up slowly behind us. They were really bringing it on today. They were everywhere.

The federal agent pulled his damaged car to the side of the road. I sat in the driver's seat of my RV. Through my rear-view mirrors, I saw a police officer open his door. His dashboard gun mount was empty! No twelve-gauge pump there. I was fucked.

"This is it!" I thought.

The cop approached me with his weapon in hand. Briefly, I lost sight of him. Where had he gone? They were going to take me out right here and now. So this was how it would end!

No. Not this time. Not now. That was it — time for me and my forty-one-foot, big white box on wheels to get the hell out of there. I pressed the accelerator, but my RV smashed into another car that had stopped in the road. Maybe a witness, maybe a do-gooder. Probably a co-conspirator.

I found a path through the tangled traffic and took off again, a cop in pursuit, speeding along Foothills Boulevard and approaching Baseline. Speed limit is fifty-five, but I gunned it to seventy-five as the fucking cop tailed me. Ahead, the left-turn traffic signal was green. I swerved around two cars to get onto Baseline. The right lane looked clear up to Fiddyment and Walerga. If I could get to Pleasant Grove Road, I'd be in the clear.

When the Baseline and Fiddyment light turned yellow, I thought I could make it. I needed to make it! Eighty, eighty-five, ninety. Red. Fuck it all. I gunned it because I had to make it, or else it was all over...

CONCLUSION

Two months later.

Sloane and I talked by phone almost daily during the spring and summer of 2017, but I did not see her in person. She refused to meet me face to face. I did not know why. I told her we forgave her abrupt departure from our last Christmas gathering, but she did not believe me. We were puzzled and concerned, but nobody was mad at her. Sloane did not believe me.

Our conversations typically culminated in screaming and crying, but there was laughter, too. We would go on for an hour if her phone battery held up or my work allowed. Sloane was clearly upset and troubled but refused to admit it or ask for help. If I had tried to give it, I know she would have been gone forever.

As the holidays again approached, I invited her to come to my house again to celebrate. The kids were aching to see her.

"They think you're pretty cool for some reason," I teased.

"Yeah, well, what do they know?"

"So how about it?"

"I have to decline, Shane. I'm not feeling well."

"You live close. Just see how it goes. Let us know whenever you're ready."

"I really don't think I'll be feeling up for it this year, Shane. Please understand. You know I would if I could."

Like that, 2017 ended, and early in 2018, Sloane's phone went dead. She had gone dark and she was unreachable. I called her ten times a day, but the calls went to voicemail. Voicemail filled up.

I figured she and her pets again were living in her RV. The previous time we talked, I got the distinct impression that she was driving throughout North Sacramento trying to outrun the demons haunting her. I needed to check on her and was determined to begin at her Foresthill property, whether she wanted me to or not. When I arrived, her home was abandoned.

Nothing prepared me for what I saw there. I punched in the key code, drove through the gate and immediately saw eerie warnings written on the driveway in red spray paint: "JEWS GO HOME"; "CIA GET THE FUCK OUT!"; and more. The grass growing in her fields was waist-high, and vines and branches crawled up the walls of the house and onto the roof, pulling the gutters away from the fascia. Nutsedge, wildflowers and uncut fescue grew in the once-manicured and tidy area bordering the house. Saplings and weeds sprouted up through cracks in the driveway.

I parked, unlocked the front door and walked inside. The air was musty, and cobwebs clung to corners of the ceiling. The vents and window borders remained taped over. The interior was disheveled, not unlike a homeless encampment, with clothes, books and boxes strewn about. The home had four bedrooms, and one was entirely dedicated to her paranoid visions and delusions. On the walls, she had taped or tacked lab reports and medical forms from blood panels, articles from news periodicals, lists of the names of her alleged torturers, and more warning signs for the government and groups telling them to get out or go to hell or fuck off. I found similar handwritten threats and warnings taped behind toilets and in drawers.

Sloane obviously had not been in the house for a very long time.

As I was leaving, I glanced into a room she had converted into an office. Out of the corner of my eye, I saw a small, black, fire-rated safe with the door ajar. I flung the door open and staggered backward. In neat rows Sloane had stacked rows and rows of unopened, orange prescription bottles with labels reading Lithium Carbonet Tablets.

I quickly retreated and drove nervously to her Roseville residence, where I found a similar scene.

Next, I called the phone company Verizon and explained to their representatives that I was trying to contact a family member about whom I was greatly concerned. Verizon officials suggested Sloane might have blocked my calls or stopped paying her bill, but neither scenario seemed plausible.

I called on Sloane's Pacific Northwest family and reached her cousin Marie.

"Have you heard from Sloane?" I asked.

"No. Why? When was the last time you talked to her?"

"Just before Christmas."

"Has her criminal case gone to trial yet?"

Her words knocked me off balance.

"Her what? Criminal trial? What are you talking about?"

"Her trial. The one stemming from that horrendous accident she was involved in, of course."

"What accident?"

There was a sharp silence.

"Shane, you didn't know she caused major collision about a year ago? She blew a red and ran through an intersection. She wiped out a bunch of cars with her big RV. You must have seen it on the news or in the newspaper."

"No! I missed that. What? When?"

"Let me send you the newspaper article I kept. I have it in my documents somewhere. There, I just sent it. Take a look. I'll stay on the line."

I opened the link, and there was the story, a short article on B6 in the local paper, about Sloane barreling through an intersection in Sacramento taking out a bunch of cars.

Valentine's Day | Feb. 14, 2017

5 hospitalized in fiery crash that shuts down busy intersection in Roseville

The intersection of Baseline and Fiddyment roads was closed Tuesday after a motor home allegedly caused a seven-vehicle crash in Roseville.

The driver of the motor home was taken to the hospital along with five other victims and has been arrested.

Roseville police say Sloane Stevens was driving the large RV and fled the scene of a minor accident near Cirby Way and Vernon Street. A Sacramento County sheriff's deputy who had stopped to investigate the first crash chased the motor home at high speeds until Stevens' motor home hit several other vehicles in the intersection and caught fire after the crash.

How did I miss it? I wondered. Skip the evening news, choose to listen to a rock or all-talk radio station, or just barely skim through the daily paper just one day, and the story is gone.

"Why didn't anybody tell me?" I asked Marie.

"We assumed you knew. You live right in the same city. You're next of kin. You're her true bloodline. We figured since you're close to Sloane, both personally and geographically, you were handling the situation. We thought you would at least be aware of it. It seems impossible that you didn't know."

I have explained that I live on the periphery of the hundred-year-old Stevens dynasty, just an observer. I am connected tangentially to that Pacific Northwest family only by virtue of my mother and younger half-sister. Even Sloane is somewhat detached from the family lineage — or at least tries to be — mostly because her father was adopted and later shunned. I am first on the list for Sloane, they reckoned, not them. Fair enough, I thought, but this irritated me considerably.

At least she is alive, I thought. Apparently.

"None of this answers the question of where she is now," I told Marie.

"I thought you two were close."

I ignored her snide remark.

"Just tell me, was there a trial?" I asked.

"The last thing we heard was she posted five hundred thousand dollars bail. She didn't need anybody's assistance with that, I guess. She has the assets. Conrad told me she used her Roseville house as collateral, but as a condition for posting bail the judge put her under house arrest and made her wear an ankle monitor. She could only leave home for court-approved appointments. At that point, there was nothing more we, as a family, could do."

"I must have been talking to her while she was at home under house arrest," I reasoned. "That's why she refused my help and didn't want to visit or for me to come see her."

When I hung up, I quickly checked a Placer County website containing public reports for daily bookings and releases and the in-custody roster. There, I learned my sister was back in jail awaiting a competency hearing to determine if she was mentally fit to stand trial.

She rebuffed my appeals to visit her in jail, too. A correctional officer explained in a cynical tone that Sloane believed I was associated with the mafia or the gypsies and therefore did not want to see me.

But when it came time for her hearing, I sat in back of the courtroom out of her view. The jury needed merely ten minutes to find her incompetent to stand trial and the judge to suspend criminal charges. However, the attorneys required a hell of a lot longer to argue before the judge which public psychiatric facility to place Sloane in. I stayed and listened to the disposition hearing.

Based on a psychiatrist's recommendation, Sloane's defense attorney contended she that she should reside in Napa State Hospital, just an hour away, but the prosecutor went berserk over that suggestion. He hungered for revenge and her disgrace, having spectacularly lost the chance to secure a guilty verdict.

"No way!" the prosecutor said firmly. "With all due respect, your honor, she needs to be as far from here as possible, somewhere where the forensic psychiatrist can be as neutral as possible and not influenced by defense experts."

He vehemently argued for her commitment to no other facility than Metropolitan State Hospital in Southern California, four hundred miles away.

This time, he prevailed. Sloane was sent to Metropolitan, not far from Sybil Brand, where she was incarcerated thirty years earlier and her mad journey began.

"There, you both got something to take back to the office to celebrate," the judge declared. "Case closed."

I promised Sloane I would always stand by her side. I had assured her I always would be committed to her safety and comfort in this brutal life. With that in mind, I now took over the management and safeguarding of her assets as her conservator and trustee.

My first order of business was fending off a half-dozen civil lawsuits stemming from the crash. Two of the victims, a husband and wife in their eighties who suffered the worst of the injuries, were coming after my sister for six-and-a-half million dollars. They might not have three years left to fight us. They did not have the luxury of paying high attorney fees in the hundred of thousands of dollars. Therefore, they were committed to settling the case through arbitration. I had no stomach for a protracted court battle, either, so we agreed to negotiate.

Both sides bogged down in the exchange of information and documents, case preparation, gathering evidence and prepping witnesses.

Plaintiffs and defendant both finally consented to mediation.

The crash victims, my attorney and I agreed to have a retired San Francisco judge drive inland and over the Yolo County Causeway to Sacramento where he would dispose of the case in one final, definitive judgment.

We met at the downtown office of the plaintiffs' attorney. I peeked out of my assigned conference room and saw the elderly couple for the first time ever. Right then, I knew we were doomed. My obligation to handle all of Sloane's affairs suddenly was on shaky ground — with millions at stake.

Their attorney pushed the wife into the conference room in a wheelchair — she was hardly moving a muscle — while the husband, aided by a walker, hobbled along next to her at a snail's pace. They were frail. Their gray and blue sweat suits hung loosely off their feeble arms and legs like loose blankets. I again read the exchange of information. It said they had been a robust couple who played tennis and hosted dinner parties at home just a year ago, before the wreck. This, of course, is what their lawyer asserted.

I waited a painfully long time next to my legal counsel while the judge hunkered down with the plaintiffs in their war room. My hopes sank as each moment passed. The weight of my soon-to-be-broken oath cracked my heart. My pledge to Sloane — once as strong as a sinewy ship rope pulling another vessel — was now as delicate as a sewing thread ready to snap.

I heard shoes shuffling outside the conference room door where we waited. A moment later, the judge walked in. He sat down and introduced himself. My attorney and I introduced ourselves — and a revelation struck me. The judge looked familiar and his name stirred a faint memory.

"Sir," I said. "Do you happen to know Judge Scarpa from the First District Court of Appeal?"

"Judge Roberto Scarpa? Oh, of course I do. He's my idol."

"I loved him, too. My parents loved him. That low, resonant..."

"His voice! Yes, what a deep voice!"

"Absolutely."

"Judge Scarpa could command a courtroom with that baritone."

"Or an entire room of revelers."

"Yes, yes," the judge said, laughing. "I attended dozens of parties with him. At every one of them, I would hear his voice booming across three rooms — even with a band playing loudly. How do you know him?"

"Judge Scarpa's wife and my mother were very good friends," I said.

He remembered who Mom was. We shared more stories. My spirits lifted.

The judge, as arbitrator, went back and forth from room to room, shutting our door and going to the plaintiffs, then back to us. Every time he returned to our room, our conversation resumed where it had left off, and he departed in a better mood. My confidence soared. I was unshakeable, and my attorney no longer fretted.

In the end, we whittled the settlement down to one-and-a-half million dollars, and I wrote a check for five hundred thousand dollars. That was the full extent of our obligation. Because Sloane always made sure to buy the best insurance coverage and always topped out on bodily injury liability, her underwriter paid the rest — a cool one million dollars. Half a million dollars was easy for her to manage; she kept most of her money. I wanted to tell her.

When Sloane had been admitted to Metropolitan State Hospital, she signed a privacy form that allowed her to communicate with, other than medical personnel, me. Whenever I called, her unit's receptionist immediately connected me to her room.

So after the arbitrator's decision, I called the hospital to tell her the good news. She would love hearing that her financial burden had been reduced and the latest about Judge Scarpa. But my expectations of finding her coherent, let alone lighthearted, were not met. Instead of connecting me to Sloane's room, this time the receptionist put me on a long hold.

"I need to transfer you to the attending physician," she said somberly upon returning.

"Why? What's going on?"

She did not answer, and my heart started hammered. My body temperature escalated. The doctor came on the line.

"To confirm you are Sloane's brother, I just need to ask you some questions from the information on the privacy form she signed when she was admitted here, OK?" the doctor said.

Convinced I was her brother, he delivered a thunderbolt.

"I have difficult news to share. Your sister has cancer, and it has spread to her brain. This occurs when cancer cells from the original tumor site travel through the bloodstream and form new tumors on the brain."

"I know what metastatic brain cancer is, doctor. I just want to talk to Sloane. Put her on please."

"I can't."

"Excuse me?"

"You can't talk to her."

"I need to talk to my sister."

"Let me find her case manager."

"No, no, no. Go find her right now and put her on."

The doctor was gone, his voice replaced by nondescript, bland music.

The case manager quickly picked up the phone.

"You sister was remanded back to custody," she told me.

"What? What the hell is going on? She would have..."

"A forensic physician was called in to do a court-ordered evaluation of Ms. Stevens. Her condition has improved thanks to her compliance with medication and the comprehensive care of our staff. Sloane has recovered sufficiently to stand trial. Because she has regained competence, the court resumed criminal proceedings."

"What? Where is she, then?"

"Let's see. In the notes here, it says she's in the Placer County jail infirmary."

"The infirmary?"

"After the psychiatric assessment, medical doctors diagnosed her. She's in the late stages of cancer."

The words rattled me.

"This is barbaric," I said. "She needs to get out of the jail infirmary and into oncology for the best treatment. She's not going to survive if she's incarcerated."

"I'm sorry, sir. Unfortunately, it's out of our hands here. It's beyond this hospital's control."

The prosecuting attorney was evil and vengeful. He knew what he was doing when he convinced the judge to send Sloane to Metropolitan and far away from her own medical team. Unable to bankrupt her, he had vowed never to rest until he torched my sister's legacy, and burned to ashes all hope of her living a long and free life.

He got what he wanted. Sloane again was in custody and facing charges of fleeing police, driving recklessly and causing serious physical injuries.

Needing to fight back, I hung up the phone and flew into action. By Friday, as conservatorship of the person and estate of Sloane Stevens, I obtained the declaration of her condition from our lead physician, a neuropsychiatrist. His evaluation of my sister concluded that she lacked the capacity to provide informed consent to undergo medical treatment.

"Ms. Stevens had been diagnosed with metastatic melanoma, and based on review of her medical records provided to me by Ms. Stevens medical professionals it is my understanding that she is in the advanced stages of cancer," his report said. "Her life expectancy is likely only a few weeks."

The report stated that Sloane had visited Sutter Medical Center's oncology department within the preceding year, but she had not told me or anyone else.

We needed to get her back. Armed with her medical team's evaluation, my lawyer miraculously got us before a judge on Monday. Without hesitation, the judge ordered Sloane released into my custody. We raced from the Santucci Justice Center in Roseville to South Placer County Jail, usually a six-minute walk from the courthouse. But we sprinted.

The jail facility sprawls across two hundred thousand square feet and houses four hundred inmates. A correctional officer watched us approach the visitor's window inside.

"I'd like to see my sister right away, please," I hastily said to the man staffing the desk behind the Plexiglas.

I showed him the document, my hands shaking.

My attorney interjected, "This allows my client to remove this individual, his sister..."

"Please wait. I'll be right back."

We protested but the sheriff's employee rose from the desk and left without another word. He returned fifteen minutes later accompanied by a uniformed nurse.

"We called hospice for your sister on Friday," the nurse said.

"You're kidding me," I said, my voice rising with unease. "I want to see her right away."

"She's very, very ill. We are trying to manage her pain."

"What are you giving her?"

"She only wants Tylenol. She doesn't want to be pumped with anything. That's what she told us. She said she doesn't want to take anything from 'you people.' She won't follow our standardized care pathways."

"That doesn't matter anymore. See this court order. She should be in our care now. I need to see her immediately!"

The nurse looked at the sheriff's clerk.

"OK," he said, perusing the court papers. "You can see her, but we need to do a background check on you first."

"Jesus Christ. No way!"

"How long does that take?" my attorney asked calmly.

"About ninety minutes."

"Come on, man!" I shouted. "You gotta be fucking kidding me! Here's my driver's license. And here's the document that the fucking judge signed a half-hour ago. We don't have time for this."

The nurse and the clerk were unyielding. They left again, and a correctional officer came to the window and watched over us until the background check was completed.

"OK, we can let you in," the clerk said when he returned twenty minutes later.

The corrections officer called for two uniformed sheriff's deputies. They accompanied my attorney, the nurse and me through a maze of hallways into the jail and back to the infirmary.

"We're going to get Ms. Stevens on oxygen and a morphine drip right away," the nurse told me as we walked.

The infirmary was designed like a pod and we approached a desk in the middle where people worked and talked on phones. The nurse and deputies walked past the central station, so I followed them. To the side of this work area was a room with thick, bulletproof Plexiglas instead of bars, and there one of the officers stopped and faced me while the other stood motionless behind me. It appeared to be as far as they would let me go.

Through the glass, I saw lying on a hospital bed a frail form with pallid skin, jutting cheekbones and arms that appeared as fragile as a small bird's wings. Sloane was gasping for air. There was no morphine drip.

I had not seen Sloane for two years and the once graceful curves of her body were rigid angles. She appeared to weigh eighty pounds. Her chest rose and fell fitfully and without rhythm with each irregular breath. I saw no needle piercing her skin, no liquid entering to offer a gentle veil for her pain.

"What the fuck is this?" I howled. "What are you doing to her? You're all a bunch of fucking murderers leaving her like this!"

Even through the Plexiglass, Sloane heard my voice. She slowly turned her head and looked at me. A faint, untroubled smile came over her face. There I stood, once more the knight on the white steed come to soothe her pain. Her features softened, and tension in her body fell away, leaving only quiet and a serene grace.

EPILOGUE

When leaving downtown Los Angeles from the vicinity of Fifth Street and Crocker, perhaps going to LAX, you drive straight through Skid Row where the stark inequity of life is on full, heart-wrenching display. You cannot escape the overwhelming picture of homelessness, mental illness, addiction and poverty. You have no choice but to see — and feel — this profound human crisis.

Remembering Sloane's life story takes me there every time. Ironic in many ways, the single thread weaving her narrative into the experiences of most of these downtrodden individuals and families is her battle with mental illness. Despite her vast financial resources, she was trapped in a labyrinth of human suffering and the fight to survive, as they are.

After we buried her ashes in a suburban Sacramento cemetery plot, next to where Mom is interred, I hit the road alone. I needed solitude and time to think. Even before I removed my black funeral suit, I started driving to places throughout California, Oregon and Washington that hold for me memories of her life. I took Highway 50 to Lake Tahoe and from there I blazed through Lassen, Modoc, Klamath and Lane counties, finally connecting with northbound Interstate 5 North in west-central Oregon.

I traveled father north and then west to the coast, reaching the house that Sloane built in Nehalem near Eddy's. The property reminded me of a scene from a J. R. R. Tolkien novel. Overgrown bushes and hedges spilled onto the driveway and paths. Trees, heavy with uncut branches and leaves, loomed over the roof. The garden and yard were dense with untrimmed grasses, and sprawling blueberry vines so completely engulfed the house that I needed a chainsaw to cut my way to the front door. But once I got inside, I found that the place appeared pristine.

I stayed two nights before driving inland back to I-5 and streaking north to Seattle. I drove by Stevens family's mansions on the lake, but I did not call on anybody. I stopped to take a good look at the shipyards and watched the maritime activity for a while.

Next, I dashed south, back to California and Placer County. There, I walked around Sloane's Foresthill property. The neighbor she clashed with no longer lived nearby.

I did not remain in Northern California, instead following I-5 south six hours later until I hit Los Angeles.

Beverly Hills. The PCH. Malibu. Venice Beach. The beach cities were beautiful, but bad memories flooded my thoughts like tsunami inundating the coastline.

Finally, I took a spin over to Skid Row. I slowly coasted through the heart of the city's homelessness — fifty solid blocks lined with makeshift tents, tarps, cardboard, blankets, shopping carts, boxes, unwashed clothing, stuffed animals, piles of weathered belongings and hungry dogs. Also, humanity, sickness and disorders of every stripe. How many people lived on these streets? Three thousand? Four thousand? Ten thousand? Some of the saddest, dirtiest, yet most innocent, children were scattered among them, too.

I passed by boarded-up buildings and under freeways. I rolled the windows down and caught scents of body odor, piss and traces of smoke from small fires. The scrawled signs propped against signposts, light poles and shopping carts asking for help reminded me of those desperate notices Sloane placed in her home and yard — except these called for the opposite action. They wanted you to lend a hand, to come over, leave money — and then go away. Sloane's signs warned you not to come closer, to get the hell away and never come back — or else.

Some figures sitting on sidewalks or huddled on bus stop benches reminded me of my sister's appearance at her lowest. Their stories remain untold, while here, I've laid bare here Sloane's struggle. Down every street, around every corner, I felt close to her. I think about how many people in this homeless population — some sources say seventy percent

— share her mental illness.

The odds always suggested that Sloane would not end up here. She drifted comfortably in another world, the one you can see in the distance when standing on Skid Row, a remote place where expensive high-rises shimmer and penthouses shine. She enjoyed upper-class privileges, at least in fleeting moments of lucidity and fortitude.

I drove up and down every Skid Row street in Los Angeles — Third Street, Seventh Street, Main Street, Alameda, San Pedro, San Julian, Winston — for two hours. Tears filled my eyes, and my throat constricted. My chest ached as it housed my broken heart within.

Then, I had an idea, a small idea to be sure, but one of hope.

Sloane hurt many people on that day her car hurtled into the intersection at Baseline and Fiddyment. Even though we tried to make amends, Sloane's shrewdness ensured most of her trust stayed intact. The victims ultimately received payouts from her insurance coverage and personal accounts. It was less than they asked for, but it nonetheless was substantial.

I knew I could help many more people than just those hurt in the wreck. I knew I could help suffering people, like Sloane, in whom tempests raged, the sources of their pain inscrutable and unseen.

Seated in the quiet of my Mercedes, I made a resolute decision. I wished to tell Sloane and receive her blessing, and seeing Eddy's face and hearing his reaction would have amused me. As for my mother, I know she would have been pleased because of her wish to educate people about mental illness and manic depression. But only I remained alive to see it through.

As soon as I could, I put the untouched assets from Sloane's accounts into a charitable trust. As founder, I defined its mission as serving and aiding souls suffering from the schizophrenia and mood disorders that marked so much of Sloane's life — and, of course, influenced mine.

Mom once pledged to Sloane that she would help educate as many people as possible about mental illness and manic depression. Now I carry on the fight through the Sloane Stevens Memorial Mental Health Endowment.

If you need support...

Call or text 988 any time for free, confidential mental health
or substance use support.

Visit 988lifeline.org to chat with a crisis counselor online
or to find more support resources.

The official website for the National Institute of Mental Health (NIMH)
is www.nimh.nih.gov.